INCENDIO: FLAME BORN

INCENDIO: FLAME BORN

CHRONICLES OF AN URBAN ELEMENTAL™ BOOK 1

AUBURN TEMPEST

MICHAEL ANDERLE

DISRUPTIVE IMAGINATION®

This book is a work of fiction. All of the characters, organizations, and events portrayed in this novel are either products of the author's imagination or are used fictitiously. Sometimes both.

Copyright © 2023 LMBPN Publishing
Cover by Fantasy Book Design
Cover copyright © LMBPN Publishing
A Michael Anderle Production

LMBPN Publishing supports the right to free expression and the value of copyright. The purpose of copyright is to encourage writers and artists to produce the creative works that enrich our culture.

The distribution of this book without permission is a theft of the author's intellectual property. If you would like permission to use material from the book (other than for review purposes), please contact support@lmbpn.com. Thank you for your support of the author's rights.

LMBPN Publishing
PMB 196, 2540 South Maryland Pkwy
Las Vegas, NV 89109

Version 1.00, January 2023
eBook ISBN: 979-8-88541-325-1
Print ISBN: 979-8-88878-113-5

THE INCENDIO: FLAME BORN TEAM

Thanks to our Beta Readers:

Malyssa Brannon, Mary Morris, David Laughlin, John Ashmore,
Kelly O'Donnell, John Scafidi, Jim Caplan, Larry Omans

Thanks to our JIT Team:

Dorothy Lloyd
Christopher Gilliard
Dave Hicks
Jan Hunnicutt
Daryl McDaniel
Diane L. Smith
James Caplan

Editor
SkyFyre Editing Team

AUTHOR NOTE

Welcome to *Incendio: Flame Born*, book one of the Chronicles of the Urban Elementals series.

This series is written as a starting point for a new series but is also a continuation of the chaos and mayhem that began two years earlier in the timeline with another cast of characters living in Toronto.

If you're the type of reader who wants the full experience, you'll want to check out *A Gilded Cage*, book one of the Chronicles of an Urban Druid. That series leads into the Case Files of the Urban Druid, where we first meet Jules, the main character of this series.

If you're game to jump in with both feet, read on.

Either way, thanks for joining us. Happy reading. We hope you enjoy our stories.

Auburn Tempest and Michael Anderle

CHAPTER ONE

"I know who you are! You're one of them. She's one of them!"

I grip the shoulder of my tweaked-out, freaked out, twenty-something skater dude and encourage him to keep marching up the station's ramp. "Yep, you got me. I'm one of those crazy cops who bring in nakey guys gone wackadoodle on pharmaceutical."

He shuffles ahead of me, his bare-footed steps sloppy with whatever synthetic feel-good wave of wonder he's riding.

Rene steps out the station's door and winces, bringing his hand up to shield his eyes. "For the love of all that's holy. Where the fuck are your clothes, kid?"

Nakey Kid lifts his cuffed hands and I yank him back to keep him from getting touchy-feely. "There's no hiding from me. I see all."

"Nobody *wants* to see it all," Rene snaps, averting his gaze. "Damn, kid, cover that shit up."

I chuckle and head inside. "Have a good one, Rene."

"You too, Gagne. Keep our city safe."

"You betcha. One streaker at a time."

The buzz of the station on a busy night feeds my cells. *This* is my drug of choice. Fighting the good fight. Sweeping the streets. Corralling the whacked and weird and keeping them from ruining the night of innocent, hard-working folks.

"Inspector Gagne."

I cringe at the pronunciation of my name and glance at the desk sergeant on duty. The old girl has been living in Montréal long enough to pick up on French pronunciations by now.

Hell, I've gone over it a half-dozen times for her. "Betty, it's pronounced 'gahn-yay' not gag-knee."

She slides a disparaging look over me that says how much she doesn't care.

Yeah, nice talk.

Of course, it's Betty on the desk on the night I smell like a sewage-vomit love child and have been wrestling with Nakey Kid. If it were Mitchell or Stanton, those old warhorses would think it's a hoot that funk covers me tits to toes while I frog-march a flasher.

Instead, it's the precinct's matronly mother.

Betty somehow has the finely honed ability to berate me, my position on major crimes, and my successfully single lifestyle all in one steely gaze.

Suck it, Betty.

I pass the desk, chin up and spine stiff, and head straight for holding.

Montréal's Twenty-Third Precinct isn't sexy or flashy like a couple of the downtown houses. It sags in a few places and shows the wear and tear of its struggles in a few others—much like the cops who work here.

Still, we've got a great bunch of dedicated officers. Not only do they work the job, their blood runs blue.

"*Calice*, Gagne, you smell like de dumpster behind my building."

I laugh and keep my kid walking. "Because that's where I camp out on my days off, Morin. By the way, I found your blow-up doll while I was on my stakeout. You really wore her out."

The guys get a kick out of that one.

Marx pops his head up from his cubicle like a scruffy, balding gopher. "Don't you have dat big family dinner tonight, Gagne?"

"Yeah. It's the twins' birthday."

Anna and Micah are two teenage kids I pulled from a flophouse during a raid a couple of years ago. They aren't related by blood but bonded over their rough beginnings and were about the same age.

Since neither of them had a suitable family to claim them, I hooked them up with my adoptive aunt. She raised my siblings and me after our adoptive parents died in a car crash.

Charlotte Gagne, or as everyone calls her—*Charlie*.

My adoptive father's younger sister has a life rhythm that flows to a different beat. When most would zig, she's solidly a zag girl. She's odd and spontaneous, and we were lucky to have her.

The night I landed back at our childhood home and introduced her to the kids, she asked them about themselves and deemed them twins. She declared that day was their new birthday and sent me to the ice cream parlor to get them a cake.

'New lives deserve a new birthday to celebrate,' she stated, welcoming them inside.

That's the way Charlie rolls—no one gets left behind.

"Oof, we can't send you home for a family party looking and smelling like dat." Morin waves in front of his mustache. "I'll run de kid up to holding so you can shower and hit de road."

I chuckle. "And in return?"

He runs his thumbs under his beltline and tugs the waist of his pants around his pot belly. "Well, de courteous thing to do when someone does you a favor is to return dat favor."

"Uh-huh, and what does that look like?"

He glances at me sidelong and smiles. "Bring us some of your aunt's baking, and we'll call it square."

I laugh. These boys are slaves to Charlie's baking. "Done deal. Tell the guys upstairs to let Nakey Kid sleep it off until morning, and I'll write him up before I leave. Tomorrow, I will deliver your bakery bribe."

Morin grins and waggles his brows at his partner, Marx. "Dat's how it's done, assholes. You see?"

Marx chuckles and leans back in his chair. "Ah, *oui*, I see. I see your belt moving to de next notch."

"I know who you are!" the kid yells again as Morin carts him off.

His declaration hits home. Normally, I'm guarded enough that the shit flung at me doesn't stick. Except I've been thinking about the twins today…where they came from…where *I* came from… Huh, I guess I opened old wounds.

I know who you are.

That makes one of us because I sure as hell don't.

I head into the locker room, doing my best to get Nakey Kid's words out of my head. I grab a change of clothes from my locker and take them and my cleanup kit into one of the private shower stalls. Once I've shut myself in, I strip down and toss my stanky clothes into my canvas backpack.

I kind of miss being a uni because now when I get grimed up, it's not police-issued clothes getting wrecked.

It's my wardrobe.

I lean into the shower stall, crank the water as hot as it'll go, and give it a second to heat up.

The guys rib me about my "molten lava" setting preference, but hey, this is me. I love the singe of water on my skin and the humidity of the air filling my lungs.

Who needs a spa? This is a poor girl's sauna.

Just because their delicate skin can't deal with it doesn't make me wrong. I've always liked my showers near scalding. Besides, if any day ever called for a truly hot shower, it's this one.

"Man on deck!" Marx's voice rings out as he pushes the locker room door open.

All officers use the same locker room, men and women. It's not like I've ever cared if any of the guys see me getting ready or winding down after a shift, but the men still call out whenever they enter, just in case I've suddenly sprouted a debilitating case of modesty.

"*Calice!* It's a sauna in here. You trying to steam press our uniforms again, Gagne?"

I flick water over the grungy curtain, hoping I get him. "What are you doing in here in the middle of your shift, Marx? Forget your shoes again?"

"Har-har. *Très drôle.*" Marx has three girls, all under five, and I don't think he's had a full night's sleep in years. It's no surprise he occasionally makes it all the way to the station in only his socks. "Dat only happened once."

"Once is too often for an officer of the law to leave his boots at home, don't you think?"

He chuckles. "Talk to me when you've got two kids kicking around in your bed all night because a dumbass cousin thought it was fun to watch scary clown videos."

I laugh. "The next time Charlie teases me about finding a man and settling down, I'll flash her your badge picture. The bags under your eyes are epic."

"Happy to be of service." The echoing metal-on-metal *clang* signals him shutting his locker and the conclusion of his business. He takes his leave, still razzing me about how hot it is.

"You know what they say, old man. If you can't take the heat, get out of the locker room."

I stand under the water until the filth from my shift swirls in the drain, then a little longer. The tension I carry in my muscles releases bit by bit.

The pipes squawk when I shut the faucet. I run my hands over my head and shake off the excess water. Toweling off and getting dressed is the work of a moment.

I slide on my black tactical jeans, a white tank top, and the thin gray hoodie I've worn almost threadbare.

With all my lady bits covered, I gather my shit and exit my shower stall to finish getting cleaned up in the locker room.

After another rough pass of the towel over my head, my hair hangs straight to my shoulders, and I grab my brush and make a quick pass.

I've never been a mousse and style kinda girl. Why bother? In five minutes, I'll have a helmet on anyway.

I toss the towel into the department laundry bin in the corner and my brush into my locker. The hollow *bang* of metal echoes against the space's hard surfaces, and I take that as my cue to leave.

The silver buckles of my cool-as-fuck motorcycle boots snap closed across my ankles. My leather trench is next. It's snug over the hoodie but better when I reach back and pull the hood free from my collar. The coat falls to the back of my knees, and I have to hike it up when I sit so it doesn't touch my pipes.

A small price to pay.

It's badass.

After shrugging on my backpack, I grab my helmet and keys and head out into the Montréal night.

I'm not a huge fan of shifts that end this late, but when you're trying to catch cockroaches, it's gotta be dark out.

Still, the hour makes the ride home more fun.

My boots drum out a steady rhythm as I close the distance to my most prized possession.

Scarlett—my Ducati Multistrada V4S motorcycle.

Fire engine red with black detailing, she's about the sexiest thing you've ever seen. Straddling her seat, I get things started and let her purr for a moment while I finish getting suited up. Helmet on, Bluetooth synced up, gloves on.

I ease off the station property, the engine purring with the knowledge that as soon as we're clear, we'll be gripping and ripping.

Scarlett is a beast. A sexy, glorious beast.

I make my way north, dodging the traffic hemorrhaging from Olympic Park stadium.

There must have been an event tonight.

By the look of the crowd, it was a big one.

Doesn't matter. After six years on the force, I know all the side streets and alleys, and dodging obstacles makes the ride more fun.

With the wind whipping around my helmet and the lights of the city glittering around me, I zip down Rue Hochelaga. I wave at the regulars getting their late-night fix at Poutine Centrale. On another night, I'd stop for a delicious plate myself.

With Charlie cooking tonight, I don't dare.

Notre-Dame Street runs along the river and is my favorite way to cross the city. I'm booking it in the eastbound lanes when I catch the flickering strobe of lights breaking through the trees of Rougemont Park.

I might be off-duty, but it never hurts to keep an eye out for mischief in the parks late at night.

Especially these days.

Gearing down, I take the parking lot entrance faster than I should. Scarlett handles the challenge like she's on rails.

Yeah, baby.

Sure enough, as soon as I turn off my engine, I hear the laughter of youth. Dismounting, I leave my bike under a light pole in the parking lot and head along the path to check it out.

It wasn't so long ago Kenzie, Briar, Zephyr, and I used to sneak out to drink and let off some steam in the local parks with friends.

I know, cliché, right? Adopted kids bucking the system and getting into trouble...shocking.

What can I say? We have a few rough edges.

I follow the asphalt path a few yards into the trees and stop dead.

"What the fuckety-fuck is this?" There must be eighty teenagers and twenty-somethings bouncing to the rhythm of a beat I don't hear. They've got their arms in the air, smiles on their faces, and are having the time of their lives.

They're not human kids.

As crazy as it sounds, a few months ago the veil between realms came down and we humans found out that not only are the myths of fairies, elves, and fantasy species true...there are members of those communities living among us.

From where I'm standing in the shadow of the trees, I see wings, tails, horns, pink skin, and glowing eyes. Hell, a couple of them even have animal faces and furry legs and hoofs.

It's a fae rave.

It's a *silent* fae rave?

Are they transmitting music on an empowered frequency that humans can't hear?

Is that a thing?

Honestly, as fae gatherings go, it's very tame.

Members of the fae community don't seem to share the same modesty or restraint as humans. In the past six months, there have been endless sex complaints. Sprites humping in the skies overhead, naked elves enjoying the nature of the park a little too freely, orgies on apartment roofs, and the list goes on.

Those are the lovers. We've also got the fighters.

Bickering between species, bar brawls, satyrs ramming people with their horns... Hell, two nixies set a McDonald's on fire because their fries were cold.

So yeah, dancing to imaginary music is tame.

Not knowing what to think about it, I scan the scene and

strike off toward the only adult I find in the crowd. The DJ working the stage seems to be in charge, so I start there.

Climbing the three steps of the raised platform, I examine the intricate swirls of the tats covering the muscled rounds of his shoulders and arms.

Wow, this guy is jacked.

I scold myself for admiring the way the ink hugs those seriously toned muscles and focus on the designs. They aren't exactly tribal. More like runes. Maybe Norse...no, that's not right. Maybe Egyptian?

In any case, they're damned impressive.

After the art appreciation portion of the evening is over, I tap his shoulder.

He straightens, tugs one of the earpieces of his headphones behind his ear, and lifts his chin. "Yeah?"

"What's this about?" I use my stern cop voice and waggle my finger at the mass of bodies. "The park's closed after dark."

The guy, about thirty, looks me up and down and I can't tell if he dislikes me because I'm human or because I'm holding up my badge. "It's a fly-your-flag freedom celebration."

"Yeah, well, do you have a permit?"

"We're just dancing."

"Dancing to what?" I stare out at the crowd of swaying bodies.

"Music. Obviously." The level of sarcasm dripping off his response is admirable.

"Dude, why are you busting my balls?"

"Why are you busting mine?"

"Did you miss the part where I'm holding a badge, and you don't have a permit for an event on municipal property?"

His mouth quirks up into a crooked smile. "Actually, it's less about me missing it and more about me not giving a shit."

"Nice. What's your name?"

"Gareth."

"All right, Gareth. At the risk of receiving the lashing of another sharp-tongued retort, what music?"

He reaches into a bowl at the front of his table and hands me an earbud. I hold it at the opening of my ear—because hello, it's an earbud in a communal party bowl—and yeah, okay, I hear the music.

"So, everyone's got earbuds in and are just dancing and having a freedom celebration?"

"Ding, ding, ding. Give the woman a prize," he says, sounding simultaneously condescending and bored. "Look, we're not causing any trouble."

"Except for the part where you're trespassing during hours when the park is closed."

"But that's the whole point. This is a freedom celebration. These kids have been getting heckled and ridiculed so much lately, they needed to have some fun without judgy humans around."

I check my watch and exhale. *I'm sooo late.*

This is the absolute last thing I need tonight. "Okay, I'll make you a deal. I have to call it into the station, but I'll make it clear you're all being cool and that I'm giving you a chance. My station will send a patrol car, but I'll pick who comes."

His jaw clenches, and he folds his arms across his chest. "Yeah. Who will you pick?"

"Good guys who won't give you a hard time."

"Cops always give empowered a hard time. Haven't you heard we're evil and don't belong here?"

"Not me or my guys. Look, if you keep up your end, and there's no trouble, I'll give you the okay to have your celebration until midnight."

"Midnight? Fuck, Grandma, that's when things start getting interesting."

I shake my head. "That's the deal, Cinderella. Midnight and

then your magical ball is over, and your DJ setup turns into a pumpkin."

Everyone stops dancing and he curses and flicks a few switches. When things start up again, he turns to me and frowns. "Give me a break. We're not doing anything wrong."

"Sorry, dude. Trust is built over time, and for right now, I don't know you. I also don't have time to babysit."

His eyes flicker to flame red, and I'm not sure if it's a trick of the lighting or if I'm glimpsing the beast behind the tall, dark, and dangerous exterior. The hair on the nape of my neck stands on end, and my instincts scream the latter.

He leans closer and pegs me with an intense gaze. "Why don't you head out and forget all about us and our private party?"

A rush of heat awakens my cells, and I feel the weight of his suggestion tug at my mind. I push against the invasion and stand my ground. "Nice try, big guy. I'm calling it in. I can request a patrol car to join the fun and keep an eye on things until midnight, or I can shut you down now. Your choice."

His head tilts and his crooked smile returns. "What are you?"

"What are *you*, big guy?"

He chuckles. "As you said, I don't know you, and trust is built over time."

Touché. "All righty then, what's your choice?"

He glares at me and huffs. "You aren't giving me a choice."

I give him a shit-eating grin. "Ding, ding, ding. Now you're catching on."

Before I walk away, I pull a business card from the pocket of my leather slicker and hand it to him. "We'll build trust over time, Gareth. Next time, give me a heads-up and maybe I'll extend the curfew."

He reads my name aloud. "Inspector Juliette Gagne."

"Call me Jules."

"Well, Jules, not only are you a cocky pain in the ass, you're a killjoy."

"I won't argue the pain in the ass part but a killjoy? Ouch. I'm the coolest of cool."

Tossing my loaner earbud back into the bowl, I jump off the stage and dance back to the parking lot. I feel the heat of his gaze on my ass and give him a little extra sway.

Coolest of the cool. *Shit yeah, I am.*

I call back to the station and ask Marx if he and Rene can swing by and keep an eye on the fae freedom rave. Rene has been working with the mayor's office on a special fae task force.

He'll treat them right.

With that done, I wash my hands of things and get back to my regularly scheduled evening.

Not cool? Seriously? That guy doesn't know what he's talking about. Look at my spank motorcycle.

Scarlett is way cool.

Kicking my leg over the leather of her seat, I pull on my helmet and fire my girl to life. Leaning into my planted foot, I crank the throttle and burn a smoking one-eighty before launching into the night.

Suck it, muscle boy...that was cool.

CHAPTER TWO

The thundering power Scarlett unleashes makes my heart beat faster. The untapped power she holds in reserve makes me yearn for open roads.

Not very cop-like, I know.

When I signed up for the force, I knew I'd face a career of whacked and weird. Cops see a lot of people on their worst days, and on those days, behaviors and circumstances are less than pleasant.

I didn't realize that I was pledging to serve and protect a city full of newly awakened empowered folks and the non-magical people afraid and appalled to share the streets with them.

Six months ago, the world found out magical beings exist. There was a once-in-a-millennium rebalancing of power called the Time of the Colliding Realms, and the veil between our world and the fae realm dropped.

The big question now is whether or not the powers in the know can reinstate the veil and change it back.

That's over my pay grade, but I'm guessing not.

There's no *un*knowing something this big. And even if we could, "normal" people have transitioned since then. These awakenings have shocked not only the non-magical folks but the people affected.

Even if the people in charge restore the magical veil between realms, I can't imagine it will undo the triggering of bizarre powers and physical traits.

I lean into the bend in the road and give Scarlett more throttle.

Worst of all, now everyone and their brother thinks they have magic inside them. It's made life as a city cop crazier than usual, and that's saying something.

A shooting pain zaps behind my left eye.

My vision fritzes and I gear down fast and slow my roll. Laying down my bike in the street while moving at a clip like this would break my heart. Breathing slow and steady, I ride out the explosion of daggers going off behind my eyeballs.

Dammit, that's not the first time I've felt like my cranium might split open.

What the hell?

My head is pounding worse than when I have a squad party hangover and my muscles and bones ache too. Maybe I'm about to morph like all the other poor saps caught up in the mysterious magical wave sweeping the planet.

Maybe I've got some awesome power about to break free inside me.

Maybe I'll be able to fly or be indestructible or something. Ha! Who are we kidding?

I'm likely coming down with the flu.

I think about Nakey Kid and the time I've spent the past couple of days searching dumpsters behind that building for a lead.

Yeah, I'm probably incubating at least a half-dozen new strains of mystery ick.

When the malaise eases, I go back to becoming one with my motorcycle. I loop onto the Trans-Canada Highway and rev it up.

The St. Lawrence River stretches like a ribbon of spilled ink, a void of darkness cutting through the twinkling lights of nighttime Montréal. I live on the other side of the water, which means twice a day, I get to take my bike over the Lafontaine Bridge or through its massive tunnel.

The air chills as I cross the river and I breathe deeply.

The day's worries, race hostilities, increased drugs, and death rates—they all melt away.

That's the thing about riding Scarlett. When I go fast enough, my troubles can't keep up.

On the other side of the bridge, I take my exit and slow down through my neighborhood. If Charlie catches me racing home, she'll lose her mind.

As it is, she sends me statistics on *murder*cycle accidents and links to reliable, safe cars for sale on the regular.

We agree to disagree on modes of transportation.

Besides, I have June Bug, my old VW beater, for the winter months if I need to get somewhere in a car.

When I get home, I gear down and roll into the driveway on momentum alone.

No need to poke the Charlie bear. She's easy-going and good-humored—until she's not.

Once I'm in the driveway, the sensor in my backpack triggers the opener for the big, metal firehouse door. Normally, I would slow down more, drop my feet, and putter inside.

Tonight, the sweet sixteen party of two very sweet sixteen-year-olds occupies the bays.

I steer my bike to the side of the driveway instead.

My sister's electric car and my brother's old truck are Charlie-approved, but both are boring next to my beloved Scarlett.

I park alongside them, careful to avoid tripping over the long cord coiling out of Kenzie's car. I don't have to worry about Briar's truck. Even if I ride directly into the side of that thing, it won't make a noticeable difference.

Doesn't matter. Form follows function.

It gets him to and from construction sites and holds a ton of supplies. It also gets him to the late-night MMA cage fights he thinks I don't know about. I appreciate that he tries not to involve me, but hey, I'm his sister, not his keeper.

"Honeys, I'm home!"

The first to respond to my shout-out is Backup, the moody and aloof bull mastiff we all share. He lopes over, sniffs me up and down, and doesn't seem impressed.

What else is new?

"Hey, big guy." I scratch him behind the ears, and he flicks his head to get away.

"Finally!" Anna follows Backup, bounding over to grab my arm and tug me toward the party. "We waited for you."

I snort and hold my ground. "No, you didn't. Charlie knew I had a late shift and there's no way your brother held off eating."

I take off my helmet and set it on the seat, unbuckle my boots, toe them off, and set them on the mat below my hook for my jacket.

"We waited on the cake," Anna amends, grinning.

"Yeah, that's what I thought."

The moment we step through the doorway, the rich scents of Charlie's cooking and the lively beat of the music hit me. We've all had enough shit piled on us that we know life should be lived and enjoyed.

This is the Gagne way.

"Jules, finally." Micah rushes over to offer me a fist bump. "Hey, can I show my friends your gun?"

That earns him a disapproving look from Charlie. "No guns and no thug talk, brat. You might be another year older, but I can still take you."

"Not a chance. Have you seen these guns?" Micah holds up his arms and waggles his brows as he flexes with all he's got.

Charlie snorts. "Fine. I'll instruct Briar to take you down."

Micah sobers. "That I believe. B is a freakin' tank."

"Well, if you don't want to be mowed over by the tank, behave."

Micah laughs and spins away unaffected.

Charlie grabs my arm and drags me through the crowd of friendly faces toward the tables set up with food. "I know you do important work, but even so, you're late. This is a big night for the twins. They're sixteen. You remember what that was like, right?"

"You mean me sneaking out at night for backseat sex in Timmy Renaux's Kia?"

"Exactly. Now, if they're late for their afterparty sexcapades, that's on you."

I hold up my hands. "My bad, but if I was on time I would've smelled like a dumpster. Then everyone would've left, and all your hours of cooking efforts would've gone to waste."

"Impossible." Micah rushes to join us at the table. "We somehow manage to eat despite your stank every other time you come over."

I laugh, grabbing a plate. "I'll let you have that since it's your birthday. But I'll have you know my offensive odor was worse than usual today."

"Hard to imagine."

"Right?"

I stop clowning around and admire the huge spread. The big table is laid out edge-to-edge with aluminum catering pans holding lasagna, tourtière, cabbage rolls, chili, scalloped potatoes….

I heap on my selections, thankful there's still food left. "There are more people here than I expected."

Micah chuckles. "That's because unlike you, Anna and I know how to be sociable and make friends."

"Rude. I have friends, brat."

Anna laughs. "The guy at the morgue doesn't count. Geez, Jules, your best friend is a dead guy doctor."

"He's a forensic pathologist, and so what? Luc's good people. Besides, you guys are my friends too."

"Family doesn't count either." Anna reaches out and touches my damp, helmet-flattened nest of hair. "Seriously, would it kill you to pull a brush through this before you put your helmet on?"

"It likely wouldn't kill me, no. Does that mean I'm going to do it? Also no. And, if you remember, I'm the oldest. You should learn to respect your elders."

"This is why you're turning thirty and still single."

I can't win. "I'm twenty-seven, not thirty, and I enjoy being single. I love my life."

"Keep telling yourself that."

Rude. Little sisters...amirite?

She's back to flicking my hair and frowning. It seems Kenzie has recruited her to the haircare cause. "Seriously, Jules, you shouldn't hide your prettiness."

I fork in my first bite of food and groan at the savory bliss making love in my mouth. "My job performance focuses on how many criminals I can get off the streets, not how moisturized my hair is."

"It's not an either/or scenario."

Ignoring her, I add a couple of biscuits to the top of my plate and mingle with the rest of the party people.

Buying Papa's decommissioned fire station after his death was the best decision we ever made. This building is a huge part of our history, it gives us space to spread out, and there's the bonus of a fun pole to slide down later when the drinking takes hold, and Charlie takes the twins home.

"Yo, sister from another mister." Zephyr has an empty plate in his hand and the rim of a beer bottle pressed to his lips. The youngest of what we call the first four, Zephyr is a six-foot-two wiry hippie rock star type. He's the wild child of our bunch and is always getting into scuffles.

It's not that he's a bad guy.

He has a good soul but is volatile. I can't count how many times he's lost his cool and gotten fired from jobs. If there is a wrong and rash choice to make, you can bet your balls he'll make it and need me to help clean up the mess.

"Here, take my seat." He moves to make space for me to park it.

"Thanks, bro. How's the party?"

He snorts. "Baller. What's not to love about a family tween party?"

I sink onto the couch next to our sister. The last to arrive and join our adoption foursome, Kenzie is black and beautiful with the grace of a ballerina and the refined taste of a debutant.

She's calm, patient, and pretty much the polar opposite of me in every way.

Naturally, we're besties.

When I settle, I realize she's pointing at my head with a sheer look of horror. "What the hell is with that hairdo scare-do bird's nest on top of your head, Jules? Did you forget we have company tonight?"

I fork in a chunk of tourtière and savor the flavor a moment before answering. "By company, you mean you invited someone you want to set me up with, and I'm not meeting expectations?"

Kenzie rolls her eyes. "Could you work with me? Why does everything have to be so difficult with you?"

"A question I've been asking her for years," Charlie interjects. "If you figure out the answer, let me know."

"Thanks for that." I give my sister the finger and fork in another mouthful.

"Fine. Sorry. You do you."

Dinner is delicious, *naturally*, and after my second plate, I work through the crowd having fun chatting with Anna's and Micah's friends and learning the dirt they won't want Charlie to know. They have a cool circle.

They were right when they pointed out I don't spend enough time cultivating friendships.

They were wrong too.

First, Luc Leclerc is the bomb, and the fact that he runs the morgue gives us more time to hang out. Isn't sharing interests an important part of friendship?

Hells yeah, it is.

Second, since Zephyr, Briar, Kenzie, and I are all within three years of each other, we grew up hanging out together. They are my best friends.

Charlie ranks up there too. She's known us since we were babies when her brother and our foster mother adopted us and took us in.

When they died, we were too young to live on our own. She became our legal guardian and saved us from going back into the system.

She is our hero.

Our odd, Bohemian, scattered hero.

Charlie brings out a massive cake with sixteen candles burning brightly on each side. When she steps over the dog, her toe catches, and she pitches forward.

The world kicks into gear and slips into slow motion all at once. I jump up to help. Briar spins and curses. Charlie stumbles forward....

Three-inch flames flare off the candles, and I pull my face back as I grip the edge of the silver platter. Thankfully, my hair doesn't catch fire, and my eyebrows don't singe.

After setting the cake safely on the table, I draw a deep breath. "*Shit*, Charlie, are you trying to set me on fire?"

Briar chuckles and points at the inferno flickering wildly on top of the cake. "I love the trick candles. Well done, Charlie. Very dramatic entrance."

Charlie clears her throat and straightens with all the dignity she can muster. "For my next trick…"

Briar hands us each a fresh beer and shrugs. "We live in a fire station. No harm done."

He's right, although right now, it looks more like a frat house than a fire station.

Our adoptive father used to be the captain here, and we visited while he worked. When they closed this station house five years after his death, we bought the building with money from his death insurance payout.

I think he would like that we saved his building.

The four of us had been talking about moving out of our childhood home, and we couldn't bear to let Papa's building go.

Upstairs, we each have a private living space that spills out into a communal kitchen and a big living room. On the ground floor, we have the fire truck bays where we park and plenty of space left for our workout equipment and a pool table.

Tonight, the cars are parked outside, and the gym has been pushed against the wall to make room for the party. It's not a fancy space, but it holds fifty people easily and still leaves enough room for a dance floor and tables for food and refreshments.

Micah and Anna wait for the cake to be down and secure, and each blows out their half. We all cheer when the candles go out and sing a round of Happy Birthday.

When the last note is still hanging in the air, Briar claps and waggles his brow. "Now that that's done, let's carve this sucker up."

"This cake is delicious, Charlie," I tell her a few minutes later, scooping up a forkful heavy with frosting. "Can I take some to the precinct? They're always asking for your cooking."

Charlie grunts. "I don't doubt that but the more they eat the slower they'll be on their feet. I've seen Morin's waistline. If he gets any fatter, you'll have to roll him out of the cruiser."

I laugh. "He's not that bad. Besides, he's got a new girlfriend who's trying to get him on keto."

Briar snorts. "I can't see that happening."

"Yeah no, but hey, love makes people do crazy things, amirite? If I can sneak him some food at the office, I don't mind."

"If they wanted food, they should've sent you home on time," Charlie retorts.

"Unfortunately, junkies and criminals have no respect for shift change or evening plans."

"If only they could schedule their crimes to be more convenient for you," Briar deadpans.

Anna chuckles. "Charlie, she made it in time to eat and sing for the cake. Isn't it more important that she's here and safe?"

Charlie grunts. "I don't understand why a smart, beautiful woman like you needs to work a job that gets you home halfway into the dead of night."

"It could be worse." Zephyr grins. "She could be a true woman of the night and not get home until morning."

Charlie pegs him in the head with a dinner roll, and the rest of us bust up. "Don't even joke about that and certainly not in front of the twins."

Zephyr grins at me and winks. "I meant as a night nurse, Charlie. Geez, what were you thinking?"

Okay, that was funny.

Still, it doesn't derail her rant for long. "And riding home on that dangerous machine in the dark, for what? So, you can get up the next day to be threatened by vicious thugs?"

Ha! The scrawny, naked, completely out of his gourd kid I

arrested tonight wasn't a pinnacle of viciousness or even all that threatening.

"It's not that bad. Besides, I love my job."

"You could love another job too. A normal job that lets you have a social life and time to meet men. You could be a bartender —you'd meet lots of men then—or work in the Harley store. Lots of men there too."

Uh-huh.

"Don't roll your eyes. There's nothing wrong with wanting you to have a work-life balance."

"I like the way things are weighted in my life. I have goals for the city and ways to make things better for people who can't make things better themselves."

Kenzie holds her hands up in the universal sign of calling a time-out and grins. "Getting back to the birthday party...hey Zephyr, will you play us some music?"

"Subtle, Kenz." Zephyr laughs and finishes his beer. "Sure, let me be your dancing monkey."

I snort. "You wish. Monkeys are cuter."

"Monkeys are pesky assholes," Briar interjects.

"Oh, then that works."

Zephyr gives us both the finger and laughs.

"Language," Charlie snaps.

"Charlie, that was sign language, not swearing. Big difference." Zephyr gives me a friendly shove as he passes me to grab his guitar.

"Assaulting a police officer is a criminal offense."

Zephyr snorts. "Yeah, so is *impersonating* one, but you do that every day."

"Hey, I'm legit. I have a gun and eat donuts and wrestle perps and everything."

Charlie mutters something under her breath, and I decide she's wound up enough for one night.

I grab another piece of cake and sit on the arm of the couch beside Anna. "Aren't you playing, chickie-poo?"

"Nah. Not tonight. I'll let Zephyr hog the spotlight."

Zephyr winks. "I promise to delight your guests and treat them to a great show."

I bump shoulders with Anna. "Wow, he's talented *and* humble."

Kenzie sits on the floor to lean against Anna's knees. She's got her bongo set with her and sets them in front of her crossed legs. "Yeah, Zephyr's the poster child for self-effacing humility."

Briar claps his massive hands together and pulls out his harmonica. "Come on. Let's make some music!"

CHAPTER THREE

As my siblings play music into the night the sixteen-year-old crowd thins, and our adult friends start to arrive. It's well-known in our circles that once you get the Gagnes going, we don't stop. There are worse reputations to have.

I enjoy a few drinks, sing a few songs, and the stress of the past weeks and months slips away.

This. I need more moments like this.

Since the fae veil dropped, it seems like there's never been enough downtime.

Thus, me feeling like roadkill.

When it's time for Charlie and the twins to head home, we walk them out, sing another round of Happy Birthday, and thank them for a good time.

After waving our goodbyes, Zephyr and Briar rejoin the party, and Kenzie and I walk around back to wind down with some drinks on the patio.

Our firehouse isn't exactly prime real estate. It's a giant square brick building with high fences and no curb appeal, but it's spacious, it played a big part in our childhood, and I love its location.

We're near the St. Lawrence River, close enough for me to see the islands from my bedroom window. Backup and I jog over to Boucherville National Park and enjoy the wilds of forest life in the city when the weather is on my side.

Besides, this is where my siblings are so there's nowhere I'd rather be.

I sink into my patio chair, lean back, and stare at the pink haze of fae magic that covers the moon.

It's so weird how the city's ambient energy pulses all around us. I didn't notice it as much when the veil first fell, but the more Rene tells me about what's going on behind the scenes, the more I see and feel it around me.

Thinking about it makes the hair on my entire body prickle and stand on end. It's like the world around me is charged with a low level of electricity.

It's not quite uncomfortable, but it is freaky.

Speaking of freaky—the pink air smells like cherry Coke. It makes me thirsty.

I'd bet the sales of the real deal have gone up a bazillion percent since this all began.

Who doesn't like cherry Coke?

"I'm worried about Zephyr." Kenzie runs a finger through the condensation on her bottle. "Something seems off with him."

"Are you sure it's not, you know, Zephyr being Zephyr?"

He's always been the wild one of our quartet. We don't know what happened to him before his adoption into our family—and he's not alone in having his background be a mystery—but we know he's always been moody and prone to stormy outbursts.

Plus, there are his dreams.

Zephyr has violent night terrors. Once he got big enough to do damage in his sleep, he started wearing wrist restraints and a bite guard at night to keep from hurting himself or others.

Kenzie shakes her head. "It's something specific. Something

recent. I know he's always been...well, Zephyr...but something is wrong."

"Have you asked him what's going on?"

Kenzie looks at me like I've suggested that she try teaching Backup how to read. "He swears there's nothing. Then he avoids me like I've got the plague."

I lift my cooler and let a long swallow of fruity bliss pass over my tongue. I share Kenzie's concern for our brother, but if there's one thing I've learned in my years on the force, it's that you can't change someone else's mind. If Zephyr wants our help, he'll ask for it.

We can't make him take it.

"I thought maybe you could poke around and use your police contacts?"

I snort. "Yeah, no problem. I'll fire up the twenty-somethings database and see what's trending with broody troublemakers."

Kenzie laughs. "Maybe check that database for yourself too, but instead of broody troublemaker, try mouthy cranky pants."

She's not wrong. "Sorry, I feel like cat hack."

"Well, then, maybe listen to Charlie for once and take some time off to rest."

"Nah, that's much too sensible. Where's the fun in that?"

She rolls her eyes. "Right. You should keep on keeping on until you drop."

"That's my plan."

"You're impossible."

"Hey, look at the bright side. With Zephyr and me in the mix, you'll always be the golden child."

"Well, someone's gotta keep Charlie's hair from turning completely gray."

"I think Zephyr has rendered that noble pursuit entirely useless."

"You're probably right." Kenzie twirls her bottle, her pink nail polish glinting in the light of the patio lanterns. "He's always getting into trouble. Maybe I should wait for whatever the Mischief of the Month is to die down."

"I'll keep an eye out," I tell her. My siblings and I might rib and tease each other, but at the end of the day, I trust Kenzie, and I love Zephyr. If she thinks something is up with him and wants me to help, I won't say no.

"Thanks." Kenzie takes another sip and finishes her drink. "How about you? What was that thing about smelling like a dumpster today?"

"Oh, no big deal. Just another day at the office." I tell her about the crazy naked kid and make her laugh when I describe the gibberish he was spouting. She laughs even harder when I recount Rene's reaction to the kid's boy bits swaying in the night breeze.

For some reason, I leave out the part where he claimed to know who or what I was. I know it was the drugs, but still, it hit too close to home.

"Well, at least your job is never boring," Kenzie offers.

"That's for sure." I yawn and check the time on my phone. "It's not that late, but I'm bagged."

"You've had a lot of excitement today."

"Yeah, and I think I'm coming down with something." As much as I hate the idea of getting out of this chair, there's a memory foam mattress waiting for me upstairs. "Happy birthday party, sista. Enjoy what's left of the night."

"Happy birthday party to you too." We *clink* bottles and haul our butts out of our chairs.

Stepping back, I let her go first.

I take two steps when heat flushes on the back of my neck. My cop instincts kick in hard, and I stop to assess my surroundings.

Glancing around, I search the shadows of the night. The original fences of the fire station stand eight feet high and block out any line of sight from our neighbors.

Despite the sensation that I'm being watched, there's no one there.

Ha, now I'm bringing work home with me.

I used to be unflappable, but the world is getting too weird. It's likely the effects of the flu kicking in. Leave it to me to mistake cold symptoms for a paranormal phenomenon.

The muffled screams of terror have me jolting out of a dead sleep. Without thought, I'm bounding off my bed and racing barefoot across my room and out the door.

Straight across the kitchen, I push past a gawking Barbie girl in Briar's T-shirt and join the big guy in wrestling Zephyr to the mattress.

The first thing I check is that his wrist restraints are clipped shut and secure.

They are.

The next thing is that Briar has a good hold on him.

He does.

"It's okay, Z. We've got you, buddy. Come back to us." I scramble to keep the arm I'm securing from flailing, and it astounds me once again how strong he is when he's in a fit like this.

Kenzie arrives and grips both of Zephyr's ankles and starts to sing *Carry On My Wayward Son* by Kansas.

It was a joke for our benefit the first time she sang it. We were all big *Supernatural* fans and loved the song, but since then, we've found it's the only thing that calms him down other than fighting us and wearing himself out.

Once Kenzie's voice takes hold of him, the fighting eases, and he falls still. He doesn't wake up. His eyes flip open for a moment, then his head lolls to the side, and he starts snoring.

I nod at Briar, climb off the mattress without disturbing Zephyr, and go back to bed.

The next morning, I wake and double-check that a dump truck hasn't run me over. Feels like it. I lay there for a bit, trying to gather the strength to get vertical. I wonder how Nakey Kid is feeling this morning. Whatever drugs were in his system can't have left him feeling much better than me.

At least I didn't spend any time yesterday naked and shrieking nonsense.

After dragging my ass out of bed, I shuffle across my bedroom floor. "Morning, you two."

The two goldfish swimming around in their bowl on top of my dresser pause and look at me, waiting for me to feed them. Every morning, it's the same thing. I tell them about my dreams during the night or my plans for the day, and they make lazy circles until I sprinkle some flakes of food on top of their water.

Today, though, I don't feel all that talkative.

My head is throbbing, and if I had any dreams before or after wrestling Zephyr, I sure can't remember them.

I skip to the part where I drop some food into the bowl, and they swim up to nibble it with their rubbery little mouths.

"Now, Jack, leave enough for Jack."

Both goldfish are named Jack. One's Reacher and the other is Ryan. Don't ask me if I can tell them apart.

They're fish.

I set the tub of fish flakes down and stretch. It's my day off, but I've never been one to laze around. Out the window, I can see Boucherville National Park across the water. I could really go for a light jog.

In the state I'm in, that doesn't seem wise.

Better see how I feel after a cup of coffee, at least.

I get dressed but skip the shower, having already scrubbed myself nearly raw last night. I must've slept weirdly because my hair is bent and sticking up in every direction. "Meh, whatevs."

Kenzie will have something to say about that. She's been begging me to sleep on a silk pillowcase for ages.

That's what happens when you belong to an adopted family with siblings of every race and color. You get your black sister giving you curly hair care advice while your blond, broad-shouldered brother teaches you how to pull off a great hockey deke.

None of them are around when I go out to the kitchen. I'm either up early enough that everyone else is still in bed or late enough that they've left for the day.

"Which is it, Backup? Breakfast or brunch?"

Backup has no answer for me. He comes over and gives me a thorough sniffing, sticking his nose in places he has no business invading.

"Dude, personal space."

He sits in front of me and stares like he doesn't like what he's smelling.

Rude.

Am I paranoid or is my dog judging me?

"Oh, there's a note." I head over to the countertop and read the smooth and swirling cursive.

Left you an iced mocha in the fridge.

Cool. "Thanks, Kenzie."

I'll leave that for a late-morning pick-me-up. For now, I need something hot and bitter to beat out my headache. I turn on the coffee machine, listening to it *whirr* and drip as it prepares my morning beverage.

The silence of the kitchen bugs me. I'm used to the bustle and bullshit of the precinct or at least one of my siblings bouncing around in the firehouse.

The only recourse is to put on some music. At least having the kitchen to myself means I get to pick the tunes. Lately, Zephyr has been insisting on helping us broaden our horizons by playing some horrendously experimental noises on his speakers.

I'm more of a classic rock gal.

Not streaming from Spotify—vinyl rules.

Each of us gets one wall of shelves in the main living room. Mine houses my record collection, along with some awards and memorabilia I've earned during my time on the force.

I shift through my Led Zeppelin, bypassing the ones with too much heavy drums and bass. Right now, my head couldn't handle anything but their gentlest stuff.

Today calls for III, with its bluesy Celtic sounds.

Once I've got Plant, Page, Jones, and Bonham to keep me company, things in the kitchen feel much homier. I fix myself a bowl of sugary cereal off Zephyr's shelf in the pantry, grab my coffee mug, and head to the sofa where I've left a dusty cardboard banker's box packed nearly to bursting with file folders.

It might be my day off, but that doesn't mean I'm not working. Charlie would kill me if she knew, but as far as she's aware, I'm sleeping in and taking Backup for a safe, leisurely jog around the park.

Truth be told, these files need attention and I need a distraction. When the captain let me bring a few boxes of cold case files home, he didn't expect much.

He also didn't know me very well.

When I started this side gig a couple of years ago, there were eighty-nine unclaimed bodies at the Montréal morgue over eighteen months.

That wasn't something I could let go. The cases stuck in my head, and I knew the only way to get them out of there would be to solve them.

Now, in my off hours, I figure out who these people were and how they ended up at the morgue. I contact their families if I can and try to give them closure.

Those eighty-nine unclaimed dead bodies I started with?

Now there are only seventy-two. I intend to keep driving that number down until it's at zero. At which point I guess I'll have to find a new hobby.

This sort of stuff is what rocks my socks.

Helping people whose identities are lost.

Helping figure out who they were.

No Freudian analysis needed. I know what it's like to be disconnected from the people who should have rooted you in your past.

I flip through a few files, but I can't focus. The coffee has dampened my headache somewhat, but I still feel tired and sweaty.

Plus, I went over these files a few days ago. Nothing new is ready to jump out at me.

I draw a deep breath and try to shake off the pent-up energy buzzing around in my cells. Soon, I'm back over at my shelf, standing in front of my album covers.

I pull out a worn jacket of a Bright Eyes album I loved as a teenager and take it back to my spot on the sofa.

Propping it open, I slide a hand inside and pull out the four papers that sum up where I come from.

The first is a police report of what they believe to be an arson case at a nondescript house in a neighborhood on the city's east end. I was found in the fire and rescued from the inferno by my adoptive father—a firefighter.

That's how I ended up a Gagne.

The other people in the building weren't so lucky. My father pulled me from the arms of a guy who was dead by the time firefighters came in looking for survivors.

They never IDed him, and no one ever claimed him.

I still have his picture, though. That's document number two. There's not much to learn from the image. It's like every photo taken at the Montréal morgue, a body on a cold metal table.

Something is different about this guy.

Markings cover his skin, but due to the graininess of the photo and the fact that he was burned pretty badly, I've never been able to figure them out.

I can't tell whether they're wounds, like knife slashes, or whether they were there on purpose, like runes or tattoos.

The next piece of paper is the intake form for "Baby Doe." That would be me. Aside from listing my approximate age—six months—and the fact that I had black hair and hazel eyes, it lacks information.

No DNA match to the dead guy. No hospitals with a record of birth that lined up with my age. No one who ever came looking for their missing baby.

No one ever discovered who I was or how I got to Montréal with that man. The answers died with him.

The last paper is my emergency foster placement with Laurette Deschamps, who by the grace of all things right and just in this world, took me in and loved me every day of my life.

Over the next year, the handsome firefighter who saved me dropped by enough times that sparks ignited.

Voila, we were the beginnings of a family.

I stare at the foster form, the first piece of evidence that I truly existed as part of a family. By then, I wasn't listed as "Baby Doe" anymore, but under the name Maman gave me. Juliette.

Of course, by the time the other three arrived a few years later, it was clear to them such a delicate, feminine name didn't suit me.

I went from "Baby Doe" to "Juliette" to "Jules."

I've been Jules ever since.

Whether I was called something else before, if that man with the strange markings knew me by a different name, I guess I'll never know.

The buzzing of my phone jerks me out of my thoughts. I read Luc's name and swipe green. "Dude, surely you have access to the departmental calendar. It's my day off."

"And here I thought we were at the 'anytime day or night' stage of our relationship."

I laugh. "Sure, we are, but you know how I like to relax on my days off."

"You're full of shit. You're working that box of cold case files, aren't you?"

"Maybe."

He laughs. "Thought so. No, seriously, I've got something you'll want to see."

Luc has me dead to rights. He knows I love a good mystery, and if he says he's got something for me, there's no way I can say no.

"All right, give me forty-five minutes."

CHAPTER FOUR

When I'm ready to leave, I go back out to the kitchen to grab my bag and notebook. Briar and Kenzie jump apart like their asses are on fire and halt their whispered conversation. The two of them busy themselves looking nonchalant, and it's not suspicious at all.

Seriously? "What's up with you two?"

Kenzie blinks at me, feigning innocence. "Nothing. It's fine. Everything is fine."

"Uh-huh. Did you two forget I solve mysteries for a living, and I've known you both since we've all been old enough to walk and talk?"

The guilt on their faces clinches it.

"Seriously, what's going on?"

"It's nothing." Kenzie waves at me as if her Ben Kenobi impression will wipe my suspicions away.

"It's fine." Briar holds out his arm.

There's a gnarly dry patch covering most of his forearm. I lean in to take a closer look. It's almost like someone poured concrete over his skin and let it cure. "What the fuck is that? Did you touch a chemical or something on a construction site?

"I build houses, Jules. I don't work in a laboratory."

"Well, what did Charlie say about it?"

When in doubt, we Gagne kids always defer to her wisdom. If she thinks you need a doctor, you probably do. If she thinks you can walk it off, then you definitely can.

"I didn't show her," Briar mumbles and tugs his sleeve down to cover things. "I didn't want to ruin the party."

He sounds genuinely worried. Briar is our gentle giant. He's a brawny, six-foot-four linebacker of a brother but he's also really damn sweet.

I can't stand to see him scared.

I side-hug him and pat his shoulder. "It's fine, bro. Nothing a little lotion and maybe a checkup with a dermatologist can't solve. Don't panic."

Kenzie pegs me with a look but goes with it. "Yeah, Jules is right. I'll stop by the pharmacy this afternoon and see what I can find that might help."

He seems encouraged by that, so we'll call it a win. I change the subject. "Is your sleepover guest gone home?"

Briar leans back in the chair and sighs. "Yeah, sorry. I don't like that she came out and saw Zephyr like that. I told her to stay in bed, but she didn't listen."

"People are drawn to a train wreck."

Kenzie scowls at me. "Don't say that."

"You know what I mean."

"Yeah, we do," Briar says. "And yeah, she's gone."

That's good enough for me. "Where is Z? I couldn't believe he let me play an entire Zeppelin album without coming out to explain to me that I'm missing out on the current decade's most irritating screech rock."

Kenzie glances at his door. "He's still sleeping."

I check the time on the stove clock. "It's almost eleven."

Briar nods. "After we all went in at four, I had to go in again at half-past six. Took a while to get him sorted, but he calmed down enough to sleep through the morning."

I love Zephyr, but I'm glad Briar is around to help manage him during his night terrors. Both of my brothers are strong, but Briar is a beast. "Sorry, I didn't hear a thing during round two. I must've been out cold."

Kenzie glances anxiously at the two of us. "They're getting worse. Even when he has a bad night, he only sleeps until nine or ten."

"He'll be up soon." Briar's reassurance falls flat because he doesn't sound convinced.

Okay, now I'm worried.

Kenzie adds, "Charlie thinks he ought to try herbal supplements before bed, but he says it's a bunch of *l'enterrement de crapaud.*"

Briar chuckles. "Charlie has never met a problem she can't solve by feeding you something."

True story.

"Speaking of…where'd you put the leftovers? I gotta pack some up to bring into the precinct."

Briar flashes me a look. "This is your day off. Remember what Charlie said. You've gotta work on a balance."

I hold up my hands. "I have balance. I'm dropping off some goodies. I promised."

"And you're not working?"

"No."

"So, just to the station to deliver cookies, then straight back?"

When I don't answer, Kenzie moves to stand behind Briar and crosses her arms. "The whole truth and nothing but the truth."

I laugh. "I'm not in court, and you're not a judge."

"No. We're family and family doesn't lie to family."

I make a face at them. "Fine, I'll be coming home after I drop off the food at the precinct and make a quick stop at the morgue. Only because Luc called. He's got something he needs to show me."

"There it is." Briar chuckles.

Kenzie rolls her eyes. "You need to take some chill time. Since all this 'empowered world' craziness, you've been running ragged. You look like hell."

She's probably right but being tired and achy is no excuse to get nothing done. "I'll come back as soon as I can, and we can all loaf and watch a movie. Is that chill enough for everyone?"

Kenzie arches a brow and looks me up and down, her gaze landing on my hair. "While we watch the movie, can I do something about that horror show?"

"Deep hydration, ancient oil techniques, whatever. You can go nuts. My head is yours. Deal?"

"Fine. Off you go, Detective Toe Tag."

I cringe. "You know I hate that name."

Briar chuckles. "Then stop hanging out at the morgue."

He's got me on that one. Knowing there's no way I'll make any headway with the two of them on the same side, I have no choice but to accept the nickname with as much grace as I can manage.

I wave over my head as I duck into my room to grab my bag, then shinny down the pole to land quickly on the first floor.

"Buh-bye, you two," I call as I tug on my motorcycle helmet. "Love you."

The guys at the precinct are thrilled to be the beneficiaries of Charlie's cooking. Morin declares we're square in the favors department, although Marx and Rene insist that a delivery like this should count for another few favors, at least.

Knowing there will be hell to pay from Kenzie if I linger long enough to get pulled into a case, I say my goodbyes and duck out.

I don't mention that I'm on my way to the morgue again. The last thing I need is the Detective Toe Tag moniker following me around.

It's an easy enough ride to the coroner's office, a squat, Brutalist building near a nondescript row of warehouses. All I do to get inside is flash the top edge of my badge at the very bored-looking clerk.

I'm here often enough that I could probably get away with wandering in from the street and betting someone inside will recognize me.

The familiar smell of eau-de-cleaning-up-death hits my nose, and my stomach squirrels.

Maybe Kenzie and Briar are right. Maybe spending too much time in the morgue with all the embalming chemicals is pickling me from the inside out.

I make a mental note to see if I feel any worse after checking in with Luc.

The white-tiled hallways are always the same, buzzing with fluorescent lights at all hours of the day and night. Luc's lab is the second-to-last door on the left, and he's sitting at his desk with his back to me.

Luc is thirty going on seventeen in many ways—most of them involving the opposite sex—but he loves his job and is great at it.

The electronic music he's pumping into his massive, LED-lit headphones has him bopping as he works, his focus fixed on the computer screen in front of him as he finalizes a report.

"Hey, man." I tap his shoulder.

He jumps and spins. Tugging off his headphones, he lets them hang around his neck. "Fuck, Jules. I nearly pissed myself."

"You knew I was coming. You're the one who called me down here on my day off."

"Right, right." He stands and walks toward the autopsy table before jerking backward. He hasn't taken off his headphones, and now the long, black cord is tangled around him and his chair.

"These things! I'm starting to develop a bondage kink after so much time wrapped up like this."

"Why not go for wireless?"

Luc looks at me like I recommended he jump naked into a vat of raw sewage. "Yeah, great idea. Or I could listen to my music on a seven-year-old CD player with more dust stuck up in it than an old lady's coochie."

"You're nasty."

"So are wireless headphones. With that sound quality, you might as well hammer nails directly into your eardrums."

"Whatever you say."

One of these days, I've got to get Luc and Zephyr in a room for the great audiophile battle of the century. The loser will have to buy me a new turntable for my record collection because they're both wrong and vinyl is truly superior.

"I'm not here to talk about the specifics of audio technology. You called me down to see something?"

He takes a moment to untangle himself from the headphones, and when he finishes, he runs his hands over his head to smooth down his long chestnut hair. "I waited for something wild before calling you down. If I let you know about every weird thing coming through here lately, you'd have to move in."

"Not in your wildest dreams."

Luc grins. "Never say never, beautiful. Anyway, since the fall of the veil, I've seen all sorts of crazy stuff. For one, there's been a big uptick in suicides. Nearly every time I complete the autopsy on one of these poor saps who decided to punch their exit ticket early, I find evidence of recent change on a cellular level."

"Hold on." I have no idea what change on a cellular level looks like, but I'm still stuck on the first thing he said. "How big of an uptick in suicides?"

"We're seeing seven or eight per month. Compared to two or three monthly before everything happened."

"Are they all newly emergent types?"

"Just about."

"Wow. People would rather die than be magically empowered?"

"Seems so."

I can't imagine what it must be like to have your world, your body, and your entire sense of self completely change overnight. Even still, would I rather die than ride out the storm?

Yeah no, I don't think so.

"The guy you called me in about…is he one of them? A suicide?"

"I'm not entirely sure. Cause of death is drowning. The crime scene unit pulled the guy out of the St. Lawrence yesterday evening, but there's no way of knowing whether he ended up there due to an accident, on purpose, or with someone else's help."

"What is it you have to show me?"

"Look." Luc leads me to the body, which a white sheet covers, and tugs it back.

"Holy crapamoly."

Luc grins. "That's what I'm talkin' about."

All over the body are markings similar to—no, almost identical to—the ones on the man who died in the fire I was rescued from as an infant.

These are clear, though. Visible. Fire didn't damage them, and the guy wasn't in the water long enough for his body to bloat.

For the first time, I can tell they're not slashes or accidental marks—they're purposeful.

"They're almost like letters, like a language."

Luc moves in next to me and grins. "As soon as I saw him, I knew I had to call you."

I'm lost in my thoughts and muddled memories. I don't usually share the details of my history, let alone the specific photos and documents in my slim personal file, but it's clear now that I did the right thing to show them to Luc. "Yeah, thanks."

"Do you know what any of the markings mean?"

I shake my head. "Until I saw this guy, I wasn't sure they meant anything."

"I can't imagine they're aesthetic. Maybe ritualistic?"

I take a closer look. "They definitely mean something. They're symbols. Runes."

"I tried running them through the databases—gang signs, known tattoos, even the old symbols nomadic travelers used to carve into trees or stones. No matches."

That doesn't surprise me.

I've been searching my whole life for any information about those runes, and as far as I could tell, that photo in my file is the only record of anything like them in the world.

With the unidentified body here, now there are two.

"Do we know anything else about this guy?"

Luc walks around the body, gesturing. "Male, Caucasian, likely in his mid-thirties. Found floating in the water last night near the Old Port of Montréal. The water in his lungs was a match for the area. Figured he'd been dead for a few hours and in the water for the same amount of time."

"No ID?"

"Nope. He was wearing casual, nondescript clothing, had no phone or wallet, and nothing in his pockets."

"Didn't leave a note?"

"Unless he shoved it up his ass—actually, scratch that, we look everywhere during an autopsy—so, I can say with certainty that he didn't leave a note."

I roll my eyes, but it's nice to have Luc's company in times like these. Nothing seems to faze him, and he's never met a situation he couldn't make a bad joke about.

"Anything else you can tell me?"

"A fisherman found him last night while he was hauling in his catch. The body's condition is pretty good, aside from the whole being dead part. The guy was in relatively good health but shows signs of a high-stress lifestyle. Although, these days, if I got a body in here that didn't, it would be more remarkable."

"What about that other thing you mentioned—molecular whatever?"

"Visible evidence of a change on the cellular level," Luc corrects me. "This department doesn't have the budget for equipment to let me look at molecules. Although if you could put in a good word somewhere, that would rock."

"A random precinct detective doesn't have the sway for brass to cut checks so the local coroner's office can get fancier toys. Sorry."

"Well, if you ever get a chance to sleep your way to the top to pull strings, be sure to pull mine first, all right?"

I smile. "Speaking of favors, I know you're not exactly supposed to be handing out files, but is there any way I could get a copy of this guy's paperwork?"

Luc wanders to the printer, a machine that looks about as beat up as I currently feel, and grabs a slim stack of papers from its cracked output tray. "It's almost like I can read your mind."

"You rock my socks, dude."

"That's what *she* said."

"I'm sure she did."

File in hand, I step out to get some fresh air.

I know Kenzie and Briar are waiting for me at home, but if I go home straight from the morgue, I'll smell like embalming fluid, and they'll fuss at me about it.

Better to spend some time outside.

It'll let my clothes air out.

With the police file tucked under my arm, I wander down to check out the scene where the fisherman found the body. The Old Port of Montréal is along the St. Lawrence River, and in many ways, it's the reason we have a city in the first place.

These days, its huge Ferris wheel and tall clock tower are popular tourist destinations, and the Old Port is full of cool stuff to do. Back in the day, it was one of the most important shipping ports in the world.

Everything from grain to fur came through there, and Montréal's entire economy and infrastructure grew from the Old Port.

It's nice being at the center of my city's history. Especially as someone who doesn't know anything about my heritage. I've always liked how the Old Port connects me to the past.

I flip open the file. It says the body was floating near the Concorde Bridge. I hop on a ferry to Parc de Dieppe and walk down to the shore, poking around. Maybe I'll see something that wasn't noted in the file.

Sometimes police work is about the thrill of the chase. Other times it's about slogging through the minutia of information with no idea what you're hoping to find until it flies up and smacks you in the face.

CHAPTER FIVE

Nothing. I kick pebbles around, my shoes getting stuck in the river muck every time I stray too close to the water. Yuck. Now I smell like the inside of a morgue *and* the bottom of the St. Lawrence. It's an excellent cocktail of aromas, and I'm sure Kenzie will have a lot to say about it.

Maybe if I smell bad enough, she won't want to fuss with my hair.

I spend as much time as I can walking the shore and peering out at the water, but I can't find anything. Well, anything that points to the identity of our mystery body.

There's plenty of other weirdness, though. A pile of stones stacked so high and balanced so perfectly it looks impossible, which all vibrate and hum as soon as I get close to them.

Then some marshland grasses appear to have grown around the bodies of shorebirds, trapping them in a bizarre green cocoon of death.

Nasty, but not all that surprising.

Nature magic has gone haywire, especially down here. Ever since the big global reveal of magic after the fall of the fae veil, the St. Lawrence River has been a central hotspot for paranormal happenings.

People have reported glowing fish, bizarre power surges, and strange miniature hurricanes only a few feet in diameter roving around on the river's surface.

Not to mention the influx of the awakened migrating into the area. Entire camps of tents and cardboard shelters have developed, full of people whose powers got them kicked out of their homes.

Sometimes it's a discrimination thing. In other cases, it's folks who don't know how to control their powers yet and keep doing stuff like shorting out all the lights or drawing thick clouds of flies and mosquitoes in through the windows.

I feel for them, but I also know that if Briar or Zephyr woke up and started attracting huge swarms of snakes into our house, I might pitch them a tent in the back yard until they got control of that shit.

Having had enough of Dieppe Park, as its name translates to in English, I take the ferry back across the water. Once it pulls up to the Old Port, I notice a commotion on the pier.

My cop instincts take over, and I hold up my badge as I push through the crowd of curious and concerned onlookers.

A man has stumbled out of the Moriner's House, shouting like he's equal parts frightened and angry. On any other day, that would mean there's a fight about to break out, so I look around for the other potential perp.

No one is there.

The man is talking to himself.

I move in and hold up my hands to show I'm not threatening. "Hey, buddy. What's going on?"

"It hurts!" The man screams, then twirls, grabbing something on the back of his neck. "Get it off me!"

I'm about to ask him what hurts when he twists, and I see the problem. He's sprouting gills.

The sides of his neck are bleeding, and a strange spiny fin is poking out of his back. The fin must be sharp because it shredded the back of his shirt.

The man continues spinning, his arms flailing wildly behind him as he tries to grab the spines.

"It's all right." I tug his shirt to help him get it off. Without it, the spiny fin is no longer tangled up, and he finds some relief. His breathing slows and evens out a bit.

"My name is Inspector Jules Gagne. I'm here to help."

He pegs me with a look of pure panic storming in his wide green eyes. Then he makes a weird croaking noise. The gills on his neck flare out.

"Is he going to be all right?" A uniformed security officer from the Moriner's House shows up on a little scooter. "We heard there was a disturbance."

"Yeah. I've got him." Sure, it might be my day off, but this poor guy is in no shape to be tended to by a rent-a-cop whose experience is mostly talking drunk tourists out of jumping into the river.

I put a gentle hand on the man's arm, and he makes another croaking noise. "We're going to get you some help. Just down here a few blocks, all right?"

Thanks to my job, I know all the walk-in centers that deal with awakenings. There's one around the corner, set up in the basement of the Notre-Dame Basilica.

The scuffle and shuffle down the waterfront have a few dicey moments, but in the end, we get there.

I escort the guy in, ensuring he gets connected with one of the nicer nuns, Sister Abigail. She knows how to keep a freaked out newcomer calm. It helps that she was one of the first people in the area to get her powers, so she knows her way around an emergence.

She asks him his name, but all he can do is make that odd, strangled sound with his gills.

"It's all right. We'll get you wrapped up in cool, wet towels, and you'll feel right as rain soon enough. Walk with me slowly here, and try not to gasp in big deep breaths, okay?"

Sister Abigail leads him down the hallway, the spines on his back making me wince. They look painful.

I'm glad that's sorted, though. I go back outside, but as soon as I start down the Basilica's steps, a wave of dizziness hits me, and I need to sit.

Turns out that getting out of the morgue did nothing to help my aching body and fuzzy head. Since coming down by the water, my skin's tingle has worsened.

It's like a thousand red hot needles poking and piercing all my internal organs.

I must be coming down with a fever. I wipe my forehead, and my hand comes away cold and slick with sweat. I'm definitely coming down with something.

Time to head home.

I feel like absolute shit. My body aches and the strange hot tingling across my skin is worse. Back at the firehouse, I let myself in quietly so I can put away the file from the morgue and change my clothes before Kenzie and Briar get a whiff of what I've been up to.

In my room, I rummage under my bed looking for my old first aid kit. Jack and Jack watch me, floating side by side in their bowl.

I find a thermometer and stick it under my tongue until it beeps. The little screen tells me I'm running a fever of...a hundred and eight degrees?

That can't be right.

The normal human body temperature is ninety-eight-point-six. A fever that high would mean I'm dead…or at least unconscious and having seizures.

Since I'm none of those things, I have to assume the thermometer is mistaken. I give it a couple of hard shakes, then try again.

A hundred and eight-point-three.

Well, that's just wrong.

I toss the busted thermometer in the trash and head to the kitchen for a cold ginger ale.

As I pop it open and let the cool carbonated goodness slide down my sore and scratchy throat, Kenzie joins me in the kitchen.

"Yikes," she says when she sees me. "Dead woman walking."

"I don't look as good as I feel? And here I was getting ready to enter myself into a beauty contest."

"What's your talent going to be? Haunting graveyards?"

After what I spent the morning doing, hanging around bothering dead people doesn't sound too far from my day job.

"I'd haunt your closet," I tell her. "Give you bad dreams any time you stole one of my sweaters."

"Like I'd want any of your clothes."

She has a point. When we were kids, Kenzie was always raiding my stuff. Now she has a different sense of fashion, which is cool and girly and full of bright colors. All she'd find in my drawers is workout gear and worn-out gray shirts with SPVM on them.

Say what you will about the budget for the Service de Police de la Ville de Montréal. They ensure we get our yearly T-shirts to thank us for our hard work.

"Here, this might cheer you up…or it might put you out of your misery. It's too close to call." Kenzie hands me an envelope. It's addressed to Zephyr, and there's a glossy booklet inside. "Zephyr did all of us."

I squint at it. "What do you mean, did all of us?" I tug the booklet out of the envelope and read the business header at the top of a detailed printout: *MyAncestry DNA Testing—Juliette Gagne*.

Kenzie holds hers up too. "It's pretty disappointing. After almost three decades of wondering, my DNA origins are inconclusive. What did you get?"

I scan the summary on the first page. "Inconclusive."

"What a bullshit scam."

"Well, apparently Zephyr has money to burn." I scrub my hand over my head, my headache taking another crack at splitting my cranium. "Charlie is going to be pissed he did this."

Zephyr was always getting into trouble with our parents, asking about his past and trying to find out more. One time, he called everyone in the phone book named Marie Claude because that was the name of the EMT working the ambulance on the night he was found.

Not that he found her before Papa found him with the phone. He was grounded for a month for that.

Our parents were adamant we don't stir up our past.

The rule bothers me too, but I got the sense it was more of a safety issue than them being possessive of their status as parents.

All of the adopted Gagne kids have violence associated with our beginnings, so it makes sense not to go poking around about our families of origin.

Still, now that Z has gone ahead and done this, I can't help but be curious. I take the booklet and my ginger ale back to my room. My phone buzzes as soon as I flop down on my bed and flip through the pages.

It's Zephyr. "Hey, Z. How's things?"

"Hey, Jules, are you busy right now?"

He's speaking quickly, breathily, into the phone, and all my instincts kick in. "I'm home with Kenz. Is everything okay?"

"Yeah…I mean, I think so. Maybe. There might be a problem."

That's Zephyr talk for "I've gotten myself into big trouble." I rub the bead of sweat off my forehead with the back of my wrist. "What's going on?"

"Well, there's this guy. He's been creeping around, sort of stalking me."

"*What?* Zephyr, for how long?"

"Doesn't matter."

"Uh yeah, it *does* matter."

"Never mind. I'll tell you about that later. The important part is that I saw him down by the water, and he didn't see me, so I tracked him. I followed him to an old house down in LaSalle."

Irritation with his recklessness and concern for his safety battle in my head. My little brother is an expert at making me want to kill him and rescue him at the same time.

"You tracked *him?* You're not a cop, dumbass. What do you think you're going to do now?"

"Call my sister who *is* a cop to come back me up."

Great. Glad to know I was Plan A.

"On my way. Text me the address." I toss the envelope on my bed, grab my shoulder holster, and press my thumb against the biometric scanner on my bedside gun safe. After retrieving my sidearm, I pull all the moving parts together and slide down the fireman's pole to go find my brother.

LaSalle is a borough south of the city near where the St. Lawrence River bends. I don't come down here often—it's not part of the precinct I serve—but as I ride my motorcycle down its cracked streets, it's clear that the weirdness we're dealing with up near Boucherville is also affecting things here.

Ever since the fae veil dropped, things have gotten out of control.

The plants are wilder, the animals are more aggressive, and even the city's geography seems to be in flux.

I could have sworn that the last time I rode down to LaSalle it took a lot longer than this. It feels like something deep at the foundation of the world shifted.

At this point, I wouldn't be surprised to wake up one morning and see the river suddenly flowing in the opposite direction.

I arrive at the address, and it's all kinds of creepy. Vines are growing up the house, pulling back the paint, and cracking through the windows. Some lights are on inside, but they're a sickly pale green, like the kind of illumination you see with glowsticks at a concert.

Pulling out my phone, I call Zephyr.

It rings a bunch of times, but he doesn't pick up.

I curse him and send out a prayer for him at the same time. Loving Zephyr is an effort in contradictions. After texting him that I'm here and heading inside, I step up onto the porch. The wood creaks under my feet.

It's spongy and rotten in places.

I peer into the front window, but the glass is covered from the inside. What does that mean?

Grow op maybe...

I breathe deep, testing the air for the stench of a skunk's asshole. Nope. Nothing.

The front door is unlocked and cracked open.

I tiptoe to the threshold and lean forward to peer inside. It's dark, and I don't see anything, but I hear a weighty *thunk*.

Well, that can't be good.

I consider calling it in, but when it comes to my baby brother, I'm never sure what Zephyr's gotten himself into. Involving the police—aside from myself—might not be what he needs right now.

Deciding to investigate first, I step inside.

With my hands positioned ahead of me, I aim my gun and hold my phone up so the flashlight sweeps the scene. The deeper I proceed, the eerier it gets.

The house is empty of proper furniture, but people have been living here anyway. There's trash on the floor, piles of blankets, and clothes pushed up in the corners.

Clothes aren't the only thing discarded on the floor.

I've got a body. A man...

Panic surges and adrenaline rushes through me like hot lava. *Zephyr.*

The floor shifts beneath my feet and I lean against the wall with my hand splayed to keep me from assplanting and blacking the fuck out.

It's not Zephyr. It can't be. I won't let it be.

The world can't be that fucked up. Because finding my little brother dead like this would be too much.

When the world's spin slows, I get my boots moving and do a drunk man's shuffle across the floor. *Calice.* Nerves and my fever are making my palms slick with sweat. My grip on my gun isn't solid.

I'm a wreck. Doesn't matter. This isn't about me. This is about the guy on the floor...who, now that I'm closer, is too brawny to be my brother.

"Buddy? Are you all right?"

No. He's really not.

I bend to check for a pulse, but there isn't one. With the heel of my boot against his shoulder, I roll him onto his back to check for wounds or weapons.

Nothing visible.

I take a few deep breaths and calm myself enough to examine the body.

It's obviously not him.

Whoever this unlucky soul is, he's older than my brother, and he's dressed in drab, worn-out clothes that, ironically, Z would never be caught dead in.

The presence of a body means I can't protect my brother from whatever nonsense he's tumbled into this time. I have to call it in.

I check my surroundings and make sure I'm alone. I have a speed dial to dispatch, and I engage the call. "Dispatch, this is

Inspector Jules Gagne, off-duty, badge number 361. I've got a body at 614 Rue Fontaine and request a unit to respond."

I finish with dispatch and am making up a story about how I ended up here that doesn't involve my brother playing do-it-yourself private investigator when I notice something.

Peeking out from the sleeve of the dead guy's shirt is ink on his skin. Like a scar, but in perfectly straight lines.

It looks familiar.

I bend and tug his shirt sleeve back. Yep. That's a rune. Like the ones on Luc's nameless body. Like the ones on the man who died in the fire.

I point my phone, trying to hold it steady even though my flu is taking hold. My hands are shaking, and I could faint at any moment.

Not yet. I need to take a picture of this.

Strange clicking sounds behind me. Adrenaline surges. I pivot, throwing my hands out toward whoever might be there. A blinding flash of light ignites, and a roaring wall of orange fire blows me back behind an explosion of flame.

Then I black the fuck out.

CHAPTER SIX

I wake up in a hospital bed, my head pounding and my body aching worse than ever. My first thought is that I passed out from the fever and the headache, but if I was brought to the hospital to treat whatever illness I have, they're doing a damn terrible job.

"Welcome back, chickie." Charlie's sweet, gentle voice pulls me out of my internal groaning.

"What happened?" I try to sit up, but the moment I move, a riveting pain threatens to blow my head wide open. I grimace, close my eyes, and flop back onto the flat hospital pancake pillow.

"Many people are waiting to ask you the same thing." Charlie leans closer. "Your colleagues are in the hall. What the hell did you do?"

I crane my neck, and sure enough, there are a dozen cops outside my door. Many I recognize from the station, my squad, my union rep, my acting staff sergeant…and a female detective I don't know.

Shit la marde. Zephyr landed me in it this time.

"Charlie, where's…" I'm about to ask Charlie about Zephyr,

but with cops watching us through the glass window and about to come in, I don't want to single him out and get him in trouble.

The last thing any of us need is police trouble.

"Where are Kenzie, Briar, and Zephyr? Are they here?"

Charlie shakes her head. "The twins tried calling them but couldn't get in touch. What's going on, Jules?"

She's getting panicked, and I don't want it to seem like there's trouble. I wave at Marx and Morin and play things off like nothing's wrong. "We all had today off. Maybe they went to the beach or something and are away from their phones."

Charlie flashes me a disbelieving look. She's one of us and hears the lie in my excuse.

Briar might leave his phone behind, but Kenzie is practically surgically attached to hers. Zephyr called me to tell me about the guy he followed to that creepy old house. He had his phone on him.

Something is wrong.

Charlie's not stupid. She understands what I'm not saying and squeezes my wrist. "Don't worry. The twins left messages. They know you're okay. They'll visit when they can. You focus on feeling better."

She flashes me a fake smile and grabs her purse.

Since I couldn't bail Zephyr out of whatever mess he's facing, he might have called Briar or Kenzie.

I bet the two of them are out looking for him. Or worse, trying to help him confront the guy he thinks is watching him.

I groan and struggle with the sheets, freeing my legs to get out of bed. "I should come too."

Charlie presses a solid hand on my chest and pins me against the mattress. The woman is scary strong when she needs to be. "Lay back. You're not going anywhere, Juliette."

"Charlie, I'm fine. I'm a cop."

"And I'm your guardian."

"You *were* my guardian. I'm an adult now."

"An adult that needs to rest. Seniority rules. Stamped it. You're staying."

I protest, but the female detective I don't recognize pokes her head inside the door. "Excuse me, Ms. Gagne. Could I have a moment to speak to your daughter?"

Charlie laughs and looks at me. "You think this pain in the ass came out of my vajayjay? No. My girl parts are in pristine condition. I could crack walnuts with my hoo-ha."

The look on the detective's face is too funny.

"She's my aunt," I clarify.

"Oh, my apologies, I must've misunderstood. Would you mind if I spoke to your niece?"

"Sure, and if she tries to get out of bed, I give you permission to shake her down and cuff her. She is too stubborn for her good."

The cops from the hallway pour in. Rene, Marx, Tremblay, and Morin present me with a bouquet of wilted flowers and a box of chocolate glazed Timbits. Those little donut holes are round pockets of sugary bliss.

"How're you feeling?" Marx asks.

I look down at myself. "I think I'll pass on the beauty pageant."

That gets a chuckle from my precinct buddies.

My staff sergeant informs me, "The doctor said you'll be fine in a few days, so quit your whining."

"Glad you're not dead, kid," Marx adds.

"Yeah. What would we do without your shiny disposition to keep us in line?" Morin claps my shoulder before reaching for one of my Timbits.

Then the woman I don't recognize steps up and introduces herself in French. "I'm Inspector Jean Carnelian. I'm the investigating detective on your case. Do you mind if I ask you a few questions?"

"Knock yourself out."

"Do we really need all these people in here?" She looks around at my buddies with one eyebrow raised.

"Everybody out." Acting Staff Sergeant Peter Trent shoos everyone out of the room.

Soon it's only me, the lady inspector, Peter, and my union rep.

The fact that Peter thinks I need a union rep present is alarming, but I try not to dwell.

The inspector sets herself up at the end of the bed and poises her pen over her little black notebook. "Start at the beginning. You know the drill."

"There's not much to tell you, Inspector. I was in that house, found a body, and called it in to dispatch. Then something exploded."

Carnelian presses her lips together but doesn't write anything down. "What caused the explosion?"

"No idea. I was examining the body, heard something behind me, and when I turned around...*shazam* there was a wall of flames throwing me backward."

"You heard something? Something or someone? Was there someone else there?"

I remember the clicking noise. Was it a person?

It could've been...or it could've been an animal...

"I don't know. I came in the front door, made my way into the living room, and found the body. There was evidence of squatters, but I hadn't had a chance to clear the house. There could've been people upstairs or in the back of the house."

"So, you heard a sound. What kind of sound?"

I try to describe it, but it's impossible to capture. She scribbles a few things down, then looks back up at me. "Why were you there in the first place?"

"I got an anonymous tip that something weird was going on at that address and I should check it out."

"A tip from who?"

"I can't say."

She frowns, but I meant it. I can't say…or really, I won't say, but that's semantics.

"All right, so your mystery tipster says you should check out this house. What happened next?"

"I stepped onto the porch to look. The windows were covered, but the door was open a crack. I heard a weighted *thud* and proceeded inside."

"Didn't you think you should call it in?"

"Since the veil dropped, we've been bombarded with more anonymous tips than the glory hole at Central Station."

She blinks at me.

Yeah, well, this is me. "These days, everyone is convinced their neighbor is turning into an elf or a centaur. I figured I'd poke around and see what I could see."

This makes my union rep cringe.

Peter has his arms crossed, glaring at whatever the detective writes in her notebook.

"Did you smell anything strange? Gas, odors, maybe chemicals?"

"No."

"You mentioned squatters. Did you see anyone?"

"No. No one."

"Except the dead guy."

"Right, except the dead guy."

"You didn't see what caused the fire?"

"Still no. I'm sorry, but I told you everything I remember." I close my eyes, wishing she would stop asking me questions. My head is about to blow apart and barf my gray matter all over this bed.

Man, my fever is raging, but I've also got chills and have started to shiver.

My awful state doesn't go unnoticed, which works for me. She gives me a sympathetic but annoyed look, then pockets her notebook.

"All right." She sets her card on the nightstand beside the bed. "Thank you. I hope you feel better soon. Get in touch if there's anything more you remember."

Inspector Jean Carnelian leaves my hospital room with my union rep following close. Now it's only my boss and me.

"Jules. Now that they're gone. What happened? What really started that fire?"

I groan. "Not you too. I'm telling the truth. I honestly have no idea."

"Look, Gagne. I like you. You're a good officer. You know I need you on the squad, now more than ever. But there's a limit to how much I can help you here."

"Why do I need help?"

Peter blows out his cheeks, sounding exasperated. "Gagne, you were found in the same room as a dead body with a house burning down around you."

"I'm the one who called *in* the body."

Peter looks like a statue with his arms folded and his eyes narrowed. "Come on. Your story has holes in it. You need to do better than *I don't know*. Tell me straight—why were you at that house in LaSalle?"

"I did tell you. I got an anonymous call."

"From whom?"

Now it's my turn to act exasperated. "That's the anonymous part."

Peter throws up his arms and heads toward the door. "Fine. Stonewall me. I'm trying to help you here."

I feel bad for the sarcasm.

Peter's a good boss, and he is trying to help, but I feel like a pile of steaming dog vomit, and I've got my three siblings to worry about right now too. "I'm sorry. Honestly, I've told you everything I can. I'm sick and cranky as fuck. Can we end this?"

"Take a few days." Peter stops with his hand on the doorframe. "Don't argue. You're injured, and now you're at the center of an active investigation. Lay low and take it easy."

"Fine."

"I mean it, Gagne. No consulting with your pal down at the morgue, no sifting through cold case files, no popping in to hang around the precinct. I want you to stay home, eat some chicken noodle soup, watch old movies, and see if you can remember anything more about this house fire. Got it?"

"Got it, Sarge."

Peter leaves, and I breathe a sigh of relief.

Alone at last.

My eyelids feel as heavy as bricks. The urge to track down and throttle Zephyr for getting me caught up in all this fills me, but there's no way I'd have the energy for even a mild throttling.

All I want to do is sleep and munch on the sweets the guys brought me.

Fortunately, the nurse wheels in with the med cart, and the little blue capsules send me floating into dreamland before I can finish my Timbits.

Normally, I wouldn't take the out and lay around in a hospital bed, but I received strict orders to rest and take it easy from Charlie, my boss, and the doctors. Plus, there's something very not right with me. It's not from the fire or whatever knocked me out back there. It's this bug I caught a few days ago that's been wringing me out ever since.

The doctors are freaked out about my fever. It's been slowly coming down, but they can't figure out why it isn't frying my brain or sending me into convulsions.

Even though the thing I'm technically here for isn't the primary reason I feel like crud, I decide to stay. No matter what's going on, I can't imagine that some rest and fluids could make it worse.

Being in the hospital gives me plenty of downtime, which I'm not used to. I worry about Zephyr. In my mind, I flip through everything I can remember from my box of cold cases, and I think about what exactly happened to me back in LaSalle.

In the afternoon, as I'm watching the same dumb pigeon hop around on my tiny hospital windowsill, the image comes to me more clearly. I remember the specific rune I saw on the guy's arm right after I pulled his sleeve back.

I was trying to get a picture when everything went to shit—that clicking sound, me turning around, and the blast of fire.

Reaching around, I pull the bag of my personal belongings out of the drawer and scroll through my phone.

Marde. I only got one blurry photo.

I need to talk to Luc.

"Jules, why are you calling me? Aren't you in the hospital? Didn't someone try to flambé you last night?"

"It was more of a quick sear and flip. Yeah, extreme heat was involved."

"Are you bored?"

"Out of my freaking mind."

"Which means you're obsessing about things."

"Yeah, about that body from the morgue and the body in the house. I think they're related."

"Related as in sharing a familial bond?"

"No, dumbass. I think the *cases* are related."

"How so?"

"No idea. It's a gut feeling."

"Aren't your guts supposed to be taking it easy and not obsessing about dead bodies and cold cases?"

I chuckle and press my head back against the pancake pillow. "What would be the appropriate topics for my wandering mind, princesses and daffodils?"

"Couldn't hurt. If you're into manifesting, could you conjure a sexy princess for me? Blonde hair, giant boobs, low expectations...."

"I'm not creating a masturbatory fantasy for you in my head. Do that on your own time."

"I try, but then I'm interrupted by phone calls from cops bugging me about dead bodies."

I laugh but regret it immediately. My throat feels like it's made of hard mud cracks in the desert.

I swallow to moisten the scratchiness in my throat. Luc takes his job at the coroner's office seriously but considers our efforts to solve mysteries a distraction from his skirt-chasing and anime-watching.

"Very sorry to ask you to do your job, Leclerc, but I'm not letting this go. I don't have my files here with me. Could you take some photos of those weird markings and send them to me?"

"On your personal phone?" Luc busts a gut. "You know I love you like a stripper—I mean, a sister—but there's no way I'm doing that."

"Since when have you been a stickler for rules?"

"That's not the reason. The talk is that the house fire you got caught in was a real blaze. You're in the hospital for a reason, Jules. I'm not sending you work while you're supposed to be recovering."

I groan. Luc thinks this can wait, but my instincts say it can't. I'm impatient, restless, and cranked up, but this is important.

"What if this is the key to figuring out who I am?"

"Then it's waited twenty-seven years and can wait until tomorrow."

I'm about to argue when someone shouts in the hall. "Hold on. Something's happening. I'll call you back."

"You're off-duty, Jules. Seriously. Stay in bed. It's none of your busi—"

Call it curiosity, call it a sense of duty, call it me being pissy and having a terrible bedside manner. Whatever the reason, I gingerly hoist myself out of bed, grab my IV pole, and creep toward the door.

A tall, slender woman in a blue hospital gown stands in the hallway shrieking like a banshee. Her hair flies around like Medusa's snakes trying to escape from her head. "It's happening again."

An older nurse shuffles up the hall at a brisk pace. "*Madame*, please calm down. You're disturbing the other patients."

"Then help me!" The woman throws her arms out, and her feet lift off the floor. Inches become feet, and her hands bump on the ceiling. "Get me down!"

"We're here to help you, *madame*." The nurse seems unfazed by the helium balloon routine.

She also sounds exhausted.

"Here we go. Back into your room. You've got to stop taking off your leg weights, *madame*." The nurse grabs the woman's leg and tugs her back down to the floor like a kid with a balloon at a carnival.

I chuckle and head back into bed.

The world gets weirder and weirder.

I pop one of the blue pills the nurse told me to take when I want to sleep and hope when I wake up the past few days will have all been a bad dream.

No, back that train up.

Let's rewind the past five months, not only the past few days.

When I wake up, it's dark outside. I pick up my phone and check for messages. There's a text from Briar telling me he's glad I'm not dead and that I need to call him or Kenzie. There are three missed calls from Kenzie.

Message one:

"What the hell happened? We thought you were lying down, but you were getting blown up in a fiery explosion. What the serious hell?"

Message two:

"Jules, did your fiery explosion have anything to do with you know who? Because we can't find him and he's not answering his phone."

Message three:

"Seriously, Jules, we've looked everywhere. I know you're supposed to be resting, but we're losing our shit here. You need to shake off whatever pill-addled mind-haze you're in and phone home."

Okay, the staycation is over.

At some point during my nap, someone took out my IV line, so that makes things simpler. I flip back my sheets and head to the little closet. A young nurse with a brown bob pulled back in a barely there ponytail comes in while I'm getting dressed.

"Going somewhere, Ms. Gagne?"

I pull my jeans on under my cotton nighty and reach back to pull the drawstrings behind my neck. "Yeah. I'm checking out early and heading home."

"I don't think that's a good idea. The doctor hasn't cleared you yet."

"I'm fine."

"Let's see what the doctor has to say, all right?" She hustles out, and I hurry things along. Unless he's a hot and hunky guy allergic to shirts, I'm not interested in what the doctor says.

I pull off the johnny I'm wearing and grab my top.

"Inspector Gagne." The doctor glides in with a smile and catches a good eyeful of the girls. I'm not heavily endowed up front, but my curves will rock a man's socks if I do say so myself.

The doctor spins the other way and steps back behind the corner. "Sorry. Nurse Monica said you're hoping to get discharged."

I chuckle, finish getting things covered up, and pat the sheets looking for my phone. "Something got lost in translation there, Doc. I told Nurse Monica I'm leaving."

"As your doctor, I'd prefer it if you stayed."

I tap his shoulder and give him the all-clear. "I'll sign a discharge form saying it's against your medical advisement. Don't worry. I'm not a sue your doctor kinda girl. I need to get home. We've got a bit of a family emergency thing going on."

He adjusts his glasses and studiously tries to lock in eye contact. A couple of times his gaze dips, and his cheeks flush, but I give him points for trying to keep it professional. "Your fever only just dropped into an acceptable range, but we don't know what caused it. Also, there was a problem in the lab. Your blood work needs to be retaken."

I chuckle. "I got cold-cocked and knocked unconscious in a fire. What's bloodwork got to do with it?"

"It's standard practice to run certain tests, and with everything changing in the world right now, it's even more important."

Everything changing?

A wave of nausea swamps me. I manage a weak laugh as a hot flash sets in. "Nah, sorry, Doc. I haven't got powers. I just got knocked on my ass."

"Still, I'd like to rerun the tests."

"Not necessary. I'm good. Thanks though."

Nurse Monica returns and tries to say something else, but I deke her out like a forward on a breakaway and bolt for the door.

"Inspector, please," Doc says behind me. "I can't force you to stay, but I need to stress the importance…"

As I push through the ward doors, I run almost directly into my brother's broad, muscular chest. "Briar, excellent timing. Tell me you got my Uber pickup request on our sibling psychic link."

"Almost. Charlie told me to bring you dinner." He holds up a paper sack with some greasy fingerprints on the outside. "Aren't you supposed to be in bed?"

"Nah, I'm fine."

"Is that what the doctors said?"

"If it wasn't exactly that, it was damned close."

He chuckles. "Uh-huh, and aren't cops supposed to follow the rules?"

I wave a finger and get us moving toward the parking lot. "Cops follow laws, not rules. Big difference. So, since you're here, give me a ride home. Tell me what's going on with Zephyr. Have you found him?"

Briar sighs. "No, and Kenzie is crazed. Between the call finding out you were being taken to the hospital and Z missing, she's losing her mind."

"All the more reason I need to be home."

"Charlie will kill me if she finds out I broke you out against the doctor's orders."

I wave that away. "She doesn't have to know. Did you hear the doctor tell me I needed to stay?"

"No, but—"

"Exactly. I'm telling you I'm cleared to leave, and that's all you know and all you need to tell Charlie."

Briar thinks about it for a moment, but our sibling bond is too strong for him to leave me here or rat me out. Besides, I've kept plenty of his secrets from Charlie over the years. He owes me.

He stops when we get to the truck and waits to unlock my door. "Jules. I'm serious. I'm only taking you home if you promise to take it easy, okay?"

"Oh, for sure. I'll be the poster child for chill."

He snorts and unlocks my door. "You're such an unbelievably frustrating asshole."

I chuckle. "I love you too."

CHAPTER SEVEN

I dive into Charlie's care package on the way home. The spicy smells of her home cooking fill Briar's rattly old truck and make my stomach growl in appreciation.

"No sign of Zephyr?" I ask through a mouthful of smoky brisket.

"No, nothing. What the fuck is going on with him?"

"No idea. One minute I'm lying in my bed feeling like cat hack and the next, he calls me and says he's got a stalker and tracked him to a house in LaSalle. He said he needed me to come and ghosted me. Not cool."

"He wouldn't leave you if he knew you were on the way. That's really not good."

As annoyed as I am with our little brother, I agree.

Zephyr is a lot of things, but he's not careless with our safety. "I need to go back to that house and look around."

"When Charlie told us what happened, we wondered if Zephyr was mixed up in something and we went there. We didn't find Z, but we did bring home your bike."

"Thanks for that. Scarlett gets homesick."

He laughs. "Charlie said we should claim it was a casualty of the fire. I swear, she hates that motorcycle more than she hates my girlfriends."

"And you defied her murderous intent? Thanks, bro."

Briar grins at me sitting in the shotgun seat. "Truth be told, I don't know who scares me more these days. You or Charlie."

I laugh. "Don't let her hear you say that. She'll take it as a challenge."

There's a quiet pause in the truck while I eat and Briar maneuvers us through the narrow streets of Boucherville.

"I really am worried about Zephyr." He hits his turn signal and turns toward the river. "I know he runs in questionable circles and drops off the grid occasionally, but with all this extra weirdness going on, it's especially scary. He didn't even come home when we left him messages that you were in the hospital."

That's not a good sign.

As a cop, I know too much about what befalls someone in our city's dark alleys and back streets. The fact that Zephyr called me to a house with a dead body, then disappeared, is really bad news.

Still, I don't want to freak Briar out.

I'm the oldest of the Gagne kids, and it's my responsibility to keep a cool head. Everyone is already worried enough. "Maybe his phone died," I suggest.

"Maybe." Briar pulls up the driveway, and the big bay door opens into the wide garage of the firehouse. He doesn't say anything more, and he doesn't need to.

We all know the score.

Right now, Briar and Kenzie need me to be the big sister who knows how to safeguard the city's streets. So, it's fake it 'til you make it time.

When I drop out of Briar's truck, I check my bike for scratches, then haul my exhausted ass upstairs.

"You're home!" Kenzie drops the polishing cloth and rushes over to hug me. "I don't even care that you should probably still be in the hospital. I'm glad you're a stubborn, cranky, pain in the ass. I need you here."

It's tough to breathe through the crushing pressure of Kenzie's anxiety hug, but I let her use me as her stress ball. "I'm here, Kenz. Yeah, I'm supposed to rest, but I can rest better in my bed with my laptop."

Briar chuckles. "I think they call that working from home, not rest."

I ease back from having my ribs bruised and shrug. "For me, working is rest. It's doing nothing that winds me up."

My body might be wrecked, but my mind is sharp.

I grab my laptop, prop up my pillows, and flop into bed. I pull up the blurry picture I took of the dead guy before I got clocked.

My laptop doesn't have any of the high-tech software we have at the precinct, but I try to see if I can clean it up.

I zoom in and click around, looking for anything in the photo that could help me find Zephyr. Then I get the clearest view of the rune I can manage and take a screenshot.

I compare that image to the file Luc gave me from the guy pulled out of the river, then I search the Internet for anything about ritual tattoos, scarification, and runes.

Nothing.

Ads for a video game involving runes pop up, and I'm distracted by the women with gigantic breasts. What exactly does their titty armor protect?

Unhelpful on multiple fronts.

Next, I search for the owner of the house and go that route.

Yeah, police work is glamorous.

I wake on the littered floor of the flophouse in LaSalle. It takes a minute to orient myself. Instead of leaning over the dead body, I'm lying next to him. He has his arms around me like I'm a child, but I don't feel safe.

The clicking noise sounds.

It's coming from all directions. I turn my head but can't see what's making it.

My heart is racing and a burst of adrenaline hits.

There's a blast of heat and flames surround me. Funny. Engulfed in a rush of amber fire, I do feel safe.

I jolt upright, breathing heavily, with my sheets drenched in sweat. Holy hell that felt real.

I kick my feet, struggling to untangle my legs from the twist of my covers.

Fire. Heat. The man with runes…

What happened back there? How did I make it out completely unscathed? I lift my hands and study the flesh on my arms. Not a burn or a scar on them. What about smoke inhalation? Shouldn't I cough up soot and have my throat and sinuses seared?

I swing my feet off the bed and draw a few deep breaths. Wait…did I light my tea light candles?

They're burning. I don't remember lighting them.

Marde. Life is getting too weird.

Maybe Kenzie came in and lit them for me. She knows how much I love candles. Maybe she wanted me to relax and take it easy.

I reach toward the flame, still curious about how I escaped unscathed from the inferno they rescued me from.

I hold my hand over the flickering flame and…

I don't feel anything.

Is it nerve damage? Do I not have a thermostat in my skin that registers concentrated heat?

I lower my palm until the flame bends, pushed down by the presence of my hand.

Still nothing.

No pain. No burn.

Turning my palm back so I can inspect it, I find it completely unharmed.

This is officially too weird. I blow out the candles, grab some fresh clothes, and head into the shower. Once I've cleaned up, I check my phone again to see if there's anything from Zephyr.

He's still incommunicado.

I call him, but it *clicks* over to voicemail. Nope, his mailbox is full, so I'm instructed to call back.

"Damn it, Z. Where are you?"

Briar and Kenzie are out in the living room when I emerge from my suite with my hair wet from the shower.

"She lives!" Kenzie throws her hands into the air in a mock hallelujah.

"How are you feeling?" Briar asks.

"Better. I'm heading out to look for Zephyr. Figured I'd start at his usual hangouts. Where's my helmet?"

Kenzie glares. "Well, that's not happening. You're supposed to stay home and rest."

"I did that. My resting tank is full, I promise."

"It's too dangerous," Kenzie insists.

"If only we knew someone who had the training and experience to face Montréal's criminal element. Maybe a cop who knows the players on the streets…."

Kenzie throws me a droll stare. "Okay, Inspector Sasshole, we get the point."

Briar stands and takes his dirty dishes and his empty snack bag to the kitchen. "We're not letting you go alone. If you're looking for Zephyr, we're coming too."

The three of us pile into Kenzie's electric car, whirring toward Zephyr's best friend's house. Max and Z have a music studio set up in his garage where they like to jam and record.

"I've never understood what Zephyr sees in this guy," Briar says.

I laugh. "Remember when Papa caught Max sneaking Z out of the house in the middle of the night when we were kids? I'm surprised Zephyr's not still grounded."

Briar grunts. "I remember how he ogles Kenzie. That boy has been carrying a torch for you for years, sis."

Kenzie grimaces. "No thank you."

Briar chuckles. "Okay, he's not your rockstar romance Romeo, but maybe you should be the one to knock on the door. You could use a little of your sweet Kenzie charm to get us information."

"That is disgusting." Kenzie punches his muscled arm. "You're pimping your sister."

Max answers the door bleary-eyed and smelling of weed. He blinks at us a few times, his eyes red-rimmed and bloodshot.

"Hey, Max. Is Zephyr here?" I ask.

Max shakes his head.

"Have you heard from him?"

"Nah."

"Are you sure?" Briar presses. "We need to find him. He's not in trouble or anything."

"Sorry, man." Max offers an apologetic smile before closing the door. I'm pretty sure I hear the bubbling of a bong being hit inside.

"Well, that was a bust." Briar squeezes his massive frame back into the car.

Kenzie shrugs and starts it. "To be fair, thinking Max could help us is on us. Name one thing he's ever been useful for."

Nope. I've got nothing.

We drive by Zephyr's favorite coffee shop, the burrito place he hangs out at, and around Boisé des Citoyens. He likes to play his guitar in the park there for pocket money.

He's nowhere to be found.

He's also not at the pawnshop where he sometimes helps repair musical instruments.

"Come on, Zephyr. Where are you?" I don't like the strain in Kenzie's voice.

Briar must have caught it too because he reaches over and pats her arm as she drives. "We'll find him. Maybe we can take a break and eat."

Yeah, I like that idea. "Two birds one stone. Let's stop at Casse Croûte, grab a bite, and check for Zephyr."

It doesn't take much convincing.

Kenzie hits her turn signal and steers us to our favorite pub. Casse Croûte, named after the local snack bars in the area, has great food, fun company, and live music.

Zephyr plays there sometimes.

As we pull the door open and step inside, part of me hopes we find him munching on poutine and flirting with the bartenders.

I scan the dim pub interior—no sign of Zephyr.

We claim a booth, and we're ready when Sam comes over to take our order. "What can I get for you three?"

Briar takes the lead on that. "A pitcher of honey lager and two large baskets of wings and fries to share."

"Sauce?"

"Half honey garlic, half devil's inferno."

"You got it. Anything else?"

"Is Cami on the bar today?" I ask.

"She hasn't started yet, but she's in the back. Do you want me to tell her to come say hi?"

"That would be great, yeah."

We settle in and wait. A couple of minutes later Camille delivers our pitcher and sets it on the table. "Hey, guys. You're one sibling short. Is Z meeting you here?"

"That's why we wanted to talk to you." Briar pours for the three of us. "We've been all over town looking for him. We hoped he might be here."

"He hasn't been here in a while, but you're not the only ones looking for him."

"What do you mean?" I ask.

"Someone was in here last night asking about him."

"What time was this?"

"Early…maybe seven? The dinner crowd was easing off, but the night crowd hadn't started yet."

That makes sense with my timeline. "He called me soon after. He said he spotted a guy who's been stalking him, and he followed him to that house."

"Maybe he spotted him here," Kenzie suggests.

"That's what I'm thinking too."

Cami glances around and leans toward us. "I don't want to sound judgy, but I'd bet money he wasn't from this world. Also, he was nothing like the fae you see on TV—no bunnies with wings or men who turn into wolves. This guy was straight-up scary."

"Do you know anything about who he was?" I ask.

"No, but after he left, people got talking. Rumor is, he's behind the new drug on the street—Second Sight."

Kenzie frowns. "That's the one they say lets people see beyond fae glamors, isn't it?"

I roll my eyes. "That's the pitch they use to sell it, but if you ask me, it's simply a fancy hallucinogen. It makes people see the whacked and wild of the world, but that doesn't mean users can pick out fae from the crowd."

"That's what the kid was on the other night when you arrested him, right?" Kenzie asks me.

Briar chuckles and wiggles his finger. "The one that made your night with his willy waggle?"

I snort. "Please. A guy has to do more than waggle his cock at me to make my night."

Kenzie laughs. "How would you know? You haven't seen a cock in what…six months?"

"Silicon and batteries are just as good."

The bark of a deep laugh rings out, and my attention goes to the booth across from us. The hot, tats DJ guy from the park the other night lifts his glass. "Hello, buzzkill."

I rerun the conversation in my mind and die a little inside. "You stalking me, Gary?"

His amusement fades to black at an impressive rate. "Not my name, and, no, I was here first."

"I've never seen you here, and we come all the time."

"Guilty. I quoted a job across the road and thought I'd enjoy a quiet drink after a long day. This is the first, and likely the last time I'll be here. It seems this bar will let anybody in."

"Seems like it."

He finishes his drink, stands, and tosses down some cash. "Inspector, if silicon and batteries are just as good, you need to raise the bar on the men you invite into your bed."

My mouth falls open, and I want to say something incredibly quick-witted and sharp-tongued, but my traitorous mind blanks out on me completely.

I watch him leave, annoyingly aware that his muscled legs fill out his black jeans too well.

"Who's the dark and haunted hottie?" Kenzie asks.

"No one." I ignore the looks and the heat flushing my cheeks and tend to the dryness of my mouth. Staring at the rim of my glass, I busy myself drinking beer. "Now, where were we?"

"We were discussing Second Sight and your altercation with Nakey Kid," Briar says.

"Right. Yeah, he was high as a kite. He claimed he could see all. It's the *en vogue* drug of choice, but that doesn't mean it delivers on what they claim."

Kenzie sighs. "You're sure it was the empowered drug dealer looking for Zephyr, Cami?"

"I'm sure a bad news guy was intent on tracking down your brother, but the drug dealer part is hearsay."

"Did you tell him anything?" I ask.

Cami shrugs. "There was nothing to tell. I didn't know where he was. Haven't seen him for a bit. I told the guy if Zephyr came around, I'd pass the message along."

"Does that mean he left contact info?"

"Yeah, a card with a phone number."

"Can I get that number, please? I'll trace it and see if we can find out who the creeper is asking about our brother."

Sam brings our baskets of wings at the same time our family WhatsApp chat room buzzes with a message from Charlie.

Emergency family meeting. My house. Now.

Kenzie and Briar are checking their phones too.

"Not good. Either she found out Briar busted me out of the hospital AMA, or she knows Zephyr's missing and we didn't tell her."

Briar grabs his beer and guzzles it down in several quick gulps. "We're dead either way."

Kenzie groans and hands the baskets of wings back to Sam. "Check, please. We're going to need that phone number and these wings to go."

CHAPTER EIGHT

Freaked out about the cryptic message from Charlie and even more worried about the trouble Zephyr has gotten himself into, we pay our tab and head out. Kenzie takes us back through Boucherville toward the house where we grew up and where Charlie still lives.

From the passenger seat, I sit back and study the tree-lined streets and broad pastel-colored houses. Tall stone and brick buildings, mostly schools and churches, dot the corners and seem to gather the houses around them like a mother hen.

The four of us went to school in a building like that, shaded by centuries-old trees. The chiming of the church bells would ring out in the afternoons as school ended for the day.

Our school was close enough for us to walk home, but *Maman* insisted on picking us up every day, waiting in her big silver van for us all to pile in.

Kenzie pulls up to the wide driveway, and I can't help but draw a heavy breath at the sight of the house. It's a historic two-story built after the big fire in 1853. Zephyr used to climb the tall stone pillars in the front, scrambling around like a lizard. My old room on the second floor overlooks the yard with the tire swing Papa made for us.

"I wish *Maman* and Papa were here." Kenzie echoes my ache of nostalgia.

"Me too," Briar agrees.

But they're not. Our adoptive parents died in a car accident when I was fifteen. They might not have been our biological parents, but they were the best parents the four of us could've hoped for.

Charlie tried to fill their shoes, but she was more like a scattered aunt or a wild older sister than a parent. Still, she's the glue that held us together when child services snooped around after our parents' deaths.

"Let's get this over with."

We leave Kenzie's car, and Briar opens the side door, stepping back to let us go first. It's either chivalrous or cowardly. I'm not sure which.

Part of me hopes Zephyr is inside and Charlie has called us in to give us a proper dressing down for not telling her what was going on.

Our brother is nowhere in sight.

Instead, Charlie is standing in the living room talking to our dog, Backup. Sure, we all talk to the dog at times, but I get the feeling they're having a conversation…or at least she thinks they are.

It's weird that Backup is here, but then again, if Charlie wants to have a family meeting, it's not out of the question that she swung by our place to get him so he would be included.

She does shit like that.

"What's going on?" Briar asks.

Charlie spins and looks at us. "It's been a clusterfuck kind of day. That's what's going on."

Kenzie rushes forward. "Why? Is it Zephyr? What happened?"

"No, I haven't seen Zephyr since the twins' party. Why? What's going on with him?"

"Is it the twins?" I divert the conversation.

"No. Not the twins either. They're out with friends at a school football game."

"Then what?" Briar asks.

"Well, to start with, I called the hospital to check on you, and they said you left."

I nod. "That's true. I'm much better—"

"You look like roadkill."

"Uh…thank you?"

Charlie rolls her eyes. "So, being the last to learn you checked yourself out of the hospital, I went over to the firehouse, and things got worse and worse."

I make a face at Kenzie and Briar, trying to see if they know what she's talking about. They look as lost as I am. "What happened at the firehouse?"

"He happened." She gestures at Backup, looking wildly freaked. "He told me what's been going on and showed me these."

I glance down at the papers and photos on the coffee table. It's the MyAncestry printouts Zephyr had mailed to our house.

"What were you thinking?" Charlie sweeps her hand over the papers. "What did you do?"

"That wasn't us." Kenzie points at the glossy folders. "Zephyr sent our DNA off without us knowing."

Briar jumps in. "It all came back inconclusive, so it's not like we know anything anyway. No harm done."

"No harm done?" An unflattering mottling of color is creeping up Charlie's neck and jaw. "Your *maman* drilled it into you from the time you were little to leave the past in the past, or it would bring the danger you escaped into our lives."

"Now Zephyr's missing," Kenzie says.

Charlie's eyes widen, and I draw a deep breath and try to head this one off. "We don't know what's going on with Zephyr. It's best not to jump to conclusions."

Kenzie shakes her head. "We know Zephyr wouldn't fall off the map knowing you're hurt."

Charlie cusses in a long string of French and points at me. "Tell me what really happened with the fire at that house, and don't you dare lie or leave anything out."

I'm about to explain when something within the pile of MyAncestry packages catches my eye. There's a picture of a dead body with runes on his arms.

I reach forward and pull the contents of the police file Luc gave me to the top. "What the hell? You can't go into my room and sift through my things. This is part of a confidential police file. You overstepped, Charlie."

She shakes her head. "If you didn't want me investigating on my own you shouldn't keep secrets."

"What are you talking about?"

"These files, this case. You said nothing about looking into any of this."

"Why should I? It's police business."

She juts out her chin. "Really? What business is it of the police to have photos from your infancy?"

I clench my fingers into tight fists. "This is a personal and a professional violation. I'm an adult, and yes, these pictures are about what happened to me as a baby, but they're also my job."

Charlie shakes her head and looks at the dog. "You let it go on too long. You should've come to me sooner."

I cast a sideways glance at Kenzie and Briar. Yeah, they're finding the conversation with the dog strange too. Did the pressure of raising troubled kids finally snap her mental wafer?

Kenzie stands. "Charlie, maybe you should sit—"

Charlie points at the photo of the dead guy with runes. "Laurette told you a thousand times you were survivors of terrible things and nothing good would come of picking at old wounds. You shouldn't be involved with this."

"What *is* this? Three days ago, a body got pulled out of the port. Then, the night before last, I found a dead guy in an abandoned house with the same runes. I don't know what any of it means yet."

"Exactly my point. You shouldn't be digging into things you don't understand." I know she's getting pissed because her sentences are now a broken Frenglish of half French and half English.

I throw up my hands. "I'm a police investigator, Charlie. That's my entire job."

"I've told you it's not the right job for you. Your parents would never have approved."

I bolt to my feet, my blood running hot in my veins. "That's not your call…and it wouldn't have been our parents' call either. You all raised and watched out for me—and I will be forever grateful for the life and love you gave me—but you don't get to decide who I am."

As I shout, the candles twinkling around in the living room flare, and the fireplace, which has been cold and unused for months, blazes into a roaring fire.

The room goes silent.

Briar and Kenzie are trying to melt into the sofa, and Charlie sends the dog a horrified look.

"What's with the fucking dog?" I can't take it anymore.

"Language, Jules."

"Fuck that. There are times to behave, and there are times when you need a strong word or two to convey how truly messed up the situation is. This is one of those times."

Charlie meets my glare with an impressive amount of hostility and after a couple of deep breaths, looks at Backup. "Are you going to help me here?"

Her mental wafer has definitely snapped.

"The talking to the dog thing is creeping me out," Briar interjects. "You need to cut that shit out, Charlie. Seriously."

Kenzie nods. "If it's the stress of having teenagers, we can do more to help. The twins can sleep over with us on the weekends to give you a break."

Charlie raises a hand. "The twins are amazing. Loving them is easy. They're human."

I stall out on that one. The way she says they're human makes it sound like… "Are you saying we're *not?*"

She sits on the arm of the recliner beside the fireplace. "Jules, Briar, Kenzie…there are things you need to know. Perhaps I should have told you earlier, but your parents swore me to secrecy."

I'm going numb. I think somewhere inside me, I've known for months. I was too afraid to let the thought take hold. "Okay, we're listening. Tell us now."

Charlie draws a deep breath. "When the veil between worlds dropped, everyone became aware of the existence of the fae, but there are many more magical realms beyond that."

I nod. "I worked with a Greek immortal and the alpha of the Moon Called shifters of Toronto a few months ago. We tracked down a witch who could help us take down the vampires causing trouble in the Montréal government."

"You what?" Charlie snaps. "Why is this the first I'm hearing about this?"

"Because when I mention things that happen on the job, you react like this."

"I'm not sure that's helpful, Jules." Kenzie looks at me and shifts to the front of her seat. "Charlie, what we need for you to understand is that we are adults. It wouldn't be healthy for us to run to you every time something happens."

"I know you think that, but you're wrong."

I sigh. "No. She's right. We're more capable than you give us credit for. You have to start believing we can take care of ourselves."

"I'm not a helicopter parent," she argues.

"Then what is it?"

"Laurette said the four of you are special and I swore I'd ensure your well-being if anything ever happened to her and my brother."

Briar clears his throat. "No offense, Charlie, but it's part of the parent handbook to think your kids are special. Whatever *Maman* said, you don't need to watch over us."

"To a degree, but in your case, it's true." She holds her arm out and pulls up her sleeve. As we watch, a golden dragon appears, coiling up her arm. "I am more than your guardian by law. When Laurette died, I became your fae guardian as well."

I stare at the magical tattoo, and something inside me clicks. "I've seen this before. Where have I seen this?"

"On the hilt of the dagger hidden in the space under the floorboards." Briar sits up.

Charlie looks stricken. "You went into my private space and snooped?"

I point at the photos on the table. "We were kids, but that's a kettle-pot scenario here, lady."

She has the good sense to drop her indignation. "Fair point. Fine. The past is the past. From here, we are honest, and there are no more secrets or lies."

"Except there are more secrets and lies, aren't there? If you're a fae guardian, you're about to tell us the reason we're special is that we're...*what*? What are you hiding from us and when did you find out?"

Charlie lifts her chin and meets my gaze. "The four of you are elemental fae."

Kenzie and Briar look lost, but I've always been the best at rolling with diversity and have already pieced that much together. "Which means what?"

"It means we're being punked," Briar says.

"I don't think so, bro. I think this is why I've felt like crud and Zephyr's night terrors are worse and likely why you've got that patch of leprosy on your arm. We're having awakenings, and Charlie knew it this whole time."

I can't help the anger leaching into my words.

"Zephyr has been struggling, and instead of telling us the truth, you gave him some bullshit advice about taking magnesium before bed."

Unbelievable.

Charlie pegs me with a look. "I need you to listen to me, Jules. You've always been terrible at listening."

"Not true. Listening is a key skill in police work. I spend all day listening to people, taking statements, and figuring out the truth. The problem is, to listen, the other person has to tell me something, and you're too busy keeping *Maman's* secrets."

"Don't blame this on Laurette."

The three of us glance around, searching for the owner of the male voice we just heard.

"Who the fuck said that?" Briar jumps to his feet.

"I did."

I search the room but...

Briar points at Backup. "Either I'm losing it, or the dog is talking."

I follow Briar's pointed finger to the mastiff sitting up and glaring at us. "What? No. I think you're right, bro. I think someone is punking us."

"No one's punking you," the dog says. "I'm not a dog, and my name isn't Backup. My name is Azland, and I was placed in your home to watch over the four of you."

My jaw drops. Backup, the annoying and broody dog we've lived with all this time, is some kind of fae bodyguard? Seriously?

My mind spins out on that one, and I glare at him. "Hold on, Kenzie and I change in front of you! I've had guys over and taken showers, and…all the time you were sitting there watching us… you were actually sitting there watching us? Gross! Not cool!"

Azland sighs. "I never looked, and I certainly never wanted to listen. Didn't you ever wonder why your dog went into the closet if I got caught in your room when a guy was in your bed?"

I always thought that was funny, but now…gross. "Still, it would have been nice to know our pet dog was…whatever the hell you are."

"Now you know," Azland says. "So, can we move on? Your brother is missing, and we're wasting time."

I'm not sure I appreciate his attitude, but he's not wrong. Dysfunctional family drama aside, Zephyr's what matters.

"I assume if we need this big reveal, whatever is going on with Z has to do with the fae world?"

"It does," Azland—formerly known as Backup, my dog—says. "I suggest you let Charlie continue."

"I can't even." Kenzie stares at Backup. "I hear the words coming out of your mouth and see your mouth opening, but it's too weird."

"*Waaaay* too weird," Briar agrees.

"Zephyr's more important," I remind them. "Let's try to focus."

Charlie sighs and takes control of the conversation again. "Thirty years ago, six dark world creatures brought an army of assholes into the elemental kingdoms and wrought a level of devastation those lands had never faced before. They were the offspring of a fae queen and a demon king and possessed traits of both origins."

"Is that possible?" Kenzie asks.

Briar groans. "Demons are real now too?"

The dog growls. "Yes, demons are real. Now listen to your aunt."

Charlie continues. "The six Poreskoro children—or The Six as they became known—consume their prey like demons but because of their fae side, what they crave isn't blood or soul. The

Six have an insatiable hunger for elemental power, a natural force that connects certain fae to a specific nature magic."

"They consume magic?" Briar repeats. "How does that work?"

Charlie holds up a finger to delay the question. "After they feed, they have the power and strength to multiply, creating a race of lesser dark creatures. Those are called the skoro."

"That's seriously messed up," Kenzie says.

"You're not kidding." I try to imagine how this multiplying works. Is it like birthing or does another being split off them? Is it a mogwai eating after dark scenario where we end up with gremlins?

"The more The Six fed, the more offspring they created to do their bidding and create havoc."

"The Six are assholes. What does that have to do with us and about Zephyr missing?" Briar asks.

"Let me finish, and you'll find out!" As chill as Charlie can be, when you flip her switch, she's equally scary.

Briar backpedals and holds up his calloused palms. "Sorry, Charlie. Go on."

"As their numbers grew, The Six sought to feed their endless hunger. They took on the fae kingdom of Draíocht, consuming the elemental magic of that kingdom, and moved on to Biotáille."

"So, they drank everyone's magic and took down entire kingdoms?" I ask. "Couldn't they be stopped?"

"At the time, no. They were incredible fighters and with the mutation of their powers, possessed strengths no one in the elemental kingdoms could win against."

"What did the elementals do?"

"They decided the best chance of keeping their races from being wiped out entirely was to bind the powers of the elemental young, glamor them as humans, and send them as far away from the fae kingdoms as possible."

"They ensured the survival of their species and at the same time cut off the food supply," I clarify.

"In effect, yes. The numbers of the skoro dwindled and died, but the Poreskoro children didn't. The Originals—which is another name for them—are still very much alive and as dangerous as ever."

My head is spinning with all this information, but I do my best to keep up. "How many elemental children are we talking about?"

"Laurette said that at the time there were hundreds. Now? I can't even guess. Two dozen…maybe more."

"We're elemental young who were bound and sent away?"

Charlie nods. "That's what Laurette told me."

Kenzie brightens. "Do we have family? Are our parents alive in a fae realm wondering what happened to us?"

Charlie shakes her head. "I don't think so. From what Laurette said, the adult elementals battled against the Poreskoro six and were destroyed."

"And the young?" Briar asks.

"Trusted fae scouts took them as far from the fae world as possible. Those children were to be raised in secret among the humans and protected from The Six to ensure elementals did not completely disappear."

"The veil dropping changed things." Azland twitches his ear. "When it unleashed fae power in this world, the glamors began to fail, and the elementals began emerging."

Beside me, Kenzie and Briar are tense, nearly vibrating with questions.

"So, were *Maman* and Papa fae elementals too?" Briar asks.

Azland shakes his head. "Laurette's father was a forest lord. She had great earth magic and trained to be your fae guardian. Scaith Warrior is a designation, not a species."

"What about Papa?" Kenzie asks.

"Marcel was a human firefighter who saved a baby girl and fell in love with the woman who took her in. He was human and a hero and a dear friend to all who knew him."

I sit back and try to let that all sink in. "How long have you known about all of this, Charlie? Because this explains a lot and might've been nice to know instead of us always feeling like a part of ourselves is out of sync."

"It was important to keep you safe," Charlie insists. "I'm not trained as a Scaith Warrior. This appeared on my arm when your *maman* passed, but that doesn't mean I was prepared to take this on. I did my best."

The frustration is clear in her voice, but we're frustrated too. "You still should've told us."

"Your parents made me swear that unless something happened, you weren't to find out."

"Now something happened," I say.

Azland looks down his nose at the MyAncestry printouts. "You really shouldn't have done this."

Briar huffs. "Zephyr's been searching for answers and struggling. You can't be surprised he colored outside the lines."

Azland growls. "It's too late now. Fae run most DNA heritage sites and use them to track humans. When they got the DNA for you four, they likely sold the information to a member of The Six and they took Zephyr."

What the hell?

I thought Zephyr got himself caught up in his standard trouble. Now he's been kidnapped by magical fae beings who consumed an entire kingdom of fae elementals and want to eat his energy?

What the hell do I do with that?

They didn't cover this in the police academy.

CHAPTER NINE

Briar runs rough fingers through his blond hair. "This is insane. It can't be real."

"It's very real," Azland counters.

My mind is spinning. "How did *Maman* end up with all of us? If it was a point of survival that elemental children were to be absorbed into the population, doesn't having four of us in one household work against the objective?"

Charlie sighs. "From what Laurette said, even after the young arrived in this realm, hunters were tracking you. When she sensed elementals in danger, she interceded. Each of your handlers was killed. She took you in and used her powers to shield you from detection."

My brain stumbles over the facts of my reality. "I can't believe you've known this for twelve years, Charlie. You never thought to share this with us? We were supposed to be family."

She offers me a sad smile. "I would've loved to. Honestly, I almost told you a hundred times, but Laurette was adamant that knowing about the fae world would put you all in danger."

Briar shakes his head. "No way. There's no way I'm an elemental whatever. It doesn't make sense."

"What doesn't make sense is our parents lying to us for years," Kenzie snaps.

"And Charlie," I add.

Charlie's big green eyes are glassy. "I'm sorry. I love you guys. You know that. I did what they begged me to do. I kept you four safe and the fae world out of your lives…until I couldn't."

There's no mistaking her sorrow, but that doesn't mean I'm not still pissed. With so much going on, I can't worry about that right now. "What is an elemental fae?"

Briar waves his hands around. "Yeah. What powers am I supposed to have?"

I draw the conversation back to Backup. "I hate to be rude, but how the fuck does a talking dog fit into all of this?"

"Language, please, Jules!" Charlie says.

Kenzie holds up a hand. "In her defense, if there was ever an appropriate time to swear, it's when we're stunned and reeling because we've found out we're fae disguised as humans because there are demons who want to suck out our magical essence."

"I understand that this is overwhelming." Azland's voice is gentle but firm. "You three can be as angry as you want at us later. The most important thing right now is finding Zephyr."

None of us can disagree with that.

He turns to me. "Jules, you said you heard a clicking sound when you were in that house in LaSalle?"

I nod.

"Describe it to me."

I do my best, but it's a strange, intangible sound that is hard to describe.

Thankfully, Azland understands. "That's the sound a skoro scout makes before it attacks."

"It wasn't one of The Six?" Briar asks.

Azland shakes his head. "No. The scout likely tracked and killed the man you found in the house."

"Who was that man?" I ask. "He had those runes on him, the

same ones the guy in the river had. After twenty-seven years of having no clues to my past, two men in two days have the same rune markings as the guy who shielded me as a baby. I don't get it. What's going on?"

"Those men were Scaith Warriors, sworn to protect elementals. The massive influx of fae energy in Montréal is causing a huge surge of awakenings. Other elementals are unlocking. They will sense them and come to ensure their safety."

"Do you wear the same runes?"

"No. I had warrior training when I held a humanoid form, but that was years ago."

"How long have you been a dog?"

"For the past twelve years."

Great. I finally have answers to the questions I've been searching for, but there's no way I can solve the case. I can't report that my siblings and I are highly sought-after fae beings and that I found this out from my talking dog who used to be a warrior before he—

I hold up a finger. "Wait. You were a warrior until twelve years ago?"

Briar frowns. "That's when *Maman* and Papa died in the car accident."

My mental cogs are all starting to click together. "Only, it wasn't a car accident, was it?"

Charlie shakes her head. "The local fae guild made it look like that, but no."

Briar runs his hands over the thighs of his jeans, looking like he might explode. "Then what happened? Is there anything about our life that isn't a lie?"

Charlie frowns. "When the four of you hit puberty the binding on your powers started to fail. Scaith Warriors and skoro scouts started popping up. One of The Six came too. There was a terrible battle to protect you."

The room falls silent as we all let that sink in.

Our adoptive parents died to protect us.

Charlie became our guardian to protect us.

Our entire lives, people have been lying and working behind the scenes to protect us.

That ends right now.

I peg Backup with a glare. "Is that everything? Are we up to date on our lives now?"

He nods. "There are small details about my life, but that's ninety percent of everything and one hundred percent of what you need to know for right now."

"Okay, so what about Zephyr? How do we find him?"

Azland frowns. "Before they can siphon off his elemental power, they'll have to unlock it. That will take time, and once they do, I'll be able to track it."

"We don't have to wait," Charlie says. "Laurette was proactive. She had each of them chipped."

My mind stalls out on that. "Exsqueeze me?"

Briar curses and I can tell he's as offended as I am. "We weren't her fucking pets."

Charlie shrugs. "Don't kill the messenger. I'm telling you what I know. You each carry a tracker, and I have the tracking receiver."

Azland grins. "Even better. Get that for us, and in the meantime, I'll remove the glamors so you can access your powers."

Briar holds up a finger. "Didn't you say The Six need to unlock our powers so they can consume it? Doesn't unlocking them make it easier for the enemy?"

"In one sense, yes, but more importantly, it gives you a chance to survive."

Kenzie's eyes bug wide. "What do you mean, remove our glamors?"

"Exactly what it sounds like. These bodies you wear are illusions to mask your true selves."

Briar huffs. "Fuck that. I'm rather fond of my skin and face. I won't be made into some kind of freak from another planet."

Azland scowls. "Not another planet—another realm. Briar, you're from the fae kingdom of Litaui and are infused with the elemental power of earth. You were the prince of the kingdom and heir to the throne. If there were still a kingdom to rule, you'd be the King of Litaui."

Briar's shock would be hilarious if any of this were funny. "Oh, great, well, that solves everything. I'm a king freak. That's much better."

"I'm not sure that difference will matter much when you look in the mirror and have no face," Kenzie says.

Azland growls. "Relax. No one is losing their face."

Charlie shakes her head. "Laurette said in the fae realm, your true form is the embodiment of your element, but as long as you're in the human world, you'll likely keep a humanoid form even without glamors."

I hear the upbeat tone in Charlie's voice, but I'm not buying in. "Likely? She didn't know?"

"There's no way to know for sure," Azland interjects.

"Well, I can't show up at the station on Wednesday and be a...what exactly *am* I?"

"You are the descendant of a great warrior from the Lasair empire. It's the kingdom known for the elemental connection to fire."

"Ah-ha! That makes sense," Kenzie chimes in. "Lately, I swear she's a walking furnace. Then there's the weird flaming candle stuff that's been happening around her."

Okay, yeah. I buy that. "So, I'm the Human Torch, and Briar is the Thing...what about Kenzie and Zephyr?"

"Mackenzie's mother was a great magical healer of the water empire of Uisce, and Zephyr's father ran the training academy for Gailleann, the people of air."

I chuckle. "Air? Like…easy, breezy, that sort of thing? Doesn't sound much like our Zephyr."

Charlie sighs. "Zephyr is an air elemental, but he's more perfect storm than summer breeze."

True story.

Azland stands. "We can't sit around talking. I need to remove your glamors so you can access your powers and help me get Zephyr back."

I hold up my hand. "Wait a minute. I don't know you, dude. Like, at all. Maybe you're a great warrior protector or maybe not. Either way, there's no way releasing powers suddenly makes Kenzie and Briar tactical fighters ready to take on minions of the Hell realm."

"What do you suggest? Should the two of us take this on alone? Should we ask your cop friends to challenge powers they don't understand and can't comprehend? What exactly do you think we should do?"

Am I really arguing with my dog about a raid and rescue? The insanity of the moment is too much.

I feel like death, discovered that magic-eating hellborn fae kidnapped my brother, and learned the only way to get him back is to unlock my fire side and "likely" remain recognizable as my human self.

I search the faces of my siblings and hate everything about this. "Fine, we'll unlock our powers, but Kenzie and Briar sit this one out. That's non-negotiable."

"Then how do you think we'll get your brother back?"

"I'll think of something."

We walk out into the back yard, shaded by trees. The birds are singing, and the pond next to the cluster of birch trees is emerald green. We all used to hang out back here as kids, climbing trees and trying to catch the frogs that lived in the pond.

As an adult, it seems smaller but no less special.

"All right, Jules." Azland sits up and raises his front paws. "You're the oldest and your powers are already breaking free of their bonds. You first."

Hating this whole thing but unsure I have another option, I hold my hands out. He rests the pads of his paws in my palms and meets my gaze. For the first time, I glimpse the watchful dog companion who tagged along by my side for years.

He closes his eyes, so I close mine too.

As he speaks in tongues, something wild and powerful builds inside me.

Either he's calling it or irritating it. I can't be sure.

My blood grows hot in my veins, and my hands shake. Azland continues to speak, but the powerful thrum of something inside me determined to be set free drowns out his voice.

When he finishes speaking, it's like he unlatches the cage door and the beast within me explodes toward freedom. The surge of power that hits me is incredible.

It's like a firehose of energy has opened full-bore and a pressure I didn't realize had grown so strong spews out of me in a violent funnel.

Distantly, I hear loud voices, but the relief is so exquisite I'm lost in the sensation.

Hands out in front of me, I release the burning, my palms hot and tingling.

Then, a strange sense of history takes hold in my mind. It's a connection. A vision of a huge castle flickers behind the lids of my closed eyes. It's like I suddenly have a homeland I'm attached to.

The relief that washes through me is almost orgasmic.

Drawing a deep, steadying breath, I open my eyes, exhale, and —"What the hell?"

The grass is scorched in a long line from where I stand to where the fence is charred and smoking a hundred feet away. Small flames are licking up from the ground, and the air is rife with the scent of a bonfire. "Did I do that?"

Kenzie's mouth is hanging open.

Briar nods. "You sure did."

"Yikes. Sorry. I didn't mean to torch the back yard."

Azland trots around to stand in front of me. "It seems your powers have built up a lot over the years of containment. Not to worry. Now that they're free and we'll be working them, that built-up force should dissipate to a more controllable level soon enough."

"Not soon enough for Charlie's lawn," Kenzie points out.

I look at Briar and Kenzie. "Other than me being a flamethrowing menace, am I also a mutant freakazoid?"

Briar shrugs. "No more than usual."

Good. That's good. "I felt things click into place when Azland unlocked the glamor. I have access to a part of me that's been locked away for too long. It feels good."

"You still have a face," Briar says.

"And yep, the same old hair," Kenzie adds.

Man, if Kenzie's hair changes, she's going to lose her shit.

Azland has Kenzie step up next. They repeat the palms and paws thing, and both close their eyes.

I watch, wondering if I can see anything happen during the unlocking. I can.

Blue patterns shimmer across her warm brown skin. They're like ripples on the water's surface, ebbing and cresting before they fade.

She opens her arms to the side as Azland moves away and raises her face to the sky. A sun shower sprinkles down on her. It's delicate and brings with it the scent of summer rain.

Briar and I are standing five feet away with Azland, and the water doesn't touch us. It's only for her.

Kenzie opens her eyes, blinks a few times, and reaches up to touch her curly hair.

"You're still you," I reassure her.

"Unfortunately," Briar teases. Our big bear of a brother chuckles at his joke and grows serious. "What if…what if I don't want to do this? What if I'm happy living as a human?"

Azland sits in front of him and lifts his snout. "The man you know is only part of who you are. Resisting or denying your magical heritage won't make it any less real. It will try to force its way to freedom. In the end, there won't be any stopping it."

I grunt. "Trust me, that sucks. I've felt like shit for weeks."

"And now?" Briar asks.

"S'all good, bro." I hold up my hands and grin.

At that, Briar sighs, then steps toward Azland. He holds his arms out, stiff and awkward, but he lets our dog give him his paws.

I'm watching for the visual cues of Briar's elemental unlocking when the ground beneath our feet rumbles. At first, it's a shimmy. Then it's a quake.

Azland moves back, and I widen my stance, gripping Kenzie's wrist. The ground is having a seizure beneath our feet. Kenzie and I take a couple of steps farther away to distance ourselves from the seismic activity.

"*Tabarnak*, look at that." I point at where the earth is splitting apart in a long, jagged line leading from Briar's feet toward the charred spot on the fence.

Wow, Charlie's back yard is taking a beating today.

"Rein it in, Briar." Azland watches the fissure widening at his feet. "Yes, it feels good to release the energy, but earth is also about healing and growth."

Briar's forehead creases for a moment, but he pulls his hands back and shakes them out. As he comes back to full awareness, the earthquake ends.

Azland sits pretty and looks at us. "Well done. That's the first step done."

"What's the second step?" Kenzie asks.

"That's up to Jules. Have you thought of a better plan than mine? Do you have a way for us to infiltrate a skoro compound and get your brother back without getting ourselves killed?"

"I have." I pull my phone out of my pocket and feel surer of my plan with each passing moment.

After searching through my contact list, I find the entry for the one person I trust to help me with a problem like this. I hit send and wait for her to answer.

"Hey, Fiona. It's Jules Gagne in Montréal. I've got a family awakening emergency. Any chance Team Trouble can help me out and keep things private?"

"Of course. How many of us do you need and what are we up against?"

I give her a quick rundown of what we know.

"Yeah, text me the address. We'll be there in five."

CHAPTER TEN

Azland isn't happy about me calling in outside help, but I know Fiona and her team from the vampire attacks on City Hall last month, and I trust them. They run the fae policing arm for the Toronto area, and since the fall of the veil, they've been acting as fae liaisons and bridging the gaps between fae and humans.

"This isn't their business," Azland gripes.

"That won't matter with Fi and her people. This is what they do."

Fiona appears out of nowhere. "And we do it quite well." Six other warriors in leather battle gear, cloaks, and designer jeans accompany the red-haired druid. Five men and one woman.

Fi comes over to shake my hand and smiles. "It's good to see you again, Jules. How has your awakening been going?"

She says that like it's the most natural thing in the world. "You're not surprised?"

She winks. "Registering fae power is one of my gifts. It was obvious things were about to change in your life."

"How about a heads-up next time."

She chuckles. "Luckily, an awakening is a one-time-only kinda event."

Her team fills in behind her, and I recognize several of the faces. "Thanks for coming, guys."

Fiona raises a hand and gestures at her group. "Everyone, this is Sloan, Nikon, Tad, Eva, and my brothers Calum and Dillan."

They each nod in turn.

Sloan is the love of Fi's life. He has stunning, mint-green eyes that contrast with the mocha brown of his skin. If I remember correctly, he's a master druid.

Nikon is the blond and beautiful Greek immortal.

I haven't met Tad before. He's a tall, blond guy with piercing blue eyes and a thick Irish accent.

Eva is a full-figured beauty with a radiance that's hard to explain.

Calum and Dillan both look like Fi, although instead of red hair and blue eyes, they both have black hair and emerald green eyes.

I'm so relieved to have them here.

Having fought with Fi, Sloan, and Nikon, I know what they're capable of.

I return the favor and do a round of intros too. "This is my brother Briar, my sister Kenzie, and our dog Backup who we found out an hour ago is a fae guardian named Azland."

Fi blinks at me. "An hour ago. Wow, so this is very new for you."

"Yes, very. I might still be in shock, but if I believe what we've been told, I'm a fire elemental and the skoro we're taking on eat my particular kind of fae energy."

"Yes, they do." The blonde with the scythe nods, her ringlet curls bouncing beside her full cheeks. "They're a low-level opponent, but their makers are quite a bit more powerful."

"Like Asmodeus powerful?" Fi asks.

"No. Not greater demon strength by a long shot."

"Okay, then we're good to go."

Charlie returns, raises her brow at all the extra people, and hands me a device that could pass for a television remote. "I'm not sure how it works, but all four of you should be trackable with this thing somehow."

"Trackable?" Fiona repeats.

"Yeah, apparently our adoptive mother knew what we were and had us all chipped along with the cat."

"Which also explains how she always knew when we were out drinking instead of studying," Briar adds.

Dillan laughs. "Been there."

Fiona chuckles. "Well, today, you being chipped is a good thing."

"Aye, it is." Sloan comes over to see the device. "If this can narrow us in on an address, Nikon can look it up, and we'll be on our way."

Maman's tracer leads us to a rundown building near the Hydro-Québec Électrium and Research Institute. It used to be part of the hydroelectric plant but was abandoned in favor of new technology.

The building is massive, with concrete walls and almost no windows. Inside is completely dark.

Fiona lifts her nose. "Is it my imagination or does the air smell like burned cookies?"

I wrinkle my nose at the odor of scorched sugar and wonder what's been going on in this place.

"That's the skoro," Eva explains. "They smell like burned cookies, crossroads demons smell like a bonfire, and funnily enough, Princes of Hell smell like S'mores."

I blink at Fiona and lean closer. "How does she know all that?"

"Eva is an angel of the Choir who used to work for Death as a

Reaper. As well as being part of the family, she's now our guardian angel."

"That's amazing."

Fiona nods. "You'll discover a lot of amazing people and things in this world, Jules. Yes, it can be violent and scary, but it can also be incredible."

"Did you always know what you were?"

Her laugh is more like a harsh bark. "Hardly. My brothers and I only found out two years ago."

Two years? "Wow. I'm impressed. You guys got really good in two years."

"I have no doubt you and your siblings will be no different."

Maybe. I'm not so sure. I can't see Kenzie tearing up a battlefield with the drow, goblins, or any of the fae nightmares surfacing around the city.

The wind picks up, and Fiona's massive animal companion forms next to us. The grizzly bear lifts his snout and grumbles and grunts. Fiona, her brothers, and Sloan nod and follow.

I wish I spoke grizzly bear.

Feeling useless, I pull out my gun and do a quick check on things.

When the bear dissolves into the air again, Fiona turns her attention to Azland and me. "My bear Bruin says there are close to thirty inside, all heavily armed. Zephyr is tied up in the back, and it appears they're in the process of opening a portal gate to another realm."

"To take him somewhere else or bring someone here?" Nikon asks.

"No idea. Either way, let's not let that happen."

"Agreed," Sloan says.

The group settles and looks at Fi.

She stretches her neck, and a growing black fretwork suddenly covers her skin. It looks like a tree's roots, branches, and bark have covered her entire body.

I've seen her body armor before, but it's still freaky.

"Tad and Calum, you're on the door. Take down the guards, get inside, and get Calum to high ground. Dillan and Eva, you're on demon distraction and destruction. Nikon, shut down that portal gate. Sloan, Jules, Azland, and I are going for Zephyr."

Everyone nods and the group breaks.

Single file, we creep along the building. Calum and Tad make quick work of the guards. Tad *poofs* them into position, they take them out from behind, and Tad grabs them and *poofs* out.

A moment later he's back empty-handed.

I have no idea where he dumped them, but honestly, I don't care.

When Sloan swirls a hand in the air and speaks in tongues, the tingle of magic settles over us.

"A concealing spell," Fi whispers. "To keep us unseen as long as we can."

We sneak inside the unguarded door and make our way through the factory's front office area and into the power plant behind.

There is plenty of abandoned, rusted-out machinery and shelving to give us cover as we move, but that goes both ways. Our opponents can be hiding too.

Clicking sounds close by, and an icy chill runs down my spine. "I hate that noise."

Azland is trotting close to my heel. He lifts his nose to sniff the air. "You and me both."

A skoro comes around the corner, and we freeze.

How much will Sloan's spell hide us? We're not exactly in the open, but in another moment that thug will look right at us.

The smell of burned cookies is nearly overpowering here. I briefly wonder why I didn't smell it before the attack in the house in LaSalle. Maybe it takes time for the scent to build or a concentration of skoro to taint the air. I push that question away for later.

Now is the time for us to focus.

The approaching skoro looks human, but its black, beady eyes give it away. It also moves with a weird twitchiness that would never be mistaken as human.

Fi raises her clenched fist in the universal hand signal for "hold position."

I glance around my aisle, searching for something I can use as a weapon. My gun is great but not quiet. It'll alert those thirty men in the back that there is trouble if I fire on this guy.

I need a piece of metal or a chunk of wood or something. Hell, even an ax in a firehose case would be great.

A quiet whistle sounds and the thug is thrown back by the impact of an arrow to his chest. Sloan rushes forward, snaps the man's neck, and drags him behind one of the storage racks.

I watch as fluttering black magic seeps out of the dead guy's nose and eyes and gets sucked through a crack in the floor. "That's not creepy at all."

Fi chuckles. "I know, right?"

"You're free to move," Tad says behind us.

How did he get there? Is he a ninja?

Fiona flexes her hand, and a wicked spear with a jagged green marble spear tip appears in her hand. "Let's go save your brother."

We're halfway down a dark corridor when something heavy crashes in the distance and chaos ensues. A rush of wind sweeps past us and Fiona nods. "Bruin says Zephyr's through this next door at the back."

As we approach, a rush of skoro pushes through the door, and we're exposed.

"Busted." Fi goes for the first one.

Her bear materializes and corners two more.

Sloan has his hands up and zaps them with energy balls of blue magic.

I straighten and squeeze my trigger. Hellborn or not, a kill shot to the head ends the fight.

The noise will attract more attention, but there's no helping it. Two skoro jump over a stack of crates and launch themselves at me. I lean back, swing my aim, and catch one in the shoulder. I can't get a second shot off before gravity wins and they're on top of me.

I go down hard, dropping my gun to brace my fall. Somehow, I manage not to smack my face against the concrete floor. Yay me.

The attacker I shot is cursing and pounding on me.

The other is pinning me down and leaning in like a zombie about to eat my brain.

"Like hell." Adrenaline ignites inside me as I push against them with all my might. Like flamethrowers exploding from my palms, both launch into the air behind a ten-foot flame.

Holy shit. I'm a fucking rocket launcher…

"Man, that feels good." I scramble to my feet and embrace the flames. All the tension and anxiety of feeling off and trapped is released. My hands glow in swirling hues of yellow and orange, and I can feel the power of my fire eager to consume.

Grappling opponents doesn't burn or harm them. Then I remember they are born from The Six and have a demon king daddy.

Sadly, fire might not be the weapon of choice against them. Too bad because this feels *gooood*.

"We've got this, *a ghra*," Sloan shouts. "Take Jules and get her brother."

Fi tries the door, but it's a no-go. "Bruin, get us through here."

Fi's bear rears up on his hind legs, drops, and takes a powerful gauntlet run toward the door. The wood shatters into toothpick-sized splinters, and we advance in a rush.

A handful of skoro turn and look surprised that we've

managed to get through. Did they think they could keep me away from my brother?

Ha. Not bloody likely.

I run straight for the gaggle of skoro, my heart pumping the blood in my veins, and...*whoosh!*

Without intending for it to happen, my wreath of flame burns hotter and brighter around me. It's got a mind of its own, and it's pissed right now. "Get away from him."

Zephyr is bound to a funky dental chair, looking ragged and thoroughly beaten to shit.

He shifts his head to look at me through the slit in his eye where he can see beyond the swelling. "What the—"

"I'll explain later." I'm about to grab him by the wrist when I realize I'm still on fire. "A little help here."

Fi's bear barrels over, swipes with one of his massive paws, and slices Zephyr's bindings with his dagger-sharp claws.

Fi joins us and frowns. "Jules, deep breaths. Dial back your fire, girlfriend. Tad, get them out of here."

I do as she says and try to pull my flames and heat inside me as quickly and thoroughly as possible. "They don't want to extinguish."

Fi meets my gaze and smiles. "You can do it. Power is often tied to adrenaline. Calm yourself. Tell your inner warrior that all is well and as soon as you gain control, you and your brother will be on your way home. Deep breath. Release your instinct to fight. Take your brother back to your siblings."

Damn, she's good. "Yeah, okay. I've got this."

The blond Abercrombie guy appears next to us. He sets one hand on Zephyr, one hand on me, and tilts his head to Backup at my side. "I need one of ye to finish the circuit if ye will."

Once Zephyr touches the dog, magic washes over me and we appear in the back yard of my childhood home.

"You did it!" Kenzie shouts, rushing over to hug us.

"Don't touch me. I was on fire and might still be hot."

"Ye definitely are." Tad shows me the hand he used to grip me for transport. It's burned red and blistering.

"Oh, dude. I'm so sorry."

He waves that away. "Not an issue. Sloan will heal it up as soon as he gets back."

Kenzie abandons the idea of hugging me and moves to where Zephyr is lying on the grass. Briar is sitting next to him, checking on him. He waves off Kenzie's intentions, and she deflates.

"May I hug you?" She looks at Tad. "I need to hug someone, and you took one for the team."

"Och, I'd never turn down a hug from a lovely lass."

That's exactly the right answer. Kenzie beams and wraps her arms around him. "Thank you for bringing them home safe."

"I'd say it was my greatest pleasure, but yer thanks is even better."

Kenzie eases back and bites her bottom lip. "Mmm, I like you. Charm sounds so much better with an accent."

Leave it to my sister to turn the rescue of our brother from a kidnapping into a dating game.

Within five minutes, everyone is back from the power plant, and other than goopy black ichor staining their clothing, no one looks any worse for the excursion.

Sloan heals Tad's hand. Nikon gives me back my sidearm. And Fiona gives us the nod that all is well.

When the dust settles, my cop instincts come back online. "We can't leave all those bodies there. That warehouse is now the scene of a massacre. Not to mention an abduction. Should I call it into the precinct?"

Fiona waves away my concern. "Not to worry. Dillan and Eva will take care of the cleanup. Put the whole thing behind you."

Nikon snaps us back to the fire station, where everyone plops down on the big sofas in the living room. Zephyr fills us in on what happened to him, and we do the same, explaining our elemental status and the fact that Azland unlocked our powers.

"And everyone survived," Briar adds, bringing out an armful of beers. He looks Zephyr over. "If just barely."

Sloan is magically healing him, and Kenzie is glued to the scene. Since finding out she's the daughter of a great healer, she's pretty sure that while Zephyr and I are destined to be fighters, she's supposed to heal.

"Jules, come here to me if ye will," Sloan calls.

I set my beer down and join him at the other couch. He points at a particularly nasty puncture wound on Zephyr's thigh. He had it wrapped, but now that the pressure of the binding is gone, it's pulsing blood at an alarming rate. "Shit, should we get him to the hospital?"

"No need."

"That's not the kind of injury you can slap a bandage on and call it a day," I point out.

"No. That's why ye'll cauterize it."

Zephyr, who had previously been lying back with his face pale and his eyes closed, sits up. "Absolutely not."

"Don't be silly," I tell him.

Sloan looks at me. "Yer a fire elemental. I'll guide ye through it, but now that yer powers are unlocked, it's important ye take every opportunity to expand yer knowledge of what ye can do. Stoppin' excessive blood flow is a valuable skill."

"She only unlocked those powers, like, an hour ago!" Zephyr protests. "I'm not letting her light me on fire. I'd rather be bleeding than cremated."

Seriously? After everything I've done and been through to save him, he's dissing me? "You're about to be both, asshole. Do you have any idea the shit you stirred up this time?"

Briar groans and steps into the mix. "He's losing too much blood to argue. Fix him first. Yell at him second."

"Fine. What do I need to do?"

Sloan places my hand over the bloody gash and lays his hand over mine. "Ye need to sear the flesh to close the wound and sterilize the area. The trick is to do that without burnin' any healthy skin."

"I can do that." It's not bravado. I think I can get this done. Except…my powers are new to me…and I don't have control yet.

Sloan senses my hesitation and smiles at me. "Yer powers have always been part of ye. They're newly awakened, aye, but they are an extension of yer will. Ye don't want to hurt yer brother, do ye?"

"Sometimes…but no, not now."

"Aye, then follow my instructions and ye'll be fine."

"Is it going to hurt?" Zephyr asks.

I chuckle. "No, you've been stabbed and are gushing blood, and now we're going to use magical fire to sear the wound closed. It'll feel like bunny rabbit tickles."

Zephyr flashes me a middle-finger salute. I push my hands against the wound and focus on bringing heat that will sear and seal, not flames that will leap and lick.

He cries out, then sags to the side and catches his breath once I finish.

"You big baby. That wasn't so bad, was it?"

The look he pegs me with is filled with the storm of his emotions. "Wait until I get my powers, Jules. I'm going to catch you in a hurricane and spin you until you puke, then keep spinning you while you get splattered by your vomit."

Fiona laughs. "That is so something my brothers would say. Hilarious."

Sloan chuckles and waves Kenzie over. "Now, I want ye to try yer powers too. Water has a great many healing properties. Send some flowing over the spot Jules closed."

"She'll get the sofa all wet," Briar grumbles.

I chuckle. "No worries, I'll blast some hot air and dry it off. Man, these powers can come in handy."

Sloan nods. "Kenzie, control is the key. Release only a little of yer water power. Envision the outcome and manifest the result ye want."

She looks at me and waggles her brows. "Here goes nothing."

She focuses her intention on Zephyr's leg, and sure enough, she soothes the angry red. He falls back against the couch, letting out a long breath.

"That feels really good, Kenz. Thanks."

Maybe Kenzie's right, and she was supposed to be our peacemaker all along. She's always been the one to soothe hurt feelings and calm tempers.

Sloan continues tending to Zephyr's injuries until the doorbell rings. Briar jumps up and smiles. "It's the pizza delivery guy. Time to replenish our energy."

When he's laid out the boxes on the table and everyone has dug in, Zephyr sits up and takes a bite of meat lovers. "Sorry, guys. I didn't mean to cause so much trouble."

"Not your fault." I take a bite of Hawaiian bliss and savor the pineapple. "*Maman* knew those black-eyed freaks would come and try to eat our power, so she bound our fae sides and lied to us our whole lives. That's not on you."

"Charlie lied too," Briar adds. "You'd think she would've come clean, knowing your nightmares were getting worse, but nope. She kept up the lies."

"And Backup isn't a dog. He's an undercover fae guardian spying on us," Kenzie snaps.

Zephyr blinks at me. "Are you fucking with me, Kenz? Because I've really had a day."

I finish chewing and swallow. "Nope. That's the gist of things. Yeah, you might have tipped them off to us by sending in our

DNA, but if we'd been privy to our information, you wouldn't have been searching."

Kenzie reaches over and squeezes his wrist. "And your night terrors were your powers trying to escape the binding. Once your powers are free, you might be good on that front."

A battle between hurt and fury mars Zephyr's expression. "I don't even know how to process that. She told me to take supplements."

Backup trots in from the hall. "It's not Charlie's fault. She loves you four and believes in your parents' right to safeguard you. Don't be too hard on her."

Zephyr stares at our mastiff. "Our dog is weighing in on this."

"I told you—he's a fae spy keeping an eye on us," Kenzie repeats.

Zephyr takes another bite and chews. "That's going to take some getting used to."

No doubt. "Next time someone is stalking you, how about you come to me first and not track them into a situation where you're alone and vulnerable."

"Done deal. In my defense, at first, I thought it was someone I pissed off or owed money to, but they never asked for anything. They wouldn't stop, like, touching me and sniffing me."

"They were likely trying to consume your elemental powers," Azland interjects. "Luckily, they hadn't figured out how to unlock them."

"What would've happened if they did?" Zephyr asks.

"Then you would have been lost to us, and our enemies would have grown significantly stronger."

Zephyr takes a long swig of beer and holds up his bottle to the group. "Then thanks again. I'm glad I wasn't a fae energy drink."

The room falls quiet as everyone eats and lets that little ray of sunshine blow over. "How'd you get from the house in LaSalle all the way out to Hydro-Québec?"

Zephyr drinks another long swig and swallows. "Remember the guy who was stalking me?"

"The drug dealer?" Kenzie asks.

Azland growls, turning a furious glare on Zephyr. "You have a drug dealer? *Tabarnak de câlisse*, are you that self-destructive?"

Zephyr shakes his head and raises his palms. "No, I swear. No drugs. I don't know what they're talking about. I caught a guy following me a couple of times. I have no idea who he is or what he's into."

Even though I'm still annoyed with him, I jump in for the save. "We went to Casse Croûte, and Cami said some creepy dude was trying to find you. A few regulars pegged him as the source of the new street drug that gives people fae vision."

"Second Sight," Fi says.

"That's the one."

Zephyr reaches for another slice of pizza. "I followed that guy to the house in LaSalle, and I called Jules. I was going to wait outside for her to get there, but I heard something inside the house."

"Like a weird clicking noise?" I ask.

"No, it was a fight. I went inside to see what was going on, and someone grabbed me from behind. Creepy stalker dude was there, and it was two against one. They dragged me into a car and tossed me in a room in that busted-up electrical plant."

Briar shakes his head. "I wish you could go one day without tumbling headfirst into trouble."

"I didn't mean to drag everyone into this. I wanted us to know more about our heritage."

"Well, you succeeded in that," I tease. "Thanks to your MyAncestry stunt, we all found out that we're fae elementals in hiding and had our magical powers unlocked by our dog—who, did I mention, is a fae spy who's been lying to us for more than a decade."

"But we're not bitter," Kenzie adds.

"No. Not at all."

Zephyr snorts. "Tell me more about my air powers. What have I got to look forward to?"

"You'll find out soon enough," Azland replies. "Finish your dinner, and we'll go outside and get that glamor off you. Once that happens, you need to start training—all four of you—as soon as possible. Without your glamors, The Six will be able to sense you, and they'll be here before you know it."

I finish my beer and grab another. "So, Fi, how do we train to be urban elementals…asking for a friend."

Fiona and her Team Trouble Toronto team spend the next couple of hours with us, decompressing and answering questions about what we should consider for our next steps.

"Training. Training. Training," Fi says. "When we first got our powers, the five of us trained with either my father, Sloan, or our other mentors for hours every day."

Calum chuckles. "Aiden, Dillan, Emmet, and I are all cops, but training with our powers and our new weapons was the only reason we survived our first battles."

I groan. "I need to talk to you guys about how you balance work and your empowered life. I'm freaking out about that."

Calum offers me a warm smile. "Fi will give you our numbers. Call us anytime."

"I appreciate that."

Kenzie sighs. "I'm not looking forward to this. I'm a lover, not a fighter."

"Maybe ye haven't had the right trainer," Tad suggests. "If ye like, I can stay on a few days and see that ye get off to a solid start."

Azland growls. "That won't be necessary. Now that they are

unbound and know who I truly am, I'll train them in the ways of their people."

Kenzie scowls at the dog. "How are you going to show us how to hold a weapon or to break out of a hold? You're a dog."

"I was a warrior before I took this form. I'm very capable of teaching you four what you need to know."

"It can't hurt to have a second set of skills to add to yer regimen," Sloan says. "Druid and elemental powers are similar in many facets. Tad could be a big help."

"Then it's settled." Kenzie glances at me, Z, and Briar. "Agreed?"

I nod. "Yeah, I'm good with it."

"Me too," Briar confirms.

"I like the idea of having a guy who can portal in our house," Zephyr adds. "If bad guys come calling, we can get out of Dodge."

I smile at Kenzie and nod. "Good call, girlfriend. Looks like we've got ourselves a private trainer."

CHAPTER ELEVEN

Work the next morning is a shit show. There's a plastic kiddie pool in the middle of the bullpen with a bunch of baby turtles swimming around and climbing to bask on "rocks" that, upon closer inspection, are old helmets used by the equine mounted unit.

"Gagne," Morin shouts. "Tell Marx he can't set up a turtle pond in de office. Those tings have germs."

"Uh, what's going on?"

Tremblay laughs. "Marx and I caught the first call of the morning. It was a pet store robbery."

"But dispatch got two calls from de same shop at de same time," Morin interjects. "De robber was also trying to call de cops."

"Turns out," Tremblay says, "the shopkeeper and his wife are super anti-empowered, like, they absolutely hate anyone with magical powers."

"Why?" I ask.

Marx shrugs. "Their son got into a beef with de newly awakened kids who hang out in a nearby park."

"What does this have to do with turtles?"

"Patience, Sasshopper. So, de lady shopkeeper is in fighting with a lady customer, and de customer is yelling dat they need to release de fish back into nature."

"Sounds like a nutter," I say.

"I thought so too, but then I noticed her hair is seaweedy and she's got webbing between her fingers," Tremblay says.

"It was gross," Marx says. "So, she says we need to liberate de sea life, and she's telling me she called me down to report animal abuse. Meanwhile, the shopkeeper is screaming dat she's stealing fish right out of de tanks and wants us to arrest her."

As they relay the story, one of the turtles climbs over the rim of the kiddie pool. It lands on the tile floor with a wet *smack* and scuttles toward Tremblay's shoes.

Morin scrambles to climb on top of his desk. "Augh…it's loose. Put it back!"

Marx laughs. "What are you afraid of? Dat it's going to cute you to death?"

"I told you. They carry germs."

Tremblay joins the chaos and laughs. "I've seen you eat a donut that was in the break room for a week. Don't tell me you're worried about germs."

"So, there's this mermaid lady trying to rob a pet store," I prompt, wanting to return to the story's point. "What happened then?"

"She said she could communicate with the critters and they were crying out for freedom. I offered to call animal control, but she peeled off her dress and climbed into the biggest tank. There she was, in just her underthings, swimming around and blowing bubbles."

The guys are now thoroughly busting up.

"Anyway, we finally got her hauled out of there and off to a resource center for the newly awakened—I gave her the benefit of the doubt that she isn't currently in her right mind. Then animal control showed up and told us the turtles were illegal, and we needed to impound them."

"What's illegal about a turtle?" I ask.

Morin is sitting on his desk with his feet on his chair and his arms crossed. "You won't be laughing when you're out for two weeks with salmonella."

"Hell, for a two-week vacation, I'll make out with one of those suckers," Tremblay says.

I laugh. "Gross, but I'm strangely intrigued by that."

"You would be, you freak."

I shrug off the jibe. Tremblay doesn't know how right he is. "Really, what makes the turtles illegal?"

Rene shrugs. "I guess sea turtles are a species you're not allowed to have. They're endangered."

"So now we're turtle-sitting," Marx says.

"Why couldn't animal control take them?" I ask.

"They were headed to a seizure call for exotic animal parts at de airport. I offered to babysit these guys as a professional courtesy until they swing back around to pick them up."

I bend over, looking at the baby turtles sitting on the Mountie helmets. "They are rather adorable."

"Welcome to Montréal's Twenty-Third Precinct," Morin grumbles. "Police station by night, turtle rescue and adoption center by day."

"Would it make you feel better if we named one after you?" Marx picks up one of the little turtles, which swings its tiny legs in the air. "This one looks suitably grumpy. What do you think? You wanna be Morin Jr.?"

"Don't touch them," Morin shouts. "Go wash your hands, or you'll take us down with you."

"Maybe they'll let me keep one. Do you wanna come home with me and be my best friend, Morin Jr.?"

"I'll arrest you for illegal turtle harboring," Morin threatens.

"All right, you guys enjoy your time with the turtles. I've got actual police work to do."

No sooner have I plopped down at my desk than my phone rings. I see the extension number and curse. Picking it up, I force as much calm and cheer into my tone as I can. "Hey, boss, what's up?"

"In my office, Jules. I'd like a moment."

"On my way." I hang up the phone and sigh.

So much for riding under the radar.

This is going to suck.

The distance from my cubicle to Acting Staff Sergeant Peter Trent's office is about fifty feet and one right turn away. It feels like a death row walk today. I hoped I would have longer to settle in and figure out what I would tell him.

Yeah, well, best-laid plans.

"Jules, come in. How are you feeling?" He's standing behind his desk as I come in and gestures at one of the two chairs opposite him.

"Better, thanks."

He raises an eyebrow. "You sure about that? You don't look much better than when I last saw you."

I chuckle. "I'll try not to take that personally. No. Really, boss, I'm fine."

He sits back in his chair and tents his fingers. "Did you figure out what happened with that house fire? I'm getting pressure from the brass and would like to close that file out."

I draw a deep breath and exhale. "Yeah, actually. I did. A lot has happened in the past forty-eight hours."

"Oh? Care to share?"

"It turns out I'm a fire fae. I didn't have any idea, but there was something, or someone, in that house who tried to attack me.

Apparently, I accidentally let loose a burst of flames with the adrenaline rush."

Peter sits there staring at me.

"Yeah...so...there's no arson case or anything to worry about. The fire is on me. My powers came through when I felt threatened."

Peter rubs a hand over his mouth. "Damn. I never saw that coming. I'll have to document this, but you won't be on the hook for whatever happened. I'll take care of it."

"Thank you."

"Are you all right?"

"Yeah, I think so. I feel different since my powers unlocked, but it's not bad. It's more like my cells can finally rest. If that makes any sense."

"As long as you're all right."

"I am. Or, at least, I will be."

He picks up his pen and rolls it between his fingers. "The current protocol with awakening powers is seventy-two hours off from active duty."

"Since I just had three days off, can we count that?"

Peter thinks for a second. "On one condition."

"What's that?"

"Take it easy and ride your desk for a day or two. Work those cold case files. Work from home if you need to. Rest if you need to. I don't want you on the streets or out in the thick of it yet."

"I don't know," I say jokingly. "I hear we've got people slinging illegal reptiles. Are you sure you don't need all boots on the ground?"

He rolls his eyes. "Don't even get me started. I swear if those things aren't out of here by shift change..."

"I'll look up recipes for turtle soup." I wink.

"Seriously, though, Gagne. Be careful. Things are getting hairy out there, and violence against empowered folks is on the rise. I know you'll still be a great officer, but…I don't want to see you get hurt."

I salute Peter agreeably.

With evil Poreskoro trying to capture and consume our powers, he doesn't have to tell me twice to stay off the radar.

I spend an hour at the morgue, checking in with Luc and catching him up on everything he missed since the last time we talked.

"Seriously? You've got powers?"

"Yeah. I guess I've had them since I was a kid, but my parents blocked them so I could grow up human."

"Do you know what the block was?"

He's a scientist, always trying to find answers to questions and solutions to mysteries.

"Magic?"

"You feeling like roadkill was them reacting to the veil dropping and wanting to emerge?"

"That's the theory."

As much as I want to share everything, I've decided not to get into the specifics of me being an elemental and a delicacy for a family of half-demon, half-fae royalty. The fewer people who know, the better.

I do, however, make sure he knows that if anyone comes sniffing around about me or our cases, to tell them nothing and to let me know immediately.

"Sure thing. Snitches end up in ditches and all that. You know me. Nothing leaks outta the vault."

Hilarious. "Dude, you're constantly letting me see and copy confidential files that aren't technically related to my cases."

"Yeah, but that's *you*. I'm not telling every bozo who wanders in here about the secrets of the universe."

"Do you know the secrets of the universe?"

He holds up his hand and ticks off his fingers one at a time. "Women like it when you take your time, cheap tequila will get you just as drunk, and car salesmen are always lying. You're welcome."

"You're a veritable guru. You should write a book."

"With your powers and my wisdom, we could take this show on the road."

"And give up the glitz and glamor of our lives? Never." I wave at his autopsy table and the row of stainless steel sinks behind it.

Luc grins. "We do live charmed lives. Speaking of, did you ever figure out what those strange symbols were?"

"Oh, not exactly. I know the men with them were fae guardians, and they're coming because they sense the awakening of elementals or other fae like us. I don't know who killed them yet, but I'll let you know if I find out."

"And I'll let you know if anything interesting comes across my table."

"Done deal."

I'm not going to lie. I'm relieved Luc took the news so well. Since finding out I'm empowered, I've been nervous about how people will treat me. There's still so much we don't know, and there is a lot of growing mistrust among Montréal's citizens.

I leave the morgue, ready to return to the firehouse and spend time with my siblings. Maybe we can flop on the couch and have that movie night Kenzie was planning.

Hell, at this point I'd even let her braid my hair.

When I get there, everyone is out in the back yard with Azland. The sun is high in the sky, and the air is singeing hot. I love it.

Briar and Zephyr are hauling a huge metal crate up from the basement while Kenzie is flirting with Tad.

"Good, you're home early," Azland gruffly greets me.

"How'd it go with the cops?" Zephyr asks. "Are you in big trouble?"

"Nah, I told my boss what happened, and he said he'd take care of it. He also told me to take it easy the next couple of days and that I can work from home. He doesn't want me in the thick of things until I can control my powers."

"Perfect," Tad observes. "That brings us back to Fi's advice. Training. Training. Training."

Zephyr and Briar drop the crate on the ground with a loud *thunk*. Azland trots over to it, stands on his hind legs, and waves a paw over the top. A string of runes illuminates and briefly glows on the metal's surface before something *clicks* inside it.

"What's in there?" I ask.

"We'll get to that in a while," Azland deflects. "Right now, we're going to see what you four can do."

"Jules can set the grass and fence on fire," Kenzie volunteers.

I give a little bow. "True story. I can also torch birthday cakes, light candles while I sleep, and burn down flophouses. Quite an accomplished resume for my first week as a fire fae."

Briar laughs. "You've always been a showoff."

"You're just jelly."

"Who wants to start?" Azland asks.

Briar volunteers and Kenzie, Zephyr, Tad, and I step out of the way to watch.

Azland starts with a long and boring speech about the importance of respecting our elements and nurturing a bond with nature. "All four of you spread out and face away from one another. Then, close your eyes, and connect with your element."

"There's no fire here for me to connect to," I protest.

Tad shakes his head. "Yer lookin' at it wrong, Jules. In my case, I'm a guardian of nature. I have a bond with the natural world around me and the power it holds. It's not the same fer elementals."

"How so?" Kenzie asks.

"The four of ye *are* yer elements. Yer water. Yer fire. Yer air. And Briar is earth."

Azland nods. "When I tell you to connect with your element, that's not external. It's internal."

I *am* fire.

Huh. I let that little tidbit settle over me.

The ground rumbles beneath our feet, the earth and rocks around us shake, and tufts of sod rise in small, uneven mounds.

Briar holds his hand over the earth, moving a little lump of grass as if he has it on a string. "I thought that would be bigger."

"That's what *she* said," Kenzie and I say at the same time. We high-five and chuckle at Briar's droll stare.

"I meant it was anti-climactic."

"That's what *she* said," we chorus again.

Briar gives us each the finger.

Tad waves away his annoyance. "Yer learnin' balance. When ye first unlocked yer element, ye caused tremors and tore a fissure into the earth."

"Which I repaired." He holds up a finger.

"Aye, ye did. While creating massive effects can be useful, other times subtlety will work better."

"When is massive effect better? I nearly created a seismic fault in the middle of the city."

"Aye, it got away on ye at first, but earthquakes and fissures are great ways to distract or gain distance from yer enemies. Or, if need be, to swallow them or hide bodies."

I frown. "You know I'm a cop, right?"

Tad shrugs, unrepentant. "In the empowered world, the creatures and beings that come at ye won't hesitate to kill ye. They won't be held in a police station or go to prison. It's a different set of laws for survival. Most importantly, at the end of the fight, ye want to be the ones still breathin'."

"Yeah, that will take some rewiring of my instincts."

"Aye, I suppose that's true."

Briar sighs. "What if I'm not a weapon guy? I don't know if Jules or Kenzie mentioned it, but I dabble in MMA and cage fighting. I like to use my fists."

"Then do that," Azland encourages. "Clench your fingers and focus on your fist being as hard as stone."

Briar's gaze narrows on his fist and before our eyes, it hardens with that gray concrete skin rash that's been bugging him the past few days. After a moment, he releases the stone fist and shakes his shoulders. "Whoa, that was super cool."

"Was it heavy?" Zephyr asks.

"No. Not really."

Azland flicks his ear and scares off the fly bugging him. "With practice, you'll be able to turn any part of your skin to solid stone. It will act as armor to protect your flesh and give you a tough weapon to hit enemies. Who's next?"

"Jules," Kenzie and Zephyr chorus, pointing at me.

"Consider me voluntold." I leave my siblings and join Azland in the middle of the open back yard. "Okay, what am I doing?"

"Fire is strong in you, Jules, but it's exploding out of you, and we don't always want an explosion. We're going to work on more of a passive flame."

"What does that look like?"

"Like a sheath of flames enveloping you. Like a fiery aura that burns from every inch of your skin."

Holy crap. "I can do that?"

Azland blinks. "Jules, if you give into your true form, you'll shed your body completely and be a living flame."

Okay, that scares the hell out of me. "No thanks. A fire aura will be plenty, thanks."

"For now. Don't underestimate what you can do. Being an elemental is an incredible gift."

Yeah no, I'm not there yet. "Okay, let's do this."

Azland steps back. "First, stand in a strong pose, back straight, feet apart. Now think about your blood, the heat it carries, the power coursing through your veins."

My blood? "Briar got to landscape with his mind, and I'm focusing on my pulse?"

"Just try it," Azland insists.

I close my eyes, draw a deep breath, and focus on the blood in my veins. The warmth it delivers to my extremities. The power.

I feel it.

I feel each pumping beat of my heart. I can sense the branching shapes of my capillaries.

"Now bring that heat to the surface," Azland instructs. "Not in a burst, but as if you're turning up the dial on your stove element."

I do what he says, picturing the blood racing through my veins, drawing the heat to my skin, and turning up the heat.

Kenzie and Briar gasp and I open my eyes.

Oh, cool. I'm on fire again. Flames wreath my skin. Yesterday, I had no idea how to control it, and it streamed from my hands.

This time…it's all of me.

"Does it hurt?" Kenzie asks.

"Nope. Not at all. I feel pleasantly toasty."

Briar snorts. "Toasty? You're on fire, Jules."

"I know. Cool, eh?"

Azland trots around me, tail wagging. "This power is called *Searing Skin*. You should practice calling it to activate it on demand. Don't do it inside or you'll risk burning down the house."

Zephyr steps into my view, leaning in to get a better look. "I've got a question. Since she's all fire woman and wreathed in flames, what happened to her clothes? When she lets the fire of her skin die, she's not going to be naked, is she?"

I blink and peg the dog with a glare.

Azland frowns. "Uh…probably, yes. In Lasair, everyone wore clothing woven with magic so it didn't burn off. I never thought about that."

Seriously? "What the hell, dude? I can't end up naked after every battle. Where do I get Lasair clothing and what do I do now?"

"Well, you won't be able to put on human textiles until your skin cools down, so you'll have to get used to being naked. Honestly, people don't worry about such things in the elemental kingdoms, much like the fae and shifter kingdoms."

"Yeah, but I'll be battling with my brothers and friends. Not cool."

Tad *poofs* out and returns a moment later holding a heavy beige fire blanket. "I've got ye covered, Jules. Release yer flames, and I'll wrap ye up. Then ye can practice calling flames to your palm for now until we figure out a wardrobe."

When he holds up the corners of the thick blanket, I step in close and release the fire energy keeping me aflame. Grabbing the edges of the blanket, I pull it around me. "Thanks, Tad. I owe you one."

Tad winks. "Not a problem. Glad to help."

Azland doesn't seem to care either way. "Kenzie, it's your turn."

Kenzie seems more excited now that she's watched Briar and me go.

"Hold out your hands and conjure water. Envision the soothing, cool droplets appearing between your hands, suspended in the air."

"Where will the droplets come from?" Kenzie asks.

"Gather them from the air around you, the cells within you,

or if you're close to a body of water, use it to increase your strength."

I tighten my blanket around me and tilt my view to see what's happening between Kenzie's palms. *She's doing it.* A sphere of water the size of a golf ball is suspended between her hands.

"Now, while still holding it suspended, control its movement. Make it ebb and flow between your hands."

Kenzie's focus is locked on the water as she flattens it out into a ribbon of fluid and moves it through the air, manipulating it in all sorts of graceful motions.

"I'm doing it." She grins.

"Hells yeah, you are," Zephyr agrees.

"How does this help me in a battle?" she asks.

"Think about making it cold. Keep the water under your control until it freezes. Then send sharp icicles out and throw them toward the fence."

Kenzie frowns. I know what she's thinking. How on earth is she supposed to do all that? Still, something about Azland's instructions makes sense. I didn't think picturing the blood in my veins would do me any good, but once I started trying, it came naturally.

"You can do it, Kenz!" I shout.

"Remember that winter camping trip when we went to Cape Breton?" Briar asks. "Zephyr broke his sled, so he was sharing yours, and we all tipped over onto the ice. Remember how cold it was?"

That's enough inspiration.

Briar falls silent as the moisture under Kenzie's control crystalizes. She manipulates it for a few seconds and sends a delicate but deadly sharp icicle directly into the wooden fence.

"Well done." Tad claps. "That was exceptional."

"My turn." Zephyr shakes out his hands. "What can I do?"

"Let's start by having you conjure a bit of wind," Azland says. "Like Jules, you need to work on control."

He makes a face at me, and I laugh. Yeah, the two of us have always been the problem children.

"There's already a breeze, so you don't need to do much. Call only the slightest wind to yourself and see if you can control what you build up."

Zephyr closes his eyes and holds up his hands. A moment later wind tugs at my hair, and I raise a hand to keep it from whipping me in the face.

The power of his little vortex is wild and unruly, and I'm not the least bit surprised. It feels like the same energy that has been busting to get out of him since he was four years old.

"Now, I want you to run across the yard and have the wind push at your back. If you control it, you should be able to increase your natural speed."

Zephyr grins. "I'll have super speed?"

"It's called *Wind at Your Back*, but yes."

"You're a superstar, Z. Dooo it. Dooo it," I chant, rooting him on.

"Dooo it. Dooo it." Kenzie and Briar chime in.

Zephyr tries it but is more jogging than running. He flails his arms, and the wind picks up, but he doesn't super speed across the back lawn.

When he runs out of lawn, he scowls, looking as disappointed as that same four-year-old.

Azland frowns. "Try again. This time, put your hands down and run like you're not an idiot. Will the wind to push you without all the semaphore signals."

Zephyr flips him off. "You were nicer as our dog."

True story.

"You got this, Z." I pump my fist into the air as a sign of solidarity.

Zephyr shakes out his hands and runs, then seriously picks up speed.

"Holy shit, he's going to hit—"

"Slow down—"

"Stop the wind—"

Right before Zephyr's going to smash face-first into the fence at super speed, Tad *poofs* in front of him, disappears, and reappears at the far end of the lawn so he can stumble to a stop.

Briar busts a gut. "Can you believe this is our life? Zephyr would've super speed faceplanted into a fence if our friend hadn't portaled him to safety."

I giggle. "We should be journaling this. We can write a book later and sell it as adventure fiction."

Kenzie laughs. "Because no one would believe us if we put it out there as non-fiction."

Zephyr and Tad jog back over to join us.

"Good save, druid." Briar raises his fist for a bump. "Although the faceplant would've been hilarious."

"He would've broken his nose and likely his jaw at that speed," Azland points out.

Briar shrugs. "Still hilarious."

Zephyr laughs. "Yeah, thanks for the save, man."

The Irishman shrugs, waving off the accolades. "I'm here to assist wherever and whenever I can."

Briar rubs his hands together and addresses the dog. "What's next, oh, mighty mentor?"

Azland glances at the metal case. "Weapons training."

Briar claps and waggles his brows. "Hot diggity dog. This day gets better and better."

CHAPTER TWELVE

After I run inside and get dressed for round two of training, I come out to find Briar and Zephyr digging into the metal box they brought out earlier. With the lid flipped open, the two are all "Ooo and Ahh," so I hustle over and join them peering into the box.

"Yep. Weapons."

"Really freaking cool weapons," Zephyr amends.

Azland trots over and sits. "We'll try each of you with a variety of weapons and see which ones suit your powers and fighting style best."

I'm not sure how I feel about taking on a new weapon as well as learning how my powers work. Maybe I could focus on that for a while…and on getting a fireproof wardrobe.

"I'm good. I have a weapon I'm proficient with. Issued to me by the Twenty-Third Precinct."

Azland shakes his head, his ears flapping against the side of his boxy head. "Human technology won't do much for you when you flame up and melt your gun into a pile of goo. Look inside and see what speaks to you."

I never thought about that. Leaning over the edge of the box, I pull out two long, curved swords. Placing one in each of my hands, I step back and give them a few test swings, cutting through the summer air.

Azland points at a target at the other end of the yard. It's a magical manifestation, shimmering in the sunlight. Even though it's semi-translucent, I can tell exactly what it's supposed to be.

A skoro thug.

A huge one, too, with heavily muscled arms and a face like a cinderblock. It looks human except for the eerie coal-black eyes.

"Go for it, Jules," Kenzie encourages.

Azland nods. "Let's see what you can do."

Closing my fingers around the sword hilts, I rush for the fake enemy. As I bring the swords forward, their unexpected weight takes over, and they smash together. Distracted by the *clanging* awkwardness of my weapons, I fail to land my attack and get knocked onto my back by the snarling skoro.

My manifested opponent makes a couple of aggressive *clicks* and disappears into thin air.

Zephyr cringes. Briar and Kenzie look concerned.

"That wasn't good," Azland says.

"Thanks for the constructive feedback." I get to my feet and shake out my arms before picking the swords up from the ground. "Maybe I don't need two of these things flying around and banging into each other. Let me try it with one."

"They are meant to be wielded as a pair."

"Well, forgive me for my lack of knightsmanship. The police force doesn't require me to work with medieval weaponry."

"Try this." Azland hands me a twelve-inch dagger, much shorter than the swords. It has a vicious-looking double-sided blade and feels steadier in my hands.

"Better. I dig the dagger."

"Go again," Azland instructs.

I grip the dagger, gauging its weight and balance. The skoro reappears and lunges at me as it did before.

This time, I get the dagger straight in its belly. It grunts and howls, then wraps an arm around my neck and drags me to the ground.

I continue to stab and twist with the dagger until my foe disappears.

Azland crosses his arms. "Better, but it still took you down."

"I'd say it was a mutual taking down."

"If you kill your enemy while it kills you, you both end up dead," Azland states matter-of-factly.

"No shit, really? If I get killed, I die? What a concept."

Kenzie frowns in admonishment. "Dial back the cranky pants. He's trying to help."

I huff. "Fine, then you take your shot."

Kenzie steps up and takes her turn with Azland. He first gives her a bow and arrow, standing behind her to coach her into the right form and posture to use it. She's an okay shot but doesn't seem able to combine her water magic with her archery.

"Unlike your siblings, you don't want to be a fighter. To compensate for that, I'd like you to have a weapon to use in conjunction with your powers. One which you can infuse with your element," Azland explains.

"I'm not following."

"If I weren't a dog, I would show you."

"I'll show ye what he means." Tad steps forward and picks up the bow and arrow. He widens his stance, mutters something in Gaelic, and releases the arrow.

As it sails toward the magical skoro opponent, it ignites, and when it hits the target, it goes up in flame. He shoots another, and it does the same thing, only this time when it hits, it encases the skoro in ice.

Azland nods. "Exactly right. Magic and weapon become one."

Kenzie never quite gets the hang of the bow and arrow and has the same issue with nunchucks, swords, daggers, and throwing stars. She does her best with each weapon Azland pulls out, but ultimately, she gives up. "Why can't I use my powers by themselves?"

"All right, Mackenzie," Azland says. "Show me your idea of an attack."

Kenzie squares off with the target, locks herself in, and sends a blast of water directly into the skoro's chest. The hit knocks our opponent backward, and she rushes in and pins it down. From above, she splays her fingers, and the water she's commanding becomes spears of ice.

She impales the skoro, and he disappears.

"Winner, winner, chicken dinner," Briar says.

Kenzie beams. "That felt much better."

Azland stands on his hind legs and glances into the metal box. "Do you see that banged-up carved wooden case in the corner? Someone pull that out."

Zephyr gets it and hands it to our sister.

Kenzie lifts the lid of the wooden box and pulls out a silver bracelet with a little blue orb charm dangling from its chain. "What is it?"

"Magic bling," Zephyr deadpans.

"Not helpful."

"But not wrong," Azland corrects. "You wear it, and when you need it, you enlarge the jewel. Try it."

Following Azland's guidance, Kenzie puts the bracelet on, then holds her hands in a cupped position. Sure enough, the little blue charm grows to be about the size of her fist and hovers above her hands.

"Now send your magic through it," Azland tells her.

When she lowers her chin and focuses, a single jet of water shoots out with such an intense force it makes a hole in the tree trunk in the back corner of the yard.

Kenzie squeals. "Holy hell! Did you see that?"

"It works defensively as well," Azland adds. "Try creating a wall of water to shield your siblings from attack."

On Kenzie's first try, she encases us in a sphere of water like a fishbowl. It collapses when she realizes none of us can breathe, leaving us all drenched as it fades into the ground.

On her second attempt, she rectifies her earlier mistake and creates a bubble to surround us. We're inside, separated from the rest of the world by a wavy water force field.

"Excellent, Kenzie. You practice that, and we'll look for a better weapon for Jules."

"I like the dagger."

Azland ignores me, looking around in his box. "There, the eight-foot whip. Try that."

"Which one is the eight-foot one?" I see three in the weapons box.

"The one that's eight feet long?" Zephyr offers.

Azland growls at him and turns his attention back to me. "The black one with the oxblood grip."

I pull out the woven leather whip and unfurl its length. The handle is hefty and thick but easy to get my fingers around.

"How does that feel?"

"Fine, but I like the dagger."

"You have two hands. An eight-foot whip is good to start with and build skill. If you like it and get good, I'll move you up to a ten-foot. Get the feel of it for a minute while I sort out your brothers."

While he does that, Tad comes over and shows me several techniques to handle a whip.

It's cool and feels badass when I snap it in the air.

Once I begin to get the hang of it, Tad hands me the dagger. "It sounded like he wants ye to practice with a weapon in both hands. So, whip in yer dominant hand and dagger in yer other, to use if the enemy gets in close and personal."

We practice some more, and Azland comes back to check in. "Are you ready to try again?"

I nod at the spot where the fake skoro has been appearing. "Yeah, let's do this."

When the sparkling illusion appears, I dart to the side, faking it out. In the few seconds it takes to adjust, I swing the whip. It hits hard against the skoro's face, making it reel back.

It's not only me wielding the weapon. As I attack, I feel magic surging in my veins. It feels ancient and full of information. Like it's downloading a "how to" manual into my cells as I go.

I snap the whip again, wrapping it around the skoro's shoulders, and yank it forward to the ground.

At the same time, I lunge and plunge the knife into the back of its neck.

I'm breathing hard when the mirage fades, but Azland looks pleased.

"Excellent. Those will be your weapons."

I stand, crack the whip, and smile at the sharp sound it makes. "Damn, that's sexy."

Zephyr whistles through his teeth. "Have you ever thought of moonlighting as a dominatrix? You're a natural with that whip and in your bike leathers... Booyah!"

Briar grimaces. "Dude! That's our sister."

"Yeah, but there are plenty of guys who aren't her sister who would pay a pretty penny to feel the loving kiss of her leather."

Briar covers his face. "That's wrong on so many levels. No one talks about their sister like that. I'm gonna need therapy."

"Fortunately, Jules will be able to help pay for it with all her sexy kink money," Kenzie adds.

Briar groans. "Not you too."

Azland growls. "That is a powerful magical weapon, not a tool to be used for sexual gratification."

"Well, not with that attitude," Zephyr jokes.

"Focus. I need you four to take this seriously."

Zephyr shrugs. "Back up, Backup. Why so hostile? We're doing great. It's crazy, but this all feels so natural. Is that weird?"

Tad steps in. "Weel, it's certainly different. Druids begin learnin' our skills as wee children and start with the basics. Yer powers are strong and incredibly respondent to yer will, even though ye've only just unlocked them."

"Why is that?" Kenzie asks.

"Because you are elementals," Azland explains. "The four of you aren't humans with dominion over the elements. You *are* the elements. Kenzie *is* water. Jules *is* fire. Briar *is* earth. And Zephyr *is* wind. It's within you. It's like your brain sending a signal to lift your arm, only it's telling it to conjure ice or flame. Do you understand?"

Zephyr grins. "Yeah. You're saying we're badass inside and out. That we don't need training wheels because we're naturals."

I snort. "I'm not sure that's what he was saying, Z."

"I'm pretty sure that was the gist of it."

Azland arches a brow. "If you're so confident, I guess I can raise the bar."

Oh, boy. Zephyr and his big mouth.

Azland tenses and the fur on his hackles stands on end. All of a sudden, our back yard is transformed into a battle-scarred wasteland. Towers of black smoke choke our lungs, and jagged boulders surround us.

"Look out!" Briar shouts. A whirling tornado of fire is coming our way. He grabs Kenzie and me and yanks us behind one of the stones.

It might seem like we're safe, but the heat is getting stronger, and the tornado is about to come around the corner and engulf us in flames.

"Kenzie, use your water."

She steps up and holds her hands out, sending a huge ball of water rolling toward the tornado. It extinguishes the fire, but three skoro were using the flames as a shield. Now they're coming for us, and they're all swinging silver chains that crackle with electricity.

Briar steps in front of Kenzie to shield us and holds his arms out. His broad torso and muscled arms turn to stone, and he uses his body to block the chains.

As they attack, he clenches a fist and uses his connection to pull one of the boulders toward us. It crushes two fake skoro attackers, but the third is still barreling toward us.

It jumps on me, yanking my hair.

"Ow." I raise my dagger and try to fend the thing off, but it's got me in its grip. I slash and stab at it, covering myself in sticky black ick that stinks like burned cookies.

"Close your eyes!" Zephyr shouts.

I do, and a surge of air whips around me. When I open my eyes again, the skoro is down and clutching the ground to keep from blowing away.

"Hold him," I shout against the gale.

Zephyr smiles triumphantly. "Baby, I could do this all night. Do you know how good it feels to let this chaos out? It's orgasmic."

I scratch the last statement from my mind and plunge my dagger into the heart of the illusion.

It stops moving and disappears.

In a dizzying swirl of shifting reality, the battlefield, the fire, the smoke, the boulders, and the skoro all fade away. We're back in the yard, with Azland looking smug.

"What the hell was that?" I ask.

Azland shrugs. "Expect the unexpected. Things get dangerous with elemental powers involved. This is why we need to get everyone up to speed with their weapons as soon as possible. Zephyr, you're up."

"I want something cool," Zephyr insists.

Azland mutters something to Tad, and the druid pulls out a gnarled wooden staff.

Zephyr raises his eyebrows. "I don't need an old man's walking stick. Do I look like Gandalf?"

"You shall not pass," Briar booms.

"Right? I've got two legs that work fine. Why not a cool sword or a big-ass whip? I bet I could wield a ten-footer." He waggles his brows at me. "We could be a Dom team."

"Try the staff," Azland growls.

Zephyr grumbles, grabs it, and walks into the center of the yard. He gives it a few tentative swings, but it's a half-assed effort at best. "Nah. I'm not feeling it. This doesn't work for me."

Instead of giving him advice or coaching, like he did with Kenzie and me, Azland watches silently with his arms crossed.

"Come on." Zephyr groans. He taps the staff on the ground a few times. "This is lame."

Azland smiles. "Your father ran the elemental training academy for an entire kingdom. The staff was his weapon of choice. I have no doubt there's some part of you that will have an inherited affinity for it. Open your mind and try it."

That strikes a chord in him.

All of us have yearned to know our origin story but none of us so much as Zephyr.

Mention of his father being a great warrior lights something up in him. He picks the staff up and starts to spin it. We all stay silent and still and let him dig deep.

Is an inherited affinity for fighting a thing?

"Stop thinking of it as a stick," Azland barks. "It's an enchanted staff designed to respond to air elementals. It will adopt your personality. Right now, it's mirroring your attitude, and all you're getting back is stubborn and difficult."

Zephyr frowns. "Rude."

"You can do this, Z," Kenzie calls. "Turn that frown upside down. Make friends with your staff."

Briar and Tad both laugh.

"Yeah, bro. What she said. Charm that shaft of wood. You got this."

Okay, now Kenzie and I are laughing too.

Zephyr raises his middle finger and directs it at each of us so we're all included.

"Ignore the peanut gallery," Azland snaps. "Focus on the staff. You're the master. It's the conduit of your intentions."

Zephyr turns his back to us and holds the staff at arm's reach. There's a moment of tense silence, and a whoosh of air gusts past us and knocks him off his feet. He stumbles forward, staggering to reclaim his footing before he sprawls over a bush in the back corner.

The staff promptly gains its freedom and flies off in the opposite direction to land on the grass.

"What the serious fuck?"

"Dust yerself off, sham," Tad calls. "Calm yer mind and try again."

Zephyr extricates himself from the shrubbery and brushes himself off. He stretches out a few kinks and reaches down to reclaim the staff.

As soon as his hand touches wood, it shoots into the air, dragging Zephyr along. A gale-force gust of wind propels him around the yard before dumping him on his ass in front of us.

"Dude, are you okay?" I rush over to check on him. "That staff's really got a mind of its own, doesn't it?"

"No. It doesn't," Azland corrects. "It's picking up on Zephyr's mental chaos. You'll need to sort that out before any enchanted weapon works for you. I thought releasing the binding would've settled your powers, but I suppose it'll take time."

"So, I don't get a weapon?" Zephyr snaps.

"Right now, you *are* the weapon. The Storm Staff is yours to claim, but today won't be the day you wield it."

Briar offers Zephyr a hand up, and we get him back on his feet. His hair looks positively eighties Guns N' Roses rockstar, but other than that and a few scrapes, he's relatively unscathed.

"Ye'll figure it out." Tad pats him on the shoulder. "I'll help ye.

With a few meditation sessions, we'll have ye wieldin' that staff like Merlin himself."

"Thanks, man, I appreciate it." Zephyr tugs his shirt down from where it's tangled up around his ribs. "What I don't appreciate is being bound and left to twist for the past twenty-five years. Maybe if someone had given enough of a shit about me, they could've seen I was in a bad way and helped me before now."

Azland sits there looking up at him. "Like we told you. It was deemed necessary by the elders of the kingdoms to keep you shrouded and protected. That wasn't my call or my edict to break."

"That's a bullshit cop-out, and you know it." Zephyr grabs the staff off the grass and storms off to the house.

Azland takes that as his cue and trots off around the other side of the building.

"So ends training for day one," I quip.

"Ye did grand," Tad says. "Good on ye. It takes druids years to train our powers to respond the way yers did. At this rate, ye'll be fightin' fit in no time."

"You really think you can help Zephyr calm his mind?" I ask.

"Och, fer sure. Don't give it another thought. I'll have yer brother wieldin' that staff within the week."

That makes me feel better. I don't want the three of us to have success and leave Zephyr behind. He needs triumphs more than us.

It's always hurt him that he struggled so much.

"Looks like *Maman* got her wish." Kenzie chuckles. "When we were kids, and Zephyr got into trouble, *Maman* would throw her hands up and wish that one day he'd have a child half as difficult as him."

Briar chuckles. "That staff is *Maman's* revenge, all right, but it'll be good to see him release his turmoil and learn to control his inner storm."

"Yeah, it will." I feel sorry for Tad. "He's going to be difficult to work with. He's volatile and angry."

Tad lifts a shoulder and offers us a sad smile. "Don't worry. I have plenty of experience bein' the angry wild child. He's in good hands."

I'm not sure what that means, but I get a sense his hunky designer rich-boy exterior isn't all there is to know about Tad McNiff.

"Well, I'm sure you'll have better luck than Azland," Kenzie adds. "Zephyr has trust issues, and he and Charlie fucked that up royally."

"Aye, I picked up on that. How did Azland end up bein' yer dog?"

The three of us regard one another, and we've got nothing.

I shrug. "After our parents were killed, Charlie brought home a dog to cheer us up."

"Was he a puppy?"

We all shake our heads.

"You named him Backup?"

Kenzie chuckles. "Yeah, Kenzie and I were big Veronica Mars fans, and when Charlie first took over as our guardian, she was paranoid and overprotective."

"Which makes more sense now," Briar says.

Yeah, it does. "When we got the dog, she insisted he go everywhere with us. Take Backup was our little joke."

Briar grunts. "Now that we know he's not a dog and he's some kind of warrior guardian, it's much less funny."

Kenzie exhales. "And that our parents didn't die in a car accident."

"Another of their lies," Briar agrees.

Zephyr walks in and scans our faces. "What really happened to *Maman* and Papa? I missed the conversation, and nobody said."

I exhale. "According to Charlie, hunters were tracking us. When *Maman* sensed elementals in danger, she interceded. Each of our handlers was killed. She took us in and used her powers to shield us from detection. Our powers fluctuated when we hit puberty, and the enemy found us. The local guild covered up their deaths and made it look like an accident."

"We're going to find out all of it, right?" Zephyr asks. "I'm done being lied to about our lives."

All eyes fall on me. I read their expressions and nod. "Looks like I've got a new cold case to solve."

"Unless Azland or Charlie want to tell us the truth, for once," Briar adds.

"What are the odds of that?" Kenzie snaps.

I'm about to chime in with the griping when a loud cry rings out from across the street.

"Help! Someone, help!"

CHAPTER THIRTEEN

The five of us race around the side of the firehouse, burst through the back gate, and book it through the midday traffic. A mob of almost twenty people is trying to push into the Korean barbecue restaurant across the street.

We've known the owners, Mr. and Mrs. Seong, forever. Back when this place was an active fire station, they often donated huge platters of barbecue for cookouts. Mrs. Seong also makes the best lavender lemonade, which I crave on hot summer afternoons.

The mob is shouting something about the fae freaks who run the place, which seems odd. We've never seen any indication the Seongs are empowered.

As we try to sort out the situation, I get a closer look at some people in the crowd. Their eyes are glassy and weirdly shiny.

Uh-huh. I know what that means.

"They're high on Second Sight."

Some industrious guy grabs a rock and is about to smash the front window. Briar sees it too and raises his palm, calling the rock to his hand.

The crowd's attention turns to him. "Get them! Get the freaks out of our neighborhood!"

The group leader is a dark-haired woman standing at the front of the crowd. Her eyes are completely glassed over, and she's screaming like a banshee.

Well, she's not the first drugged-out hostile I've dealt with. I step up, flip my badge, and engage. "Ma'am, I'm Inspector Gagne with the Twenty-Third Precinct."

I barely get the words out of my mouth before I have to deke to the side to avoid getting assaulted.

"Hey," I shout at her and the crowd closing in. "Stand down and step away from the building."

"Fuck you, pig. You're a cop, and you want to protect them! Do you understand how messed up that is?"

"You mean the family who has been part of this community, working their business and feeding our neighborhood for twenty years? Damn right I want to protect them."

Her drugged gaze narrows and she surges forward. "You're one too. They've infiltrated the police! No wonder you protect them."

The crowd turns.

Fantastic.

Glass shatters, and Mrs. Seong screams inside.

Shit. I spin to address the mob now smashing the plate glass, breaking it to get it out of their way. "Inciting a riot, damage to private property, hate crime, the charges are piling up here, people. Back the hell away from the building. This is your final warning."

"Don't listen to the cop. She's a mutant freak!" The woman rushes me, throwing a punch. I dodge the hit and shove her with both hands so she ass-plants on the sidewalk.

Kenzie does her water bubble thing and encases her, then turns the sphere to ice. "Time to cool off, bitch."

The crowd goes mental. "They're all freaks!"

"Get them!"

"We can see you!"

I hold my hands up, the sudden rush of adrenaline spiking the tingle of fire beneath my skin. "You don't want to do this. I'm still a cop, and on top of getting your asses whipped, you'll be charged with assault if you don't back down and disperse right now."

That doesn't deter them.

The moment one takes a swing, the situation dissolves into a free-for-all.

"We need backup," Kenzie says.

"The dog or the police?" I'm confused.

"That's not my name anymore," Azland shouts, racing in to join us. "But I've got you!"

"Me too." Zephyr comes in fists flying.

Then it's on.

"Hold them back. I'm going inside!" Briar's skin solidifies to gray rock, protecting him from the sharp edges of glass. He pushes through the broken front window and is gone to secure the Seongs.

Another rock is flying at the building when a gust of wind changes its course. The gale force blows it off into the crowd and several of the protestors stagger, stumbling from the hit.

"Sorry." Zephyr makes a face. "I'm new to this. If you don't want to get clouted, you should disperse. I can't be trusted not to do damage."

Another rock.

Another gust of wind clobbers rioters.

When one comes toward my head, I get caught in the wake of the wind, but Zephyr redirects the hit into the window of a parked car.

"Sorry!"

"If it's a window or my head, I choose the window. Thanks, Z."

He winks and gives me finger guns. "I got you, sista."

Kenzie conjures a wall of water and uses it to push the crowd back from the building.

I race through the door and find Mr. and Mrs. Seong huddled behind Briar. He's got his arm braced in front, and it has morphed to create a massive stone shield.

"Look at you, Captain America."

He grins. "If I'm going to be a superhero, we'll have to talk costumes."

I laugh and check in with the elderly Korean couple behind him. "Are you two okay?"

Before they have a chance to answer, Kenzie screams outside. "*Incoming.* They're breaking through!"

Sure enough, the crowd shoves through the wall of water. Emboldened by the drugs or the mob mentality, they push toward us, soaked but undeterred.

I can't help how my annoyance grows. The moment my adrenaline kicks in, I feel my control slipping.

Dammit. "Close your eyes and stay behind Briar!"

I don't want to hurt anyone, but the glowing coals from Mr. Seong's massive slab barbeque start flying through the air. The burning projectiles start pegging off the irate invaders. They are responding to my mood, regardless of it not being my intention.

Chaos ensues as people scream and try to defend themselves. One lady grabs a plastic tray to shield herself while a real gentleman pulls another woman in front of himself to take the brunt of the damage.

This is *not* the way I wanted this to go.

Channeling all my self-control, I summon the coals and try to harness their fiery burn. I take their intense heat into myself, and though it's not much better, now it's only rocks pelting them.

With all that heat building inside me, I push my palms toward the crowd. The rush of scorching air I send their way pushes back our attackers.

The building is left mostly undamaged, although some posters on the wall are singed and curling at the edges. I walk forward, forcing dry heat at the mob.

They recede outside, frantically patting the ends of their hair and hissing as they touch their eyebrows. Or, more accurately, the scorched skin where they used to have eyebrows.

"Go home right now!" I shout and repeat it in French. *"Retournez chez vous, toute de suite!"*

They remain unfazed.

They're hopped up on drugs and crazed with hatred. There's so much division between the empowered and the non-magical citizens that they can't let it go.

"Push them back more, Jules!" Zephyr's command has me searching, and I find him standing in a truck's bed in the parking lot.

Wind swirls around him in a crazy vortex, but he looks calmer than I've seen him in years. I'm not sure what he's got planned, but hey, I'm happy to pass the torch…so to speak.

Kenzie is dousing people a few meters away, her orb hovering in her hands. "Go, you. End this, Z."

Focusing on the fury heating my blood, I summon my strength and release another blast of heat into the crowd. As soon as they back away, Zephyr spins his hands, controlling the hot air and using it to corral them into a tight circle.

Kenzie takes that as her cue. She conjures a ribbon of fast-moving water around them, binding them into a crowded ball of haters. "Briar, now!"

Briar is back outside. He drops to one knee, solidifies his fist into rock, and drives it to the ground. The ground rumbles beneath our feet. Earth and rubble float up and mix with the water.

Mud encases the group from shoulders to the ground. I step in and add the final touches. I splay my fingers and touch the wet earth, drying it rock-hard around the rioters. "You are under arrest."

My hands are hot, but my clothes are intact. Yay me.

I hold my palms up for Kenzie to cool and when I'm sure I won't melt my phone, I pull it from my pocket and call the riot in.

I let the guys at the precinct know we need the prisoner bus because a bunch of Second Sight rioters are ready for their evening at the iron bars hotel.

"You're safe now," Briar reassures Mr. and Mrs. Seong as they come outside. "We'll stay until Jules' friends come and get those folks."

"Thank you so much," Mrs. Seong says tearfully. "We didn't know you kids had powers."

"Neither did we," I tell her. "It's very new."

"For us too," Mr. Seong tells us. "We can grow things." He holds out his hand, and a tiny green stem emerges from the center of his palm. It buds into a beautiful pink blossom, and he bows his head as he gives it to me.

Mrs. Seong smiles. "Herbs, too. Good for more lemonade." She pulls her hair back, and I see a sprig of lavender poking out behind her ear.

It breaks my heart that people tried to hurt them because they suddenly gained the power to grow plants.

"We'll make sure none of those jerks come back," Zephyr reassures her. "Call us if anything happens, okay? Day or night, we're only across the road."

Mrs. Seong nods and hugs each of us. She insists on bringing out a huge pitcher of lavender lemonade, and we sip it as we wait for the police to come and pick up our prisoners.

"Jules? Does Second Sight always cause this much trouble?" Kenzie asks.

"It's hard to say. The ones who take it and cause trouble get noticed. We have no idea how many more are taking it if they're not causing trouble. Marx's theory is that it enhances a person's natural tendency. So, if they're violent and aggressive, they become worse. If they're happy and odd…"

"They strip their clothes off and become Nakey Guy, doing the dangle wrangle with you in the street." Briar's massive chest bounces as he laughs.

"Something like that. Either way, I'm determined to get that shit off the street."

Azland finishes trotting around the encased prisoners and sits with us. "Then realign your priorities, Juliette. Your job is to survive and protect the lineage of the fae kingdoms, not to get involved enforcing the human laws about drugs."

"Getting them off the street does both. This drug lets any jerk who takes it expose anyone on the empowered spectrum. It draws more attention to us and puts innocent folks in danger."

Kenzie reminds us, "Plus, if Cami's right, one of The Six is behind the drug. They might be using it to find us."

I finish my glass of lavender bliss and swallow. "The drugs, the skoro who kidnapped Zephyr, the threat against us...it's all connected. If we're right about those connections, once we find the person responsible for Second Sight, we'll be closer to ending this."

"What's our next step?" Briar asks. "Go back to the bar and ask around?"

"Let's go home, take a breath, and I'll check in with Fi. Even if she doesn't have any specific information about Second Sight in the Montréal market, she might be able to shake loose a few ideas."

"Och, Fi's always good fer that," Tad agrees.

I nod. "Okay, you go home, and I'll give my statement to the guys. I'll be up in a bit."

It takes twenty minutes to get the rioters sorted and for me to explain what happened. Tremblay will write up the report but send it to me tonight for fine-tuning before he files it.

Upstairs, the taste of Mrs. Seong's lemonade is still on my lips when I flop on my bed and dial Fi's number.

Typically, when I'm lounging in bed chatting on the phone, Backup would be curled up somewhere in the room. It pisses me off he was likely there to eavesdrop.

Still, he and Zephyr seem to have patched things up for the moment, and he's in the back yard teaching my brothers about magical weapons.

Things are so weird around here.

Fi answers on the second ring.

"Hey, Jules! What's up? How's today going for you?"

"With us, good. With Montréal…less good." I tell her about everything happening in our streets, our belief that it's one of The Six behind Second Sight, and how the drug is making it more difficult for everyone, including us.

"We've had a few episodes in Toronto, too. Not as bad, but it's here. We anticipate it getting worse before it gets better. You've got it worse than us though, simply by Montréal's geography."

"How so?"

"I don't want to bore you with a bunch of technical magic stuff, but it has to do with ley lines and the Laurentian River Systems. Together, they've deposited more prana into the system than any other waterway in Canada."

"Can we block it? Or slow it down? If it's coming from the river, maybe there's a way to get a handle on it."

Fiona laughs gently. "There's no controlling the elemental forces of magic."

I groan, frustrated. "It's crazy, you know? Last week I was a regular human police officer with a handful of goofy adopted siblings. Now I'm conjuring fireballs and learning about my secret fae ancestry."

"Oh, I get it. When I discovered we were druids, it wasn't like I could isolate and curl up with a *History of the Empowered World*. I had all sorts of enemies I didn't know about. And they were all trying to kill me."

"That sounds familiar."

"It's not easy."

"You made it through, and now you're a badass druid. What's the secret for getting from here to there?"

"My family was my lifeline, and we gathered powerful friends as we went. I quickly learned who I could trust, and once I found those people, I held on for dear life."

I draw a deep breath. So far, our only ally is Azland, and I'm not sure we can trust him.

"Now that I've built my crew, we handle anything that comes at us. We've got each other's backs."

"Clearly." I chuckle. "Save the world. Save Montréal. Save my brother."

"You'll get there," she assures me. "Trust your instincts and do what's right. You'll attract the right kind of people, and you'll build your team."

"Thanks, Fi. This talk has really helped."

"I'm always here to chat. I hope Tad's been helping too. If he's only there to flirt with your sister, let me know, and I'll reel him in."

"Oh, no. He's been great. I'd love to keep him here longer if you don't mind us hogging him."

"Not at all. He's a skilled fighter, an amazing computer hacker, and an all-around guy you can count on. He's been going through a rough time, and I think helping you guys could help him in return. Plus—and you didn't hear this from me—he's easy to look at."

The two of us share a laugh. "I might have noticed."

"Hey, it just occurred to me…you should probably connect with the Guild Governor of the Guild of the Laurentians, too. Remember when you escorted Mayor Tremblay and our group to the Basilica to meet that tall Viking?"

"Yeah."

"You stayed in the background of the conversations, but Bakkali is the head empowered player in your area."

My head is reeling.

It was hard enough to learn the organizational structure of the police force. Now I need to connect with the Guild of Governors for the empowered world too?

I respect Fi and like she said, gathering powerful friends was important for her to establish herself in the empowered world. Why would I ask her advice and not take it?

"Cool. I'll do that. Thanks, Fi."

"Anytime."

CHAPTER FOURTEEN

When I finish my call with Fiona, I join the others. Kenzie is making a tray of mid-afternoon snacks in the kitchen. She sets out beers for the boys and coolers for the girls.

"Great idea."

Kenzie grins. "Thanks. What did Fi say?"

"Mostly normal rah-rah stuff. It takes time for things to settle. Be careful who you trust. Gather the right kind of allies."

"All sensible things."

"Yeah." I claim one of the coolers and lead the way to the stairs. "She also mentioned that I should contact the local Guild Governor and get him onside."

"I didn't know there was a guild in place."

"There is. I met the man a month or so ago when I was working on the protection detail for the mayor's office. I wasn't privy to chatting with him, but I'd know him to see him."

"Do you know how to contact him?"

"Nope, but I'm sure Fi can arrange it."

The two of us emerge into the mid-afternoon sunlight. I turn my face up to the ball of fire in the sky and soak it in.

"I swear the sun feeds my cells."

"Of course it does." Tad works his hands in a series of motions as he walks the fence line. "Yer a fire elemental. Other than the molten core of the planet and the active volcanos it feeds, the sun is the next most intense fire source in nature."

Kenzie and I stop and enjoy the view for a moment. Fiona's right. It's no hardship watching the man work.

"What are you working on?" Kenzie asks.

"I thought this place could use a bit more cover. For privacy's sake and all."

"Wonderful idea." Kenzie grins at me. "It's always a pleasure to see you work your magic."

I take a long drink and lean close to whisper. "That was very subtle."

"Oh, sister mine. There's no need to be subtle when you see something you need to have. Make your intentions clear so there's no mistake."

The two of us sip our cocktails and watch Tad work the yard's perimeter. He waves over some of the hedges, thickening them. With a few strong gestures, he raises some of the trees to be taller, making sure they block all sightlines into the yard.

All the while, he's mumbling in a smooth and seductive Irish lilt that has Kenzie and me hot and bothered.

"What are you saying?" Kenzie asks. "Because whatever it is, don't ever stop."

He flashes her a flirtatious grin. "I'm spellin' the yard so no sounds or sights will get through to nosy neighbors. Once I finish, I'll set up a proximity alarm against dark magic users. If anyone breaches the perimeter who ought not to be here, ye'll know right away."

"Cool. Carry on."

Tad finishes the wards, and even Azland looks satisfied with his work when he finishes.

"I feel more secure already," Zephyr says. "Now can we get back to training? Azland promised I'd get to beat up Briar."

Briar chuckles. "No, he said we'd train in hand-to-hand combat."

"Yeah. That's what I said."

Briar barks a laugh. "As if, storm boy. When we wrestled as kids, I always pinned you first."

"That was because *Maman* would come in and make us stop fighting before I could put my signature moves to use."

"Well, *Maman's* not here to protect you now, little man. Let's see what you've got."

"After we work on weaponry," Azland interjects. "Zephyr, collect your staff. Jules, put your drink down and pick up your whip. Briar, try this."

Briar picks up the sledgehammer he indicates and tests its heft. "I wield one like this at work. Are you sure this is a weapon?"

"Depending on the wielder, yes."

Briar swings the hammer. The muscles in his arm flex as he holds it aloft. "Yeah, I'm good with this."

Zephyr spins his Storm Staff in his hands and chuckles. "First a shield and now a hammer. Are you Captain America's and Thor's love child?"

"It's better than being smashed around by my weapon. That thing is so crazy I half-expect you to start dating it."

I bust up laughing. "Harsh, but hilarious."

The girls Zephyr dates tend to be nuts. If he has as many fights with his weapon as he does with his girlfriends, we'll be in big trouble.

Zephyr scowls. "No. Not hilarious. That was uncalled for. Besides, Stormy and I get along better now that Tad and I have been focusing my chi."

Briar snorts. "Like all your girlfriends. It's the calm before the storm, brother. Hey, you can't blame her. Her name is storm."

When our brothers start whaling on each other, grunting and

rolling around on the grass, Kenzie and I pull up lawn chairs and cheer them on.

"Zephyr, don't whack him with your hands. Use them to channel your powers."

"Nah, I think I'd rather whack him."

Tad laughs.

Azland glowers.

"What about the wee lasses?" Tad grins at us, holding his hands up in a fighting stance. "Do the two of ye want to have a go?"

"Both of us?" Kenzie asks.

"Sure. No powers this time around. Ye need the physical conditionin' to defend yerselves in any situation."

Kenzie looks at me, and I hold up my drink. "I box and have training partners at the station. I'm going to get my buzz on. You two have at it."

"If you're sure," Kenzie says. "I'm new to the whole self-defense arena. You'll have to show me some moves before I'm ready to take you on as an opponent."

Tad winks. "Och, yer in good hands, lass. Come here to me, and I'll show ye a few things."

We spend the rest of the afternoon working out. Between Azland and Tad, we get plenty of advice on things like stances and posture. We also see Zephyr hauled around upside down after trying to ride his Storm Staff like a witch's broomstick.

"That's a firecracker of a brother ye got there," Tad observes as we watch him trying to reposition himself despite the staff's sabotage.

"No." Kenzie laughs. "Jules is the firecracker. Zephyr, for some reason, is aligned with the element of air."

"That surprises ye?"

Kenzie shrugs. "I always thought of air as a calm breeze. You know—refreshing. Air doesn't usually make much of a fuss. You can't see it."

"Ye ever gone a minute or two without takin' a good deep breath?"

Kenzie nods. "We used to dunk each other in the pool as kids."

"Then ye know how fickle and rowdy air can be."

"It's new to us," I remind him. "I'm glad you're here to answer questions and help us sort things out."

"Well, it's Azland who knows the most about the natural magic of yer people, but I'll do my righteous best to help ye out whenever I can."

"I'm sure you will." My phone buzzes in my pocket and I pull it out to read the incoming text. It's from Fi.

Got u an audience with Bakkali 4 tmrw afternoon. Sending u the deets now.

U rock. I reply.

Thankfully, the meeting with Bakkali isn't until tomorrow afternoon because I'm half-buzzed and floating on a raspberry vodka high.

I tell the others about the meeting. My siblings seem pleased. Azland doesn't. Huge surprise there.

Uninterested in hearing his rant about ignoring the world around us and focusing on our lives of isolation, I gather the empties and head back inside.

Even though I'm on a small boozy bender, I call up the contact info for Malia Davis. I met Malia at the academy and touch base with her now and then. She went to Narcotics, and from what I've heard, she's blazing a trail and getting the attention of the brass.

"Hey, Davis, it's Jules Gagne."

"Jules! How's it going at the Twenty-Third? I hear things are wild down by the river."

"You don't know the half of it. That's why I'm calling. We've had a spike in problems with folks taking Second Sight. I wondered what you could tell me."

"The stuff is toxic. We need to get it off the street."

"Agreed. I'm working on tracking down the source. Have you got any theories or leads that might help?"

"Very little. A CI on my beat says the runners pick up their supplies from a bike messenger downtown. Somewhere between the Basilica and the Old Port."

"Any ID or description of the messenger?"

"Not yet but we're working on it."

"All right, thanks. Let me know if you come up with anything more substantial and I'll do the same."

"Will do. Give my love to the Twenty-Third."

"Sure thing. We'll talk soon."

I hang up and flop on my bed. The room is spinning in a deliciously slow swirl, and I close my eyes and let exhaustion take me.

I wake in my clothes, still starfished on my mattress, and feel around on the bed for my phone. Finding it tucked under the ruffle of covers, I hold it up and check the time. Seven-thirty.

Huh. That has to be a record.

Either I was drunker than I thought or this whole awakening transition thing knocked the shit out of me. I'm leaning toward door number two because I don't have a headache and feel better than I have in weeks.

After a quick shower and change of clothes, I head out to the common area of our home to find Briar flipping pancakes while Kenzie sips a cup of coffee at the table. Tad wanders out a few minutes later like a barefoot blue jean god. His blond hair is tousled, and he looks like he had one hell of a night.

I study Kenzie, but she's not giving anything away.

I grab a plate from the rack and snag a fork before sitting down. Briar sets the stack of pancakes down, grabs the syrup, and joins the rest of us at the table.

"How's everyone feeling this morning?"

"Amazing." Kenzie beams.

I watch Tad's face, searching for any micro-expressions that might give me an idea of whether the two are now actively doing the down-and-dirty.

Nothing.

Damn. He's good.

"Yeah, I'm good too. I slept straight through for like, what… thirteen hours? Sorry I missed the midnight excitement shift."

Briar stabs four pancakes off the main plate and drops them in front of himself. "You didn't miss a thing. We didn't have any midnight theatrics. Our boy slept through."

I swing my gaze to Zephyr and raise my palm for a high-five. "That's amazing, Z. You must be so relieved. What does it feel like to sleep through the night?"

Zephyr lowers his mug and swallows. "Honestly, I'd forgotten what it was like to get a full night's rest. I feel wild and bright-eyed this morning."

"It'll be good fer our next meditation session," Tad comments. "Yer mind will be clearer than if yer knackered."

"I'm thrilled for you, Z. Here's to new beginnings." I raise my juice glass, and my siblings and Tad each raise their drinks of choice.

"To new beginnings," Zephyr toasts. "Is it too much to hope that the storm inside me is free?"

I pour the syrup and pass it to Briar. "I don't think so. I think it's perfectly reasonable to hope the stormy battles are over."

"You've been through enough," Kenzie adds.

Definitely.

The five of us eat pancakes and bacon and drink coffee and juice. I have to admit this is the most relaxed meal we've had together...I think ever.

"What cases are you working on today?" Kenzie asks.

"I'm trying to track down the supply chain for Second Sight. I called a friend in Narcotics last night, and she says a bike messenger drops the drugs off to the runners downtown, but they have no idea about any of the particulars."

"It's a shame *Maman* and Charlie raised us so well," Briar observes. "None of us have any close contacts among the criminal underworld."

"What about that guy you told us about the other day?" Zephyr asks. "The naked one."

"It's not a bad idea. There's always Max too," Briar suggests. "He's always smoking or inhaling some chemical or another."

Zephyr frowns at us. "I'll ask him. He thinks you all hate him. I don't know if he'd help you even if he could. Well, maybe Kenzie."

Kenzie rolls her eyes. "Could you please show him the futility of pursuing me? I don't know where he got the idea that we'd make a good match."

"Likely during a chemically altered state," I snark.

She nods. "That must be it."

After I've consumed my pancakes, I open my laptop. Once I log in, I connect with my precinct files. I take out the address of Mr. I See All and take a picture on my phone. "I'm off to visit the Earl of Nakeyville. I'll start at the bottom of the food chain and work up."

"With any luck, today will be a pants day." Kenzie takes her mug to the sink to rinse. "I'm off too. I've got a new client coming in for a consult this morning. See you at six."

"Unless the universe detonates on us," Briar adds.

I nod. "Unless that. Everyone keep your phones handy in case there's an emergency."

There's a high-pitched *ding* in the spare room, and Tad brightens. "Hold that thought."

He *poofs* out of existence, rustles around in the spare room, and reappears where he was with a laptop.

"That's so freaky." Briar blinks at him with an awed smile. "Not sure I'll get used to that."

"Sure, ye will." Tad calls up something on his computer and nods. "Och, this is good stuff. It's not fer public consumption, but Garnet granted me access to some of his lab's research findings."

I scan the triangular LGEO logo and read the banner. "Laboratories of the Lakeshore Guild of Empowered Ones."

"Look here." Tad clicks on a file and opens what looks like a bunch of letters and numbers strung together in tiny text. He scrolls down to some graphs, pointing at one chart that shows the drug's ingredients and their purposes.

"It says fer the most part, Second Sight is a regular feel-good party drug. Except this one's got two extra magical components."

"Which are?" I lean in, trying to read the tiny font on Tad's screen.

"One's a rather complex spell that removes the glamor of any fae livin' as humans and reveals the presence of any fae magic."

"And the other?"

"The other triggers aggression."

Kenzie is swinging her purse over her shoulder and pauses. "Why aggression?"

I sit back in my chair. "When people on the drug notice an empowered person, they go out of their way to get hostile."

"Whoever made this stuff is a real asshole," Briar points out.

Tad lifts a shoulder. "They're hellborn. Bein' assholes stands to reason."

CHAPTER FIFTEEN

Briar and Kenzie leave for work, Azland trots off to take care of his business, and Zephyr vows to stop by Max's place on the way to the music store. That means it's Tad and me on today's mission, which is to track down Michael Dove, better known as Nakey Kid.

"His apartment building is near the Old Brewery Mission. Which, conveniently, is close to the Notre-Dame Basilica of Montréal."

"Where the drug messenger is thought to frequent."

"Exactly. We'll spend time there too. With you transporting us, it will be quick and easy for us to get around and cover more ground."

"Only it won't." Tad shakes his head. "I can only teleport to places I've already been. I need to be able to 'lock on' to the place I'm headed to. It's like an internal GPS."

"Oh. How'd you get here, then?"

"Nikon brought us. His teleportation is different. He can be anywhere he sees, so as long as there's Google Earth, he can go anywhere. He also doesn't exhaust his power to travel. Sloan and

I are Wayfarers, so we need a few days to recharge after a long distance."

I let that sink in. "What's considered a long distance?"

"If I go home to Ireland, I'm there for the weekend."

I laugh. "Oh, so really long distance. Cool. I get it. Looks like you'll be getting the deluxe tour of the city today. If anything happens, I don't want you handicapped by a lack of GPS information."

"Sounds good. Kenzie mentioned ye have a kickass bike. I don't suppose ye have two and we can tear up the streets?"

"Sadly, no. We can take public transit or my off-season car, June Bug."

He chuckles. "June Bug. That sounds entirely tough and masculine on a mission against hellborn."

"Maybe it'll work as us being undercover."

"Aye, let's go with that."

Because he's still excited about it, we both take the pole down to the garage bay. I have to admit, it never really gets old.

"To the Batmobile." He's grinning so easily that I hope Fi's right and being here helps him through the tough times she mentioned. She said he's a really good guy and I feel that down to my fiery core.

A long whistle echoes in the massive bay and Tad goes to my girl. "Oh, she is a beauty."

"Thank you. Do you ride?"

He nods. "I've got a couple of beasts back home. Maybe I'll have Nikon take me back tonight, and we'll bring one here. Are ye up for givin' the new guy a tour of the city that way?"

Now it's me who's grinning like a fool. "Finally, someone who speaks my language. Hells yeah."

"There's nothin' like the thunderin' rush of a hundred and fifty horses catapultin' ye down a bendy road to get the blood pumpin' and clear the cobwebs."

"Amen, brother."

The two of us are sharing that glorious rush when he catches sight of June Bug, and yeah, I understand the letdown.

"She's a means to an end." I brush a hand over her mismatched quarter panel. "She might not look like much, but she's never let me down."

"Beggars and choosers as they say."

"Right you are. We'll get you all toured up, and June Bug can hibernate for a few more months before the roads get icy and I need her."

June Bug starts a little rough, but after a few heavy stomps on the gas and her coughing out some black smoke, we get moving and head downtown.

It's still early enough that I highly doubt our target will be awake, so we swing by the Basilica to wander around first.

"It's gorgeous," Tad whispers and cranes his neck to look at the gleaming gold of the domes high above us.

"Notre-Dame Basilica is the prize jewel in Montréal's crown. All the biggest and most famous dignitaries have their services here."

"The fountain is elaborate." He's glancing up at the bronze statue at the top. "Who's the man sportin' all the swagger?"

"That's Paul Chomedey de Maisonneuve, the founder of Montréal."

He walks around the four statues at the base of the monument. "And these blokes?"

"They represent four famous contributors to the city's establishment."

He takes his time soaking it all in and points at the church. "Is it public? Can we peek inside?"

"Sure. Are you religious?"

He shakes his head. "Most people in the empowered world are more spiritual than religious. I've met Mother Nature, and we've come up against Death and Loki. After a while, it becomes more about believin' in a code and yer friends."

"What about family?"

A shadow darkens his stunning visage. "Fer some, maybe. Not fer me."

"Well, I've never met anyone from my blood family, but Briar, Kenzie, Zephyr, Charlie, and our adoptive parents filled that slot as well as anyone could."

He nods. "That's what I'm workin' on too. Ye can't choose yer blood family, but ye can certainly choose who becomes the family of yer heart."

"Truth."

I lead the way up the front steps and inside the center of three arched wooden doors. The inside of the historic cathedral is even more magnificent than the outside, and I kick myself for not coming here more often.

Tad's eyes widen. "Och, she's breathtakin'."

"She is at that," I agree.

"Thank you for appreciating her." A tall, blond man stands from the pew at the back of the church. A braid falls from each of his temples, and the scruff of a clipped beard covers his chiseled jaw.

I recognize him immediately. "Mr. Bakkali. I'm sorry…we didn't mean to disturb you. I was showing Tad around the city."

The Viking strides over to join us, and there's no mistaking that he might be a true Norse raider.

He shakes Tad's hand and gestures at the opulence around us. "The cathedral's interior is renowned throughout the religious and artistic worlds. The azure vaults, the golden stars, the reds, purples, silver, and gold. It's incredible, don't you think?"

"Without question," Tad agrees.

"To allay your concerns, Ms. Gagne, you didn't disturb me. I come here most mornings to sort my thoughts and prepare for the day ahead. We can either talk now or this afternoon as originally planned."

Part of me wonders how he remembered me but then again, he runs the magical community of this entire region of Quebec.

I'm sure he's quite magical himself.

"Now works if we're not keeping you."

"People begin vying for my attention the moment I emerge in the morning, but the boon of being the top dog means I choose with whom I spend my time." He casts a scrutinizing gaze over Tad. "So, Mr. McNiff, the son of the man who thought to grab the ring of power."

Tad stiffens, and the warm, approachable, hot, and handsome guy shuts down. He straightens and lifts his chin. "Aye, well, I had no say in who my father was or what he became. I'd ask ye not to hold me to the same standard. I assure ye, I'm my own man."

Bakkali continues to study him. "Garnet said as much. Still, I warn you. If you bring that darkness to my door, I won't hesitate to end you as a bad seed."

My jaw drops open. "What the hell? You don't get to talk to him like that. This was obviously a mistake."

Tad shakes his head and raises his hand to stop my steamed exit. "It's fine, Jules. It's nothin' I haven't encountered a dozen times over the past year."

Bakkali smiles at me as if he didn't kick my friend while he was down. "Stating expectations is important to lay the groundwork for future encounters. With that said, come, sit with me. Tell me why you had Fiona reach out on your behalf."

The three of us move to the back pews, and I slide in beside him while Tad sits on the next one forward. I'm still trying to assess what the hell that was about Tad's father, but this is neither the time nor the place.

I let that go and get back to the regularly scheduled program. "I'm not exactly sure how you can help us. My siblings and I are only three days into our awakenings, so we're still coming to terms with most of it."

"So, the rumors are true. The powers of Laurette's quartet

have awakened." There's a slight smile on his lips, but nothing about his eyes or voice makes that sound like a good thing. "Yes, Fiona was right to direct you to me."

"How so?"

"Let me ask you this. Are you aware of the dangers you face from within the empowered world?"

"Our dog and our aunt told us about The Six and their food preferences, yes."

He nods. "This explains the influx of Scaith Warriors and skoro showing up dead around the city."

"I know of two instances. One was a man dredged from the Old Port and one was a body I found in LaSalle the night my brother Zephyr was kidnapped."

"The wind elemental," he says matter-of-factly.

"You know a lot about my situation already."

His grin widens, and there's a cruel edge to it. "I know pretty much everything that goes on in my city, Juliette. I've needed to in order to keep the balance and hide our existence for the past centuries."

"That's a lot of moving parts."

"That it is."

"So, yeah, we're playing catch-up, training, and trying to ready ourselves and our lives for the incoming threats."

"As you should."

"One major thing that might help is to track down the source of this new drug on the street."

Bakkali arches a flaxen brow. "You're going after the manufacturer of Second Sight. Do you realize that might take you directly into the lion's den?"

"I do. The thing is, Second Sight is making things more difficult for both the empowered and human societies. I mean, it's magically designed to cause division."

"How so?"

"We've recently learned there are magical components designed to penetrate fae glamors and incite aggression."

"And where did you learn this?"

Tad said that information isn't for public consumption, and I wonder if I've stepped in it. I glance at him to gauge if I should continue or backpedal, but he seems to want to take it from here.

"I'm one of Fi's Team Trouble warriors. Garnet's lab techs filed their report about an hour ago and copied me. I'm sure once Garnet sees it, he'll forward it to you too."

Something hostile flares in the man's eyes. "No. You'll forward that to me right now."

Tad doesn't hesitate. "I'll need a secured email. Guild files are encrypted."

Bakkali reaches into the pocket of his dress shirt and hands him a card.

"I'll be right back." Tad *poofs* out and is gone for a very tense moment before he *poofs* back and nods. "Ye'll have access to it now."

"I'll read the report and take it from here."

I wait, but he doesn't elaborate. "Excuse me for asking but what does that mean?"

"It means I am the leader of the empowered community living within the Laurentians. I'll direct my Guild Governors to inquire among their communities, and they will pursue the matter."

"What do you expect us to do?"

"Nothing, Ms. Gagne. By your admission, you are a fledgling in our world, and you need to catch up. Work on your abilities and safeguard your quartet. Perhaps reach out to other elementals to help them ready for the dangers ahead."

I hadn't thought of that.

"Are there other elementals having awakenings in the city?"

"Indeed. The prana rivers flow wild and fast within the Laurentians. We are tasked with following its flow and receiving its magical gifts."

It's hard to think of anything from the St. Lawrence River as a *gift*. So far, it's coughed up a dead guy covered in runes, a freaked out sailor sprouting gills, and the chaos of awakenings sending the city into a tailspin.

"Okay, well, I might be a fire elemental, but I'm also a cop. I can't and won't sit around doing nothing. You talk to your Guild Governors, and I'll investigate the Second Sight distribution in the streets. Maybe between the two of us, we can shut this down."

"Be aware that you're opening yourself up to unmitigated danger by pursuing a powerful foe who is searching for you."

"I understand the conundrum. Consider me warned."

Bakkali nods. "Very well. Until we meet again, Juliette Gagne. Be well."

After our meeting with Bakkali, Tad and I meander through Old Montréal, popping into a café for maple and bacon donuts before heading north toward the address on file for Michael Dove.

It's a rougher neighborhood, but the architecture is no less classic Montréal. From the towering Old Brewery Mission to the nearby courthouse done in a Brutalist style, there's always plenty of culture in our buildings.

"Definitely not the streets of Dublin," Tad remarks as we walk the sidewalk toward the rundown building.

I rap my knuckles on the door and wait.

No one answers.

Heading out, we stand on the front stoop before targeting three guys standing on the corner. "Hey, boys. Any chance you know a kid that lives in this building?"

"Sorry lady. We don't know anyone."

Tad chuckles and pulls out a billfold. He pulls off the clip and flips through the red of fifties into the brown of hundreds. "Are ye sure? We'd be very thankful to the first person who could tell us where to find Michael Dove."

Three hands come up fast and point at a convenience store down the road. "There's a video room in the back where he hangs out."

"Och, that was grand, boys." Tad pulls three C-notes and passes them around.

The boys take them and eye what's left in the billfold. "What's stopping us from claiming the rest of that stack?" one of them says.

I chuckle and pull back the nylon jacket I wear to cover my gun and badge clipped to my hip. "This for one thing."

Tad chuckles. "And this, fer another. *Fréamhaithe i Bhfeidhm.*"

The boys sound off as the two of us strike off toward the convenience store. I glance back to see what the problem is and chuckle as they twist and strain to pull their feet free from the sidewalk.

"What did you do?"

"The spell is *Rooted in Place*. It'll last long enough fer them to reconsider jumpin' strangers in the street."

I look again and laugh some more. "I'm sure it will. Magic is fun."

"Aye, at times it is."

CHAPTER SIXTEEN

Tad and I find Michael Dove in the back of the store, working the joystick and button combo of a retro '80s standup table of Centipede. Thankfully, Kenzie was right and today *is* a pants day, so it spares me a repeat exposure to Michael's male parts.

"He'll recognize me from the other day and likely try to bolt. Any chance you can root him to the floor so we can speak to him?"

"Aye, of course. Consider him a captive audience." Tad goes in first, does his thing, and I follow.

"Hey, Michael. Nice to see you again. Even nicer that I'm not seeing the goods this time."

His buddies all burst into howls of laughter.

Nakey Kid glares at me.

"Why are you here? Haven't you done enough?"

I chuckle. "Are you pissed that I arrested you while you were flying high and flashing your wiener and beans?"

"Do you know how mad my mom is at me right now? She's off the rails."

"Well, there's a life lesson in that. Don't do drugs and waggle your Peter pointer at a cop."

He shifts and frowns at his feet. "What the fuck? Why can't I move my feet?"

"A little precaution in case you were thinking about making a run for it. Don't worry. S'all good."

He continues to fight with his feet, and it's a little sad.

"Dude. Forget about the feet thing. We'll release you once you tell us what we want to know about the drugs you were on when I brought you in. Where'd you get the Second Sight and from who?"

Nakey Kid's friends are happy to stand around and mock him, but as soon as we start talking about the drug dealer, they suddenly have somewhere else to be.

Michael frowns and scowls at the empty video room. "I can't tell you that. I ain't no snitch."

Tad chuckles. "Then I guess yer good to spend the next few days rooted in place. How will yer mam react to that?"

He grumbles. "Seriously? That's cold, dude."

I cross my arms and settle in. "Tell us where you got the drugs."

He glances around, but there's no one to save him. He realizes it and sighs. "Friend of a friend. A guy named Santa. Don't know his real name."

"People call him Santa?"

"You'll get it when you meet him."

"Where do we find jolly ole St. Nick?"

"He moves around depending on the day of the week. Today's Monday, so he'll be hanging out around the Basilica somewhere."

I jot that down. "And Tuesday?"

"Old Montréal."

"Wednesday?"

"The Old Port."

"Thursday?"

It goes like that until I've written down the schedule of the local seller. "That's very helpful, Michael."

He shakes his head. "No. It wasn't. Seriously, I wasn't helpful. You didn't get anything from me."

I nod. "Deal. If the intel pans out, we won't tell Santa you put him on our naughty list. If it doesn't, we'll boomerang back here, and we won't be as understanding of your predicament."

Tad releases the kid's feet, and he storms off, cursing us under his breath.

"Guess we're off to the North Pole."

Tad chuckles. "I guess so."

As it turns out, Tad and I don't need to go to the North Pole to find Mr. Claus. Santa turns out to be a pot-bellied man with a scruffy white beard and a ratty old Santa hat.

"I'm underwhelmed," I say to Tad from a distance.

"He looks more like a homeless man than a drug dealer," Tad observes.

He's not wrong.

"Hello, Santa."

He's sitting in the Basilica courtyard throwing bits of bread at pigeons. He scans me with a wary gaze but says nothing.

"Bread isn't good for birds." Tad eyes the loaf in Santa's hand.

"Nah, they love it." Santa tosses another handful of bread toward the chubby birds.

Tad glares at the man. He whispers something under his breath, and the birds take flight in an instant, leaving the courtyard empty.

"Aw, man." Santa groans.

"Well, now maybe we can talk," I say. "We heard you knew where to get Second Sight?"

"Who told you that?"

"A little birdie." Tad holds his hand up. A pigeon lands on his hand and coos as it rubs its head against his thumb.

"Well, I can't help you. Santa delivers presents to good girls and boys but has nothing left for the fuzz."

I take liberties, pick up his red man purse, and peek inside. He's not lying. Beyond stale bread, he doesn't have anything in there. "Where could we get more?"

He eyes me and shrugs. "Not sure what you're talking about. I'm an old man feeding pigeons in the park."

I notice the ink on his wrist when he snatches back his bag and smile. "Okay, big man. Have it your way."

Leaving him to his bread and birds, I turn and leave the courtyard.

"Ye picked up on somethin' I take it."

"Yeah. The stamp on the inside of his wrist is from a Lion's Den party. It's a weird trendy club. Very posh. Invite only."

Tad laughs. "That gobshite qualified?"

"Exactly."

"Well, I suppose if he can get an invite, we can get ourselves on the guest list."

"You think?"

"Aye, leave it with me. I'll see what I can do."

I'm not sure what he can do, but Fi said he was a marvel. The two of us take the scenic route from the courtyard of the Basilica back to where I parked June Bug. I figure the more of Montréal he experiences, the better it will be for portaling in the long run.

I point out some historical highlights along Notre-Dame Street as we pass from the Basilica area through Old Montréal to the Old Port.

As Tad and I make our way across one of the raised wooden bridges that gives us a spectacular view of the island, I draw a deep breath of fresh air and stiffen. "Do you smell that?"

Tad searches the surrounding area and frowns. "Burned cookies."

"Maybe we should get off this bridge. I don't love the idea of being trapped between two pinch points where energy-sucking creatures can swarm us."

"Bein' trapped isn't a concern. I can portal ye out quick enough. It's whether or not ye want to take a few more players off the field. That's the question."

I think about that for a moment, and yeah, he's right.

The empowered world doesn't play by the same rules as the human world. As a cop, I try to diffuse and avoid conflict. As a fire elemental, there are enemies who think it's open season on me and my siblings. "Taking a few off the board sounds good to me."

Tad mumbles a few incantations and the trees above crowd in, giving us more cover. We creep toward the edge of the bridge, our heads on a constant swivel.

As we're about to make it onto solid ground, two skoro cut us off and rush forward.

Tad puts himself between the opponents and me and raises his palms. He casts a spell in tongues, and a tangle of plant vines scurries along the ground and grabs the ankles of our surprised guests.

When the flora pulls their feet out from under them, we follow as it drags them, chasing them to the small treed area off the beaten path down by the water's edge.

They aren't the bravest of foes.

They *screech* and *click* and flail their arms. I'm not sure if they are surprised the predators have become the prey or what their problem is, but they should suck it up and not embarrass themselves.

I call fire to my palm, move in, and throw it. The ball of flame catches my opponent square in the chest but does little more than burn off its clothes.

Right. Hellborn. I forgot.

Tad holds out his hand, and a thick branch flies into it. A

shimmering glow overtakes the wood as he infuses it with his druid magic and brings it down on his attacker's head with a *thunk*.

I don't want to discharge my gun in the middle of Old Montréal, and I don't have my dagger or whip.

I didn't realize I was so woefully unprepared.

Tad takes out the second guy and points. "Ye'll be able to fry them now. Get rid of the bodies."

"Excellent. I don't like being left out of the action."

I move in and press my hand against the fallen. When my heat gets molten, they go up like kindling, leaving only a scorch mark and a pile of ashes.

Tad comes in behind me and presses his palm to the ground. His lips move with his whispered command. The ground churns and swallows the ashes. When he straightens, the grass fills in thick, and there's no evidence that anything happened here.

"Well, other than the baleful screaming, that went smoothly," I say.

Tad frowns. "What the hell was that ruckus about?"

"I have no—Behind you!"

Tad whirls and is in full fighting mode when I rush forward and send a few blasts of fire to help out.

Fire might not be the most effective against this particular brand of opponents, but the force of my strikes still makes them stumble backward and knocks them off-balance.

"I think I know what all that vocalization was about." I grab a fallen branch and wield it like a bat. "I think that was skoro for phone a friend."

Tad chuckles. "I think ye might be right. Try to toss them into the water. Didn't Azland say they weren't great with water?"

He did.

"On it." I blast one of the guys closest to the water, then run and give him a solid kick into the drink. The splash is epic, and he spits and sputters, but he stands waist-deep and remains very much alive.

"That's disappointing."

"Let me see if I can help. Keep them off me." Tad sticks both hands in the water and closes his eyes.

I fire bolts and balls of flame, keeping the remaining skoro from getting too close while a huge school of fish rises from the depths, surrounds the man in the water, and drags him under the surface.

"Nice." Distracted by watching Tad do his thing, I lose focus. Two guys close in on me, and I call *Searing Skin*. Flame wreaths my skin in a fiery aura, but it's not all that effective against our opponents.

One punches me in the stomach while the other drags its claws down my neck. I scream as hot blood washes the front of my shirt and the world around me starts to swim.

"Feckin' hell." Tad is back at my side, and a moment later we're standing in the firehouse's kitchen. "Azland, I need ye, sham."

He lunges toward the stove and grabs a dish towel, wrapping it around my throat as he curses with his lovely Irish lilt.

His hands are slick with blood, and the crease in his brow is getting more pronounced. "Is anyone here?"

My feet slip out from under me, and he scrambles to lay me on the floor before I fall.

"Och, fuck this."

Another wave of his power hits and the world shifts again. This time, I'm lying on the floor of someone's living room. "Sloan! Fi! Is anyone home? Anyone?"

I wake up sometime later with a blanket thrown over my upper body, Fiona mopping the floor, and Sloan's hand cupping the side of my neck. His touch is warm, and the magical healing energy he's using on me makes my skin tingle in all the right ways. "Hello, Jules. Welcome back. Ye had a bit of a rough go there, did ye?"

I blink and let my mind catch up with me. "Tad brought me to Toronto?"

"Aye, that's right. It seems ye had a bit of a run-in with some nasty folks with very long claws."

I swallow as the memory comes back. "My fire doesn't work well against skoro."

"No. I suppose it wouldn't." He moves back and helps me sit up. "Now, don't rush. Ye lost a fair bit of blood before Tad found help."

"Where is he?"

"I'm here, lass." I follow Tad's voice to one of the chairs in the kitchen across the room. "I owe ye an apology. I should never have encouraged ye to fight with so little trainin' and understandin' of your limitations. This is on me."

I shake my head. "No, it's not. We put up one hell of a fight and made the world a little safer for the elementals of Montréal. I need to figure out my fighting strategy against other fire-based empowered. That's not on you."

He doesn't seem convinced.

"Can I get a drink?"

"Of course," Fi says, finishing with the mop. "What would you like? Water, soda, alcohol?"

"Coke, Pepsi, Sprite, whatever you've got handy."

Fi goes to the fridge and brings me a can of Fresca. I crack the tab and drink, letting the tart citrus bubbles rush down my throat.

When I finish, the world stops spinning. "Am I patched up, Doc?"

Sloan winks. "A little food in yer belly and a few hours of rest and ye'll be good as new."

I squeeze his wrist. "Thank you."

"It's no trouble. I'm happy to come to yer aid, but if I could make a suggestion... If yer life ends up bein' anythin' like ours, ye'll need a healer within yer ranks. It might be prudent to seek one out and start buildin' a relationship."

Fiona chuckles. "That's his tactful way of telling you that standing against the forces of dark fae is a dangerous and bloody endeavor. Having at least one healer is a must. Having two or three with medical skills is even better."

"Ye'll always have me to fall back on in an emergency," Sloan adds.

"And his father in the event that it's direr than that," Fi advises. "The Mackenzies are great healers, but I'm sure there will be someone in your area who will fit the bill."

Tad chuckles. "It just dawned on me...Jules's sister, Kenzie, is the healer of their family and her full name is Mackenzie. Maybe it's somethin' in the name."

Sloan chuckles. "Maybe."

My phone buzzes in my pants pocket and I pull it out to see who wants me. There's a text from Zephyr.

911. Get home. Kenzie is losing her mind!

I chuckle. "Speaking of Kenzie, it seems she's having a meltdown of some sort. Am I good to go?"

Sloan nods. "Safe home."

I glance down at the blanket wrapped under my arms to cover my chest. "I'll have to get this back to you. I haven't sorted out the flaming clothing problem yet."

Fi chuckles. "Don't worry. I've ended up naked a few times after battles. No harm done. Off you go. Call us if you need our help."

CHAPTER SEVENTEEN

Tad portals us back to Montréal and we take form in the firehouse. Being teleported while holding onto Tad feels like being at the top of a roller coaster, where you start to feel that little tug at the center of your stomach.

It's pretty fun.

We materialize in the center of the living room. Kenzie is sitting on the couch, holding one of the multi-angled mirrors she uses to do her hair and shrieking in alarm.

I immediately see why she's so upset—she's blue.

Not, like, having a bad day metaphorically blue. She's literally blue. Her skin, which used to be a rich dark brown, is now the pale blue of a clear summer sky.

Zephyr rushes in, his arms full of makeup from Kenzie's bathroom. "Oh, thank fuck you're here," he calls when he sees us.

"None of that will help," Kenzie wails. "It's all made for black skin! Human skin! Where the hell is my skin?"

As she looks up, I notice that her eyes have also changed color. They used to be the brown of garden soil, and now they're a deep ocean blue.

"Maybe with all the new powers awakening, they'll start a skincare line for blue people," I suggest.

"This isn't a joke!" Kenzie drops the mirror on the sofa and covers her face with her hands. "I can't go to work like this—I'm *BLUE!*"

"It's quite fetching, though, if I do say so," Tad says.

"Yeah, you look great." I adjust the blanket around me, ease down beside her on the sofa, and hug her. "Blue is in right now. Plus, you can make ice. Remember how popular Elsa from *Frozen* was?"

"I'm not a Disney princess," Kenzie cries. "I want to be *normal.*"

"Hey, if you saw the stuff Tad and I saw today, you'd realize how normal you are compared to all the other wackiness out there."

"There's a great Eiffle 65 song about that," Tad remarks. *"Blue Da Ba Dee."*

"I love that song." Zephyr nods. "You can tell everyone they wrote that song about you."

Kenzie is not amused by this musical interlude. She buries her face in a pillow.

Zephyr is sitting cross-legged on the floor, digging through the pile of makeup. "Does mahogany brown eyeliner go with blue skin?"

"I don't want a new makeup routine!" Kenzie yells. "I want to be *myself* again."

"Ye are yerself, lass." Tad tries to soothe her. "This is the most yerself you've ever been. All that's happened is the glamor hidin' yer true self faded away."

Not helping.

Kenzie groans and flops against the sofa as tears fall on her sky blue cheeks.

"I'm calling Charlie." If sibling sass can't cheer Kenzie, it's time to break out the big guns. After all, when the world falls apart, and nothing makes sense, everyone needs their mom...or at least their odd, overly protective adoptive aunt.

I secure my blanket, pull my phone out of my pocket, and send a text asking her where she is. When the reply comes back, I meet Tad's gaze. "Do you remember where Charlie lives?"

"Aye."

"Please go get her."

Tad is back in less than a minute with Charlie, her hands still dusted with flour and carrying a big container of freshly baked brownies.

"Oh, chickie-poo," Charlie says when she sees Kenzie crying. She hands the brownies to Zephyr, scoots me over on the couch, sits, and wraps her arms around Kenzie. "It's all right."

Kenzie sobs, blinking up at her. "I'm blue. Nothing about that is all right."

Charlie rubs circles on her back and shushes her. "Now that the glamors are gone, we expected you might experience physical changes."

Zephyr interjects, "Last time I had a parent figure sit me down and tell me to expect 'physical changes,' I was thirteen and covered in acne. As long as this doesn't make me break out all over, I'm fine."

"Ugh, I really cannot handle a second puberty right now," I moan.

"Remember how boy-crazy Kenzie was at that age?" Zephyr reminds me. "I swear she came home from school with a new crush every day."

Kenzie sniffles. "That's not true. I crushed on Justin Livingstone for, like, months in the ninth grade."

Zephyr and I laugh. Justin Livingstone was a kid in Kenzie's class who, for some reason, she was completely obsessed with.

One day Papa agreed to drive her and Justin to the movies for a date. Apparently, he was so lame and boring that Kenzie came straight home and never mentioned Justin Livingstone again.

"Will I be blue forever?" Kenzie has calmed down enough to return to the topic at hand.

"I don't know, honey." Charlie holds Kenzie's hand. "It's possible you'll get stronger in your powers and able to manipulate your appearance."

"Then that's what I'm going to work for."

"This is yer true form," Tad repeats. "Yer beautiful. Don't confine yerself to the ideals of humans. Yer so much more than that."

"At least we haven't taken our true elemental forms," Zephyr remarks. "Azland gave me a book, and in our elemental forms, we are crazy scary-looking. Or maybe that's coming, but it hasn't happened yet."

"That's not reassuring," I mutter.

"Have any of you experienced the same kind of physical changes?" Charlie asks.

I shake my head.

Tad frowns. "Uh, actually... Durin' the fight, yer eyes had flames in them."

I blink and pick up Kenzie's mirror. "Seriously?"

"Aye, but they faded by the time ye woke up after the healin'."

"What's this now?" Charlie leans over and peers into my face. "What fight? What healing?"

"Nothing worth worrying about. We had a bit of a run-in. Look away."

"Is that why you don't have a shirt on?"

I grin. "Thankfully, I was just flaming up in the fight when I got taken out. I'm not naked. Score."

"I'm not sure being taken out early in a fight is a win, Jules," Zephyr contradicts.

I wave away his comment and change the subject. "What about you, Zephyr? Any changes we should know about?"

He shrugs. "Nothing yet, but Azland released my powers later than yours. Who knows, maybe I'll wake up tomorrow and be ten feet tall with clouds for hair."

"They'd match the clouds in your empty head," I tease.

Zephyr chuckles.

"Do I smell Charlie's brownies?" Briar comes up the stairs while pulling off his sweaty shirt.

Charlie rushes over for a close look at Briar's chest, arms, and back.

"Awkward. Why are you all up in my business? And why—holy fuck—is Kenzie blue?"

Kenzie presses a pillow over her face and screams.

I make eyes at him. "She's a little sensitive about the situation, so can you tell her it's not so bad?"

Briar flashes me a crazy look. *She's fucking blue!* he mouths.

I'm aware. Say something nice, I mouth back.

"Uh, yeah, sis. For sure. Blue's cool. You can be like that Disney princess all the kids love."

Kenzie pulls down the pillow and glares. "Is that what I've been reduced to—a Disney character? I'm so much more than that. I'm a kickass lawyer, I'm smart, I'm funny, and I can play the drums and carry a tune like nobody's business."

"Aye, and I think that's yer answer, luv. Yer more than the beautiful package that went from black to blue. If people don't see that, it's on them."

She looks at Tad, draws a deep breath, and sighs. "That was a pretty perfect thing to say."

He winks. "I meant every word. Yer not the first person of color I've come across. Nixies are blue or green. Faeries can be pink or purple. I've dated women who shapeshift and others who turn into animals. Yer perfect just the way ye are."

"Ow, seriously, Charlie, back off. Stop picking at me," Briar snaps.

"Your rash is taking on the texture and appearance of stone.

Your abs and chest look like you've been dipped in concrete or carved out of granite."

"I'm aware. I worked the entire day without taking off my shirt. Now I'm hot, sweaty, and hangry. Give me some space."

"Is it painful?" she asks.

Briar reaches for a brownie and puts some distance between himself and our aunt. "Nope. Only weird."

Charlie is about to say something when a blaring horn goes off, and a male voice with a thick Irish accent shouts, "Feck off, ye have no business here. Feck off, ye have no business here."

"What the hell is that?" I stand from the sofa and look out the windows into the back yard.

"Something tripped my wards," Tad snaps.

"Not just something." I take in the sight through the windows. "We're being invaded. Dammit. I need a shirt."

Tad *poofs* the boys out to the back yard while I run for a shirt and Kenzie pulls herself together. The two of us meet at the pole, slide down, and are headed outside a moment later. "Stay inside, Charlie," I shout.

"Be careful," Charlie replies.

Half a dozen raiders are forcing their way through the reinforced hedges and climbing over the fences. Our druid-on-loan leaps into action with a heavy kick at one of them.

Azland is there too. He's running on all fours with his fangs bared. "Jules, behind you!"

I whirl, and a big man with long hair is coming for me. His arms are outstretched, his claws extended. I rush forward, tuck my head to protect my neck, and slam into him.

As soon as we make contact, I summon flames to my skin. We roll on the ground, leaving scorched patches in the grass as I work to pin him down.

"Jules. The yard is spelled to swallow noise. Use yer gun if ye want to."

"Excellent. That's the best news I've heard in days." I draw my gun and fire a round ending the struggle.

Rolling off my dead guy, I take stock.

Kenzie has her hands raised, and sharp spears of ice are dropping from the sky, cutting into our enemy. Gooey black blood stains the grass and the stench of burned sugar is cloying in my nostrils.

Briar and Zephyr are holding their own. They've got a bunch grouped and cornered near the back fence. Briar lifts jagged rocks from the soil and Zephyr uses hurricane force to pelt the intruders. They have things well in hand.

Until the tides change.

A dozen more ebony-eyed men arrive. They scurry over the fence like cockroaches to get to us in the back yard. Up close, I can tell they're not people, so I don't feel bad about ending them.

The point here is to survive.

The new wave of enemies sees Zephyr and Briar kicking ass and moves in that direction. Now Briar and Zephyr are trapped behind a crowd of nearly fifteen opponents.

Yeah no. I don't think so.

I run toward them, gun raised, and pick off attackers one by one. I'm fast, but before I can get my brothers clear, one of them grabs Zephyr's arm, twists him around, and slams him onto the ground.

There's a sickening *crunch*, and Zephyr screams a string of obscenities.

"Tad, Zephyr's down. Get him and Charlie out of here."

Tad flashes me a thumbs-up, and the two of them disappear. I don't know where they've gone, but it'll be safer than here.

I move in to help Azland and Briar, with Kenzie tight on my six. I'm emptying my Glock into these assholes shot after shot, but even with the three of us giving it, this is a losing battle.

Tad reappears, checks the scene, and reappears closer. "Come here to me! All of ye!"

I'd love to go to him, but two skoro are leeched around Kenzie's waist, trying to pull her toward the fence.

Briar kicks his opponent off and rolls to his feet. He and I get to our sister at the same time. With his adrenaline flowing and how he rushes in and grabs her wrist, I'm surprised he doesn't pull her arm out of its socket.

"I've got her," I shout. "You get them."

"My pleasure." He hardens his fist to stone and thumps the shit out of them.

The moment she's free, we rush to Azland and Tad.

As soon as we're in contact with Tad, he *poofs* us away. I feel that same exciting tug in my stomach. Then I stumble to stay on my feet, surrounded by the massive arches and domes of Notre-Dame Basilica.

"What are we doing here?" Briar asks. "I think the last time I visited this place was during a third-grade field trip."

"Jules and I visited earlier today," Tad explains. "I can only teleport to places I've been before, so my choices were limited to our tour of the city or Charlie's house. If the skoro forces found yer home, I had to assume yer childhood home is compromised too."

"The twins." Fear strikes me cold.

Charlie meets my gaze. "They're camping this weekend with their friends for their birthday."

Good. That's good.

We all take a beat, finding pews to rest on while Kenzie tends to Zephyr and I help cauterize the various wounds that Briar, Azland, and Tad sustained.

"So, we're all safe for now," Briar says.

"Well done, McNiff." I cast him a thankful smile. "We owe you."

"S'all good, folks. It's what we do."

I move over to Zephyr. He's cradled his arm against his chest and is sweating badly and gasping.

I check in with Kenzie. "Is it as bad as it looks?"

"It's dislocated. I don't think anything's broken, but I'm a total noob at healing, so what the hell do I know?"

Zephyr curses. "Could you at least pretend to know what you're doing?"

"Oh, sure thing." She forces a smile and pats his thigh. "You're fine. It'll heal. Once we put the shoulder back in place, I'll heal you right up."

"That was good. Much better."

Tad comes over and nods. "All right. Let's get that shoulder back in place, shall we?"

Briar arches a brow. "You say that like you know what you're doing."

"I do. I might not be much of a magical healer, but I'm Irish. I've been in enough donnybrooks to set a shoulder and straighten a broken nose. This is child's play."

Excellent. That's exactly what I need to hear.

I stand and shake out my hands. Adrenaline is still pumping fast in my bloodstream. The last thing I need is to burn down the jewel of Montréal.

To avoid combustion, I strike off to burn some nervous energy. I do a lap around the church, sticking to the outside walls. Thankfully, on Monday night there's not a large crowd, and there's no service.

As I pass one of the candelabras near the altar, the candles burst into brilliant flame.

Up until now, I've always protected those around me. I'm a good cop, a good sister, and a good friend. Now, I barely recognize the world and the people I love are getting hurt.

This isn't what I want for my life.

Or for my powers.

I need to get a better handle on this. I'll stop giving Azland a hard time—whoa, that's crazy talk. Okay, I'll give Azland *less* of a hard time.

I need to grab this situation by the horns, get control of my powers, and do better.

For myself. For my city. For my family.

Thankfully, when we tell the priest an abridged version of what happened, he invites us to hang out in the Basilica for as long as we need to regroup. I call Rene, and like a true friend and fellow cop, he drops everything and comes running.

"Are you all right?" He looks me over and glances at where Zephyr is recovering with his head on Charlie's lap. Briar and Tad are chatting, and Kenzie is kneeling on one of the prayer benches having a private word with a higher power.

"We survived."

"You should've called me sooner, Jules. You don't need to go through this alone. The entire point of my task force is to help fae citizens when their lives get turned upside down."

"Well, we nailed that one. We're as upside down as it gets. Add a few death spirals and a head-over-heels, and you'll find us there licking our wounds."

"This is what the fire was about?"

"It was the start of things, yeah. Now we've got skoro after us, and The Six know who and where we are, and I have no idea how to proceed."

"Are they still at the fire station?"

"When we left, they were still in the yard. Now…I have no idea."

"How many were there?"

"At first…maybe ten, then another two dozen. We got our asses kicked."

"Well, yeah. Even if you four were at full strength and

comfortable with your powers, six against thirty-four is ridiculous. Don't beat yourself up because they forced you to retreat. Be thankful you have a man on your team who can portal."

I glance at Tad and smile. "Believe me. I am."

He pats my shoulder. "For now, we'll assume the fire station and your childhood home are overrun. I'll put you and your family up in our safehouse and send a couple of units to both locations to check the status."

"Thanks."

"Not a problem."

Kenzie comes over with a sheepish smile for Rene. "Hey, so, I guess Jules filled you in. Sorry for the freak show."

Rene shakes his head. "You are as stunning as ever, Kenzie. Blue might be different, but it certainly isn't bad."

I nod. "We keep telling her that she looks cool."

"I look bizarre," she argues.

"Ye look like an heir to a great fae water kingdom," Tad corrects her. "Even by those standards, ye stand out as resplendent."

I'm thankful Tad's here to say all the right things to Kenzie. I have to remember to send Fi a thank you fruit basket or something.

What says, Thanks for loaning us a druid?

Meat trays maybe.

Kenzie and Tad break off to sit on one of the pews.

I rub my face and yawn.

Rene pegs me with a worried gaze. "You're bagged. Let's get you all set up for the night, and we can talk more in the morning."

"Hey, I know cops don't hug cops, but can I make an exception without it getting weird?"

Rene chuckles. "Sure."

I hug him, thankful he's my friend and my peer. "I never

expected my life to look like this, but now it does. I'm a freaky fire mutant."

"No, you're not. You're still you, Jules. You're the same motorcycle-riding, sarcastic, pain-in-the-ass, dedicated cop you've always been. Only now you can throw flame, and evil hellborn fae want to suck you dry like a juice box."

A bark of laughter escapes and I ease back from the hug. "Yeah. Same ol' story. No big deal."

A priest in a long black robe comes out to get our attention. "The Basilica will be closing shortly. Would you like me to contact the homeless shelter around the corner in the Old Brewery Mission?"

I field that one. "Thanks, Father. We don't need to take up space in the shelter. We have somewhere to stay for the night. We're good."

CHAPTER EIGHTEEN

The safehouse Rene takes us to is across the road and down a bit from Casse Croûte. Rene unlocks the door, and we follow him inside and up the back stairs. The apartment is sleek and decorated in a modern minimalist style. Very different from the firehouse's homey, cozy atmosphere.

"All right, then." Zephyr crosses the floor and sinks into the recliner. "What's the plan?"

Rene answers, "You stay here where it's safe for tonight. Tomorrow, after you all get a good sleep and restore your health, I'll be back to report on the status of the fire station and your childhood home."

Kenzie raids the sleek white cabinets, pulling out every bowl, jar, and flower vase she can find. "Help me fill these. Now that we have some privacy, I'm going to try to heal Z's shoulder."

Briar and I fill all the vessels from the faucet, then arrange them on the coffee table next to the Lay-Z-Boy where Zephyr sits.

Rene says good night and I walk him out.

Tad and Azland work on the doors and windows, spelling for privacy and setting up wards.

By the time I get back to the couch, Kenzie is moving her hands, drawing water out of the bowl, swirling it around her hands, then letting it flow back in.

Charlie watches with wide eyes.

I don't remember Azland teaching Kenzie this trick. It seems she's figured out a few things on her own.

A twinge of embarrassment niggles at me.

I haven't experimented with my powers in my free time like they have. In my defense, it's not like I've had much free time lately, but maybe if I'd been practicing, I could've done more to the bad guys than lightly toast them.

The seven of us crash. Battling with our powers is still new and takes a lot of energy. Kenzie's wiped from healing Zephyr, so she claims one of the bedrooms with Charlie. Zephyr zonks out on the couch, and Briar and I crash on the second bed.

I'm disoriented when someone taps my knee sometime later. I wake with a start and blink up at Tad's apologetic smile.

"Sorry to disturb ye. I got a response about that club ye wanted to crash downtown. There's an event tonight, and we've got the details if yer still up fer it. Or, if we're in fer the night, I can try to get us an invite fer another night too."

I sit up, run my fingers over my face, and push my hair back. "No. I'm good. If we've got an in, let's do it."

Briar grunts. "We're supposed to stay inside and off the radar."

"Yeah, well, Rene knows I don't listen."

Briar laughs and sits up. "Everyone knows you don't listen. Give me two minutes to splash water on my face. If you're going, I'm going with you."

"Sounds good." I glance down at myself and frown. "We're not dressed for a trendy club."

"Too bad we don't have a fashion stylist with a rack of clothes handy," Briar says as he rolls off the bed.

"What's this?" Kenzie rushes to the open door of the bedroom. "Does someone need my expertise?"

I chuckle. "Actually, yeah. We need to get hot and sassy for the Lion's Den, and we can't go home to raid our closets."

Tad chuckles. "Not true. I can. Tell me what ye need, and I'll pop back and round it up."

Kenzie grins. "Yes, just pop off to get stuff. Do you know how crazy that sounds?"

"Aye, weel, welcome to the fae world, lass. Where the impossible is made possible every damn day."

Tad cleans my jeans using a spell. My black lace bra works as my top, and with the addition of a black leather dog collar and wrist bracers, I'm sexy and edgy in a flash. Kenzie is in her glory, teasing my hair and vamping up my makeup. Once Briar and Tad take off their shirts and get guy linered, we're good to go.

Kenzie thinks being blue is too conspicuous and decides to stay home with Charlie. Zephyr is still recovering from his injuries, so he and Azland will stay and keep the girls company.

The deep *thrum* of bass greets us from across the street as we approach the old warehouse retrofitted into the super hip club. If I'm right, the only business a slug like Santa would have here is to obtain or sell his supply of Second Sight.

Briar grumbles as we approach the building. "Why do I feel like everyone I hated in high school is inside that club?"

"Because they are," I retort.

The Lion's Den is in what used to be an old fish factory. Decades ago, before any of us Gagne kids were born, poor women in Montréal would work in cramped conditions, cleaning and packaging fish to sell in the markets.

Now, it's Montréal's hottest rave. We get in line, surrounded by young Montréal citizens in neon gear. The girl next to us has dreadlocks with glowsticks woven through them, and the flashing in the corner of my eye might give me a seizure.

Man, I feel old.

When we finally get to the door, the bouncer—a short woman wearing aviator sunglasses and a headband with alien tentacles—looks us up and down. "Is this your first time at the Lion's Den?"

"Nah." Briar is effortlessly cool. "Our brother has played here a few times."

The bouncer tips her glasses down over her nose, getting a better look. "He's a musician?"

He nods.

"With what band?"

"I doubt you've heard of them. They mostly play invite-only underground pop-ups."

Her eyes widen. "Did he play in the Alexandria Tunnels last week?"

Briar waves that away. "Only sell-outs play the tunnels."

"Right, yeah. Anyway, welcome to The Lion's Den."

She waves us through the doors, and we step into a massive open space. Tall concrete walls with no windows work to block out the moonlight.

In The Lion's Den, it's always the dead of night.

Music pounds and bodies sway. Giant metal hoops hang from the ceiling with acrobatic dancers twisting in them. On the main floor, dancers pulse to the music.

At least a third of the people are sporting the glassy-eyed haze of feel-good drugs.

Tad looks at me and chuckles. "Why did we bother with Nakey Kid? This seems to be drug central."

He's not wrong.

"Now what?" Briar shouts over the pounding music.

"Now we figure out who's got the drugs," I reply. "Everyone

go mingle and make friends. See if anyone has Second Sight for sale."

Briar laughs. "Excuse me, Inspector, are you sending me out onto a dance floor to find drugs?"

"Find them, yes. Don't take them. Big difference."

Briar is still chuckling when he disappears into the mess that is the Lion's Den clientele.

When he's gone, I turn to Tad. "Why are you still here? Aren't you going to find the drugs?"

"I think if yer anythin' like Fiona, I'd better stick close. Mayhem seems to follow her, and it's lucky she has five people in her posse who can portal because that's the only reason she's still breathin'."

I wait a moment to see if he's kidding.

He's not.

Who am I to argue with his desire to keep me alive? "All righty then, let's see if we can find the owner."

We force a path through the crush of people until we get to the bar in the room's far corner. While we wait for our turn to speak to the bartender, I check in with Tad. He's frowning and staring at the floor.

"What's wrong?"

"My shoes are stickin' in some kind of muck. I'm hoping it's a spilled drink."

I glance down, but it's too dark to see anything. While I'm distracted, a drunk and handsy guy cops a feel of my ass. I sigh and elbow him in the ribs. "Not cool, dude. Wait for an invite for moves like that."

Tad shrugs. "Looks like neither of us will make it out of here unscathed."

Looks like it.

The bartender comes around and points at us. "You're up. What can I get you?"

"We're looking for the man in charge."

"Can't help you."

"Can't or won't?"

"Can't. Everyone here got an Internet interview and is mailed our shifts. We've never met any decision-makers, and as long as my money is in my account every other Friday, I don't care."

"Seriously?"

He nods. "It's a great gig. Steady work. Good pay. No boss breathing down my neck."

That's so not helpful.

"Is there anyone who's here all the time, maybe a regular who knows what goes on?"

"You can try Dandy."

"Sure. Where's he?"

The bartender points at one of the acrobatic dancers in the silver hoops.

"That's the guy we need to talk to?"

When the bartender shrugs and goes back to serving the next person, we push away from the bar and find a quiet corner to watch and wait.

After a while, one of the other twirling hoop dancers dismounts, climbs to a suspended platform, and another person in spandex and glitter takes their place.

I track where they exit and make my way over. "Hey, excuse me. Is this where people get on and off those hoops?"

"They're not open to the public," one of the dancers tells me from behind a privacy gate. "If you want to learn the art of tantric rhythmic acro-hooping and bodywork, come back on Thursday at ten in the morning."

"No, I only need to talk to someone."

"The talking circle is on Saturdays at seven-thirty."

I blink at Tad. "Is it me or is she annoying?"

The crowd parts and Briar tromps through the parting of the sea, looking sweaty and exasperated. "I found one girl who said she'd do Second Sight with us in the bathroom, but she had no idea where she got it."

"How could she not know where she got it?"

"I'm not even sure she had it. When she showed it to me, it was a baggie of jellybeans."

Perfect.

"What did you find out?" he asks.

"There's no official owner on site, but the guy dismounting that hoop is a fixture around here. We're waiting to talk to him."

"Ye think he's more than a regular, aye?" Tad asks.

"Sure do. What better way to keep an eye on your investment than to perch above the crowd and watch what happens every night?"

The song winds down, Dandy climbs the rope holding the hoop, then teeters on a rickety catwalk over to us before descending a poorly made ladder leaning against the wall.

"Nothing in here is up to code," Briar mutters.

I laugh. "I don't think proper construction practices are a major concern here."

The three of us wait until our man in royal blue harlequin tights ventures down to the main floor. When the server finishes handing him his drink, she hustles back through the privacy gate, and I'm ready and waiting.

I catch the gate before it latches and let myself inside. "Hey, Dandy, can I speak to you for a sec?"

As he stops and turns, I get a good look at him. Dandy is short and sinewy, with curly black hair and perfectly round glasses. He's wearing skintight pants and nothing on top except a heavy application of body glitter. "Do I know you?"

Tad flashes him a charming smile. "Not yet, sham, but we hope ye'll help us with somethin'. Any chance we could talk somewhere quieter? Maybe a little more private?"

Dandy takes a towel from one of the other dancers and pats

his face and shoulders dry. He eyes us up and down and starts back up the ladder. "Sure, you can join me in my office."

The three of us exchange a glance, but when it comes down to it, we've faced more dangerous things in the last twenty-four hours than an out-of-code ladder.

"Why bother?" Tad holds out his hand. He *poofs* us up to the narrow catwalk, and we're waiting when Dandy makes it to the intersection at the ceiling of the old fishery.

"Nice trick."

We follow him to a wide platform where he's created a yurt with walls of tie-dyed fabric and one giant woven rug.

Once we push through the fabric that makes up the door, it muffles the sound from the club enough that we can have a regular conversation.

"Welcome to my humble abode," Dandy says.

Inside the weird ceiling yurt, there's a pile of fluffy pillows scattered around the floor, plus blankets and the occasional stuffed animal.

Dandy flops down on a beanbag chair and reaches for a tall purple glass hookah, which he lights and puffs on. "Want some?"

"No, thanks." I wave the sickly sweet smoke away from my face.

"So, despite the cleavage, you're obviously a cop. What do you want and how do I get you to leave and not come back?"

Dandy is direct. I can get behind that. "I'm looking into who's supplying the city with Second Sight."

Dandy leans back on the beanbag and closes his eyes. "I don't like being investigated. Unless it's a sexy lady investigating what's in my pants, you know?"

Briar chuckles. Tad rolls his eyes.

"Yeah no, that's not happening."

"Then what's my incentive to talk to you?"

"How much do you make in a night?" Briar asks.

Dandy shrugs. "Cover charge is thirty bucks. Lots of folks in and out. It's the place to be."

Tad whistles. "Thirty bucks a person, and what… maybe a thousand people downstairs. That's thirty large without counting drinks and extracurriculars. Given that you'll get some turnover throughout the night, you must be pulling in fifty easy."

"Sounds about right." Dandy takes another long drag on the hookah.

Briar cracks his knuckles and smiles. "That's a lot of green to lose because the cop in the pretty bra won't go down on you. Think about it. You've got safety violations, iffy business practices, and drugs on the premises. Are you willing to risk having her shut the place down?"

"Go ahead and try it. I've got great lawyers. I'm not just a pretty face."

He's not a pretty face at all, but that's beside the point. "I think what my friend is getting at is that even if I only ticket you and call for the liquor board and the bylaws office to investigate, you'll be shut down for a week, maybe two."

Briar laughs. "You think too highly of the municipal machine. You're looking at three weeks minimum."

Tad whistles. "Three weeks downtime. That's over a million in lost revenue, all because you wouldn't give us a name."

"You don't have that kind of clout."

I laugh and pull out my phone. Calling up a number from my contacts, I hit send. The phone rings for a moment, and a woman answers. "Hello?"

"Hello, Madam Mayor, it's Inspector Jules Gagne. I'm sorry to call so late. I hope I'm not disturbing you."

"Hello, Jules. Not at all. I'm up most nights reading reports. What can I do for you?"

"I wanted to tell you how much I appreciate and support your initiatives and outreach. I'm working hard on the Second Sight investigation and truly believe getting the drug off our streets will be a turning point in the fae/human conflicts."

"Well, you have my full support. Whatever you need to get the job done, let me know. I'll make it happen."

"I appreciate that, Madam Mayor. Thank you, and hug Bella from me."

"I will. Good night, Jules."

When the call ends, I slide my phone back into my pocket and grin at Mr. Dandy. "Let's try this again. Where do you get the drugs?"

CHAPTER NINETEEN

Dandy might not be a looker, but he's smart enough to know when he's beaten. After a sigh and a dirty look, he sits up and shrugs. "I answer your questions, and you fuck off and leave me and my business alone?"

I nod. "As long as what you give me is good and I don't have to circle back."

He considers that for a moment before giving in. "The drugs I buy for my club come in a blue truck. The shipping company is named Julian Street Crates & Trucks."

I type that into my notes on my phone. "Is there anyone you deal with in particular?"

"Different driver every time."

"All right, we'll check it out." I pull my card from inside my phone case and let it flutter to him on the floor. "I'll try to stay out of your way. With any luck, this will be the last you see of me."

"Awesome."

Tad *poofs* us onto the sidewalk outside, then back to the safe house where we each grab a shirt as we regroup. Once my girls are properly covered, and the guys put their abs away, we're ready to resume police work.

I look up the location for Julian Street Crates & Trucks. It's out in Côte Saint-Luc, southwest of where we are. It's outside the tour route I took Tad on, so we call an Uber.

It's after eleven, and the streetlights glow gold against the night sky. Briar is too big for the back seat with two other people, but our driver, Daven, isn't open to anyone sitting in the front with him.

Tad and I get wedged in beside Briar, and I make a mental note to get UberXL next time.

The streets are pretty quiet.

The partiers are in the clubs but won't be out for a few hours. The non-partiers are in their homes and won't be out until morning.

Our driver maneuvers through the streets. Briar's stomach growls loud enough to have all eyes on him. "With everything that happened, we didn't eat. My body protests when I miss a meal."

True story.

"Well, the trucking company isn't likely to be open tonight anyway. Why don't we stop for poutine before dragging ourselves out to Côte Saint-Luc?"

"I can go for that."

Briar leans forward and directs our driver down a narrow alleyway and around a sharp corner until we reach a mom-and-pop poutine shop he's been to. We pay our driver and let him go on his way.

Inside the restaurant, doodles and drawings from locals who frequent it cover the walls, and there's a little old lady behind the scratched-up counter.

Tad is eyeing the menu board like he's been sucked into the *Twilight Zone*.

"Dude, what's the issue?"

"I'm not even sure what I'm looking at."

I snort. "That's French."

"I realize half the menu is in French. I'm looking at the English side. Do ye really put cheese and gravy on all those other foods?"

"Hells, yeah, we do," Briar confirms. "I'll have the large pulled pork poutine with a Coke."

"I'll have the standard." I add to the order. I check in with Tad, but he looks no closer to being ready. "He'll have the standard too."

"And to drink?"

"I'll have water."

"Same." Tad pulls out his debit card. "It's on me, guys."

I wave that away. "You paid for the club. I'll pay for the poutine."

Tad shrugs. "I don't mind."

"Neither do I. Fair's fair."

It doesn't take long before three red and white checkered cardboard boxes filled with fried potatoes topped with savory gravy and cheese curds are set on the tray.

Okay, now that I smell it, my stomach is growling too.

We sit at one of the shop's linoleum-topped tables, each armed with a white plastic fork. Briar sorts out who gets what and we dig in.

At least, Briar and I do.

"Do ye really eat this stuff?" Tad pokes his poutine, pushing it around his box and picking at the cheese curds. "It looks like a heart attack in a box."

"You've never tried poutine?" I ask.

"No."

"Well, it's great," Briar insists, shoveling it in. "They might not have it on the Emerald Isle, but you can get it now that you're in Montréal."

I chew the flavorful gravy bliss and unscrew the top of my water. "How long have you been in Toronto?"

"Five months or so."

"Ah, since the shit hit," Briar acknowledges.

"Yep. I figured that was as good a time as any to start again somewhere new."

After Bakkali's comment this afternoon, it sounds like getting away from being associated with his father was a good choice. "Do you live close to Sloan and Fi?"

He grins. "Across the road." There's a slight sadness in his expression. He pulls out a French fry and takes a tentative bite.

"Is it good?"

"It's made with potatoes. It has to be good."

"Right?"

Tad smiles. "We Irish like our spuds, but this is pretty grand."

We finish our midnight snack and call a second Uber.

Sure enough, Julian Street Crates & Trucks is closed when we get there. Fortunately, the interior of their office is a complete mess. With Briar hoisting me up, I can peek through the window and see all sorts of notebooks, receipt pads, and printouts scattered around.

"See anything good?"

"Hold on." I hold my phone up to the window and zoom in, trying to see if I can pick up the text on any of the papers. We end up with a handful of names and addresses pulled off envelopes and receipts.

I swipe through the images and slip my phone into my pocket. "No clue if any of this means anything, but it's more than we had before."

"I can get ye in there," Tad offers.

"Nah. I'd rather not be the cop caught on their security cameras breaking and entering. If nothing pans out, we'll come back tomorrow in a more official capacity."

A train rattles past, and the ground rumbles under our feet.

Côte Saint-Luc is next to the major railway connection for the entire Montréal area, which means that a shipping and trucking company located nearby makes a lot of sense.

"Do ye think they're bringin' the drugs in by rail?" Tad asks.

"It's possible. Let's head over to the tracks and see if we see anything out of the ordinary."

Once we approach the tracks, it's clear there's plenty out of the ordinary.

Two women run past us, waving their arms and searching the night sky. "Darlene, come down here. Where are you?"

They rush toward us, breathing heavily. "Have you seen a small brown bat flying like she's had one too many Manhattans?"

"A bat?" I repeat.

"There!" One of the women points at a streetlight.

Yep, a fuzzy brown bat flutters around in erratic circles and occasionally runs smack into the pole.

"Darlene, thank goodness. Get down here!"

The three of us follow. If nothing else, it's the most entertaining thing that's happened all night.

"Yer bat is drunk," Tad says.

"She doesn't know how to fly!" one of the women cries. "Yeah, she might be drunk too."

The bat is squeaking frantically. She lands on top of the streetlight, then flaps her wings and slips off. Instead of catching herself by flying again, she plummets toward the ground.

"Darlene!"

Tad catches the little bat in his cupped hands. "Hello, Darlene. I know yer likely out of sorts, but I need ye to try to calm yerself. Trust me. When I first started with transformations, I was a hot mess. The secret is reclaimin' a calm focus. Listen to my voice, close yer eyes, and picture yerself as yer human self here with yer friends."

While Tad does his bat whisperer routine, Briar and I try to keep the girls occupied so he can get Batgirl calm.

"Is she okay?" The girls are frantic, trying to get to Tad to check on their friend.

"She'll be fine," I assure them.

Tad crouches, sets the little bat on the grass, and speaks to her in a long run of soothing words warmed with his Irish accent.

After a few moments, a woman about my age appears naked on the grass. Tad backs away so her girls can get to her.

"Darlene! Here, we have your clothes."

The three of us give them a minute. Then they glom onto Tad, clinging to their new hero.

"Let me guess." Tad chuckles. "This was the first time ye went drinking since yer powers woke?"

The three of them nod sheepishly.

"Well, ye'll need some practice with yer transformation before ye bend yer elbow again. Practice up and learn how to fly before ye hit the pub next time, aye?"

"Uh-huh," Darlene agrees.

"Do ye know anyone else with transformative powers ye can learn from?"

Darlene shakes her head.

I offer her a supportive smile. "Tomorrow, go to one of the centers for the newly awakened. They'll help you learn about your transformation ability and can find you a mentor."

"Thanks. I will." Darlene frowns and looks around. "Where are we?"

"Near the dang railyard." Her friend laughs. "You flew all the way over here from Nathan Shuster Park!"

Darlene rubs her head. "That was freaky."

"It was. Now, let's go home."

Darlene and her friends might not want to be near the train tracks, but we hope the railyard might contain some information to help us in our quest.

We leave them to the night and step over the rails. There are a dozen metal train cars parked in the yard, so maybe we can find something.

Laughter, a crackling fire, and stumbling feet on pebbly gravel draw us to the drunken revelry in the railyard.

Half a dozen men hang out beside a bonfire in front of the rail cars.

Briar raises a hand and tries to look less huge and intimidating than he is. It doesn't work, but he tries. "Hey, dudes. We come in peace. What's up?"

"We're security watch," someone shouts.

I glance at the railroad company logos on their shirts. "You all work security for the trains?"

"Yeah."

"It takes a lot of legwork to cover a yard this big."

"Or it used to," slurs a guy raising a tall boy. "Now that Kenny got himself powers, he knows when someone's coming."

"Now we don't need to walk the yard."

Kenny, a blond guy with a beer belly and three-day scruff lumbers over. He taps the side of his head. "I sense people. Now we can party together instead of watching the tracks all night."

"You the man, Kenny!" All the gathered security guards raise their cups, bottles, and cans to cheer.

"Well, congrats on the powers, Kenny. If you sensed us, maybe you sensed we're curious and need to look around."

Kenny tips back his can and swallows. "Knock yourselves out. Just so long as you don't steal nothing." He taps his head again. "I'll know if you do."

"Deal."

Tad, Briar, and I leave the partying security guards and wander around the tracks.

"What are we looking for?" Briar asks.

"How about that?" Tad points at a rusted-out green cargo car with the name Fosters and Daly on the side. "Wasn't that one of the companies on the paperwork in the Julian Street office?"

"Sure was," I confirm.

Briar uses his stone arm strength to pull the door open, and we sneak a peek.

I conjure flames in my hands to light the interior.

Nothing.

"Well, that was a bust," Tad says.

"Maybe not." I climb the steel rail ladder on the car and swing inside. There are a couple of plastic baggies on the floor.

"You think we're on the right track?" Briar asks.

"I do. Now we need to figure out who's behind Fosters and Daly."

A quick search on my phone raises more questions.

Tad's tapping his thumbs over his keyboard too and shakes his head. "At first glance, I'd say it's a fake company. I'll know for sure once I can get onto my computer."

"So, it's a dead end," Briar grumbles.

I shrug. "Maybe not. Let's talk to Kenny."

When we get back to the security guard party, Kenny is lying face down on the gravel, performing a party trick where the other guys run and jump over him, and he guesses who it was.

"That was Shaddy!" Kenny yells into the dirt.

"Bullshit. He's listening to footsteps," someone objects.

"Nah, he's got real powers, man. Shaddy, you owe us all a drink."

I think they've had plenty of drinks, but not my circus, not my monkeys. "Hey, guys, can we ask a question or two?"

The crowd insists that first, I jump over Kenny.

I don't see the point since they're saying it out loud and Kenny can hear them, but I oblige.

When I finish, Kenny scrambles to his feet, looking at me with awe. "I sensed you, but not only you. There's something else going on. What are you?"

"I'm empowered. You probably picked up on that."

"Cool. What's your power?"

"I'll show you if you can help me with something."

"Sure thing."

"You say you sense anyone who comes into the railyard?"

Kenny nods.

"That Fosters and Daly cargo car over there. Did anyone come and get stuff out of it?"

"Yeah, earlier this afternoon. Two guys with a big blue truck."

"Was it from Julian Street Crates & Trucks?"

"Sure was."

"Can you tell me about them? What did you sense?"

Kenny stops to think for a second. His brow furrows, and he seems confused. "Sensing them was hard."

"Why was that?"

Kenny shrugs. "Just...hard to tell what was up with them."

"All right. How about another question? Which direction did they come from? And where did they go?"

Kenny's grin is wide and proud. "That one, I know for sure. They hung around for a while before their train arrived for them to pick up."

"Where were they hanging around?"

Kenny points. "Dive bar around the corner. Pistachios."

One of the other guys laughs. "It's called Pinocchio's, you drunk idiot."

"Thanks, boys. I appreciate all your help."

I'm about to turn to go when Kenny and all the other security guards shout and remind me I promised to show them my powers if they helped.

"Right, right. Sorry."

I see the small fire they're burning and decide to give these drunken fools something to talk about. Focusing on the power in my blood, I call my heat forward. With one shove out and up, I turn the fire into a massive column of flame. It stretches so high into the night sky it might touch the stars.

The men gasp.

Oops. As easily as the connection to our element comes, the control isn't there yet. I draw the fire back in, reestablishing the small campfire it was before.

"Whoa!"

"What are you, lady?"

"Do it again!"

Tad, Briar, and I leave the guards to their party, armed with more information than we had before.

"It's nice to see Kenny's mates celebrating his powers rather than shunning him for them," Tad says.

I snort. "I think it's mutually beneficial. Those boys like their jobs a lot more these days."

Briar laughs. "You know what they say. When you love your job, it isn't work at all."

I snort. "Because it isn't work. They're screwing around getting drunk."

"And gettin' paid," Tad adds. "It's a good gig."

"The best," Briar agrees.

CHAPTER TWENTY

As it turns out, neither of the drunk security dudes telling us about the bar was right. The dive bar around the corner is not Pistachios or Pinocchio's, but rather Parcheesi. Inside, the tables are painted to look like classic board games, but this doesn't seem like the kind of establishment where you could play a quiet chess game.

We work deeper into the crowd.

The dim lighting makes the neon sign over the bar glow bright with its warning. Snitches get stitches.

Classy.

Twangy old country music drawls over the crackly speakers. Everyone here looks like they've come off three back-to-back night shifts or a week-long bender.

Or both.

"Welcome, darlings." A raspy-voiced bartender with a blonde beehive hairdo beckons us over to the bar. "Anything I can whip up for y'all?"

"Three pints of Guinness," Briar answers.

"What are you doing?" I peg him with a look. "We're tracking people down, not out for a night."

"Gotta blend in." Briar slides the bartender some money across the counter.

Since there's no sense in blending in if the guys from the train only come in when they're offloading, I veto Briar's plan. "Could I ask you a question?"

The beehive bartender glances over as she draws our beer. "What's on your mind, hon?"

"We're trying to track down some guys who unload at the rail station. From what we know, they come here when there's a wait for the arrivals."

"We get a lot of guys like that. You'll have to be more specific."

"They empty the Fosters and Daly cargo car and load it into the blue Julian Street Crates truck."

"Oh, sure. The blue truck boys were in earlier today. They had quite a wait. Train delays are good for business around here. They come in every week or so for work, but sometimes, they stop back for a drink or two around midnight if their schedules allow."

"Do you know their names or where we might find them?"

"Nope. To me, they're the black guy who likes cider with lime and the silver-haired hottie who shoots whiskey straight up."

"Okay, thanks, that's helpful." Or it will be if tonight is one of the nights they stop back. Not great if we end up needing to stake this place out for the next week.

We take our beer to a tall table near the far wall. I stand with my back against the windows, scanning the crowd for anyone who might be able to give us answers.

No one pops out, but apparently, we've caught someone's eye. The bartender saunters over to us, carrying a bowl of salted peanuts and pretzels.

"Courtesy of the lady at the counter." she gestures at the bar.

A woman who looks closer to retirement age than ours with her graying hair pulled back in a ponytail waves at Briar.

"Not this again."

I choke. "You've been wooed by cougars before?"

"Women are becoming more and more emboldened. Yes, this happens."

"What's wrong with women seizing their power?"

Briar rolls his eyes. "Nothing. I just wish I wasn't so irresistible."

Tad laughs. "What a problem to have."

"It can be. She's likely been to a cage fight and has all kinds of pent-up, sexy ideas of what she wants to do to me. Trust me. It's not as fun as it sounds."

I laugh, finding all of this too amusing. "Don't worry, bro. I'll protect you."

"Yeah, sure. Thanks."

"Will ye go over and thank the lady fer the nibbles?" Tad pops a couple of salted peanuts into his mouth. "Do ye think the choice of snack is subtext? Do ye think she's commentin' on yer nuts?"

Briar grunts.

"Not only your nuts." I reach for the bowl. "There are pretzels too. Maybe she's a contortionist and wants to get acrobatic with you."

"Fuck off. You're both assholes."

"Och, gettin' salty are ye?"

"Like your nuts," I add.

Briar plucks a peanut from the bowl and throws it at my face. "You both suck."

Tad laughs and takes a few nuts and pretzels in his hand before he twists back to the window ledge behind our table. The window is open for airflow, and a couple of baby raccoons and a possum sit there watching us.

"Och, I hear ye, little ones." He opens his fingers, and they scramble for snacks, their greedy little paws gathering nuts and pretzels at high speed.

I love it.

"I wish I could call on cute woodland creatures. That's awesome."

One of the raccoons runs up Tad's hand and nestles in the crook of his arm. I reach over to pet it, and it makes a contented chittering noise. "There are a few perks to being a druid beyond the power. While ye'll likely not be able to communicate with animals, Briar here will someday."

Briar grins. "For reals?"

"I should think so. Yer element is earth. I expect yer tie to nature will come naturally."

I take a swig from my glass and force myself to swallow. I'm more of a cooler lover than a Guinness girl, but whatevs. "As much as I'm enjoying myself, we've veered so far off topic we might never get home."

"Good point."

We hang out a while longer, long enough to see Nut Lady pay her tab and leave with a disappointed and longing glance at Briar.

As the next hour wears on, various people filter in and out of the bar. Some come in already stumbling drunk. Others pop in for a quick beer.

Around twelve-thirty, a man with silver hair wanders in, walks to the bar, and orders a whiskey.

"There. Keep an eye on that one."

I'm not sure he's a skoro, but he's wearing dark sunglasses despite being inside, at night, in a dimly lit bar.

"I'm going to take a closer look," I declare.

Doing my best to suppress anything about my powers that might catch his attention, I walk past, pretending to be on my way to the washroom. As I go by, I draw a deep breath.

The telltale odor of burned cookies comes back at me.

Gotcha, dude.

I can't race back to my table right away, so I continue to the washroom, rinse my hands, and check myself in the mirror.

The surface is so scratched up with graffiti I can hardly see my reflection. I scan the numbers and offerings among the scribbled chaos, searching for a code or number used to access Second Sight.

No such luck.

I check that the silver-haired heartthrob is still sitting in the same place when I come out of the ladies' room and give the man a wide berth as I return to my table.

"Well?"

"Burned cookies."

"What's our play? Talk to him? Follow him? Take him down?" Briar seems ready to move, but I'm not sure that's the best call.

"The guy at the railyard and the bartender said there are usually two. Let's not do anything until we see if there's another one coming."

And so, we wait…

Nursing our beers…

Watching our man…

Twenty minutes later, a black man walks in and waves at Mr. Silver Fox's table. The first guy stands, and the two head for the door.

"Follow them."

We slink out the front door, careful to stay in the shadows as we tail them. They don't seem aware of us and are quick to get into a truck and start the engine.

"What do we do now?" Briar asks.

There's no way a cab or an Uber will get here within five minutes. By then, our guys will be gone.

"I've got this. Head over to that old Chevy Nova." Tad *poofs* out, and when we jog to the blue muscle car, he's inside and leaning with his hands under the steering column.

The engine rumbles to life with a beefy roar, and he sits up and waves for us to get in.

Briar holds the door open and pops the seat forward.

"Breaking and entering." Briar chuckles. "Nice."

Tad shrugs. "Nothing's broken. I only entered."

"Even so, we can't steal a car," I say.

"Aye, that's where yer wrong, lass. Different rules."

"Dude, I'm a cop."

"How many bad guys have ye killed this week that ye haven't notified yer bosses about?"

He has a point.

"Either get in, or yer lead to the drugs disappears into the night."

Dammit. I watch the red glow of taillights grow more distant by the moment as my two lives war inside me.

My elemental needs win out. I growl and dive into the back seat. Briar gets in, and we're off.

"How'd you know how to hotwire a car?" I ask.

"Misspent youth, tryin' to get noticed."

"Leave your headlights off."

"Not my first rodeo, sparky."

I chuckle, sitting forward in the back seat to keep an eye on the skoro's truck. We follow them down Chemin Mackle until they turn onto Blossom Avenue, which skirts the Meadowbrook Golf Club.

It's late, and the golf club is closed.

Without lights on the paths or the clubhouse, the course is a giant dark spot in an otherwise well-lit city.

"Where are they going?" Briar asks as the truck pulls into the private drive.

"No clue. There's a side road past the third tee. You can pull in there and park. We'll be able to double back quickly enough."

Tad takes my advice, and we ditch the stolen car.

We get out and start a foot pursuit. Something about this isn't sitting right. I haven't been cold once since my powers unlocked, yet I shiver.

"Are we doing this?" Briar waits for me to lead the way.

I nod. "Yep. On me."

We double back to where the guys in the truck would've come in and see them disappearing down a pathway that runs deeper into the golf course.

It's almost pitch black, the only light in the night sky coming from a few industrious rays of moonlight escaping the dense cloud cover.

The wet and spongy grass under my feet swallows the sound of footsteps—ours and theirs.

Why did they come here?

A blinding light flares out of nowhere and I raise my hand to shield my vision. It's the headlights on one of the big gardening trucks, and it's barreling at us.

"Move!" Tad shoves us out of the truck's path.

I stagger and tumble, rolling to my feet before it swerves and takes another run at us.

"Come here to me!" Tad holds out his hands, and we grab them.

Only we don't go anywhere.

There's no magical sensation in my stomach.

There's no relocation to safety.

"What's happening?" I shout.

Tad yanks us out of the way of the truck and shoves us toward the rough. The truck is faster than us, but it can't dodge trees. We make it through the treed area and across a sand trap into the next fairway.

"My powers are blocked," Tad says. "There's something about the grass here. It's been magically altered."

I try to call fire to my palm, but nothing happens. "Did they lead us here?"

"If they did, it was because we can't defend ourselves and they knew they'd have an advantage."

"Fucking assholes," Briar snaps.

"Keep running."

We race across the golf course, heading toward the side road where we parked. If we can return to city streets and use Tad's portaling ability, maybe we can get out of here.

The muscles in my legs are burning by the time we're near asphalt again.

The moment we get to the side of the road a golf cart comes out of nowhere and crashes into us. Thrown back by the collision's force, the last thing I hear is Briar cursing.

Then everything goes black.

"Jules? Jules! You gotta wake up."

I blink at Briar and try to focus. He's leaning over me with his brow furrowed, and his grip on my shoulders is bruisingly tight.

He helps me sit up.

I'm lying on the white, tiled floor of a small room that is bare except for a rickety shelf against one wall. Overhead, the fluorescent lights flicker between grungy water-stained ceiling tiles.

"What happened? Where are we?"

"Not sure." Briar has a gash on his forehead and a rip in his grass-stained shirt. Otherwise, he looks okay.

"Where's Tad?"

Briar looks pained. "He wasn't with us when I woke up."

I haul myself to my feet, but the world does a tipsy-to, and Briar has to catch me before I faceplant.

"Easy. You've got one helluva goose egg on the back of your head."

I groan, my body aching all over. "I feel like I got hit by a truck."

"Which is pretty accurate although thankfully it was only a large electric golf cart."

"Man, I could use some of Kenzie's magical healing right about now."

"You and me both."

I try to get vertical again, and this time I manage to stay upright. *Yay me.*

"What the fuck happened?"

"I know as much as you do. Bad guys ran us down. Now we're here."

"We've got to get out of here and find Tad."

"We don't even know if he's here. He might've been left behind on the golf course or portaled away before we were taken."

I shake my head and regret it when my brains slosh around in my skull. "He wouldn't have done that. He wouldn't leave us."

"Maybe the skoro only wanted us. They might not have noticed or bothered with him."

"Or maybe they took him too, and he's in trouble. I won't leave without making sure."

Briar sighs.

I know my brother. He's got a strong protective streak, and his priority will always be my safety. But I care about Tad—he's one of us now—and I won't leave him twisting in the wind.

We have a standoff stare-down, but I'm not giving in.

When he realizes that, he sighs. "You're a royal pain in the ass. You know that?"

"Yeah, well, my prince. You're the only royal here."

He chuckles. "Doesn't that mean I outrank you?"

"You wish." The two of us agree to disagree on that. "Either way, whether there's a rescue or an escape, the first step is getting out of this room."

Briar nods. "The door is locked and reinforced."

"Can you yank it off the hinges or pound it with your stone fists? Wait, can we access our powers now?"

Briar grips his fingers into a stone fist and grins. "Tad's theory about the grass being spelled seems legit. Now that we're inside, I'm back in business. Still, the sound of my stone fists will bring them running. I'm thinking stealth over strength."

Yeah. I agree. "What about the ceiling?"

Briar hoists me up on his shoulders so I can push one of the water-stained tiles aside. Moldy chunks of debris rain down on both of us, leaving us sputtering.

I wipe my face and shake out my hair. "Doesn't look promising. It's rotted and dank up there. I doubt the framing would hold my weight, let alone yours."

"What about the hinges?" Briar asks. "Maybe you can melt them, and I can pull the door free without the noise of a Hulk Smash."

"Would that make you the Kool-Aid Man?"

"Last time we trained, you compared me to Thor. I like that better."

I laugh. "Nope. Now you're the Kool-Aid Man. We need to harness the vibe of one of his epic wall breaks."

"I could go for a cold glass of something sweet. Fine, I'll be your Kool-Aid Man."

Awesome. I've never tried to melt metal before but how hard could it be?

It's harder than I think.

Focusing my power isn't as easy as I expect. After a while, I manage a small handheld bonfire.

"Not bad but try to focus it more like a welder's acetylene torch."

Yeah, no shit.

I shake out my muscles and stretch my neck. It takes time and fine-tuning, but after a while, I'm shooting a four-inch flame out of my index finger.

The metal hinge glows bright red, then orange, and softens. A few drops of melted hinge fall on the floor near our feet, releasing a terrible stench as it hits the linoleum tiles.

"One down, two to go."

"Yeah, now if we can get it done before the burning stench of old flooring brings them around, that would be great."

"You can do it," Briar says in his best Rob Schneider impersonation.

I laugh and get back to it.

When I get the next one melted, Briar presses both hands on the wooden panel. He closes his eyes and stone ripples over his skin. "I'm going to try to push it while the middle hinge is still attached. That way it won't crash and bring the enemy running."

"Good point. Look at us, firing on all cylinders."

We push but don't get far.

The part of the door jamb that stops it for the catch plate is in the way. "Maybe I can light it on fire."

"You want to set fire to a door we have to pass through?"

"How about a *little* fire?" I hold my fingers out to show him a measure.

He arches his brows. "Sure. Have at it. If it gets out of control, you can suck it back in, can't you?"

I have no idea. "Yeah, sure. I think so."

I run my touch along the door jamb and set my flames free to have their fun. "Damn, fire is sexy. Look how beautifully destructive it is."

"Said every pyro ever."

I stick out my tongue at him and listen to the wood crackle. At least this doesn't stink. This I like.

"Okay, rein it in before we set off fire alarms."

It's a shame to end the magic I'm making, but I suppose setting the entire place ablaze is counterintuitive. I call the fire back into myself and absorb the heat.

Amazeballs.

Together, we manage enough force to tip the door on the center hinge and crawl out to the hall through the space we make. It's tight for Briar's broad shoulders, but we get there.

"All right. Let's find Tad and get out of here." I glance out the crack to see up the hall.

"What's our plan to find him?"

"I say we keep a low profile, check out the lay of the land, and look for the exits. At the same time…we'll find Tad."

Briar's eyebrow raises. "Just like that, eh?"

"Yeah. It's called manifesting."

He follows me without another word. The hallway is brightly lit, with the same white floor tiles and fluorescent lights overhead as in the small room. There's a thick smell of scorched sugar in the air with a hint of mold and antiseptic.

"What is this place?" he asks.

"I think it's an old hospital." I gesture at a broken hospital bed that's leaning against one wall.

"Creepy. No wonder they shacked up here."

We make it to the metal double doors at the end of the hallway, and I ease to the side to peer out. Briar does the same on the other side.

"Oh, shit," Briar mutters.

As soon as I glimpse what he's looking at, I agree with that sentiment.

Through the double doors, we can see an open courtyard with balconies all around it. While we're alone in this abandoned hallway, the area on the other side of the doors is bustling with movement.

Skoro are everywhere.

In the center of the courtyard, there's a swirling vortex where it looks like a fountain or sculpture used to be.

It resembles a swirling black hole, except a dozen shades of red and purple mix and blend as it turns. Men enter and exit through the portal like it's nothing more than a doorway.

"What the fuck is this place?" Briar hisses.

"It's the freaking Central Station for hellborn."

CHAPTER TWENTY-ONE

The portal in the center of the courtyard swirls in violent black, red, and purple streaks. "That's how they're getting here. No wonder there are so many of these things all over Montréal."

"We have to destroy that thing," Briar declares.

Agreed. "No way we can do that now. We'll need Nikon. Fi said he's the only one they know of so far who can take portals down and seal rifts between realms."

Dammit. Until now, we thought it was a handful of troublemakers creeping around. We underestimated the force against us and the scope of the movement taking over Montréal's streets.

This mission has shifted gears to retreat and regroup. As worried as I am about Tad, if we can't find him on this side of the door…we have to leave.

Briar is watching me, and I nod. "Back the way we came. Let's hope there's an exit we can use to get the hell out of here."

I check the doors as we go, hoping to find Tad imprisoned in one of the rooms. They're all locked, and we don't have time for me to burn off all the hinges and doorknobs.

"This place is so creepy," Briar whispers as he tries the doors on his side of the hall.

We're back to the door we were held captive in when Tad pops out to join us.

"Jiminy Crickets." I gasp and pound my chest. "We need to put a bell around your neck. You scared the crap outta me, dude. Where'd you come from?"

He points at the wonky door and the crawl space at the bottom. "I woke up in the ditch out there, asked the local wildlife where ye were taken, and followed the stench of Pyro Jules until I found yer room."

"Can you portal us out of here?" Briar asks. "We've got our elemental power back."

"No. I have my druid powers but can't teleport. They must be messin' with portal energy and blockin' it somehow. I can, however, show ye the window I climbed through to break in."

"Good enough."

After a few aborted attempts to hitchhike, we manage to hail a cab and make it back to the safe house. Everyone is wound up but accounted for.

"What happened?" Zephyr asks.

"Where were you?" Kenzie snaps.

"Are you okay?" Charlie demands.

After a frantic round of hugs, the three of us flop down on the sofa and the recliner. "We'll live," I assure them.

"Briar, your head's bleeding." Kenzie rushes over to examine the gash.

"Yeah. We got run over." Briar answers matter-of-factly. "Charlie, we're dying of thirst. Any chance there's beer in the fridge?"

"No, but there's water in the taps. That's better for you anyway."

Kenzie is scowling. "Go back to the part where you got run over. Run over by what?"

"A truck," Briar says.

"A golf cart," I correct.

"A big golf cart," he argues.

"Yeah, it was bigger than normal."

"I couldn't portal ye out of the way. I'm so sorry," Tad says.

I wave away the apology. "Not your fault. All's well that ends well."

"I hate these fuckers," Tad grumbles. "They shouldn't have been able to take over that entire golf course, and they shouldn't be able to mess with my abilities."

"The Six are very, very strong," Azland reminds us. "They can do astonishing and terrifying things."

"Like consume entire kingdoms of elementals," I agree.

Azland nods. "Start from the beginning and tell us what happened."

So, I do.

Over the next half-hour, we tell them about the Lion's Den and tracking down the trail of Second Sight. How that led us to the railyard, Darlene the Bat, Kenny the Extrasensory Security Guard, and our evening at a dive bar called Parcheesi.

"From there we followed the two guys we suspected of offloading the cargo of the rail car. That took us to the Meadowbrook Golf Club," I report.

"Somehow, they've treated the grass to block empowered abilities. It was a trap."

"Did they know you were following them?" Kenzie asks me.

"I didn't think so, but…maybe."

"Then they know you're onto them," Azland declares.

"That doesn't matter. I don't give up chasing bad guys once the bad guys start fighting back."

Azland insists, "It does matter because it makes them more dangerous."

"Even more reason to keep after them," Zephyr interjects.

"Where did they take you after they ran you over?" Charlie asks.

"To an abandoned hospital." I describe the room we woke up in and how we worked together to break out and look for Tad.

"I don't want ye doin' that again," Tad states. "I can *poof*, fight, or magic my way out of almost any situation. Yer too important to risk yer lives for mine."

Briar looks smug, but I'm not having any of it.

"Don't be stupid. That's not how we do things. The Gagnes are gatherers, and you're one of us. No man gets left behind."

It's clear that Tad isn't thrilled about that, but he also realizes it's pointless to argue.

"What did you find at the old hospital?" Charlie asks.

I tell them about the huge portal in the hospital's old courtyard. "Fifty men were coming and going...maybe more. The place was crawling with them."

"That's the source, then," Azland muses. "The rift between realms where they're coming through."

"We need to shut the whole thing down," I say.

Tad nods. "I'll call the Greek. He can close the rift."

"That won't be necessary." Azland sniffs. "I'll do it."

Tad blinks at him. "Forgive me, but I haven't known many folks who can take on a magical workload that massive."

"You haven't known many folks like me," Azland snaps. "I'm one of the last living citizens of the fifth element of Draíocht."

Tad's eyebrows go up. "The lost magic kingdom?"

Azland nods. "I've seen exactly what happens when the Poreskoro family gets their filthy hands on the entirety of a fae kingdom's power."

"I didn't know anyone survived."

"Few do. As a Draíochtian, I have skills with spatial and portal magic."

Tad shrugs. "Even in this form?"

"Indeed. I may have been forced into this form, but despite the packaging, I am still me."

"Without opposable thumbs," Zephyr adds.

I hold up my hand. "So many questions. First, what is the fifth element? Earth, water, air, fire, and..."

"It has different interpretations: spirit, space, essence. It is that which cannot be truly contained or restrained."

I guess I can get behind that. "Next question. You said *forced* into this form. What does that mean? What happened? Who made you into a dog? Are you cursed?"

"Not cursed. Your mother initiated the spell to transform me, but it was in my best interest. When I first came to Montréal, I felt your energy trying to emerge. I approached Laurette for help, and she agreed."

"Wait a minute, you came to Montréal, and *Maman* made you into a dog?"

"Not only her. One of The Six, Draven, was already here, searching for you four. Laurette had a gathering of Scaith Warriors here to help her cloak your powers again and fight them if necessary."

It still pisses me off that all this was hidden from us.

"The gathered warriors transformed me to hide my powers, and we all took on Draven."

My lungs tighten. "You were at the battle when they were killed?"

The sadness in his eyes is my answer. "Your mother was a brave and fearless warrior. She loved you four very much. She laid her life on the line with the others to take on Draven. She was a Scaith Warrior but more than that, she was your mother."

"How did Papa get caught up in it?" Kenzie's ocean blue eyes are glassy. "He wasn't a Scaith Warrior. He wasn't even empowered. Why did we lose them both?"

"You shouldn't have...but your father wouldn't listen. Your

mother told him to stay with you kids and if she didn't come back, to protect you and raise you as they planned."

Briar curses. "Yeah no, Papa was a hero himself. He would never have let *Maman* go off and fight to the death without being at her side."

Charlie speaks up. "That's when they brought me into it. They told me everything, and I swore I'd watch over you guys until they came back."

"But they never came back." Emotion is thick in Kenzie's voice, and I can't look at her, or I'll cry too.

I swallow. "What about the other Scaith Warriors? Did any of them survive?"

Azland nods. "A couple. Many people sacrificed their lives to keep the five of us alive. I try to honor that by watching over you and keeping you safe."

Well, that explains a lot.

"What about Draven?" Briar asks. "Tell me that it was worth it. Tell me they at least took the guy down."

Azland nods. "They did. The Six became five, and the realms became a safer place."

"Then came the cover-up," Kenzie prompts.

"Yes. The local empowered guild destroyed all evidence of fae battle, and we prayed the remaining siblings of The Six would never find out who killed their brother."

Mind blown.

"Do you think that's why they're converging on Montréal after all these years?" Zephyr asks.

Tad shakes his head. "That's the fault of the awakenings. More fae power means more fae energy for them to consume. They'll be drawn to it like a horny moth to a back porch lightbulb."

"So, we close the portal," Briar says.

I'm not so sure that does us any good. "If they can conjure a portal wherever and whenever they want to, won't they make another one?"

Azland tilts his head side to side. "Yes, but they can't simply create a primary portal anywhere. If we shut down the primary portal's magic at the hospital, it might take them months to find a suitable spot with enough stability to create another."

"Aren't portals opening all over the city these days?" Kenzie asks.

"Those are portal rifts, not primary portals. Rifts are smaller, less stable, and won't feed the skoro energy."

Zephyr claps and stands. "Well then, what are we waiting for? Let's go shut this shit down."

Azland growls. "We can't rush this. Primary portals are the result of a great deal of very complex, powerful magic. It's important to ensure we get it right."

I sigh. "Well, we can't get it right if we don't do anything. We've got jobs and lives to get back to—I can't spend my life on the run from thirsty magic vampires wanting to suck me dry."

Azland shakes his head, and his velvety brown ears flick against his neck. "It won't be long, Juliette. Give me time to work out a few things and what kind of force we'll need to get the job done properly."

"Okay. For now, we'll leave it to you."

In the moments I struggled in the police academy, I found my strength within and persevered. When I was a teenager and heartbroken over not having a date for the prom, I went stag and had a blast. Now that I'm an empowered fire fae having to face down a race of hellborn thugs who want to drain me of my essence...

I guess I'll have to dig deep and trust I can handle it.

"The next step is to make sure you four are ready to face whichever Poreskoro we're dealing with and his or her minions," Azland says.

"Her?" Zephyr asks. "There are evil chicks out there trying to kill us too? That's strangely hot."

I peg him with a look. "No, it's not."

Azland flashes us a confused look. "Yes, two of the five remaining Poreskoro siblings are girls, Zissa and Sasobek. Why do you look so surprised?"

He shrugs. "In my mind's eye, I pictured them all like gruesome soul-sucking creatures from Hell."

"Their mother was a fae queen. They are all considered attractive. The youngest, Razgarath, is rumored to favor his mother in temperament and beauty."

"So, one of them might not want to eat us? That's refreshing."

Azland shrugs. "Oh, he likely does, but not with the same fervor and violence as his siblings."

I laugh harshly. "As far as pep talks go—this sucks."

Azland looks at me. "It's not my job to paint you rainbows. I'm preparing you for what's coming."

Zephyr waves that away. "Fine, tell us about the hot lady hell-born hybrid siblings so we know them if we see them coming at us."

"Zissa has long red hair, graceful antlers, and natural body armor plating her shoulders like an armadillo. Sasobek could almost wholly pass as human in her glamored form...other than the glowing yellow eyes that give her demon nature away."

"Sexy."

Azland rolls his eyes. "Sasobek is arguably the most dangerous of The Six. She takes after her father more than the others and revels in nothing as much as the suffering of her prey."

"Hard pass," Briar says.

My head is spinning. "Male or female, our goal is the same. We need to keep training together until it's the right time to attack."

"Where, though?" Briar asks. "We can't go back to the firehouse. Rene says it's still crawling with those stupid things. This apartment is way too small."

"We need somewhere remote," Azland declares. "Somewhere with plenty of space, where we can move around without being seen by humans or fae."

"Not easy to find a place like that here in the city," Kenzie says.

"What about the nature reserve we went to when we were kids?" Briar suggests. "The one with all the frogs?"

"What are you talking about?" I ask.

Kenzie brightens. "I remember. *Maman* and Papa took us on a camping trip, and we helped restore the native habitat for those endangered frogs."

Tad looks very interested in this proposition. "Endangered frogs?"

Zephyr groans. "That was the worst trip ever. Everyone was muddy and sweaty, and we hardly saw any frogs."

"That's because they were rare and endangered," Kenzie points out. "That's why we were there."

"Well, they weren't very grateful for all our work. It would've been nice if they came out to let us see them."

"I don't think that's how frogs work." Kenzie laughs.

"Where is this place?" Azland asks.

"Boisé du Tremblay," Charlie interjects. "It's not far. It borders Boucherville and Le Vieux Longueuil."

"We'll have enough privacy to train there?"

I nod. "Absolutely."

Zephyr complains again about how miserable our last trip there was, but no one listens. I call up the UberXL app and make arrangements, and off we go.

Boisé du Tremblay is gorgeous.

It's even nicer than when we were kids being dragged around and made to pull invasive weeds in the service of ungrateful amphibians.

We spend some time at the welcome center, and one of the park rangers gives us pamphlets about western chorus frogs and what flora and fauna make this such a biodiverse area.

Tad loves this.

He talks to the female ranger the whole time. His eyes light up as they chat about mosses and slugs and other things that must be fascinating if you're a druid.

"Wow, she's really sucked him in," Kenzie grouses.

I roll my eyes. "Nah. It's not her. It's the topic. His intrigue is all about you, sis."

"You think?"

"You don't?"

"I did, but he hasn't made any moves."

I chuckle and lift my fingers to tick off my points. "He's only known you for four days. He's here as an envoy for Fiona to keep us safe. You've got a lot on your plate learning about your true self and turning blue. You haven't had any alone time where the family didn't surround you.

"Also, Fi told me his world imploded right before the veil fell and he's hurting. I think him being a little reserved is perfectly reasonable."

Kenzie nods. "Since when did you get so smart about boys? You're usually the hot mess."

"Yeah, well, do as I say, not as I do."

Azland trots back from his jog through the trees to search for a place fit for us to train for the day. "Come on, kids. This way. The fun is over. It's time to get to it."

CHAPTER TWENTY-TWO

We wander down the wooded pathways, passing a few moms with strollers and kids on bicycles until we reach a more remote area. Off the main trail, there is a meadow hidden mostly by trees.

"Here," Azland states. "Tad, if you can put up a few privacy wards, we should have the place to ourselves. If you can keep the fire attacks and ice damage from affecting the environment, that would be helpful."

Briar chuckles. "Yes, let's not destroy the preserve."

"Kinda goes against the whole premise," Kenzie agrees.

"Don't worry. I won't let that happen." Tad strikes off and goes to work.

"Are you going to make more fake skoro things for us to fight?" Kenzie asks.

"Not this time. Today you'll fight Tad and me."

"What? As much as I like the idea of getting in a few licks on you, it doesn't seem wise to turn our uncontrolled powers against two guys we need on our side."

"Don't worry about us. You four need practice against powerful magical opponents, not conjurations."

"What if we hurt you?" Briar asks.

"You won't."

"Or maybe you're underestimating how much we'd like to get a few hits on you, dog spy, liar, bossy man." Zephyr's grin is evil.

Azland sighs. "Go ahead, bring on the hostility, and get it out of your systems. Once you're an actual threat to me, your elder and superior, you'll be on the path toward fighting The Six."

"The Five," my siblings and I chorus.

I grin. "They should adjust their name for clarity."

Azland shakes his head. "Then they'd have to admit that someone bested one of them. I doubt that's going to happen."

"Then we'll keep score and work on the Poreskoro countdown."

"Here's to getting down to zero." Zephyr holds up his can of soda.

"Yeah, here's to that." I hold up mine.

When Tad finishes setting up the spells to ward for privacy, he comes back to join us. We explain Azland's plan for us to fight them and Tad grins. "If you insist."

We take a moment to stretch and shake out our muscles, and I call my fire to the surface. Rushing at him, I prepare to release my first burst of flame.

Once I get close to him, he disappears and shows up on the opposite side of the meadow. I skid to a stop, almost crashing into a tree.

Rude. "Yeah, run away, blondie. Are you scairt?"

Tad laughs and raises his palms. The tree I nearly ran into shoots out a new branch and punches me in the back. I tumble to the ground, winded and aching, and it scoops me up and flings me into the air.

Briar rushes in, presses his hand against the tree, and the large oak falls still.

The arboreal attack ends, but I still feel like hurling.

Before I can sort myself, a tangle of vines wraps around my

ankles and pulls me off my feet. I avoid *Searing Skin*—to keep from ending up naked—and call flames only to my hands.

The tendrils of vine smoke, crumble, and peel away.

I scramble to my knees and try to distance myself from the nearest tree.

Kenzie is by my side almost immediately. Moisture from the ground rises into clear dew-like droplets that settle over my skin.

I can breathe again.

Kenzie helps me to my feet, but there's no time for a sister moment. Azland is there, and he's cloned himself, so there are three of him about to attack.

"Only one is real!" Zephyr shouts.

"Yeah, thanks, bro. Big help."

"Here, storm boy. Let's see what ye got today." Tad tosses Z his Storm Staff and my brother winces when he grips the wooden shaft.

"You're the master. It's your tool," Briar shouts.

Zephyr slams it to the ground, tilting it toward the clones. A small clap of thunder sounds and dead leaves and dust swirl up through the air.

The cyclone of detritus hits one of the Azlands and catches, dropping or blowing across him as you'd expect. With the other two, the bombardment makes his visage flicker and shimmer.

"That one!" Briar points at the real Azland, then raises his arm and forms it into a stone shield.

Azland throws a blast of power at him, but it does little more than knock him back a few steps.

Briar comes back hard and pelts the two fake Azlands with rocks until they dissolve and there's only one left.

"Well done," Azland praises. "I see skills and confidence you didn't have a few days ago. You're quick learners."

Briar chuckles. "Maybe after this, Jules can learn how to go on a date without scaring guys away."

"Rude. Maybe I'm doing everything right, and I'm not supposed to be with a guy who's easily intimidated."

Zephyr snorts. "Is that what you tell yourself?"

"It's kinder than thinking they leave as soon as they meet my family. Maybe it's not me. It's you."

Zephyr launches, and he and I start tussling. The two of us roll around on the ground, throwing friendly jabs at each other.

Kenzie and Briar cheer us on. Tad remains stoic while he watches.

Azland grumbles, "Can we get back to training?"

"Only if Jules agrees that I'm way more handsome than any guy she's ever dated!"

I pin Zephyr in a headlock and give him a vicious noogie. "*Maman* taught us not to lie."

Tad sits on the grass.

Zephyr and I roll around in our friendly wrestling match until a bunch of bugs swarm out of the earth and crawl on us.

"Augh, gross!" Zephyr jumps up and pats himself down, trying to get the bugs off.

"They're biting me!" I try to shoo them away, but there are too many. Tiny stings erupt over my skin. I light myself on fire, and they sizzle and drop away.

Zephyr zaps a bunch of them with his electricity, but there are so many.

"Kenzie!" I yell.

Fortunately, my sister already got the memo. She's cupping her hands in the air, letting the gemstone on her bracelet channel her powers.

A huge wall of water rushes over us and carries away all the bugs. It also soothes the itch and irritation of my skin.

"That was nasty, man," Zephyr complains, glaring at Tad. "Not cool."

Tad shrugs. "Ye battle with the army on hand."

"You think a cloud of insects is a fair fight?"

Azland growls. "The enemies we're facing will bring much more horrific minions. Get used to it."

"I'll never get used to that." Zephyr is shuddering and dancing around as if creepies are still crawling all over him.

"Dust yerself off, boys and girls," Tad chides. "We go again in two minutes."

I draw a deep breath and try to shake the feeling of my skin crawling. "Oh, goody."

Many hours later, Tad portals us back to the safe house apartment and we call Casse Croûte to order takeout. We let Tad do the ordering so no one recognizes our voices, and we instruct our Irishman to *poof* over, pick it up, and *poof* back.

If he's recognized as one of us, it won't do us any good if he walks across the street and leads any onlookers straight back to us.

I watch out the window as he goes in and a shiver of awareness brings my attention to the tall, dark, and dangerous guy in ripped jeans, steel-toed boots, and no shirt. "Seriously? Is he stalking me?"

Kenzie comes over to see what I'm looking at and grins. "Oh, it's the hostile hottie."

"Yeah. What's he doing here? Does that seem like too much of a coincidence to anyone else but me?"

Briar comes over to look down.

"He's getting lumber out of a truck and carrying it into that building. He's on the job. He did say he was quoting on a job up the street. I think this is zero percent about you and completely about him being a hard-working contractor."

Oh, right.

Why am I not relieved?

Tad's back in the next moment and Kenzie rushes off to help him unpack our order.

"What did I miss?" Tad asks.

"Jules is hot and bothered checking out a construction worker on the street, but she's pretending she's not. She knows him, and he blew her off the other day. If I know my sister, that's like an asshole mating call for her. Now her blood is heated, and she's steaming under the collar."

"I am *not*."

"Me thinks thou dost protest too much." Charlie hustles over to the window to look. "Yep. He's totally rocking your usual bad decision for a good night vibe."

I roll my eyes. "I don't have a vibe."

All four of my siblings bust up laughing.

"I *don't!*"

Kenzie sets the stack of plates on the table. "Tortured soul, stormy gazes, and misunderstood."

Charlie nods. "Add some leather, chains, and chin scruff, and you're pretty much a goner."

"Bonus points if he has long hair and wears silver rings and has piercings or tats," Zephyr adds.

"And lock him down if he can play guitar or owns a motorcycle," Briar finishes.

I glance around the room, and my attention falls on the dog. "Et Tu, Brute? Would you care to chime in?"

Azland shakes and his ears slap against his head. "I'm not touching this one with a ten-foot pole."

"Good doggie."

Zephyr whistles between his teeth. "Your boy looks good working in the sun, Jules. The way the sweat glistens over all those honed ridges…I'd be tempted to jump the guy, and I'm a straight shooter."

I grab my order from the food laid out and take a seat. "You're all assholes. I'm not even listening because you're so far off base you're in the outfield."

Kenzie giggles. "No way. We're in home run territory, and before long, you'll be sliding in for a grand slam."

I groan and stick my fork into my buttered chicken. "I can't hear you. All I know is this food is amazing, and yours is getting cold."

Thankfully, my siblings give it a rest, and everyone comes to the table to eat and get back to the problems at hand.

"How long until we make our move?"

Azland jumps up on one of the kitchen chairs, and Kenzie opens his takeout container and sets it under his chin. "Patience. Whether it's today, tomorrow, or the next day, our success will come from us being prepared, not from rushing in because we're being reactive."

I know this. It's the same as building a case before raiding and moving in for the arrest.

"I'm worried. That portal was massive, and tons of men were coming and going through it. The longer we take, the worse the problem gets in Montréal. Even if we take down the Poreskoro behind it, we'll still have a city overrun by beady-eyed, drug-pushing monsters."

"That's less of a problem than you think," Azland counters. "Remember how I explained The Six gained power by stealing and absorbing the elemental magic from fae and splitting off to create their armies?"

"Yeah."

"That connection works in reverse as well. If we take down the member of the Poreskoro family behind this, all the minions they've spawned will fall as well."

Tad grins. "So, we don't need to kill hundreds. We only need to take down one."

Briar grins. "I like those odds."

Azland lifts his mouth from inhaling his prime rib sandwich.

"Except that *one* will be harder to kill than everyone you've ever come up against rolled into one."

"And we'll have to get to him," Tad reminds us. "It'll be like findin' the needle in a haystack when all the pieces of hay want to kill you."

I swallow and set my fork down. "How do we figure out who the Poreskoro sibling is among a horde of skoro minions?"

Azland finishes his meal and sits up. "Each of the Poreskoro six has a unique weakness. While the creatures they make to serve them are basically interchangeable, the Poreskoro are individuals with differing magical backgrounds."

Zephyr dips a fry in barbeque sauce. "The one that's after us… what's their weakness?"

"Therein lies the rub. Without knowing which one of The Six we're up against, we have no way to prepare to take them down."

"It's five, not six, if that helps," Zephyr reminds Azland.

"It does, but not much."

"A mystery for Detective Toe Tag to solve, maybe." Kenzie crunches on her salad.

"Detective Toe Tag?" Tad repeats.

Briar chuckles. "It's her nickname because she's always hanging out around the morgue trying to solve cold cases."

"That's my job. No one calls you Briar the Builder or Concrete Man because you work in construction."

Briar chucks a fry at me. "Concrete Man? That's the best you could do?"

"How about Sir Never Been Nailed?" Zephyr suggests.

"Mister Loose Screw," Kenzie adds.

"Back to the weakness of the Poreskoro," Azland interrupts. "There's an ancient relic that is said to weaken Poreskoro. It's called the Shard of Osheron."

"Where do we find this shard?" Briar asks.

"Sloan might have some idea," Tad offers. "Mackenzie gets off researching enchanted objects of power."

"Where did this shard come from?" I ask.

Azland jumps down from the chair he's sitting on and moves to the couch. "Legend has it that when the Demon King and the Fae Queen first declared their union, they attempted to wed under fae custom."

"Attempted to?" I ask.

"The magic of the fae universe rejected the union, and the bonding ritual failed. It's said their wedding ring shattered and the largest piece, known as the Shard of Osheron, contains the power to take down their heirs."

Hot damn. "Where do we get this shard?"

"It was secured within the vault of the Fae Archives several centuries ago."

"Then giddy-up. Let's go get it."

Azland pegs me with a droll stare. "The Fae Archives isn't a library, Jules. We can't show up and ask to check it out."

"I'll contact Bakkali and see if he can help us. He's got clout and vowed to protect Montréal."

"What should *we* do?" Briar asks.

"Rest up. We have a battle to ready for."

CHAPTER TWENTY-THREE

Early the next morning, Tad portals me and Azland to the head office of the Guild of the Laurentians in the center of Boucherville National Park. I've been to this park hundreds of times and have difficulty believing I could've missed a huge tower rising from the island's center.

But sure enough, when we arrive, I'm staring at the white stone structure of a magical building.

Sunlight flashes off the silver veining, making me blink from the brilliance. When I focus on the structure again, the light glints in a different place.

The veins of bright silver aren't embedded in the stone. They're moving around, shifting constantly.

It's like the reflection of light across the top of a lake.

I take it all in, leaning back to study the glass dome at the top of the tower. A low parapet of the same white stone surrounds it.

"How long has this been here? Azland and I have jogged here at least once a week for the past eight years, and I swear I've never seen this here before."

"That's the beauty of a magical glamor." Tad smiles.

We walk up, and although there's no door, Tad touches the smooth white stone with one hand.

"Ye've got to touch it," he tells me. "The tower won't let anyone in if it's not sure who they are."

Tentatively, I lay my hand flat on the stone wall. Azland does the same with one of his front paws.

Something *creaks* and a door appears.

We step inside the dazzling interior, and I realize how much I still don't understand about the magical world.

The whole entrance is an open concept, so the sunlight from the glass dome at the top fills the space. Light also spills in through the silvery veins in the walls, which look like translucent crystals.

Around the tower's walls, a huge silver spiral staircase connects balconies. Each balcony has a railing of intricate and delicate silver bars that form geometric patterns and draw the eye through the space.

"Um, wow. Is this a building or a work of art?"

"It's both." Bakkali comes through one of the entrances. "What brings you to my doorstep, Juliette?"

Bakkali is dressed in deep blue robes with a silver belt with runes on long leather strands hanging off it. A raven perches on top of his shoulder like an ominous parrot.

"We need your help to get the Shard of Osheron."

Without a word, he walks past us and onto one of the staircases. We follow him up the first set of stairs, and somehow, we end up on the tower's highest floor.

The view is spectacular, but I'm not sure how we managed to skip all the floors in between.

"The existence of the Shard of Osheron is a well-guarded secret," Bakkali informs us as the bird preens his hair with its beak. "What makes you think I know where it is or can help you get it?"

Azland cuts to the chase. "It's in the vault of the Fae Archives."

I add, "You've been in power long enough to garner respect on all kinds of levels. If you back us, we have a better chance to get that shard."

He peers down his nose at me. "You've been an elemental for less than a week. What makes you think you are worthy to wield one of the fae realm's most coveted and powerful tools?"

"I don't know about worthy, but I'm committed to protecting my family and city from the evil currently invading it."

"Evil invasions? I realize you've been exposed to a lot in the past week, but let's not be dramatic, Ms. Gagne."

Dramatic? Seriously?

"Yesterday, my brother and I were taken prisoner by a skoro force and held in an abandoned hospital on the city's fringe. During our escape, we found a primary portal gate hemorrhaging hellborn into this realm. We need to shut that down and be prepared to take on whichever sibling of The Six is behind it."

Bakkali sighs. "Such a shame to see a quartet with such promise walk straight toward death without even learning their full capabilities."

"Death is less likely if we wield the Shard."

"It would've been even less likely if your quartet had remained hidden behind your glamors. Your mother assured me the Poreskoro siblings would never wreak havoc on my city because of you four."

"No one could've foreseen the fall of the veil," Azland says. "That broke the spells binding the children, and with Laurette gone, there was nothing we could do about it."

I'm standing beside Tad, taking in the view from the tower and listening to how it would be better if my siblings and I were still locked down and unaware.

What a steaming pile of horseshit.

All our lives, the four of us longed to know about our origins. Where we were born, who our parents were, and what separated us from those lives.

It was hardest on Zephyr.

We thought his volatility and frustration stemmed from his adoption and having no link to his past. We couldn't have imagined he had literal storms brewing inside him that demanded to be set free.

"People have been lying to us for more than twenty-five years." I glare at the two of them. "Maybe if we'd known the truth and had trained before now, we wouldn't be so woefully ill-prepared to take on our enemies. Maybe instead of standing in your glittering tower wishing we're still bound and left in the dark, you could help us."

Bakkali looks at me. "The Guild doesn't take sides. We are a neutral governing body."

"Neutral? Powerful hellborn creatures are coming to Montréal to suck the energy of the fae citizens and drug the humans to expose more of them. They're killing innocents and causing dissension in the streets. Standing idly by isn't neutral. It's allowing evil to take hold of Montréal."

Azland throws me a dirty look.

He told me to be quiet and let him handle this. He reminded me more than once that we need to approach Bakkali with respect and tact.

Whatevs. Sometimes the truth hurts.

Bakkali thinks for a moment and strikes off again. He moves so quickly that the raven on his shoulder teeters and flaps its wings to stay perched.

He takes us down to an interior balcony that dead-ends against a solid wall. There's an intricate inlaid pattern on the floor, and tiny chips of silver and gold coalesce to create symbols, runes, and astrological designs.

The broody Viking swipes his palm against the smooth stone wall and speaks in a foreign language I've never heard. The pattern on the floor bursts to life and stretches up the wall.

A glowing circle encompasses the entire balcony.

In the center of the floor, a golden door floats in the open air.

"I will send word ahead for an attendant to meet you at the Archives. Be prepared for your mettle to be tested. If we are to trust you with the Shard of Osheron, you will need to prove your strength."

Azland bows his head. "I would expect nothing less."

Bakkali turns and gestures for me to lead our way down the stairs.

"Wait. What? I'm not leaving. I'm going with Azland to claim the shard."

Bakkali looses a long, deep laugh. "No, child. You are not. As I reminded you moments ago. You've been empowered for mere days. There will be rigorous trials to win the right to wield the shard, and you will die. Your mentor, however, might survive."

"But I…"

"He's right." Azland cuts off my protest. "No one doubts your dedication or heart, but conviction will not win this battle. Stay here and protect your siblings until I get back. Whatever you do, don't start anything with the enemy. You're not ready."

I want to argue.

Everything in me screams to go with him and prove our worth in this fight.

Tad grips my arm and shakes his head. "This isn't the battle to draw yer line in the sand. Let Azland take this on. Yer needed here."

I think about all the incredible things he and Azland do in training without even trying. We haven't gotten to the point of challenging them yet.

Dammit. I hate being sidelined.

"Fine. Go be awesome and hurry back. We can't stay locked in a safe house for the rest of our lives."

"Patience, Juliette, please."

Yeah, well, patience isn't my best event.

With that, Azland the dog spy mentor leaps over the threshold of the floating door and disappears into the fae realm.

When the door closes, Bakkali claps his hands together and gestures for us to walk. "If that concludes your business here, allow me to escort you out."

The "Don't let the door hit your ass on the way out" is implied.

As we descend the spiral staircase running the entire height of the tower, it strikes me that I might have insulted the man.

Fi told me to make powerful allies, not adversaries.

"I apologize if I spoke out of turn. I realize you balance the lives and safety of a huge and powerful community and I understand the importance of ruling with impartiality."

He accepts my apology. "As much as I hesitate to get involved, I hope you succeed. I believe the new world evolving around us will be a better place if your elemental quint is part of it."

"Quint?"

He glances at me as if I'm missing something.

"Right. I suppose Azland makes up our fifth element."

Bakkali escorts us to the entrance far below the glass dome and stops to stand in the exact center of the space. "Good luck, Juliette. I wish you well in your efforts to survive against your pursuers and to make Montréal a safer and more unified city."

"Thanks. I'll get Second Sight off my streets if it's the last thing I do."

"The truth is…it might be."

Outside the Guild Tower, Tad and I wander the grounds of Boucherville National Park to release some tension. It feels weird to have come here with Azland and to leave without him. I tell myself he knows his way around the fae world, and he'll be back, hopefully with the magical artifact that can help us take down the Poreskoro sibling here in Montréal.

"Ugh, that guy gets on my nerves."

Tad glances at me sidelong. "Who, Bakkali?"

"Yeah. He's annoyed we found out who we are because it makes *his* life more difficult. Seriously? How about welcoming us into the new world we've been thrown into."

"Don't let him get to ye." Tad slings a heavy arm across my shoulders. "He'll come around when he sees how awesome the four of ye are."

"Don't get me wrong. I don't give two shits whether Bakkali or Azland approves of us. It sucks that we got thrown into the deep end of the pool and when we sputtered to the surface, people were there trying to kill us."

"I know how ye feel. When it happened to me, I didn't understand what the feck was goin' on and had no chance to get my bearings."

"What happened? If that's not too personal to ask."

Tad takes his arm off my shoulder and studies the inside of his palm as we walk. "My Da was an elder druid, rich, powerful, had the houses and the trophy wives and it was never enough. He got lured into the endless potential of dark magic and invited a powerful dark spirit to inhabit his body and mind."

"Shit. I'm so sorry."

He shrugs. "He murdered his wife. Then he tried to kill me when I wouldn't join him. If it weren't for Fi and her team, I'd be dead, and my corpse would be rottin' in the forest of our country estate."

That sucks. "I can't imagine dealing with that from inside my family."

Tad shakes his head. "That's the thing, though, see. Da was never really family. He sired me, but he never cared about me beyond bein' part of his legacy. It's Fi and the ones who came to back me up who matter to me. That's what family means."

"I totally get that. Family isn't defined by blood and birth. Family is the people who live and die to ensure you're okay in the darkest moments."

"Aye, that's it."

"Zephyr, Briar, Kenzie, Charlie, and yeah, I suppose Azland are family because two great people found us and pulled us together to keep us safe."

"Aye, and ye did the same thing with the twins."

"Yeah, I guess I did. We might be an unconventional group, but you're welcome to join our chaos. You're good people, Tad McNiff. We'd be lucky to have you."

"Aw…thanks, sparky. Yer not so bad yerself."

CHAPTER TWENTY-FOUR

When we've walked off our mood from our meeting with Bakkali, Tad portals me back to the safe house. Rene is there, and he's not thrilled that when he arrived, half of the people who were supposed to be here were AWOL.

I shrug and snag a glazed chocolate donut from the Timmies box. "Sorry, man. Like I told you. There's too much shit hitting the fans for us to stay stuck in this apartment."

He rolls his eyes. "You do understand the concept of protective custody, right?"

"I might have learned about it in the academy, yeah."

"We want to go back home," Kenzie interjects. "I miss sleeping in my bed, and I have clients depending on me and appointments to keep."

"I have a gig this weekend and need some practice with my new guitar," Zephyr adds.

"When the ASS told me to work from home for the week, I'm pretty sure the *'work'* part wasn't optional."

Briar snorts. "You call your boss an ass?"

"No, *the* ASS. Peter is a great guy and happens to be the Acting Staff Sergeant for my precinct—so ASS."

Rene looks at us and shrugs. "Okay, so what do you think about going back and reclaiming your turf? From what we've seen, half a dozen low-level assholes are monitoring your place, and nobody has been by your childhood home. Either they didn't connect the dots, or they're only interested in you four."

Charlie brightens. "That's great news. Then take me home because the twins will be back this afternoon and I need to get ready for four days' worth of camping laundry and soggy cooler food."

I nod. "Let us clear the firehouse first, and Tad can *poof* us over to your place to be sure no one's hiding in the closets. Then we'll get everyone back to their lives in progress."

Charlie grins. "That's the best news I've heard all week. Okay, you elemental fugitives, go give them Gagne hell."

Tad portals me, Briar, Kenzie, Zephyr, and Rene to the firehouse's back yard to reclaim our turf. Honestly, being on my back foot and retreating for two days has me more than ready to fight back.

When you add that we're fighting for our home and reclaiming our lives, the four of us are highly motivated.

Then there's my beloved motorcycle. What must she think, being abandoned for days on end?

A sickening thought occurs to me, and I almost combust from thinking about it. "You don't think they hurt Scarlett, do you?"

The look Briar and Zephyr flash me makes me ill.

"They die. All of them. Make them sorry they ever came after the Quebec Quartet."

Kenzie lifts her hands in front of her chest so she's stacking her palms. The jewel of her bracelet expands on command to create three big teardrops of water, which hover in the air around her.

"Here we go, boys and girls."

"Here we go." Briar runs into the back corner of the yard and levitates a pile of rocks from around the back trees. "Come out, come out, wherever you are."

My skin is buzzing with the heat of flames licking to the surface. "It's true, Azland told me not to start anything against the enemy, but in my defense, they started this—we're the ones finishing it.

"Yo, skoro assholes. Come out and play." I grin as the anticipation of the moment has me flaming up.

Zephyr is stretching his shoulders and twirling his Storm Staff through the air. The enchanted staff is throwing off sparks, and his long hair is getting frazzled and standing at odd angles. "I think they're scared."

I laugh. "Scared? Scared of baby elementals? We're noobs. If they're scared of us, they must be pathetic."

That does it.

The patio door opens, and three skoro rush out. At the same time, several more pour into the back yard from both sides of the building.

Briar whoops and shoots his stones, pegging them in the heads and torsos. His attack is funny to watch but doesn't kill them or deal the blows that will incapacitate them.

"Try again!" I yell to Briar, urging him on.

He sends another volley of rocks into the air, but this time, I raise my Glock and take advantage of their distraction. They can't defend on two fronts with both of us gunning for them.

Well, with me *gunning* and Briar *rocking* for them.

One by one they fall. As we push closer, I ensure they are not only down but also out. Funny thing about demon spawn, you can't trust them to die nicely.

When our foes fall still, I glance around to take stock.

Zephyr is getting along better with his staff. He's gripping the enchanted weapon with one hand while using his other hand to shoot small bolts of lightning at the creatures.

Wondering how our powers might combine gives me an idea. "Kenzie, can you make rain?"

I punch a thug that gets too close to me and dodge one of Zephyr's lightning bolts.

"Like actual rain?"

"Yeah, you know, water from the sky."

Kenzie grins. "I...uh, think so."

I spin when movement rustles behind me, but it's Tad and Rene getting their groove on.

Kenzie obliges, and heavy fat raindrops soon fall all over the yard.

Perfect. "Zephyr, use the water to electrify them."

Z looks confused for a second, then twirls his staff. He hasn't quite gotten the hang of the thing and ends up giving them more of a stroke than a lightning strike, but they still drop to the grass to be ended.

The charge in the air is unnerving, and Briar and I take a couple of steps back. Maybe combining power needs to be explored more before we jump into that.

It wouldn't do us any good to electrocute ourselves.

Rene has a modified gun with a badass silencer on it. He's jogging through the yard ending the skoro, and I've never been so thankful to have him at my side.

I'm scanning the aftermath when movement by the fence has me pointing. "Runner!"

Zephyr and I take off around the side of the house.

Zephyr slams the end of his staff into the grass and a lightning bolt cracks from the sky. The sound is deafening, and all the hair on my body stands on end.

The bolt splits the pink haze of the summer sky but doesn't hit the skoro. It strikes the power pole at the side of the road and brings the whole thing down in a blaze of spark and flame.

It takes out the mailboxes on the side of the road and narrowly misses our neighbor's car parked on the curb.

Shit on a stick.

The hilarious part is that the skoro making a run for it is crushed beneath the crashing transformer and fries on the spot. His screams die out quickly as he's pinned and fried extra crispy.

"At least you got your man," Rene observes and blinks.

"Yeah, there's that."

Zephyr makes a face at me. "My bad. Jules, can you call that in to the power company and get it fixed? *Annnd* maybe handle Canada Post too?"

I glance up and down the block and sigh at the outage we caused. "Yeah, Z, I'll take care of it."

Rene casts me a sympathetic smile. "Later. You two are with me. Let's clear the house and make sure there are no surprises inside."

Zephyr and I follow Rene inside the bay door. I try to see if Scarlett is okay, but we're in the middle of a power outage, so it's dark.

The three of us run up the stairs, listening for any uninvited guests. When we enter the open area of our living room and kitchen, I suck in a breath.

The place is trashed. *Fuck, I hate these assholes.*

Rene leads us through the kitchen, and we clear the scene room by room.

"Clear."

"Clear."

When we exit Kenzie's suite, we meet Tad, Briar, and Kenzie in the kitchen. They look as angry and crestfallen as I feel.

"They destroyed our home," Kenzie snarls.

Tad reaches over and places a hand on her back. "Aye, they did a number, but the good news is, yer all alive and well. Things can be repaired and replaced."

"I suppose that's true."

I'm still taking in the destructive force of our enemies when Rene's phone rings. He sheaths his gun and answers it while I shuffle through the carnage. When he hangs up, he sighs. "I've gotta run. My team has a situation, and I need to leave."

"Do you want backup?" I ask.

"No. It's fine. You've got enough going on. Tad, is there any chance you could drop me back at my car at the safe house?"

"Aye, not a problem."

I hold my knuckles up for a bump. "Thanks for all your help, man. Good luck with your situation."

"Same. Good luck with yours."

When they *poof* out, I continue to take in our trashed home. I'm about to go into my suite when Zephyr pulls out his phone and answers a call. "Hey, Cami. You're on speaker."

"Z, is Jules with you? I left her a couple of messages, but she's not getting back to me."

Tension is thick in her voice. I jog over. "Yeah, I'm here. What's up?"

"Hey, remember how I told you guys there was some dude at the bar asking about Zephyr the other day?"

"Yeah, the one rumored to be behind the Second Sight in the area."

"Yeah, well, he's back, and he wants to talk to you."

"Me?"

"Well, all of you. He says he's not leaving until you have a chat with him. He's locked our doors and is holding everyone prisoner until you come."

"Shit. I'm sorry, Cami. We never meant for our drama to spill over on you or the bar."

"Not your fault. Like I told you before, he's sketchy."

She doesn't know the half of it.

"Okay, Cami, hang tight. Tell him we're on our way."

CHAPTER TWENTY-FIVE

Tad transports the four of us into the alley beside Casse Croûte in the blink of the next heartbeat. "I'll portal inside and try to get a view of what's going on. If you need me, shout. If not, make sure to watch yer backs and stick together."

"Awesome. Thanks." I draw a deep breath and get ready to face the enemy. "Here goes everything."

Briar takes the lead, Kenzie and I follow, and Zephyr covers our six. Heads high and shoulders back, the four of us walk to the front doors and knock.

A customer unlocks the door, and when we enter, he books it outside and down the street. One less hostage.

I spot Sir Creepsalot right away.

He's sitting at the bar, stocky, muscled, and wearing sunglasses as he twirls his bottle cap on the counter.

I stretch my neck as we approach and focus on steadying my voice. "Cami says you want to talk to us? I'm Jules Gagne, and these are my siblings."

"I know who you are." The guy tilts his sunglasses down, giving us a good once-over. He looks me up and down, his beady black eyes trailing over my curves while he licks his lips.

He gives Kenzie the same leering examination until Briar steps in front of her, blocking his view.

Yep, he's a creeper.

He might be a low-life demon drug lord, but I know how to handle drug lords, and I'm getting practice handling demons.

Same scum, different package.

"We're here. What did you want to say?"

He tilts his head from side to side. "You've been nosing around in my business so much I figured I should offer you the opportunity to join my enterprise."

I roll my eyes. "Of all the careers I considered growing up, filthy drug runner never made the shortlist."

He chuckles. "You won't be *running* drugs. You'd *be* the drugs. Or, at least, your fae essence will."

I scoff. "Tempting, but that'll be a hard pass from me." I look at my siblings and smile. "Yep. It looks like a pass all the way around."

Creepy dude grins. "If only it were up to you."

"It *is* up to us," Briar says. "Four against one, dude. It's basic math. Wait, do they teach you math in Hell?"

He chuckles. "I'm from Pittsburgh, you racist asshole."

Pittsburgh? Huh, I did not see that coming.

Kenzie adds, "In any case, it's a no from us."

"Do you think you have a say, blue girl? Your essences will fuel a new ruling power. The four of you will be part of greatness."

I laugh. "Greatness? Your masters eat people. That makes them monsters, not great."

"What does your elemental magic do for you in this podunk human city? Help you rescue kittens and do party tricks? Maybe you fancy yourselves modern superheroes?"

Zephyr rolls his shoulders and the electricity in the air builds. "You made your pitch and got our answer. It's a pass from us."

"We like our lives," Kenzie says.

Creepy Dude is undaunted. "You four had a good run, being hidden, pretending to be humans, playing around in this realm. Now that we know who and where you are, it would be better for you and the innocent human citizens of this city who you care so much about if you came along without a fuss."

"Yeah, we won't be doing that," Briar snaps and crosses his arms.

"Not a chance," I agree. The four of us stand shoulder to shoulder, forming a united front against the threat this guy represents.

Which, despite his bravado, doesn't seem like much.

When we got the call, I wondered if he would be one of The Six.

I don't think so.

He doesn't look any different from the skoro we've been fighting all over the city. He's got tiny, black eyes and smells like burned cookies.

Sure, he's sketchy, but he doesn't ooze lethal power.

I'm willing to bet The Six are unmistakable.

The magical energy in the air shifts and I curse inwardly. *Jinxed us. Dammit.* A portal rift opens in the middle of the bar and if I could kick my ass, I would.

The rift takes hold, and the portal opens wider.

Nope. Creepy Dude isn't a Poreskoro sibling...but that guy is.

The man who steps through the rift is everything a nightmare is made of. He stands seven feet tall and wears a long black leather slicker. He's hauntingly handsome, and I suppose that comes from his mother being a fae queen. Tad mentioned that the high fae tend to be unearthly beautiful.

The man lowers his chin, and for a moment, he locks eyes with me. I see beyond his glamor.

He's more like ten feet tall with his head, back, and arms covered in green scales that peak at the center of his head and run the length of his spine.

Two long charcoal horns come off his temples and stretch a foot above each shoulder, and his hands are fingerless and have sharp, black lobster claws.

The glimpse behind the human glamor only lasts a moment, but it's enough to send icy shards into the core of my internal furnace.

As quickly as it appeared, the image is gone, and I look at an ebony-haired man with oddly lime green eyes. "If it isn't the Gagne children. How nice to finally meet you."

Beside me, Kenzie is holding her breath. Even the random skoro who called us to the bar doesn't have anything to say as his master joins us.

"Ah, so you are the four causing me so much trouble in the streets of Montréal."

The skoro pipes up. "No longer, Lord Lamech."

Lamech. If there's power in a name, I wish I knew what this man's weaknesses are. Too bad Azland isn't here. He might be able to tell us and help us get out of this clusterfuck.

"No longer," Lamech agrees, grinning a too-wide smile as he leers at us with his freaky green eyes. "Yes, they're here now, despite your incompetence."

Creepy Dude cowers at Lamech's insult and drops his gaze to the wood floor.

There's no way I'll cower like that. I don't care who this guy is or how powerful. I don't take a knee for anyone. "So, you're the asshole flooding the streets of Montréal with fae hate drugs and hellborn thugs."

"Guilty as charged, Inspector Gagne." Lamech holds his hands in front of himself as if I could cuff him. Then he chuckles and stands at ease. "You should be flattered by all the effort to find you."

"We're fucking charmed," Briar snaps.

Lamech chuckles. "Not quite the manners of a princeling but

honestly, I don't care how nice you are. Only how good you taste and how much power we can siphon."

He licks his lips, and I shiver.

"On that note, we'll take our leave. This promises to be an afternoon to remember. Let's not dally." He snaps his fingers and a dozen skoro stream through the portal rift to surround us.

Tad rushes in from the wings, but Lamech flicks his hand and pins him to the ceiling. *Shit. Not good.*

Kenzie gets grabbed up, and Zephyr and I struggle to free her. Briar scuffles and swings his stone fists. "Get your fucking hands off them."

Fear, protectiveness, and fury mix in my blood, and I burst into flame. A wall of fire erupts from me, but they're prepared for that.

They tackle me with a silver blanket that extinguishes my flames, cuts off my view of the room, and traps my arms at my sides.

I kick and struggle, but they lift me off my feet. I can't stop them from dragging me across the bar.

Muffled sounds come through the thick fiber of the blanket. Cami shrieks, and glass shatters.

Loud *thuds* precede cursing—that's Briar.

Crackling sounds make the hair on my arms stand on end—that's Zephyr.

I'm trying to blindly follow the battle when my stomach flips with a nauseating lurch. It's like what happens when Tad portals me but a thousand times stronger.

They've pulled us through Lamech's portal.

I close my eyes and will my stomach not to empty inside this blanket tomb I'm mummied in.

That would be a whole other level of gross.

Kenzie retches to my right and I curse her as my gag reflex takes hold. Zephyr is shouting like a lunatic, so I focus on that instead.

That helps. My brother is a passionate and colorful curser.

The skoro holding me loosens their grip, and I yank the blanket down far enough to look around and see where they've taken us.

Well, shit. We're standing in the courtyard of that abandoned hospital surrounded by skoro. Far up and in the corner is the glass door where Briar and I peeked through when we watched from a safe distance.

Now, we're smack in the center of the action.

There is plenty of action.

There must be two hundred skoro crowding in as we're herded toward the primary portal. Lamech's hellborn minions are pushing closer, craning their necks to look at us.

The clicking noises they emit are nearly deafening. It's like being inside a giant typewriter. Well, if every key on that typewriter is a hellspawn who wants to kill and consume my siblings and me.

I try to flame up, but I've got nothing. Is it the blanket or do they have a dampener? "Can any of you reach your powers?"

"Nope," Kenzie snaps, fighting against the hold of her captors to my right.

"Me either," Zephyr grumbles.

Briar is using his human fists and muscles to force his way closer. I scoot toward them, pressing close within the sea of skoro. "Anybody liking these odds?"

Zephyr chuffs. "We're outnumbered fifty to one, out of our league with a Poreskoro, have no backup, and no access to our powers. Does that cover it?"

"Meh, could be worse." Kenzie grunts.

"And I'm naked," I add.

"Oh, yeah, then we're fucked." Zephyr pulls his shirt off and forces his way closer.

The sea of skoro don't care about confining us now. We're truly surrounded, so they're giving us more room to maneuver.

Briar's chiseled jaw is clenched tight as he closes the distance and the four of us are reunited.

"What's the plan?" Zephyr hands me his shirt.

I take it, pull it over my head, and hope the skoro put out my flames fast enough that I won't melt through the fabric. "I'm going with don't die and kicking their asses."

Kenzie scoffs. "That's a concept, not a plan."

"Sorry. Okay, then I've got nothing."

Lamech chuckles as he stands a yard away from us, watching. "I admit, after the trouble you've caused my men, I expected more. This was too easy."

His confidence is annoying.

I try not to let that unnerve me. Being a cop, you learn it's always best to be the calmest person in the room. I draw a deep breath and try to stall until I devise a way out of this. "What are you planning?"

Lamech smiles. "To enjoy my victory."

"There's no victory yet. Isn't your goal to stick a straw in us and drink our essence like we're elemental juice boxes?"

"That's part of it, yes."

Briar growls, pulling us closer. "You won't be so cocky when we kick your freakishly tall ass and escape this rank demon den of yours."

Lamech laughs. "Oh, good. I hoped to see what all the fuss is about. Not that fighting the inevitable will do you any good. You've lost, big man. You're as good as consumed."

"Yet, we're not." I hold out my arms and think better of it as Zephyr's T-shirt rides up my thighs and threatens to expose my girl parts.

Dammit. I need a wardrobe that doesn't burn off.

His eyes grow brighter. "There's no rush. My siblings and I have searched the realms for your kind for decades. To feed on pureblood elementals is a delicacy. This won't be a quick suck. This is a meal to be shared and savored."

Oh shit. Not only is that completely disgusting, but it's not what I want to hear. The reason he hasn't killed us yet is that he's waiting for dinner guests?

Like we're not already crazy outnumbered.

"If you're anxious to get things started, we can reacquaint you with your fae heritage. Ready for a walk down memory lane?"

Lamech gives a hand signal, and the skoro close in.

The mob writhes in excitement and presses us closer to the portal's opening. We're caught in the wake of moving bodies that will force us through to where...

Are they taking us to Hell? To the fae kingdoms?

I don't want to find out.

Briar punches anyone who comes close enough for him to nail. He's trying to give us room to gain our freedom, but there are *sooo* many of them.

Given how outnumbered we are, I don't see how we can hold them off for long.

Still, we're the Gagne kids, and we don't go down without a fight. The same sense of determination burns hot in my siblings.

"We'll make it out of here or die trying," I say.

Zephyr grins. "I know which option I pick."

"Ditto," Kenzie says.

With every moment that passes, we're pushed and jostled closer toward the swirling vortex of power. I'm searching my bag of tricks, grasping for our moment.

If I only knew what our moment looked like, maybe I could find it.

Rough hands grab and grope. We fight against the bombardment—throwing fists, feet, and elbows—trying to hold our ground.

We're not winning the battle in any way. At most, we're not losing quickly.

Lamech watches us tussle with genuine amusement on his stupid face. He's not worried. As much as I'd like to say we'll be able to exploit his confidence and use his hubris to our advantage, we won't.

He's holding the winning hand.

It's not arrogance.

It's the knowledge that his creations will win, and we'll be transported through the portal for a fae feast no matter how much we fight.

Because he's a Poreskoro.

He and his siblings raised an army strong enough to overpower entire fae kingdoms and force the dying races to send their children into exile for protection.

The four of us are resilient, but we're not powerful.

We aren't winning. We're merely slowing our defeat.

And we can't do this forever.

I'm trying to come up with a Plan B, which at this point would be more like a Plan X or Plan Y when a blinding flash lights up the courtyard.

Blinking, I study the massive, mirrored disco ball twirling in the sky above the courtyard. It's round and silver but instead of reflecting light, it's throwing off energy rays.

Shock is replaced by screams as bolts of energy pierce the depths of the skoro sea all around us.

Pew. Pew. Pew.

Magical light lasers are shooting in every direction.

That's when the soulful chords of Gloria Gaynor ring out. *"At first I was afraid, I was petrified..."*

"What the hell?" I duck, raising my arms over my head as I search for my siblings.

Skoro scatter like cockroaches, crashing into one another, and panicking as the laser light ball cuts them down. More than incredibly disorienting, it's causing grievous bodily harm.

I can't make sense of the mess of bright lights and scrambling bodies...and what's with the '70s soundtrack?

Strong hands grab me, and I'm pulled through the storm of

chaos. A moment later, I'm standing in an archway at the end of the courtyard opposite the open portal. "Got ye, sparky. Wait here."

I turn, and Tad's gone.

Pushing up on my toes, I'm searching the craziness when Zephyr and Briar join me. Then Tad's back with Kenzie. "Rally to yer theme song, people. I will survive, hey, hey."

Zephyr snorts. "What's with the Saturday Night Fever routine?"

"It's called a diversion, sham," Tad advises with a twinkle in his eye. "Learned it from Fi's brother, Emmet. Of course, I gave it my twist. I added hellborn-seeking energy bolts."

I laugh. "Very cool. Thanks for the save."

"Enough chatter!" a scruffy hobo man shouts as he rushes forward. He presses a dagger into my hand and points at the portal. "I need to close that portal. You five take care of Lamech."

Hobo Man flashes off, and I blink. "Does anyone know who that was or what that was about?"

Tad grins. "Och, aye. That's Azland back from the fae realm on two legs instead of four." He points at the hilt of the dagger in my hand. "That shiny bit there is the enchanted Shard of Osheron weaponized."

A rush of heat warms my veins as my powers come back online. "Well, all righty, folks. Gagne for the win."

CHAPTER TWENTY-SIX

With the dagger in my hand and Azland addressing the portal, the tides have turned. Tad's laser disco ball is still picking off disoriented skoro, and they're racing mindlessly in every direction as we move in to end this.

"Stop them," Lamech orders. His arm is up, shielding him from incoming lasers. He's standing on the raised platform of the old courtyard fountain with his cloak billowing out behind him. "Stop hiding and fight."

His command affects some, but not all.

The skoro who stop scattering come at us again, regardless of Tad's lasers still firing and picking them off.

Now that I know Tad's disco ball is spelled to seek hellborn, I'm much calmer. Yeah, those bolts of energy aren't coming anywhere near us.

I'm not sure if Azland got our powers back online or if the skoro jamming device got damaged in the chaos of Tad's laser light show. Whatever the reason, I don't care.

I have my flames back.

As we advance on Lamech, Zephyr sends hurricane-force winds, knocking the skoro out of our path. At the same time,

Kenzie's spray-hosing the horde of hellborn gathered under a concrete overhang to keep from getting shot by lasers.

The powerful outpouring of their powers might be out of control, but in this instance, it works in our favor.

Man, I wish my fire was more effective on hellborn.

"Briar, I feel an earthquake cave-in coming on." I tilt my head toward the cluster of attackers under that concrete porch.

My brother grins and drops to one knee, pressing his palm to the ground as he focuses on the overhang.

A tremor grows to a shimmy, which becomes a quake, and that side of the hospital wall cracks and crashes down on their heads.

Zephyr raises his hand, and sparks of lightning force Lamech's minions back and away from us.

I slice and dice through the skoro coming at us, getting a feel for the dagger's weight and balance, and reveling in how the shard's magic works on Lamech's raiders.

Briar grunts and I glance back to check on him.

Half a dozen skoro have overwhelmed him and are clawing and cutting him up.

Kenzie rushes over, grabs my hand, and thrusts her free hand into the air. "Briar, turn to stone!"

Although he's never hardened more than his lower arms and fists, he soon has his entire body encrusted in rough, gray rock.

Kenzie squeezes my hand. "Give me heat."

I release heat into her touch, and to my amazement, I don't burn her. Maybe it's her healing ability or us combining our powers doesn't affect each other, but seconds later we send streams of boiling water through the air, hosing down the skoro attacking what looks like a statue of our brother.

Unlike how they respond to my flames, they find scalding water unpleasant.

Briar's attackers sizzle and shriek, dropping off my brother.

They leave him free to shift back and start fighting again. "Not a fan of the scalding bath."

"Well, then don't get overrun," I shout.

"Fair enough." He grabs a chunk of discarded pipe from a rubble pile and starts bashing skoro skulls as if his life depends on it.

Which, considering our situation, it does.

Azland is chanting in some ancient tongue the hellborn seem to hate. They are agitated and recoiling, coming at us even harder than before.

Lamech straightens, raising his arms to the side as he shouts a counterspell. His breath comes at us in a foul-smelling, green cloud. I'm not sure if that's intentional or a byproduct of him losing his shit.

"Blow that back!" I tell Zephyr.

Zephyr has reclaimed his Storm Staff from wherever the skoro put it. He grips the weapon's middle with both hands and spins it end over end like a pinwheel in front of his body.

The whirling tornado of air he creates blows back the cloud and shrouds Lamech in the halitosis smog of his stanky breath.

"Amplify." Tad closes his eyes and throws his hand out toward Azland. Immediately, the incantation he's reciting comes at us louder and stronger.

Lamech roars and launches into the air, targeting our hobo mentor, previously known as our dog spy.

That's my cue.

I project Lamech's path, get moving, and intercept.

Lamech's neon green eyes go wide as I swipe the dagger and catch him across the back of his shoulder and arm. I get a split-second of satisfaction seeing black ichor ooze out of the wound before he spins. A look of sheer fury and confusion clouds his strange gaze.

Tad and my siblings are with me in the next second, and it's five-on-one. The odds wouldn't be enough on their own, but with the Shard of Osheron, I'm hopeful.

We tangle in a violent dance of hits given and received on both sides. The boys are working the offensive with Kenzie behind us, manipulating her three spheres of healing water.

Lamech is a fierce warrior, but so is Tad.

What Briar, Zephyr, and I lack in finesse and time-earned skill, we make up for in attitude and determination.

Once Azland finishes the spell to close the primary portal, he'll be here to bolster our offense.

Then Lamech's ass is grass.

The portal is closing, its edges darkening as the swirling vortex shrinks. It's resisting Azland's command, making a noise like a creaking door forced to close.

Many of the remaining skoro see the bridge to their world closing and leap through the shrinking portal.

Zephyr moves to block them, but Azland disagrees. "Let them go. Fewer for us to fight and they'll all die when their creator is no more."

Zephyr shifts tactics, using a cyclone of wind to force as many creatures as possible through the portal before it finally snaps closed.

Elation bubbles to life in my chest. "Nice work, hobo man. Big win for the good guys."

Azland is out of breath, his dark hair plastered to his forehead with sweat.

I refocus on my attack, knowing it'll take him a moment to catch his breath and move in for the grand finale of this battle.

"Let's finish this, boys." I push toward the finish line. "With the portal closed, Lamech Poreskoro has no way of escaping."

Tad is a freaking phenom. He's called roots from below, which are twining and wrapping around Lamech like a stranglevine on crack.

Briar and Zephyr have diverted their attention to holding off the last of the skoro force, which is rallying to save their master. I think they realize if the man who created them dies, they all do.

If that's not an incentive to defend someone, I don't know what is. They are a blitzkrieg force coming at us, hysterical and wild with mouths open, fangs bared, and claws out.

Briar calls massive chunks of smashed concrete from the downed wall and pulls them through the air. The blocks of stone crash into Lamech's minions, throwing their broken bodies sideways before being crushed.

Zephyr shouts, reeling back as a gnarly gash opens down his shoulder and gushes blood.

I reach over to slap my hand on it.

"Fuck!" Zephyr arches his back as I cauterize the wound while Kenzie jockeys closer to wash him with one of her healing orbs.

Azland scrabbles over the death-heaped cobblestone and grabs the dagger from my hand. He wields the weapon containing the Shard of Osheron with much more skill than I, and I'm thankful to have him take the lead. I don't care who deals the killing blow as long as this ends.

Azland might have been trapped in the form of a dog for the past twelve years, but it doesn't seem to have slowed his reflexes.

Attack after attack, he goes after Lamech with swift strikes and deadly focused accuracy.

Tad is making me dizzy, portaling in rapid-fire bursts to stay in Lamech's blind spot to strike. It's the most fast-paced, high-stakes game of tag I've ever seen.

"Jules, watch out." Briar takes me down and covers us with his shield as a maniac skoro goes for my throat.

"I've got him." Zephyr grunts, grapples my attacker, and thrusts him into the air. He encases him in a violent vortex of wind.

The skoro spins within the cyclone of debris, limbs flailing as he tumbles in the air. I'm not sure what velocity Z's storm power carries, but I'm going to go with a fuck ton.

While the twister moves across the courtyard picking up injured skoro and concrete debris, Briar hoists himself up and pulls me back to my feet.

I shake out my arms. My limbs feel like lead.

I've always considered myself in decent physical condition, but that's when I'm a cop in the human world coming up against human criminals.

Battling against empowered foes takes things to a whole other level of exhaustion.

How is Tad still going at it as hard as he is?

Fiona's words come back to haunt me.

"Training. Training. Training."

I scan the scene. There is only a handful of skoro left, the portal is closed, and Azland is making a bloody pincushion of Lamech.

It's only a matter of moments before this ends.

"What the fuck?" Zephyr says.

I glance over to see what has him freaked out and follow his line of sight to Lamech. "Holy hell."

The guy's eyes are getting their glow on as he discards his glamor and expands in height and width. His illusion of humanity has vanished. He's gone full green guy with horns.

"What the fuck is that?"

"He's hulking out," Briar says.

"He's busting out his true form," I correct.

Lamech—now a ten-foot-tall green and black beast of a thing—flexes his arms and bellows in a wild rage. The courtyard fills with a rancid stench and a green cloud of mist that makes us choke.

I close my eyes against the unbearable sting. It's like he can exhale mustard gas. It's so thick in the air that there's nothing to be done but cough and listen to my siblings hack around me.

"Gusting Gale," Tad shouts close by.

A wild wind picks up and siphons the green gas out of the

courtyard. I've collapsed onto all fours, coughing as my lungs and eyes continue to burn.

When it's over, Briar helps me to my feet, and we take in the scene. "Where is Lamech?"

"Gone." Tad's eyes are watering.

I scan the courtyard and curse. "How can he be gone? Where did he go?"

"I felt a rush of portal magic right after he gassed us."

"He ran away because he's a punk," Briar snaps.

Zephyr is still down on one knee trying to breathe.

"Kenzie, we need a little healing help over here." I scan the warzone, my heart sinking with every second that passes. "Kenzie? Where are you?"

Everyone straightens and focuses on our surroundings. As much as I hope to see our beautiful blue girl, she's not here.

"Shit," Briar says.

"Fuck," Zephyr agrees.

We scatter, checking every possible location in the courtyard, any spots she might have been taken down or taken shelter during the fight.

She's nowhere. Neither is Lamech.

I tamp down my panic, trying not to lose my mind. "Where did they go? Tad, you said portal magic. Did he take her to the fae realm?"

Azland and Tad shake their heads.

Azland cleans the dagger's blade on a fallen skoro's shirt. "No. He was injured and didn't have the power for a realm portal opening. He only transported her somewhere."

That's better, but not much.

"Still, if he took her, we don't have much time before he feeds on her elemental energy to power himself up to full strength again."

The heat of my firepower is coursing through my veins, and I worry I might burst into a wildfire if we don't get Kenzie back.

We have to find her.

Azland sheaths the knife and meets my gaze. "Breathe. We have more time than you might think. Between the two of us, we caused a lot of damage with the Shard of Osheron. Those injuries will prevent him from ingesting elemental power to fuel up his magic."

"For how long?"

"A few hours at most, but for that time, he'll be weak and forced to stay that way."

Good. Sucks to be him.

Once we're out of the abandoned hospital and can take deep breaths without the foul tang of Lamech's green smoke, Tad rolls his shoulders and offers to teleport us to Charlie's.

"Why Charlie's?" I ask.

"Didn't ye say that yer mother chipped ye all as kids and yer aunt has the trackin' device? That is our fastest way to find Kenzie."

"Oh, good one. Yes and no. Yes, we're chipped, but when we found out, we confiscated the tracking reader from Charlie and took it home with us."

"Och, that's fine. Back to the firehouse then?"

I check in with the others, and it seems unanimous. "Yep. Home, James." I take his hand, relieved to head home if only for a few minutes.

"Holy shit." Briar scowls at our community area when we materialize.

"Right. I forgot about this clusterfuck."

Our furniture is overturned...our sofa cushions are sliced... our fridge is dumped onto the kitchen floor...

The hair on my arms stands on end as Zephyr rushes to his corner of the living room and picks up the pieces of his brand-new Stratocaster electric guitar. "Motherfucking assholes! I saved for a year for this. I've got a gig this weekend."

"Och, sham, I'm sorry," Tad pats his shoulder. "She was a beauty."

"She was." He stands there, staring at the scattered debris of his precious guitar while Tad and Briar right the couch.

When they plunk it down, Briar scowls at the state of our home. "I have a bad feeling about the tracking reader. Where did you put it, Jules?"

"Kenzie said she hid it in her underwear drawer." I rush toward our sister's suite.

"Of course," Briar grumbles. "Because that's a perfectly logical place to hide the device that can track the four of us. Why not in your gun safe, Jules?"

I stop at the threshold of Kenzie's room and curse at the mess. It's crazy how destruction and disorder can scatter your mind and make even the simplest task impossible to focus on. "Kenzie will be soooo pissed."

Tad snaps me back to my task. "Aye, so let's bring her home so she can take in the destruction herself."

Right.

"What does the reader look like?"

"A bit like a pricing gun. Have you ever worked retail?"

"No, but I own a chain of ladies' dress shops."

"You do?"

"Among other things in my family holdin's."

That's a story for another day. Getting back on track, I scan the mess. Kenzie's dresser drawers have all been removed and smashed against the floor.

I search for the biggest pile of bras and panties and shuffle in that direction. When I get there, I drop to my knees and feel around in the stacks of broken bits and silky underthings.

"With any luck, they flung her drawers and didn't search the contents."

"Are ye generally a lucky bunch?" Tad joins me on the floor.

I think about that. Parents murdered. Adoptive parents dead. Life under siege. Home destroyed. "Not really, no."

I see it then. The black plastic case for the handheld reader for our tracking chips.

Crawling forward on all fours, I reach under the bed and retrieve the smashed bits of our surefire way to find my sister. "Fuckety-fuck."

"Aye. Agreed." Tad gets to his feet and extends a hand to help me up.

Briar and Zephyr are both in the doorway watching, and they curse and head back to our common area.

When Tad and I get there, I set the smashed reader on the kitchen counter and sigh. "Tad? Can you bring in the rubber garbage bin sitting at the side of the house, please?"

The druid is gone and back in a flash.

Grabbing the dustpan from the hall closet, I shovel what can't be saved and dump it into the bin. *Dammit.*

The bigger question is what *can* we save?

Briar grumbles and joins the cleanup efforts. He picks up our records, checks them one by one for scratches, and slides the ones we can salvage into their jackets. "With no tracking device, we're going retro. Where would Lamech take her?"

Azland grabs the big bag of dog kibble and drops it into the bin. "With his minions dead and knowing that we're hot on his heels, he'll go someplace where he can surround himself with whoever or whatever remains of his army."

I groan. "Great. More beady-eyed freaks."

"Where would that be?" Briar asks.

Tad grabs the broom from the hall closet and starts sweeping. "He probably had his best fighters at the hospital to guard the portal. He'll have lesser members of his force stationed around the city to safeguard his other interests."

"Which would be…" Zephyr prompts.

I toss a couple of broken dishes into the bin. "The drugs, for one. He'll have men manufacturing and distributing them. Likely the ones he thought best able to fit in with human society."

"So, we need to figure out where his Second Sight operation is based," Briar sums up.

I sigh. "We're back at square one. We've been trying to track down that info for days. We still don't have the goods to take the operation down."

"Now it's also the info we need to find Kenzie," Briar adds.

"How far did you get with your investigation, Jules?" Azland asks.

"Not far enough. We hoped following the men from the train car would lead somewhere, but that got us attacked."

"Then we hoped the meeting at the bar might give us some clues, but that got us attacked again," Briar continues.

"That seems to be a theme," Zephyr interjects.

I nod. "Yeah, an annoying one."

Azland nods. "All right. Let's start at the beginning."

CHAPTER TWENTY-SEVEN

The five of us try to ignore the mess to go over everything we know for sure and everything we suspect. Then we stand there and look at one another, hoping something clicks for one of us.

It doesn't.

My cop instincts are buzzing, and I need to clear my head. After a quick shower to remove the ichor of death from my skin, I slide into my shoulder harness, holster my gun, and pull on my leather jacket.

"Laters." I sweep through the kitchen and slide down the pole.

Thank fuck. Either the skoro who were stationed here were too stupid to figure out how to get into the bays, or they didn't realize how to truly break my spirit.

Either way, the garage and my motorcycle within it remain untouched.

"Where are you going?" Zephyr leans over the pole's opening to look down at me.

I grab my helmet and slide my feet into my boots. "To the station. I'm going to go over every piece of evidence we have on these assholes. I'll find them...and we'll take them down."

"You're not going alone," Azland declares and slides down to join me. His socked feet plant at the bottom of the pole, and—wowzers. Our dog—not a dog—is freshly shaven and wearing a pair of Zephyr's sweats and a plain black t-shirt.

Hoo-boy, it's quite an upgrade from his hobo persona from an hour ago. *Dayam*...Azland's got it going on. Dark shoulder-length hair, deep teal eyes, and a drool-worthy square jaw.

Hokey-doodle. My siblings are right. It's been too long since I've gotten laid because I'm staring at the man who was my dog like he's a tall drink of water.

Thankfully, he doesn't seem to notice. "Lamech is at large, and we don't need both of you girls missing. Take your brothers."

Okay, he's much less attractive when he opens his mouth. "I'm a cop. I can't take my brothers into the precinct to work on a case."

"Then you'll stay here. This is non-negotiable."

I want to tell him to fuck himself and his authoritative, autocratic attitude but something stops me.

He's the one who knows the most about everything we're up against, and he's likely the best chance we have at winning against The Six.

Dammit. "I liked you better as our dog."

He grins. "Be that as it may, it's your brothers or back upstairs."

I really could've used a fast motorcycle ride to clear my head. Still, when Zephyr, Briar, and Tad slide down the pole to join us, I know that window has closed.

We pile into Briar's crappy truck, and I lean toward the open window from the middle seat. "Tad, are you coming too?"

"Not this time, lass. I'll run down a few ideas of my own. I'll be close though. If ye need me, text me."

"Will do. Be safe."

"Aye, right back at ye."

The three of us zoom along in Briar's truck, and I realize how strange it is to be doing something as mundane as driving to work.

How crazy is it that a week could take me from that life to this one?

"Take a left here," I tell Briar when we get close.

"You're the boss." He hits his turn signal and makes the course correction.

"Pull in there. Parking is around back." I point at the entrance to the morgue.

"We're not going to the station?"

"As I told Azland. I'm a cop. I can't go to the precinct and work a case with my younger brothers tagging along. Also, I don't have time to tell the guys about everything that's happened."

The truth is, I'm hesitant to out myself at the precinct as part of the awakened and empowered citizenry.

Peter and Rene know, but while cops can be gossips, with something this big and the state of the world where awakenings are concerned, I'm quite sure my secret is safe.

Not that I don't believe in the guys...I do.

It's just...we've seen enough chaos caused by magic flooding into Montréal that some cops have developed a less-than-favorable bias against the fae.

Where would I start with the whole story?

Hi guys, I'm still your friend and colleague, but now I can light myself on fire and throw balls of flame. Also, I'm the descendant of a great fae kingdom, and super powerful fae/demon hybrids are chasing me down to suck my essence.

Oh, and did I mention those hybrids trying to find us are behind all the drugs and violence we've been battling for the past few months?

Nah. I'm better off checking in with my boy Luc.

The three of us sign in at the security desk, and I get my brothers set up with their visitor tags.

"Knock, knock." I push through the door and find him standing over a body at a stainless steel table.

Luc looks up and sets down his saw. "Hey, girlfriend. How's life as the human torch?"

"You know, death, demons, and drugs."

He pulls off his gloves and removes his visor and apron. Setting them over the end of the table, he goes over to the sink to wash up. "You brought your muscle with you?"

I grin. "Briar and Zephyr, this is Luc Leclerc. Luc, these are my baby brothers."

He dries his hands on the way over and extends a welcome. "It's nice to finally meet you and put faces to the names. Jules raves about you boys."

Zephyr waggles his brows. "As she should."

I laugh and point at his office, just off the lab. "Can we chat?"

"Sure, but ASS Trent said you're riding a desk, and I'm not to encourage you in any of your shenanigans."

"Shenanigans? Did he use that word?"

Luc laughs. "Yeah."

Rude. "Listen, man, I need to use your computer terminal for a while."

"No porn. I don't want to sit through another awkward conversation with HR."

I sit at the clunky desktop computer in the corner of his messy office space. "Don't worry. Nothing I look up will be as gross or seedy as your interests."

"No kink-shaming. It's magical when a giant tentacle monster falls in sweet, sweet love with a librarian."

"Your coworker is weird." Briar eyes him.

"Not any weirder than my family." I type in my credentials, clicking through to the folder of evidence about the Second Sight dealer and operation.

Please, please, please have something new.

I scroll down, scanning the points I recorded about interviewing Santa, finding the empty train car, the two guys we staked out at Parcheesi's...

There are photos I took of the blue Julian Street Crates & Trucks and the statement I took, slightly paraphrased, from Dandy at The Lion's Den.

"Come on, come on," I mutter. There has to be more here. It can't be a dead end.

I scroll down and find updated notes from Rene.

He checked out Julian Street Crates & Trucks and entered a schedule detailing their delivery routes.

He took another run at Santa and entered his notes about that too.

He also had two of his team track deliveries and shipments to the club.

"Bingo. Well done, Rene." I call up the task window, select all, and hit print.

"Holy shit, Jules," Luc sputters, pointing at the screen. "You can't print an entire investigation file. Admin is already riding my ass about how much ink I use."

"Maybe stop printing tentacle porn," Briar suggests.

"It's not the same without a hard copy in your hands," Luc grumbles.

Zephyr laughs. "You're seriously gross, dude."

"Got it." I grab the stack of papers, still warm from the printer. "Thanks, man."

"Good luck with your hard copies," Zephyr tells him. "Next time I visit, I want recommendations."

I roll my eyes. "Please don't ask my colleagues for porn recommendations."

"I got you, Jules' bro. I have some stuff that will open your world."

I wave that away. "Our world is too open at the moment. We need to close things. Thanks for your help."

Luc pouts at me. "You come, use me, and once you get what

you want, you leave? I feel dirty."

"I put money on the dresser."

"Okay, less dirty."

The three of us sign out, hop back into the truck, and get some Wendy's takeout on the way back to the fire station.

Zephyr breaks into the bag before we get home and passes out fries. "Okay, I take back everything I said about your bestie being a loser, dead guy doctor. He's cool."

I practically inhale the fries and stick straws into the lids of cups. "I told you. Luc's good people."

Briar drives us into the bay, and we hop out and hustle upstairs to eat. Who knew battling the spawn of evil would work up such an appetite?

"I can have Fi and her team out here in an instant," Tad is saying.

"We can handle this ourselves," Azland insists.

"There were six of us in that courtyard, and we still lost one of our own," Tad snaps.

"I suppose you think your Toronto team could've done better?"

"It's no comparison. Fi's lot has been kicking ass for two years, trainin' every day. They know how to fight as a unit and don't lose their people. Yer a week into their awakenings and up until today, ye were a dog. It's not a criticism. It's a fact. Kenzie deserves the strongest rescue force we can give her."

"I don't deny that. All I'm saying is there's no need to alert the entire network that Kenzie has been…misplaced."

Tad spits a long string of authentic Irish oaths, and even though I don't understand a bit of it, I can tell someone should be donating to the curse jar.

He meets my gaze as we walk in, and he looks abashed. His posture becomes less aggressive, and he softens his tone. "I really think we ought to get some help and ensure the safety of everyone involved."

"Thank you for being so passionate about our well-being. Let's see what I've come up with before we call in the cavalry."

I sit on the sofa, pat the torn cushion beside me, and invite Tad to sit. Knowing what I do about how his father betrayed him and how he values the family and friends he's made since…I understand his panic.

I share it.

He cares about us, he cares about Kenzie, and he wants to make sure he doesn't lose what we're building.

I won't let that happen.

Spreading out the printed sheets, I sort through them and try to piece together the puzzle.

The answer is here somewhere.

It has to be.

"What are we lookin' at?" Tad asks.

Briar and Zephyr sit on their knees on the carpet opposite us and join the brainstorming session.

"This is an interview statement from Santa. Rene retraced our steps and tried to fill in some of the gaps."

"Should Rene be here?" Briar asks. "He might be able to help."

"I called and left a message for him. I told him we were back and what we're dealing with. If he can come, I'm sure he will."

Zephyr nods. "So, what are these?"

"These are the delivery routes our drug dealer Santa gave up." I set that page on the top and fish for the next one. "These are the delivery routes Rene's team tracked by surveilling Julian Street Crates & Trucks. I hope if we cross-check them against the report from the stakeout, something might jump out at us."

"Well, we know this city better than most." Briar leans in to examine the routes. "If there's something here, we'll find it."

Agreed. "If we can pinpoint a central location where the shipments are coming from, we'll know where to start looking."

Tad *poofs* out and back with a city map and markers. "Here. This might help."

"Awesome, thanks."

One by one, Briar and Zephyr read off the locations on their lists, and Tad and I plot things on the map. At first, it seems random, but as we get further into it, patterns start to emerge.

"Everything seems to cluster around this area in the south of the city," I say.

"It's triangulated within these three freeways." Tad draws a line along the major thoroughfares, closing in a triangle area. "So, somewhere between the intersecting points of Côte de Liesse Expressway, Autoroute 13, and Autoroute 20."

"That's down where the St. Lawrence River bends inward, coming up toward Boucherville," Briar says.

I stare at the map. "It's a perfect spot for a drug manufacturing operation. The area is full of warehouses and factories, and it's close enough to the St. Lawrence that it would be teeming with magic."

"The river makes it easy to transport too," Zephyr points out. "There's a rail station here that could account for your shipments."

I press a finger against the railway tracks on the map and follow them along the river to where we saw the empty Fosters and Daly cargo car. "So, they manufacture here, ship it by freight car to the other side of the city, offload it into trucks, and distribute it to the bike messengers to sell."

Briar nods. "We figured it out. Now we need to find the building."

I hop up, groan as I see the horror show of my room, search through the rubble to find my laptop under the bed, feed Jack and Jack after rescuing their tank from its precarious perch, and hurry back out.

When I reclaim my seat, I fire things up and key in my police ID and password. Everyone crowds in, peering over my shoulder. "This is going to take a minute, boys. Talk among yourselves."

In truth, it doesn't take as long as I think.

"There." I point at a spot where a bunch of medical and pharmaceutical companies are based. I search the business directory for the company names in that area, and one sticks out. "This building was purchased four months ago by Poreskoro Industries."

Briar snorts. "Very discreet."

"Very creative," Zephyr snarks.

"Let's thank the stars Lamech is stupid enough or arrogant enough to put his name on the building."

"Everyone, get ready to leave," I call.

"We need backup." Tad looks at Briar. "And when I say backup...I mean more than yer friend Backup here."

"My name is Azland."

The boys chuckle, but our mentor fifth element fails to see the humor. *Whatevs, Tad's not wrong.*

"I get that yer confident we can get Kenzie back without anyone gettin' hurt, but Lamech already notified his siblin's he captured them. What if we show up and all five are there? They might've been able to heal him and be waitin' fer us to come."

Zephyr frowns. "I hadn't considered that but holy hell, that's a horrifying thought."

I nod. "We got our butts kicked against one sibling and his skoro minions. If five of them are there..."

Briar grunts. "Tad's right. We need help."

"Thank fuck...." Tad pulls out his phone and starts his text. "They left for San Francisco yesterday, but Nikon's with them. If they can be here, he'll bring them. Give me the warehouse address, and I'll post it in the WhatsApp chat."

"Isn't San Francisco currently missing?" Briar asks.

"Aye. They went to see if they can figure out where it went and get it back."

I highlight the address of the Poreskoro Industries building and turn my laptop so he can see it.

He hits Send, and the five of us rush to our corners to get

ready to leave. By the time I get to Briar's truck, the guys are there, and the bay door is open.

Tad's frowning at his phone.

"What's wrong?"

"My message isn't delivering. I tried to call them, and the call's not going through."

"Maybe it's something to do with San Francisco's issue," I say. "Maybe we shouldn't depend on Team Trouble to be able to help us."

Zephyr opens the door for me as Tad and Azland climb into the truck's bed. Then he opens the window at the back of the cab so we can still talk.

"What about Bakkali and his people?" Tad asks.

"No. He made it clear that while he wishes us luck, he's staying neutral."

"What about Rene's team?" Briar slides the shifter and drives us out of the bay. "Did you send him the address and an update?"

"I did. He's on his way."

"Good. He was telling us about the work they're doing to secure the empowered citizens of the city."

"Yeah, they're doing good work, but they're not necessarily empowered. They're cops who are passionate about the rights and safety of the fae emergent…like if they have a wife or a brother who has had an awakening. They're working on community programs and domestic support."

The look on Tad's face is making me nervous.

He hates the idea of us going into this undermanned. He's right. Kenzie deserves the strongest rescue force we can offer, and it won't do her any good if we get cut down in the process.

It's time to pull up my big girl panties.

Pulling out my phone, I sigh and open my directory. "Consider backup on the way."

"Aye? Who do ye have and what are their powers?"

I shake my head. "My guys don't have powers, but they have

training, skills, and heart." The line connects, and Marie Claire answers the phone. "Twenty-Third Precinct, how can I direct your call?"

I pull hard to fill my lungs and steady my nerves. Outing myself is going to suck...but there's no way around it. "Hey, Marie Claire. It's Gagne. Patch me through to the bullpen. I've got a situation."

CHAPTER TWENTY-EIGHT

We step out of the truck and survey our surroundings. At first glance, it's like any other factory or warehouse. It's a big brick building with no windows except on the top floor—likely where the offices are.

There's also a sloped roof on the side that drops to where a row of metal doors runs along the loading dock.

Three tall smokestacks rise from the building's roof.

Right now, nothing is puffing out of them.

It's good to know that while these guys might be polluting our streets with their nasty new party drug, they're not filling the air with toxic fumes.

Not at the moment, at least.

In the air, a faint smell of burned cookies mingles with diesel and other odors from the expressway and surrounding factories. It's faint but still stands as a warning—the enemy is close.

We watch for a while, ensuring we stay out of view of the upper-story windows and wait for our backup to arrive. White cube vans come and go in a nearly constant stream.

"Where do you think they're going?" Zephyr asks.

"Likely to the closest rail loading yard to fill freight containers."

"That's a lot of trucks for one container to go across the city."

I shake my head. "Yeah no. There's no way their only market is in Montréal. We found where the local supply goes, but I'd bet they've got other freight cars shipping Second Sight across the country."

It's sickening to see how non-stop the flow of trucks is from the factory. The moment one truck pulls away, another takes its place, all packed to the roof with Second Sight. "Even when we shut this place down for good, this stuff will be in circulation for ages."

"I guess that means job security for you," Briar remarks.

"Maybe. If I'm not ostracized for being a fae freak." I would've preferred to tell them in person, but that wasn't how things played out. Hopefully, I chose the right words, and they get it.

I'm still me.

I look around, wondering when the Twenty-Third Precinct will arrive. So far, there's no sign of them.

What if I overestimated their tolerance of me being fae? What if they don't want to get involved in my family drama?

"What kind of response time were you expecting?" Azland asks.

"They should be arriving any time."

"Will we hear the sirens?" Zephyr asks.

"No. It's a silent approach for this kind of raid. We don't want to tip off anyone inside."

"We have a break in the action," Tad says.

He's right. There's a break in the comings and goings of trucks for the first time since we arrived. If this is our opportunity to get inside without tipping people off, we've got to take it.

"Backup is on the way. We don't have to wait. They'll be here."
I hope.

I meet the solemn nods from our rag-tag team. Man, we look rough. Without Kenzie, we haven't healed from the last battle, and we took more than a few good hits.

That won't stop us from getting our sister back.

I draw a deep breath and get us going. "Tad will portal us onto the loading dock. Azland and Briar, you snap the necks of the guards before they sound the alarm. We need a silent and lethal strike. Then we move inside."

Tad holds out his hand, and we each stack our hands on top. "Right and tight, my friends. Safe home."

I give him the go, and we *poof*.

The attack is swift and brutal. Two men fall to the concrete dock like marionettes with their strings cut.

"Whoa," Zephyr whispers. "Remind me never to piss off you boys."

Azland arches a dark brow. "You piss me off all the time. So far, I've resisted the urge to spin your head like an owl."

Zephyr blinks at him. "Dude…that was graphic and overly hostile."

Briar and I pull the dead guards behind a stack of wooden pallets, and I five-star them and turn up the heat. Like the others we've dispatched back to Hell, their bodies burst into flame and disintegrate into a pile of ash.

Zephyr swipes his hand through the air, and a gust of wind disperses the evidence of skoro homicide.

Tad's the first through the door and crashes into a guard on the inside. The rest of us back out of the guy's line of sight and I grip the butt of my gun.

Our druid plays it off and launches into the thickest and most nonsensical string of Irish I've heard yet. I can't understand what he's saying.

"Huh?" The guard sounds equally confused. "This is private property. You need to fuck off."

Tad repeats another heavily accented statement, and the only thing I catch is "lost tourist."

Before there's another retort, things go quiet, and there's a muffled *thud*. "Jules, yer up."

I follow Tad's invitation and hustle inside. The next guard is lying dead on the floor. It's a matter of rinse and repeat from that point. We take down two more workers within minutes and clear the loading dock area.

We regroup at a locked garage door leading into the factory proper.

"Should we knock?" Zephyr asks.

"Absolutely not." I look closely at the lock on the door. It's a plain metal deadbolt. Nothing mechanically or magically fancy. "I've got this."

I place my palm against the lock plate, pulling all the furious energy of the past few days out and directing it into the bolt.

Soon, molten liquid metal drips down the door and pools on the concrete. It's glowing orange and has a gross burning metallic tang.

"Here we go."

The main factory floor has what was once a fancy lobby off to the left and a row of parked lift trucks to the right. An unattended receptionist's desk greets us as we pass, the slick modern chairs scattered and overturned around the area. The skeletal remains of a long-dead plant lean against a fading mural on the wall.

Innovation. Cooperation. Medication.
Samelson Pharmaceuticals
Est. 1993.

Echoes of the old pharmaceutical company speak of a time before hellspawn overtook this building.

Creepy.

We head farther inside, past the abandoned lobby and through a pair of metal doors. We're in the main factory area, surrounded by conveyor belts and scaffolding.

No one notices our entry.

The whole place echoes with the scrapes and screeches of metal-on-metal and other mechanical noises. The skoro working the assembly line are either wearing earmuffs or ignoring the noise.

"Let's get a better look." Azland points at a rickety platform overlooking the operation.

Tad waits until the contact is complete and portals us up.

"Look for Kenzie, but take everything else in." I scan the entire place, desperate to see the pale sky blue of my sister's new magical skin.

A fine white haze hangs like flour in the air.

Beside me, Zephyr coughs, and Briar giggles. It's an incongruous sound considering our circumstances.

I scowl at the bustling factory floor below. Skoro are pouring buckets of white powder into vats churning with colorful liquid.

"Jellybean drugs in the making," I say.

"The blowback is being completely ignored." Azland scowls down at them.

"Maybe Second Sight doesn't affect them," Tad offers.

As they work, more puffs of the powder rise, filling the atmosphere we're breathing in.

"Something tells me these guys aren't big on workplace safety protocols," I mutter.

Zephyr shakes his head and grins. "Yeah, it's affecting me."

Me too. Suddenly, finding Kenzie doesn't seem as dire or dangerous as it did.

Beside me, Zephyr grips his staff and swirls his hand through the air, then thrusts it up. A gust of air swirls around us and whips my hair into my face.

The air clears and hopefully, so will my head.

"I'll try to keep us from breathing in too much of it," Zephyr advises.

I tug my shirt over my nose, doing my best to block the airborne drugs from getting into my system. Everyone else does the same. It won't work once we're on the move and battling, but it's fine for now.

Now that I'm no longer inhaling a party drug, my single-minded focus on finding my sister returns.

"There." Tad points.

Our sister sits handcuffed to a lift truck on the factory floor past the rows of assembly line skoro making pills.

"She's alive and looks whole," I report.

"She looks pissed," Zephyr adds.

Azland frowns. "With her chained in the center of the factory floor, there's no way for us to get her without being seen."

That sucks. "Tad? What are your limitations with portaling? Could you *poof* down there and take Kenzie *and* the lift truck back to the firehouse?"

Tad shrugs in apology. His eyes are glazed. "Either they've got a device blockin' portal magic or inhalin' that drug has my wayfarer powers offline. Either way, I'm not much use as a getaway plan, I'm afraid."

I raise my hand and call a fireball to my palm. "I still have access to my element. Do you have your druid powers?"

Tad lifts his palms, and another breeze blows past. "Aye, I have access to my nature magic, just not my spatial magic."

Azland gets a focused look. Either he's trying something, or his bowels picked an inopportune moment to bunch up. "My spatial magic is offline too. I agree...we've either come into an area where there's a device to jam portaling, or Second Sight affects that ability more quickly or strongly than others."

I don't like it, but that's where we are. "All right, then we do this the hard way. How do we get down?"

Briar points at a set of metal stairs that wind down to the main floor below and swings his gaze to a metal rung ladder against the wall.

"Okay, divide and conquer. Good luck, everyone. Who's with me?"

"I am, lass. Lead the way."

I move to the top of the stairs, wreath myself in fire, and take the steps with enough speed that I don't melt them and endanger Tad behind me.

The bonus is my flames eat the air around us, eradicating the airborne Second Sight.

There's no time to celebrate that as a win before the skoro see me and open fire.

As a cop, I have a general distaste for being shot at, but as an elemental, it's not so bad. Despite being lit up from all angles, the bullets melt before they hit me.

Cool.

"Stay behind me, Tad. Apparently, I'm bulletproof."

"Aye, I noticed that."

The best part about their bullets not affecting me is that now all of them are focused on me and they've missed Azland and my brothers coming down the ladder behind them.

The assault continues as I push closer to Kenzie. Either they haven't realized I'm melting their ammunition, or they don't have a Plan B and are stuck with what to do about it.

Doesn't matter.

The more ammunition they use up on me, the less they'll have to shoot at my brothers.

"*Jules,*" Kenzie shouts when I make it to her side. "Took you long enough."

I snort and position myself between the hostile force and my pissed-off sister. "Yeah, well. Traffic and all that. We're here now."

Tad shifts in behind me to take care of her handcuffs. "Hello, beautiful. What's the craic?"

"What? Are you *on* crack?"

Tad chuckles. "No… Well, maybe. Sorry, it's the way the Irish ask how things are."

"Shitty," she snaps. "Things are shitty."

I chuckle. "You'll be better once you're not attached to this stupid lift truck."

"And I destroy whatever is blocking my powers. I couldn't freeze the metal, drown the stupid men, or anything."

"Och, well, I'll have ye free in a moment, and ye can drown all the stupid men ye like."

I hear the hesitation in Tad's words and glance back to see what the holdup is.

He tilts his head and points at the cuffs. "These are demonic in origin, which explains why Kenzie couldn't affect them with her magic."

"So, I'm stuck here?" she asks.

"Absolutely not, chickie-poo. The cuffs might be magic, but this lift truck isn't." I place my hand on the bar and squeeze. It melts, sliding down in a stinky ooze of paint and metal.

Kenzie pulls her cuffs free, and while they still dangle from her wrist, she's free to move, and we can deal with that later.

Tad helps her up, and the three of us take on another rush of skoro fire. I extend my arms, turning up the flames to enlarge myself as their shield. "Tad, take Kenzie and go. Once you're far enough away that your portal powers come back online, get her to safety."

Tad tugs her into motion, but my sister resists and flashes me her middle finger. "Screw that. I'm part of this, and I'm the one who was taken. I'm gonna go psycho Elsa on these bitches the minute I get these cuffs off, and I can access my powers."

Tad snorts. "Psycho Elsa, I love it."

When he continues to laugh, Kenzie looks at me. "It wasn't that funny."

I study his glassy eyes. "Ugh, the drugs hit him harder than us. He's high as balls right now."

Kenzie sighs. "I'll detox him with my healing waters as soon as possible. In the meantime, let's get out of here."

"Whassup?" Tad grins as we pull him into motion.

"There's a party over there by those doors." Kenzie turns him to leave. "Let's go check it out."

"Aye, lead the way, pretty blue girl."

We hustle out of the center and find much more cover once we're weaving through the manufacturing machinery.

As we dodge and weave, I stare at the cuffs on Kenzie's arms and wonder… "I have an idea."

I pull her and Tad out of the traffic flow and turn my fiery back to the room. "See if you can make your hands water—like Briar makes his stone. See if you can liquify and the cuffs will slide right off."

Her eyes blow wide. "That's crazy. I can't access my powers. That's the problem."

"I get that, but remember what Azland said? In our true forms, we *are* the elements. Our powers aren't to *wield* fire or water. Our power stems from the fact that we *are* fire and water."

She looks skeptical.

"I bet the cuffs are to keep you from mounting an offensive but don't try that. Focus on your hands becoming water."

"Becoming water? What if I can't make them hands again? Then what do I do?"

"That's not going to happen. Tad told us our elemental abilities are much more instinctive than other magics he's worked with, and I believe that. You have to admit, we've picked things up quickly."

"Yeah, I agree, but…"

"No buts. Just do it. Drop off these cuffs, and you can get back into the fight."

There's no missing the flair of dark promise in her eyes.

Kenzie is sweet as honey, but she has the sting of a swarm of bees if you piss her off.

"You can do this, Kenz. I know it."

While Kenzie focuses on liquifying her hands and dropping the cuffs, I scan the factory for Zephyr, Briar, and Azland. It's hard to see through the thick white powder floating in the air.

What was a fine mist when we first arrived is now much worse with the chaos of fighting and shooting stirring it up and kicking it into the air.

The metallic *clunk* of the cuffs hitting the concrete floor has me turning back to my sister. "You did it."

She holds up her arms, and I watch her wrist, hands, and fingers reform. "It's instinct, just like you said."

"Okay, then your first order of business is to call your healing spheres and give us all a good hearty drink of drug antidote cleanser before we're playing our parts in *Harold and Kumar Get Their Asses Kicked by Demons*."

Kenzie's watching Tad and giggling. "I bet it would be hilarious, but now is not the time."

I give her some space, and she holds her palms over one another as she develops an orb of water. "Here, pretty Irish man. Drink this."

"What is it?"

"It's magic."

"I love magic." He leans forward and directs the water into his open mouth.

We give him a minute, and I drink some too. I don't feel it to the extreme Tad does, but then again, he and Zephyr got the most exposure before we realized what was going on.

"What the feckin' hell?" Tad presses his palm against his forehead. "Is someone melon-ballin' my brains out of my skull?"

"Nope. Take another drink of Kenzie's healing waters and see if that helps. Then we gotta get to the others."

Tad does as instructed and we rush over to where Zephyr and

Briar are thrashing skoro, but both are trashed. I take point to get them out of the fight, and Tad backs me up.

"Hello, boys."

"Kenzie, you're alive," Zephyr calls with a dumb, blank, wide grin.

"Yep. Here, drink this. It's party water."

"I love party water," Briar says.

"Was I that gone?" Tad asks.

"Yep."

"Well, at least I still have clothes on."

"Sadly, yes," Kenzie says behind us.

He chuckles. "Och, lass, if ye want to see the show, all ye have to do is let me know."

I roll my eyes. "Dirty talk later. Killing hellborn now."

Briar and Zephyr come around by the time we finish with the minions who chose to fight.

We head toward the back of the building, rounding a corner and pushing through some white doors. Now we're in a laboratory, where counters line the walls and cabinets are overflowing with beakers, test tubes, and jugs of various colors.

The chemical smell is much stronger here, but no Second Sight powder floats around.

Alchemy formulas and runes are scrawled over the whiteboard wall. I lift my phone and take a picture of it in case we need it later. "Now, erase that shit. Hopefully, they were too stupid and arrogant to record copies."

Kenzie says something, but my focus is off.

My heart is racing, and my skin is tight. It's like I have a really bad sunburn. "What's happening? What is that? Do you feel it?"

Briar rubs his arms. "Yeah, it's bad."

Tad glances around and points at a sealed tank glowing bright pink against the far wall. "That must be the fae power manipulated to make the drug."

"It's humming," Kenzie adds.

"Aye, it's raw prana, and it's unstable. Judging by the nettles jabbing into my flesh, we need to get out of here before that blows."

"You mean like explode?" Zephyr asks.

"Exactly what I mean. Now move."

CHAPTER TWENTY-NINE

We evacuate the lab without argument and hustle along the corridor to get some distance between us and the unstable fae power source that's building to explode.

"What's that sound?" Kenzie stops when we get to a junction of two sterile white hallways.

"That's battle," Tad says.

I pick up speed to a run. "Maybe Azland found Lamech."

A petulant roar splits the air, and we dial it up to a sprint. "We're coming. Hang on."

We follow the sounds of fighting, and they get stronger and stronger. Up the flight of stairs to the floor of offices. Through another abandoned lobby.

"There, in the corner office."

We race to close the distance. The office isn't so much of an office anymore. Both its windows to the outside world and the interior walls are busted out.

Lamech is in his true form, the green, horned horror with glowing slime green eyes and smoggy breath. Even weakened and injured from our battle earlier, he's beating the shit out of Azland.

Broken glass *cracks* and *crunches* under our feet as we rush in. Lamech sees us coming and flings Azland against the window wall to empty his hands.

Azland hits the opening and flips out the window.

"Get him." My arm flies as his feet follow his limp body, but there's no chance. Without Tad being able to portal, no one is close enough to retrieve him before gravity takes over.

Lamech laughs. "Sorry, did I break your friend?"

There's nothing we can do for Azland now except finish the battle he started.

Where's the dagger?

I scan the floor, searching for where it might've fallen. Did he have it when he went out the window?

That would be a problem.

"Let's get this done." Briar clenches both fists and hardens to stone. As he did when Kenzie and I washed skoro off him with scalding water, he claims his true form and becomes earth from head to toe.

Pride bubbles up inside me.

Briar knows who he is...and that's how we're going to win this war.

We *are* going to win.

Not because Azland and I weakened Lamech with the Shard of Osheron. Not because we've taken out most of his minions. And not because he's a gross, life-sucking abomination who doesn't deserve a place in my awesome city.

He'll lose because this time, I understand.

As much as we tried to be us with powers at first, I understand our error now.

Like I told Kenzie...I *am* fire. She *is* water.

I've not only accepted my magical empowered self.

I embrace her.

Lamech thinks we're sheltered fae orphans who barely know

how to wield our powers. Maybe when we first showed up on his radar, he was right.

Now though?

Now, I get it. I know who I am.

I'm Juliette Gagne, heir to the Lasair Empire of Fire, daughter of Scaith Warrior Laurette Gagne, and human hero Marcel Gagne. I am a police officer, a warrior, and a protector of the innocent whether they are fae, human, or other. Whether they are alive or dead.

I will keep my lineage going no matter what forces of darkness try to destroy it.

There is fire inside me, and I'll use it to keep the people I love warm while burning our enemies to a crisp.

Lamech has no idea what he's facing.

I meet the gazes of my siblings, and it all falls into place. Hells yeah. We're going to do this.

Despite the glass on the floor, I dive and roll, searching under the desk and along the walls for the missing dagger. At the same time, Tad and my siblings attack.

I have faith in them. I trust them to distract Lamech while I find the weapon we need. Scrambling on my hands and knees, I push at the office debris, searching for the enchanted blade.

My hands are getting cut up, but I heat them and cauterize them from within.

A bellow of fury sounds above me and the desk I'm under suddenly flips and flies through the broken glass wall into the next office.

I see it then, the glistening of metal in the daylight. Scrambling across the debris field, I close my fingers around the dagger's hilt.

Slick with blood, it's impossible to get a good grip, but there's no way I'm letting go of this sucker now. "You're going down, demon spawn."

Lamech glares, his neon eyes filled with hate. "Do you

honestly believe you can win? You're food to us. A delicious four-course meal for my siblings and me."

"Sorry, we're not taking reservations," I tell him.

There's a moment when time stands still...

Then it's on.

Zephyr's storm throws books, binders, and chairs at him while Briar gets in close and lands a few bone-shattering hits. Kenzie is pelting the beast with ice daggers, and it doesn't take her long to realize his throat is a key point to draw blood. Tad's focused on the sky outside, and I see a massive storm cloud rolling in.

While we're all a big part of this, with the enchanted dagger in my possession, I must finish it.

Our gazes meet and lock.

His eyes glow lime green, and flames fill mine.

"Let's dance, creep."

I lunge forward, slashing the dagger through the air. He dodges. I twist and try again. He spins and grabs my wrist, yanking me hard. My feet leave the floor, and a moment later I face-slam into the wall.

That rattles my chains.

He's so strong.

My siblings move in, and their attacks give me a moment's reprieve to stagger back and stop the world from spinning.

"Fuck this. Kenzie, catch." I toss her the blade and shake myself. If Briar can do it and Kenzie can do it, I sure as shit can do it.

Focusing on the furnace heating my core, I turn up the heat and welcome the flame to consume me.

Tad said elemental magic is instinctive, so I go with my gut and become the human torch. If he wants my elemental essence so badly, here it comes.

There's a loud *whoosh*, and it's like I poured ten cans of kerosene on my briquettes before I lit the match. The flames that come off me fill the room in a fiery detonation that forces Tad back but doesn't seem to affect my siblings. Maybe since we belong together, we run on a shared elemental harmonic or something.

I'll think about that later.

I hold up my arms, and yeah, I'm more than wreathed in flames now. I'm a walking inferno.

I rush forward, grapple Lamech, and take him to the floor. His spiked peaks are coarse and hard to grasp, but I shift my grip to his horns and yank. Twisting his head, I fight with all I've got.

Then Briar piles on and starts pummeling.

Zephyr drives his staff down hard and shoots voltage through him. I feel the bite of his electrical charge, but it doesn't hurt me.

Amazing.

"Pile on," Kenzie shouts, tagging in to make our Quebec Quartet complete. I watch as Kenzie raises the dagger in both hands above us and thrusts it down.

Lamech arches and bellows, the cry ringing and echoing like nothing I've ever heard.

"Yeah, Kenzie," Tad shouts. "Leave the dagger in."

A horrible green goo seeps out of Lamech's mouth as he screams and thrashes to escape my grasp. I'm on my back now, with my legs and arms locked around him as Briar and Zephyr continue their assaults.

It takes all four of us to hold him down.

Because, hello, he's a ten-foot demon hybrid.

Roaring with fury, Lamech thrusts his hips skyward and tosses Briar and me into the air. I crash into the corner of a fallen bookshelf and *whoosh*, the books lying scattered on the floor ignite.

Oops. My bad.

I roll to my feet, crouch, and try to make sense of the scene. Lamech has taken massive hits but isn't giving up. He flails at my siblings with sloppy hands as they continue their attacks.

Zephyr has the dagger now and is wildly hacking long trenches of damage through skin, muscle, and sinew.

Kenzie has jagged ice spears clenched in both fists and is impaling any open wound she can get to.

Tad doesn't seem to be able to get close. He's firing bolts of blue magic from across the room.

Briar recovers and mounts Lamech's head. Squatting on the beast's broad shoulders as he fights to get to his feet, my brother grips one charcoal horn in each of his massive stony fists.

He's twisting with all his might, and it looks like he's trying to rip the guy's head off.

Damn. That's dark.

Azland, Tad, and Bakkali have all told me the rules are different in the empowered world, but yeah, decapitation seems extreme.

"Jules, get in there," Tad shouts from behind a wall of smoke and flame.

I shake off the momentary mind-mining of morality and get my head back into the fight. The Six are five and need to be four—for the safety of all involved.

Rushing forward, I punch my flaming fist through one of the biggest holes in Lamech's chest and focus on releasing as much burning damage as possible.

Azland thinks our power levels will ease off now that they are no longer bottled and building. If that's true, I might as well get the most bang for my buck while I can.

Lamech's writhing has grown sloppy and uncoordinated. He's more blood than skin at this point, and his strength finally seems to be waning.

The four of us hold steady, our commitment to ending this unrelenting. Then the most horrifying wet, tearing noise precedes Briar pitching backward with Lamech's head in his possession.

The spray of bloody ichor is the stuff of nightmares and Zephyr, Kenzie, and I are all within the splash zone.

As I recoil from the onslaught of grossness, Lamech's body falls lifeless and heavy, taking me down. I land flat on my back, covered by his incredible weight.

Panting, I try to breathe.

No one is moving.

I'm not sure we could if we wanted to. The room is still on fire. I reach out to the flames and the heat and claim them as mine.

I try to take a deep breath of the char, but I can't get anything into my lungs. "Get this dead asshole off me."

Briar starts the heave-ho. Zephyr and Tad join in, working to free me. When they do, I release my flames and—"Well, shit."

Zephyr and Briar curse and avert their gazes.

"Sorry." I flame up again and scowl. "I really need someone to get me something to wear that won't burn off and leave me naked every other minute."

"No argument," Zephyr agrees.

"We'll get ye some fire-enchanted fabric to keep that from happening," Tad promises.

Kenzie chuckles. "Yes. Let's make that a priority. We can't have Jules' girlie bits on display every time she Hulks out."

"No, we can't," Briar grumbles.

I sit there, sagging against the wall and staring at the heap of dead Poreskoro in the center of the office demolition. "He didn't disappear into a puff of ash like the skoro do when they die."

"He won't," Azland informs us as he staggers into the office and collapses on the floor with the rest of us. "The Six are superior beings to the thugs they spawn."

"Gagne? Where the fuck are you?"

"Here. We're in here."

A moment later, Rene, Tremblay, Marx, and Morin jog in. I've never been happier to see my boys in blue.

They came.

Even after finding out that I'm a fae freak with a secret past, they came. That was before they saw what I've become. I get up and list to the side but catch myself. Straightening, I stand there in all my fiery glory while they get an eyeful.

"Sorry we're late," Tremblay says. "We would've been here sooner if Morin would lay off the baked goods. Dammit, man, you're as slow as my *grand-mère*."

Morin gives him the finger. "We would've been here sooner if de building wasn't full of black-eyed freaks trying to kill us."

"There's that too, yeah."

Rene grins. "You were right about their lives being connected to their maker. We were down there swarmed and in the thick of it, and they all dropped to the floor at once."

"Likely around the time Briar ripped his head off." I gesture at the massive, dead demon in the middle of the war zone. "He was a tough one."

Morin, Marx, and Tremblay all blanch.

"You went up against that thing?"

I wave away his words. "No. *We* did. Boys, this is my family. Turns out, we're all fae, and our mother was a fae guardian. She and our papa died fighting this asshole's brother, but they took him down too. I hope that doesn't weird you out too much."

Marx shrugs. "You've always been weird, Gagne. I'm just glad you're on our side."

I hear the tension in his voice and nod. "I definitely am. Nothing has changed there."

Morin's pinched brow eases, and he shakes his head. "Dis just makes you even more badass, Gagne. Although, is it okay to say dat your fire body is freaking me out?"

"Maybe I can help with that." Rene holds up a thick fire blanket. "When you're ready, I've got you."

"My hero." I close the distance between us, and he turns to position the blanket to cut off the view as I release my flames.

When I'm me again, I tug the blanket around me and cover things up. "We're working on the wardrobe malfunctions. I know it's a lot. Don't give up on me, boys."

"Don't be ridiculous." Tremblay claps me hard on the shoulder. "Giving up on you would mean giving up on Charlie and her baking care packages. No way that's happening."

I laugh. "Well, all right. I guess I know where I stand."

He nods. "It's good to be clear about things."

My skin tightens, and that sunburn feeling is back. Only we're not in the same room anymore, so if it's happening out here, the time has run out.

"Shit, I forgot about the prana bomb. Time to go, boys. Irish, are your portal powers back online?"

Tad nods. "Aye. Whatever was blockin' me is gone now. We're good to go."

"Then let's go."

Rene is getting used to it and Marx, Morin, and Tremblay catch on quickly enough. Tad portals us outside and makes a quick return trip for Lamech's body.

By the time he returns, we've moved the firefighters and cruisers far enough from the warehouse that they won't get caught in the detonation.

The prickling grows more and more uncomfortable until the unstable prana inside blows.

The power wave that blasts past us is a violent tsunami of magic. It blows the roof off the Poreskoro warehouse like a Mentos rocket.

Fuchsia flames light up the sky.

It's beautiful and terrifying.

"Well, shit." Tremblay tilts his head back to take in the hot pink mushroom cloud. "I'm glad we were out of there before that went off."

Rene nods. "With that going up, there's not much left for us to do until fire has finished with the scene."

"Oh, I have a feeling we'll have plenty to do," I tell them. "You should have seen the amount of Second Sight they were pumping out of here. I see long days and plenty of OT in our future, boys."

"I suppose that'll be my call, Gagne." I follow the comment to where Acting Staff Sergeant Peter Trent is approaching. "The last time I checked, you were supposed to ride a desk for a few days and maybe catch up on some light casework from home."

"She's a terrible listener," Kenzie responds.

"The worst," Briar agrees.

"Can't be told a damn thing," Zephyr adds.

Rude. "While I appreciate my siblings throwing me under the bus, this all happened rather organically. I involved Rene and the team all the way. Didn't I guys?"

My boys have my back and nod to cover my ass and confirm. Damn, I love these guys.

"I look forward to reading the complete report." He eyes Lamech's body on the asphalt next to us. "And finding out what the fuck this thing is…and where is its head?"

Briar points at the spot where he dropped his gruesome trophy.

If anything about this were funny, Peter's expression would be hilarious. "That's the man behind the Second Sight production and this is where the magic happened."

Peter frowns at the body and me standing there, naked and wrapped in a fire blanket, Briar and Kenzie covered in black goo, and Zephyr cut to shit with his nipple rings glistening in the sunlight.

"Go home, Gagne. I mean it. Go home, get yourself sorted, and don't come in until you're rested and in control of whatever you do that takes down something like this. Then come in."

"Bring some of Charlie's baking," Tremblay adds.

"You know I will."

Peter strides off to speak with the fire teams, and my guys

give me a few more teasing jibes before climbing into their cars to leave.

"They think highly of ye, lass." Tad lays his arm heavy over my shoulder.

"It goes both ways."

"What now?" Briar asks.

"Now we go home, shower, pig out, and sleep for the next two days."

"Hells yeah," Kenzie concurs. "I'm in."

CHAPTER THIRTY

I take a few days off, as I promised, I rest, heal, and gather myself. When I return to the station, I meet with my ASS and present a carefully put-together case file, my full statement of the week's events, and all my supporting documentation to complete my report.

Peter takes time enough to read through it, page by page, and looks up at me. "You had quite a week."

"True story."

"This is good police work, Jules...especially because you did it while your entire world was changing."

"Thank you, sir."

"So, what now?"

"I've been thinking a lot about that. I love being a cop and serving the people of Montréal, but the world is changing. I'm not the same as when I first joined the force, and something tells me more changes are coming."

Peter looks concerned. "Do you feel okay?"

"Yeah, fine, but I've seen things and learned things. I know what's out there and there's no unknowing it now. That guy we took down, Lamech, is gone, but his siblings aren't."

Peter refers to my report. "The Six."

"Yeah, although technically they're now The Four."

"Technically."

"The rest of them will come for me, this city, and anyone like me."

Peter grimaces.

I feel like I'm the scientist in a disaster movie trying to explain what kind of threat we're facing to all the soldiers and politicians.

I don't think a human behind a desk reading reports can truly grasp the situation's severity. Peter's great and all, but I don't think he gets it.

"What do you think we should do about it?" he asks.

"I have some friends in Toronto," I tell him. "Magical people like me. They have a special task force that focuses solely on this stuff."

"A squad dedicated to the violence of the empowered world?"

"Exactly. Anyway, if we decide to do that here, I'd love to help."

"That's what Rene's task force is doing with Mayor Tremblay and City Hall, isn't it?"

"Sort of. Rene's team is more like citizen outreach. I'm talking about a magical SEAL team that gets sent in when something off the books needs doing to save lives."

Peter grins. "While that's ambitious and I think you'd do a good job, I'm not sure I have that kind of swing or that we're there yet. Sure, things have been chaotic, but I'm not sure a force squad is an answer."

I sigh. "If you change your mind, know that I'm on board and will gladly fight the fight."

"Fair enough. Until then, back to your regular cases?"

I stand and nod. "Yeah. Sure. Consider me back on rotation tomorrow."

Peter pats my report. "Again. This is really good work, Gagne. Tomorrow it is."

I say my goodbyes to the guys, and they thank me for the baking. Then I slide my backpack on and grab my helmet and gloves from where I left them on my desk.

Scarlett is waiting for me in the parking lot.

"Hello, sexy girl. Care to tear?"

I kick my leg over her leather seat and start things up. She rumbles to life with a throaty purr, and the beefy sound soothes some of my rough edges.

I rev the gas and take to the streets, likely a little faster and louder than I should. Don't care. It's been too long since I could grip it and rip it.

I weave along the tree-lined streets of Boucherville, the wind pulling at my long leather jacket. My beloved city's sights, sounds, and smells seem different somehow.

It's the same incredible Montréal architecture and history as it's always been, but *I'm* not the same.

Knowing I'm not from here makes me a little sad.

I always considered Montréal my hometown, but I'm from the fae kingdom of Lasair. I wonder what Lasair is like. I wonder what it was like twenty-seven years ago when I lived there. Do they have city streets, towering skyscrapers, or tall broad-branched trees? Could I ride my bike through the surrounding countryside?

Who would I be if I was there?

Maybe I'll go there someday. Maybe all four of us could take a tour through our ancestry.

Bakkali would make an excellent tour guide.

I chuckle at the thought. Bakkali and his governing body are interesting. They're a closed community, but I'm now a member, whether they like it or not.

I pass Rougemont Park and think about all those fae kids I saw dancing at that silent rave. Do they feel this…like they don't quite fit into the world they're in?

Images of Gareth filter through my mind unbidden. Am I a

sucker for the lost soul bad boy type? Is that why I'm attracted to him? Or is it something else?

I laugh at myself. Not that it matters…I have too much coming at me to worry about men.

Even if he's a hottie who spends his spare time giving displaced kids an outlet for fun and acceptance.

Yeah, eyes on the horizon. The Quebec Quint needs to level up and get ready for the battles ahead.

Too soon I'm back in my neighborhood. I turn the corner and approach the firehouse, uncertain about what's in store. We defeated one of The Six, but it took all of us and could've gone either way.

What if the others hear it was us and team up? Could we take four Poreskoro fighting together?

I push that out of my head. For now, everything is fine. We're safe, alive, and together.

The bay door activates and hums up on its metal tracks. A gentle honk behind me has me turning as I dismount. I pull off my helmet, set it on Scarlett's seat, and wave at Charlie and the twins.

"Hey, I guess we timed that right, eh?" Charlie steps out of her car and slings her purse over her head. "Come. Help us carry in some food."

I move in slowly, allowing the twins to see that I'm still me. Over the past couple of days, Charlie wanted us to focus on healing and recovering our strength. This is the first time the twins have been allowed to come over and experience the new normal.

I close the distance to where they're getting out on the driveway. "Hey, guys. How are you doing with all this craziness?"

Micah laughs and pops the hatch. "It's nothing we don't go through every day. Charlie's a maniac in the kitchen. I told her it's crazy, but that doesn't seem to make a difference."

Charlie grins, unrepentant. "There's nothing wrong with

wanting to make sure my charges are fed, healed, and recovering after their ordeal."

Yeah, it was the ordeal of us becoming fae that I was talking about. I guess Micah missed that…or maybe he doesn't care.

Could they really not care?

Micah lifts a couple of the insulated bags, gives Anna one of the light ones, and smiles at me. "I still can't believe you guys are the *Fantastic Four*. Wild."

I pick up a covered casserole dish. It's still warm and smells like meaty sauce bliss. "No one was more surprised than us, kid."

"They're the Fantastic Five," Charlie corrects. "Azland is part of them. He's their fifth."

Anna frowns and hits the close button for the bay door. "Now we don't have a dog. I loved Backup. Can he still be our dog sometimes?"

"You're in luck." I lead the way up the stairs. "He told us yesterday he can still take the form of Backup if the need arises. Although, now when he's our dog, it's by choice."

"Oh, like for stealth undercover ops?" Micah asks.

"Yeah, I guess."

The four of us unburden ourselves of our load and unpack the bags onto the kitchen counter.

"What have we got here?" Briar comes over to snoop. "Charlie, you don't have to go to all this trouble. We're fine."

"We *do* know how to cook." Kenzie joins us, looking apprehensive. "Hey, kiddos, so…this is me."

"Holy shitballs, you really are blue." Micah's mouth drops open.

Anna smacks him in the gut and rushes over to hug Kenzie. "Are you okay? You must be freaked out."

Kenzie accepts the hug and draws a deep breath. "I was, but I'm getting used to it. Well, as much as a black girl can get used to being blue. Tad says he can teach me how to glamor my skin so I look human."

"Handy," Anna observes.

"Hey, troublemakers." Zephyr drags himself out of his room. His hair is sticking up in every direction, and it's obvious he just woke up.

Which is amazing.

Now that his storm has been set free, Zephyr sleeps like the dead. He's off his restraints, sleeps through without night terrors, and is catching up on years of restless nights.

While everyone unpacks the food and dishes out the casserole, I wander a bit, straightening things up. There's still a faint stench of burned cookies, so I light a few candles, using the tip of my finger to set the wicks alight.

"Wow, your home invaders did a number on your furniture." Micah whistles through his teeth.

"Apparently, hellborn minions aren't housetrained."

"That sucks."

Tad *poofs* in and holds a finger to his lips.

He reported back to Toronto after everything went down and other than Kenzie and him chatting on Zoom, we haven't seen him. "Zephyr, mate, I brought ye somethin' fer yer gig tonight."

Zephyr abandons the buffet line and comes to see. "No way. Are you kidding me?"

Tad holds out the high-gloss black Fender Stratocaster almost identical to the one Zephyr lost in our home's destruction. "She deserves a good home and someone who will play her with pride."

Zephyr blinks at him. "You're serious? She's for me?"

He nods. "I picked her up during my fuck the world rebel rockstar phase. Haven't touched her since. She might need a little TLC, but she's barely had her strings plucked."

"You're sure?"

Tad nods again. "Trust me, sham. I have more than enough stuff. What I need is more happiness. If she makes you happy, then I'm sure."

Zephyr takes the gift, gives him a back-slapping man-hug, and hustles over to sit on the couch and get to know his new sexy lady.

"That was incredibly generous. Thank you." I hug Tad and kiss his cheek. "You're a keeper, Mr. McNiff."

Tad shrugs. "I'm a work in progress, but I've got my sights on the man I want to be."

"I like who you are now, so don't change too much."

"I double that," Kenzie agrees. She holds out her hand and tugs him toward the banquet of food. "Anna and Micah, this is Tad McNiff. Tad, these are the twins, the latest additions to the Gagne orphan train."

"It's a pleasure to meet ye both."

"You're the druid, right?" Micah asks.

"Aye, that's right."

"Can you show us?" Micah rushes over to the window and picks up the sad African violet that got overturned and unearthed during the tossing of our home. "Can you fix this plant?"

Kenzie frowns. "He's not here to perform tricks for us, Micah."

"It's all right, lass. The wee thing is strugglin'. It needs a little love to get it through." Tad holds his palm over the plant and speaks in the authentic Irish he uses for spell casting.

I feel the signature of his magic in the air, and the violet straightens, its leaves plump out, and pale pink flowers bud and bloom on it. "That's awesome."

Tad winks at me. "Briar will be able to do that soon enough."

Briar stops chewing. "I will?"

"Fer sure. Yer strengths go well beyond throwin' rocks, mate. Nature magic holds endless possibility."

"Nice. I look forward to it."

Anna rushes over to examine the plant and blushes as she meets the full force of Tad's stunning gaze. "Charlie said druids aren't fae, but you have fae powers. How does that work?"

"That's true. We're guardians, ye see."

As Tad settles in to explain to the twins where his fae gifts originate, I make my way back to Charlie at the kitchen table. "All's well that ends well, I guess."

Charlie grins and hands me a plate mounded with food. "That's what they say. Although this place still looks like you were housing angry jaguars that tried to claw their way to freedom."

"Meh, it's only stuff. What matters is we're still here, and we're stronger than ever."

Charlie nods. "True. Do you know what will make you even stronger?"

"Brownies!" Briar cheers.

Charlie waggles her eyebrows and pulls a layer of tinfoil off the last glass baking dish. "Right you are, Briar. Brownies for the win."

The promise of brownies brings all the rowdies back to the well-stocked kitchen table. Zephyr and Briar have their elbows up and are pushing in, impatiently waiting as Charlie cuts huge slabs of chocolate for all.

"Mmm, do I smell Charlie's cooking?" Azland jogs up the stairs looking buff in a muscle shirt and jogging sweats. No longer a muscled bull mastiff or a hobo, Azland is looking fine in his warrior form.

There's no missing the eye-fucking going on between him and Charlie, but those of us who see it try not to because *hellooo*, he's our dog.

Or was.

It's confusing.

Anyway, this is us.

The human aunt, the twins who aren't related, the druid who's reinventing himself, and five fae elementals living in the middle of Montréal and being hunted by hellborn hybrids.

I set down my plate of food and switch to a plate of brownies before they're gone.

Tad was right.

Family isn't defined by blood or birth. Family is the people who live and die to ensure you're okay in the darkest moments of life.

Yeah…if you're lucky enough to find people like that, you cherish every moment because it doesn't get any better than this.

ENDNOTE

Thank you for reading *Incendio: Flame Born*, book 1 in the Chronicles of an Urban Elemental series. While the story is fresh in your mind, and as a favor to Michael and me, please click HERE and tell other readers what you thought.

A quick star rating and/or even one sentence can mean so much to readers deciding whether to try a book, series, or a new-to-them author.

Thank you.

If you want more of the Quebec Quint, you can find book 2 in the series, *Magicae: Power Dawning on Amazon*.

THE STORY CONTINUES

The story continues with book two, *Magicae: Power Dawning*, available at Amazon.

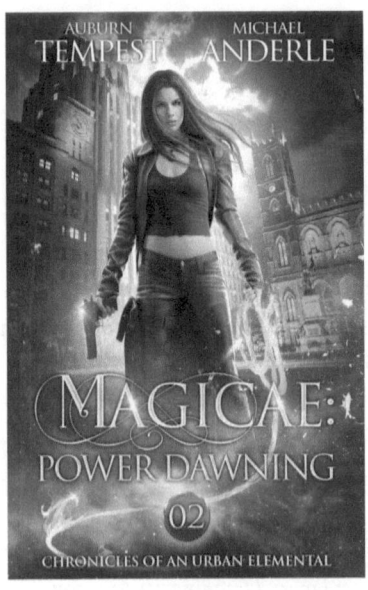

Claim your copy today!

AUTHOR NOTES - AUBURN TEMPEST

DECEMBER 15, 2022

Welcome to the Chronicles of the Urban Elementals.

The fans asked for more, and it's coming your way. For those of you who don't know, Urban Elementals is a spin-off series from the Chronicles of an Urban Druid or more precisely, the Case Files of an Urban Druid.

Jules and Rene made their appearance in book 1 of the continuation of the original series, *Mayhem in Montréal* and since Montréal was going to be affected so significantly by the influx of prana in the tributary waters, I thought fun adventures might ensue.

I'm co-writing Urban Elementals on its own merits, but it will also be a companion to the Urban Druid series and will have cross-over characters when support is needed while fighting the good fight.

Look forward to magic and mayhem, humor, and harried

moments with characters you love and others I hope you will grow to love.

Book ones are hard for me because I want to tell you everything about every character and show you their lives and their quirks. I hope you got enough of a sample that you'll stick with me for the next volumes.

As always, thank you for your support, comments, and reviews, and for entrusting your time in my characters and the stories they have to tell.

If you enjoyed it and want to keep your finger on the pulse, feel free to join the Facebook Fan page.

Or feel free to drop us a line: UrbanDruid@lmbpn.com

Blessed be,
Auburn Tempest

AUTHOR NOTES - MICHAEL ANDERLE

DECEMBER 21, 2022

Thank you for reading this book and these author notes as well!

Why do I like warm families and "found" families?

I'm writing these author notes a few days before Christmas, and I'm thinking about why I like writing with Auburn Tempest. I have decided it's about family.

Specifically, Auburn's and the ones she creates inside her stories.

As a reader, there is something extraordinary about immersing myself in the world of a fun, warm-hearted family. When I read about a group that has each other's backs and cares deeply for one another, it allows me to escape my own reality (whether my family is good or not isn't essential to having the emotions) and feel a sense of belonging and comfort.

I enjoy reading about families in the *Urban Druid / Urban Elemental* series because they provide a sense of hope and positivity. In a world with so much negativity and conflict, it is refreshing to read about characters enjoying each other's company and supporting each other through difficult times.

Further, reading about fun and warm-hearted characters

brings a smile to my face and allows me to escape into a world where love and happiness reign supreme. It is a welcome respite from daily negative news headlines, tv talking heads, and life's stresses, and it helps me feel more connected and grounded.

At least while I'm reading the story.

What if a computer created *Urban Elementals*?

I thought I'd have some fun and ask Alfonse the Idiot AI™ for three (3) examples of fictional urban elementals. I will admit I kinda laughed at his response before I thought about what he said and decided to share. The first two weren't bad. The third one, though...

FROM ALFONSE:

1) The first example of a fictional urban elemental is a character who can control and manipulate the elements of a city, such as traffic lights, buildings, and power lines. This character might use their powers to disrupt the flow of the city or protect it from outside threats.

2) Another example of a fictional urban elemental is a character who can harness the energy of the city and its inhabitants, using it to fuel their powers or to perform feats of incredible strength and speed. This character might be able to tap into the collective consciousness of the city and use it to their advantage.

3) A third example of a fictional urban elemental is a character who can shapeshift into different forms, each one representing a different aspect of the city. For example, one form might be a sleek and modern skyscraper, while another might be a rustic and organic park. This character might use their shapeshifting abilities to blend in with the city and move about unnoticed or shift into powerful forms to defend against threats.

I told you that third one was a stretch ;-)

I hope you enjoyed this book and are greedily looking forward to the next one to drop!

AUTHOR NOTES - MICHAEL ANDERLE

Chat with you in the next book.

Ad Aeternitatem,

Michael Anderle

MORE STORIES with Michael newsletter HERE: https://michael.beehiiv.com/

BOOKS BY AUBURN TEMPEST

Join us on the Facebook page: https://www.facebook.com/groups/167165864237006

Or feel free to drop us a line: UrbanDruid@lmbpn.com

Find Me

Amazon, Facebook, Newsletter,

Web page – www.auburntempest.com

Email – AuburnTempestWrites@gmail.com

Auburn Tempest - Urban Fantasy Action/Adventure

Chronicles of an Urban Druid

Book 1 – A Gilded Cage

Book 2 – A Sacred Grove

Book 3 – A Family Oath

Book 4 – A Witch's Revenge

Book 5 – A Broken Vow

Book 6 – A Druid Hexed

Book 7 – An Immortal's Pain

Book 8 – A Shaman's Power

Book 9 – A Fated Bond

Book 10 – A Dragon's Dare

Book 11 – A God's Mistake

Book 12 – A Destiny Unlocked

Book 13 – A United Front

Book 14 – A Culling Tide

Book 15 – A Danger Destroyed

Case Files of an Urban Druid

Book 1 – Mayhem in Montreal

Book 2 – Sorcery in San Francisco

Book 3 – Necromancy in New Orleans

Book 4 – Hazards in the Hidden City

Book 5 - Hexes in Texas

Book 6 - Wendigos in Washington

Chronicles of an Urban Elemental

Book 1 – Incendio: Fire Born

Book 2 – Magicae: Powers Dawning

If you enjoy my writing and read sexy/steamy romance, my pen name for the books I write in Paranormal and Fantasy Romance is JL Madore.

You can find me on Amazon.

BOOKS BY MICHAEL ANDERLE

Sign up for the LMBPN email list to be notified of new releases and special deals!

https://lmbpn.com/email/

For a complete list of books by Michael Anderle, please visit:

www.lmbpn.com/ma-books/

CONNECT WITH THE AUTHORS

Connect with Auburn

Amazon, Facebook, Newsletter

Web page – www.jlmadore.com

Email – AuburnTempestWrites@gmail.com

Connect with Michael Anderle and sign up for his email list here:

Website: http://lmbpn.com

Email List: http://lmbpn.com/email/

https://www.facebook.com/LMBPNPublishing

https://twitter.com/lmbpn

https://www.instagram.com/lmbpn_publishing/

https://www.bookbub.com/authors/michael-anderle